THE WATSON NOVELS

Emma and Elizabeth

ANN MYCHAL

Original cover design by L.J.Balter

ISBN 13: 978-0-9928795-1-8
ISBN 10: 0992879515

To Mum

Note

The use of italics in *Emma and Elizabeth* indicates that the text is taken from *The Watsons* or Jane Austen's letters.

...there is nothing people are so often deceived in, as the
state of their own affection...
Northanger Abbey

CHAPTER ONE

When a young woman, on whom every comfort in life is bestowed, has the misfortune to inhabit a neighbourhood in which peace and harmony reign, her ability to perceive and understand the world must be diminished and, consequently, in need of adjustment. Miss Emma Watson, the youngest daughter of a parson whose parish was in the village of Stanton in Surrey, lived happily until the age of five, adored, laughed at, teased and scolded in equal measure by her sisters, Elizabeth, Margaret and Penelope, and brother Robert. There she might have remained had her mother survived the delivery of a male infant, stillborn, on Christmas Eve in the winter of seventy-nine. Mrs Watson departed this life in the early hours of the morning; and while her son and daughters mourned her passing, Mr Watson took to his pulpit to announce the joyous news of the birth in Bethlehem of the Christ child.

The Watson children, left almost as orphans, disordered and bereft, had lost their anchor, for their father, who never wavered in his duty to his parishioners, rarely attended to the needs of his own family. No sooner had Mr Watson laid his wife to rest, than he looked to his eldest daughter, Elizabeth, to assume the responsibilities Mrs Watson had so lovingly discharged without complaint or reproach for seventeen years; and Elizabeth, daunted by the prospect but seeing its necessity, accepted her lot and managed as best she could, just as her mother had done before her. Assisted by Nanny in the daily chores and running of the house, Elizabeth learned what it was to raise a family. Romantic notions of the kind that filled the heads of most young women were foreign to the eldest Miss Watson, for, rather than the mending of broken hearts and the drying of lovers' tears, there were cuts and bruises to be nursed, runny noses to be wiped, and stockings to be darned. And when the daily duties were done, and the house fell silent, Elizabeth opened her journal and recorded therein the news of the day. Each stroke of the pen inscribed on the page the thoughts that were written in her heart — missives to her dear mama — who, though departed, would never be forgot.

Elizabeth's youngest sister recollected little of her early life at Stanton, for shortly after their mother had departed this life Emma had been placed under the guardianship of her Uncle Turner (the late

Mrs Watson's brother) and his wife, a woman for whom motherhood was as novel as it was perplexing. Mr Turner's choice of bride had been described by some among his acquaintance as 'singular', but to the surprise and bafflement of all who knew him, the marriage was a happy one despite differences in temperament and understanding. They neither appeared to argue nor to contradict one another, for Mr Turner was generous and compliant, and his wife was perfectly content that he should remain so. A wealthy but childless couple, the Turners owned an estate in Shropshire which was said to be one of the finest in the county.

On receiving news of Mrs Watson's passing, Mr and Mrs Turner were as desirous of easing Mr Watson's burden as of acquiring an object on which to bestow their wealth and affection. And so, when Mr Turner made an application to his brother-in-law for the guardianship of Emma, he received an immediate and gratifying reply. Mr Watson had entertained the hope that an application of the kind might be made for one or other of his daughters. Penelope or Margaret would have been more easily parted with, but it was Emma, the youngest daughter, who stole the Turners' hearts.

Emma had by far the sweetest countenance and was quickly singled out by the Turners as the child of their choice, a child who would in time inherit a large fortune and raise the fortunes of all her family. Everything considered, Mr Watson could think of nothing more fortuitous; Emma would be one less child for Elizabeth to mind, one less mouth to feed, and one less daughter to marry to anyone willing to take her for thirty pounds. Once the matter had been settled, Mr Watson was eager to avoid any delay, and so the transaction was completed within the fortnight to the delight and satisfaction of both parties. One frosty winter morning, without warning or explanation, Emma was made ready in haste, and Mr and Mrs Turner, who had little inclination to remain at Stanton an hour longer than was necessary, took the child and returned to Shropshire forthwith.

Mr Turner, a learned man who spent much of his time in his library contemplating the moral and philosophical questions of the day, knew little of the substance of a girl's education. On making the pleasing discovery that his niece was a willing scholar with an active mind, quick to learn and eager to progress, he at once decided to devote his time to her education, and he could not have done more to give her the benefit of his knowledge had he been blessed with his own son and heir.

While Mr Turner attended to Emma's education, Mrs Turner provided her with the necessary refinements that all young ladies must possess. Emma learned how to deport herself gracefully in a drawing room, a ballroom and on horseback. She learned how to draw and sew, speak French, play the pianoforte well enough to be thought accomplished, and tolerate dull conversation with good grace.

At nineteen Miss Emma Watson lacked nothing. Every advantage of rank, refinement and education that a doting aunt and uncle could provide, she possessed; indeed, she had grown into a young woman whose mind, character and temperament were as pleasing as the beauty of her countenance. Without brothers to tease or sisters with whom to quarrel, Emma Watson's world was one in which malice and rivalry were absent, and where only the purest of motives regulated the thoughts, behaviour and actions of others.

Emma loved to read, and savoured the prospect of spending a wet afternoon in the company of a spirited heroine, most especially one whose life was beset by trials and tribulations of the severest kind; and although she admired their fortitude, she was sure that wickedness, to which such heroines were universally exposed, was only to be found within the pages of a novel. Had but one such heroine spent a portion of her childhood in Shropshire — or even a day — she should not have suffered at all. And yet so great a deprivation must at once be an advantage and a defect: for to be a heroine, strange and foreign lands must be traversed, and poverty, abduction and captivity endured. When, at last, the hero (a man perfect in every aspect) should rescue her from the clutches of an evil captor, he would declare the violence of his affections and promptly make her an offer of marriage; and after protesting at length her unworthiness and astonishment at his declaration (in no less than five pages), she would at last accept him and make him the happiest of men.

It was unlikely that any such man would be found in Shropshire, for there appeared to be as severe a deficiency of heroes in that county as heroines. Emma could count among her acquaintance but five ordinary, perfectly amiable young men of differing shapes and sizes who enjoyed country pursuits, sat at cards until the early hours and talked of dogs, horses and the weather; but she was certain that among them there was not one to whom the title 'hero' could be applied. She wished that such men lived in Shropshire, but reason demanded that if they did, in the fourteen years that she had lived in that county, she should have had the privilege of making the acquaintance of (or indeed espying) one such man in the neighbourhood; and as none were apparent, even on closer enquiry and studied observation, she concluded that not only was there a deficiency of heroes in Shropshire, but that they did not exist at all.

In the end, Emma was disposed to take her uncle's view of the matter. Heroes, said he, were entirely the creation of the imagination, devised by writers of novels to provoke the dissatisfaction of young women who were not in the least likely ever to encounter one.

As she stood before the looking-glass in the grand dining hall, Emma imagined what it would be like to be the kind of heroine that she had read about in novels. The pain of separation from her family at so young an age (a necessary evil that must be endured by any heroine worthy of the name) had long ceased. Emma's devotion to Mr and Mrs Turner had grown to be as great as any that might exist between a daughter and her parents. And all might have continued in peace and contentment within the Turner household had the cruelties and uncertainties of life remained in their proper place — within the pages of a novel. It is a harsh fact that when tragedy strikes it often gives little warning, announcing its arrival when its recipients are least prepared; and so it was within the Turner household.

One bright and mild afternoon in January, Mr Turner, who had appeared to be in excellent health, and had joined the ladies for tea in the drawing room, was taken ill with a seizure, and died suddenly in the night. Grief-stricken at the loss of so kind an uncle, whom she regarded as a father, Emma began to sense what it was to suffer as her world began to fragment. The shock awakened in her a peculiar sense of abandonment; his loss would make her life the poorer, and she was sure that Uncle Turner would not have wished to make his exit from the world in so abrupt a fashion.

Emma recalled as a child her sister, Elizabeth, tucking her into bed and describing how her mother had been taken to a better place, to heaven, by the angels. 'A better place?' Emma had replied. 'What better place could there be for Mama than to be here with us?'

In the days that followed Mr Turner's passing, Emma sought solace in reading; but even the confines of a well-stocked library, and the memories contained within its walls, were of little comfort. By contrast, the shock of her husband's sudden demise appeared not to occupy his widow's thoughts for long. Mrs Turner regarded protracted expressions of grief to be of little purpose, serving only to plunge the spirits to despair; thus, being of a sanguine disposition, she was inclined to make the best of it. Adjusting more quickly to her situation than other widows might, she sought consolation of a kind that could not be satisfied by novels. Mrs Turner espoused the prospect of embarking on an adventure of her own. She still had her charms, and an estate in Shropshire that greatly enhanced them.

Mrs Turner allowed herself to be courted by a young Irish Captain of the name O'Brien. With little thought or hesitation, and to the surprise of her niece and the neighbourhood, she accepted the officer's proposal of marriage, and changed her name from Turner to O'Brien the minute propriety allowed. They planned to travel to Ireland within the month; and there they would settle on its southern shore and live out their days in comfort and ease, the means having been provided from the proceeds of Mr Turner's estate, for Captain O'Brien had no fortune of his own, nor anything more than his charm and wits to live on.

It did not please the Captain that Emma should accompany them, and so, like one of the heroines she loved to read about, Emma was dispatched to Stanton, to the family she had not seen since parting from them as a young girl of five.

CHAPTER TWO

Osborne Castle Saturday October 10th 1795

The announcement that the first winter assembly in the town of Delham in Surrey was to be held on Tuesday October the thirteenth raised mild curiosity among the inhabitants of Osborne Castle. Lady Osborne, at the entrance of the tea things, and for want of something to say, introduced the subject. Her ladyship, who in former days had enjoyed the countless delights of the assembly rooms at Bath, declared the local assembly to be a tiresome affair, having nothing to recommend it but the promise of a tolerable Cassino table and a seat by the fire. Her son, Lord Osborne, a young man of five and twenty, disliked all talk of assemblies and at the first mention of the word, retreated to the furthest corner of the room and took up a newspaper.

'My dear, have the horses been ordered from the White Hart?' enquired his mother.

His lordship, still in earshot, stiffened, and replied that they had not.

'What?' said she. 'How can I hear you when you are almost in the library? Come and sit by the fire and talk to us, for we are in need of diversion.'

Expecting, but receiving no retort, Lady Osborne turned her attention to their house guest, Miss Carr, a friend of her ladyship's daughter. 'My son is a great mimic, you know. He can replicate Mr Howard's sermon-making in every particular.'

'Of that I have no doubt. I am sure there is none as proficient in the art of mimicry as his lordship. I am quite won over by his amusing ways.'

Wishing to pay a compliment, and anxious that it be heard and understood, Miss Carr glanced expectantly at Lord Osborne. As the young woman had yet to witness his lordship's amusing ways, the remark was a curious one. But it provided Lady Osborne with some measure of reassurance: Miss Carr was easily pleased, as she would have to be if she were to set her cap at her ladyship's son.

Lord Osborne's eyes were firmly fixed on his newspaper and he gave no appearance of having heard Miss Carr at all. The young lady, though unrewarded for her efforts, contented herself with the prospect that other opportunities to gain his lordship's favour would present themselves during her stay at Osborne Castle.

Animated by the desire for amusement, and determined to have it, Lady Osborne was not a woman to give way easily. 'Will you not give us Mr Howard's sermon on the lost goats?'

'Sheep, Mama,' said her daughter, unable to suppress a yawn. Miss Osborne, a striking young woman of twenty-two, lounged languidly on a chaise longue by the window.

'Or the one we endured so valiantly last Sunday,' continued Lady Osborne.

'The sermon on the Holy Ghost?' enquired Miss Carr.

'The very one,' replied Lady Osborne. 'Oh, do entertain us for we are all quite dull today.'

Unmoved by his mother's entreaty, Lord Osborne sighed heavily and continued to read his newspaper.

'I had always supposed the Holy Ghost to be an apparition of some sort,' said Miss Carr. 'I am now quite certain that it is not. Indeed, Mr Howard was most emphatic that it was not.'

Miss Carr was a young woman whose beauty and esteem had increased in equal measure to her prospects. The event that rendered so unusually sanguine a disposition in the young woman was a propitious reversal of fortune, proceeding from the fortuitous death of her cousin at sea. There being no entail, Miss Carr had unexpectedly become an heiress. The delight she felt on receiving the news of her good fortune was made complete by a further communication: the said uncle, consumed by grief at the sudden death of his son and heir, was himself struck down by a melancholic disorder so severe that physicians held out little hope of his recovery. Mr Henry Appleby was shortly to depart this life.

Miss Carr's elevation in rank, from poor relation to young heiress, had a remarkable effect on her countenance; the young woman, whose looks were once considered 'tolerable', was now reckoned a 'beauty'. There was, however, one further accoutrement necessary to make Miss Carr's joy complete: the acquisition of a title. Among her acquaintance of rank, there was one surname that carried the day. Osborne was a surname of distinction, wholly befitting an heiress of Miss Carr's consequence. When considered from every angle, nothing could be found wanting. Osborne Castle was perfectly situated, offered every comfort, and would require little alteration under its new mistress. Indeed, the grounds were said to be some of the best and most extensive in the country. Miss Carr was determined that the surname Osborne should and would be hers, not least because the alliance of so superior a couple was certain to receive universal approval and bring joy to many.

In anticipation of Lord Osborne's offer, Miss Carr had taken pains to compose her reply. She would accept his proposal — everything that was proper would be said — the date would be set, and the banns read. Miss Osborne would receive the news with delight, and from that moment Miss Carr would no longer be 'the niece of Mr Henry Appleby', but a dear sister. The wedding clothes would be bought without delay and Lord Osborne would insist on accompanying her to town to purchase them. She would protest in the strongest of terms, but all objections would be overcome when she saw that his lordship would not endure to be parted for an hour, nor even a second, from the woman to whom he had given his heart. All that was now required to make Miss Carr's joy complete was for Lord Osborne to come to the point.

Time, it is often said, is of the essence; and Miss Carr was sensible of the fact that matrimony was a matter of some urgency. Mr Appleby must not depart this world before the marriage vows had been exchanged. It would be too cruel; for to be attired in black a full twelvemonth would be vexing indeed, but to be single and in want of a title for the same duration would be an intolerable hardship.

'I am afraid, Miss Carr, that you will receive no gallantry from my son in a ballroom, though, on occasion, he can be perfectly agreeable in daylight. Can you not, my dear?'

Lord Osborne rustled his newspaper in exasperation.

'So like his father,' continued Lady Osborne. 'I remember the first time our eyes met in the old rooms at Bath...'

'Mama, Miss Carr waits for her tea.' Miss Osborne was roused from inertia by the mention of her father and Bath, and was determined to avoid tales of her mother's exploits, which routinely followed. She endeavoured to steer the conversation back to the less disconcerting subject of the local assembly.

'Our presence is a necessary evil,' said she. 'It will dispose a great many people to attend the ball and declare it a notable success, but it will afford me very little true enjoyment. We must be content in the knowledge that we please the neighbourhood.'

'The neighbourhood talk of little else the entire season,' said Lord Osborne dryly. The ladies looked at him with surprise.

'My dear Miss Carr, do not mind my brother. He never says what he means. I must warn you, if he should propose a gentle stroll through the park, do not believe him. He will march five miles uphill and down, cross muddy fields and ditches and care nothing for the state of your feet. I have told him on many occasions that half boots are not fit for country walking of that kind. But that is his idea of a stroll.'

Miss Carr, eager to please his lordship but not wishing to give displeasure to her friend, replied, 'your brother must appear to advantage wherever he goes, whether through fields and hedgerows or in a ballroom. I confess I should dearly like to see his lordship in a ballroom for I am sure all eyes must be drawn to him.'

'That is true, but not for the reasons you might imagine,' said Miss Osborne.

Lord Osborne lowered his newspaper. 'Colonel Beresford's regiment is to winter in Reigate.'

'That is not possible,' his sister replied.

'I had it from Beresford himself this morning.'

Miss Osborne struggled to suppress her disappointment at the news of the Colonel's imminent departure. 'It is of no consequence to me, I assure you.'

Lord Osborne smiled at his sister's discomposure. Their mother, suspecting a secret to which she was not party, observed her daughter closely and added, 'It is disappointing news indeed. Beresford will be missed at cards. No one plays whist as well as he. I expect we will all miss him in one way or another.'

'Uncle Henry has a horror of public assemblies and boasts of having attended only one such ball in his life,' said Miss Carr. 'But the pleasure of a private ball, given once a year or thereabouts, cannot be surpassed, says he. There is nothing to compare to a ball where the distinction of rank is preserved. My uncle is in every particular a model of refinement in the ballroom. One is unlikely to find his equal within fifty miles of a local assembly.'

'Thank you, Miss Carr,' said Lord Osborne. 'It is now manifestly clear why gallantry in a ballroom has until now eluded me. It is entirely due to the proximity of Osborne Castle to our local assembly rooms.'

Suddenly, commotion was heard in the hallway. The sound of a child's footsteps running up the stairs dashed Miss Osborne's hopes of the visitor being Colonel Beresford. Moments later the door swung open to admit Mr Howard and his sister, Mrs Blake, a widow whose easy company and generous spirit were praised by all.

Mr Howard had a comfortable living in the parish of Wickstead and lived with his sister and her son in the rectory near Osborne Park. The parish duties were undemanding and, being situated in easy distance of London, Mr Howard had hopes of one day securing a position there, perhaps even in one or other of the royal houses.

'Mr Howard, come and sit by me,' said Lady Osborne. 'Mrs Blake, I entreat you, sit over there and do what you can to rally my son. He is in such an ill humour today. I have quite lost my patience with him. Mr Howard, we were in raptures over your sermon last Sunday on the holy goats. Ghosts. Ghost.'

'Your ladyship is too kind.'

'I must own to being in low spirits myself today,' said Mrs Blake. 'Some of my beloved husband's belongings were returned to me this morning by dear Colonel Beresford. Admiral Beresford, who is an uncle of the colonel's, you know, had arranged to send them with a young midshipman, but Colonel Beresford would not hear of it, and insisted on bringing them himself. Nothing else would do. Indeed, Colonel Beresford brought with him a note from the Admiral. Captain Blake, said he, was one of the finest naval officers and the best of men. How very kind it was of the colonel to deliver the Admiral's message in person. I wonder Colonel Beresford did not think of the Navy as a career.'

'Redcoats have the advantage in a ballroom,' said Lady Osborne. 'They look by far the — '

'Did Colonel Beresford stay long?' enquired Miss Osborne.

'A half hour or so, I believe,' replied Mrs Blake.

'Beresford sat for an hour at least,' said Mr Howard.

'Dear me! You must be right. Yes, of course you are. Colonel Beresford spoke with you and Lord Osborne at length on a matter of some importance.'

'I see,' replied Miss Osborne. 'My brother neglected to mention that he had called on you this morning. I should have liked a walk.'

'How careless of me,' said Lord Osborne. 'I forget how partial you are to mud.'

'It has rained so heavily of late that the rectory garden is now a lake,' said Mrs Blake. 'Colonel Beresford said that the potholes in the lane are the worst he has ever seen.'

'I hope it never rains again. I have a horror of mud,' Miss Carr exclaimed for want of something to say.

'What an extraordinary hope!' said Mr Howard. 'We should all die if it were never to rain again. Rain is a blessing, not a curse.'

'I suppose, after such a dry summer', said Mrs Blake, 'it must be good for the soil.'

'Neither too much nor too little of anything is good,' said Mr Howard.

Miss Carr realised the foolishness of her statement and sat in silence for some minutes before opening her mouth to speak again. The awkwardness that the subject of Colonel Beresford had aroused among at least one of those present was relieved momentarily by the entrance of Charles Blake, who bounded into the room eager to impart a very important fact.

'The staircase has fifty-two steps. I have climbed them three times. The first time, one at a time. The second time, two at a time. And you'll never guess what I did the third time.'

'Where are your manners, Charles?' said his mother.

The boy straightened his jacket and bowed awkwardly to each person present. Charles was the son of Mrs Blake. He was, according to his mother, a boisterous twelve year old who enjoyed pursuits of all kinds, with the exception of those that required extensive reading and writing, the conjugation of Latin verbs, and the observance of instructions laid down by his elders. Mr Howard was the boy's tutor, a task that had proved as arduous as it was unrewarding. Indeed, he was neither new to its demands nor unrealistic as to the outcome, for he had faced a similar challenge as tutor to Lord Osborne.

'Mama said I could go to the ball', continued Charles. 'I am determined to dance every dance. But I do not know who will dance with me. Miss Osborne, will you dance with me?'

'Charles,' said his mother, 'I am sure Miss Osborne is already engaged. Mrs Tomlinson will dance with you if you ask her politely and you may very well find someone to dance with of your own age.'

'But Mrs Tomlinson is very old.'

'She is not very old and she is very kind to you,' said his mother. 'Last week Mrs Tomlinson made Charles a pie with fruit from her own garden because she had heard how partial he was to   gooseberry tart.'

'Dancing is not the only amusement in a ballroom,' Lord Osborne said to the boy. 'There is much to be gleaned from watching others dance. The neighbourhood, and consequently the world, reveals itself in a ballroom. You may stand by me and I will point out...'

'That is absurd!' cried his sister. Then turning to Charles, Miss Osborne said, 'His lordship has no interest in watching others dance. He does not dance because he does not wish to learn.'

'Does Colonel Beresford dance?' asked Lady Osborne.

'I expect we will never know,' her daughter replied.

'He is said to be an accomplished dancer,' said Mrs Blake.

'But it is by no means certain that he will attend the ball with troop movements afoot,' said Mr Howard.

'It is true. The regiment will not be with us for much longer,' said Mrs Blake.

'Charles,' said Miss Osborne, disappointed by the news of the regiment's imminent departure, 'I shall be happy to dance with you.'

'Shall we dance the first two dances?'

'We shall.'

'And dance down every couple?'

'You have my word.'

Nothing could now dampen Charles Blake's spirits. Having secured the promise of Miss Osborne's hand for the first two dances, he knew that he would not want for partners thereafter, for others would follow where Miss Osborne led. Most of all, he was happy in the knowledge that in all probability he would not be obliged to dance a reel with Mrs Tomlinson.

CHAPTER THREE

The inhabitants of Osborne Castle passed the following day in much the same way as they always did. After sitting through Mr Howard's exhortation to cast off the iniquity of sloth, Lady Osborne and her daughter, and Miss Carr, proceeded to spend the day in languorous elegance eating cake and complaining of the lack of amusement that Sundays afforded. Lord Osborne chose to spend his afternoon alone in the library, and gave instructions that he was not to be disturbed.

The following morning brought with it the prospect of a bright autumn day. Having business in Delham that would occupy him for most of the day, thereby releasing him from the attentions of Miss Carr, Lord Osborne set out early on foot. He had neither the inclination nor the need to marry, and was content to discharge his duties to the estate and to the borough as a single man in freedom and tranquillity.

When Miss Carr appeared at breakfast, she was vexed to find that he was not present. Miss Osborne, who had been in the breakfast room some time, found little comfort in the appearance of her friend, for her mind was occupied with unsatisfactory thoughts of Colonel Beresford and his imminent removal to Reigate. As neither of the young women had anything to say, they ate their breakfast in silence.

Lady Osborne, who rarely rose before midday, surprised the young women by coming down to breakfast. 'I have a great desire to visit Lady Forbes today. She is staying with her brother at Lowford Park. I expect I shall be back before dinner. I don't intend to stay long. Am I in the right place? Tell me, have we become a nunnery? Is silence the new order of the day? What is it, my dears? You both seem out of sorts today. Has Briggs burnt the bacon again?'

'No, Mama,' said Miss Osborne.

'No, indeed,' echoed her friend.

The breakfast room fell silent once again as the two young women, lost in their private thoughts, picked half-heartedly at their food. Lady Osborne proffered a word of advice.

'There is nothing like exercise to brighten the day. Why not take a walk in the park? Better still, come with me to Lowford.'

'No, Mama. I have no wish to see Lady Forbes' brother. He talks too much and has not a good word to say about the regiment. Besides, we will find plenty to do while you are away.'

Having ordered horses to be at Osborne Castle by nine the following evening, Lord Osborne unexpectedly happened upon Colonel Beresford in a room at the White Hart. The colonel was discussing the purchase of a gun with Tom Musgrave.

'Come and look at this,' said Musgrave. 'It's a fine thing. I've almost persuaded Beresford to take it off my hands.'

Mr Musgrave's agreeable manners and modish appearance made him a favourite, particularly with the young women of the borough. It suited him to believe that most of them were in love with him, or, at some point, had been. At almost thirty years of age, Musgrave prided himself on the fact that, despite being such a favourite, he had escaped matrimony several times; and though he had once fancied himself a little in love, he had only twice given serious thought to the matter. The advice he gave to all his friends and acquaintances contemplating matrimony was the same: once an offer is made, and a promise given, it cannot be easily retracted, and is better avoided altogether.

Osborne was taken aback by Musgrave's new haircut.

'It is quite à la mode, I assure you,' replied he.

'The army does not look on this new fashion in a favourable light,' said the Colonel.

'It is of little matter to me as I have no desire to wear regimentals,' said Musgrave.

'My good man, do you not think perhaps that a little powder is needed to complete — '

'No, indeed! I counted no less than four and twenty crops at Lady Forbes' ball last month. Mr Pitt may keep his hair powder tax. It is an outrage. I, for one, shall pay not a penny,' said Musgrave catching his reflection in a mirror. 'Upon my word, it becomes me very well, does it not? And it is much admired by the ladies.'

Urgent footsteps in the corridor left no time to speculate as to their owner. The door swung open, and Mr Howard entered in a great fluster. The clergyman was in a state of heightened agitation and was about to speak when he noticed Musgrave's crop.

'The deliberations and opinions of a clergyman are always worthy of consideration,' said Musgrave. 'Mr Howard, what, pray, is your view? When shall you become a crop?'

Mr Howard made no comment. Recollecting his purpose, he turned to Colonel Beresford and said, 'Your presence is required outside without delay. Make haste, sir!'

The scene that greeted the colonel was one of uproar; as rioting protestors threw stones and plundered sacks of grain, redcoats looked on with helpless indecision. Beresford stormed towards his men with orders to break up the riot at once. Mr Musgrave and Mr Howard watched from a distance as his lordship stepped into the fray. In an attempt to help quell the disturbance, Lord Osborne was almost struck by a passing carriage. The startled coachman, seeing that the way ahead was beset by danger, brought the coach to a halt.

A young woman opened the carriage door to ascertain the cause of the commotion. As she stepped down, one of the rioters picked up a stone and took aim at a redcoat, shouting, 'We want bread, not war!' The stone missed its intended target, and struck the young woman on the shoulder, causing her to stumble and fall.

Osborne rushed to her aid and helped her to her feet. 'Are you hurt?'

The young woman felt a strange heat begin to burn in her chest as she straightened her cloak.

'It is nothing, sir. Nothing at all.'

'Allow me,' said he, awkwardly attempting to shake the dirt from the young woman's cloak.

'Sir, please do not trouble yourself on my account. I am perfectly well as you see,' said she, as she fainted into the arms of her rescuer.

A gentle breeze from an open window and the touch of cold glass against her lips brought the patient back to consciousness. As her eyes surveyed the room, she found herself among a company of strangers curious to see whether the young woman would rally or expire. A maid plumped up a cushion and placed it behind her head while the strange gentleman who had come to her assistance coaxed her to sip wine.

Lord Osborne had had some time to study his charge. There was something in her disposition that raised his curiosity. She was unlike any of the women of his acquaintance, though he was unsure in what respect; more disconcertingly, he was unable to account for the interest in her welfare that her present state of indisposition had engendered.

'The blackguard will be dealt with as he deserves,' he told her. 'You have my word.'

'I beg you, not on my account, sir. Not while there is want in this country,' she whispered.

'What do you know of such things?' said he.

The young woman did not appear, either in manner or appearance, ever to have been in want of anything.

'A little.' She sat up. 'My uncle wrote extensively on the subject. He had the finest mind of any man. If there is want, and food is scarce, what else is a man to do? How does he feed his family?'

Lord Osborne was bemused by her reply, but far from arousing his displeasure, the encounter increased his fascination. He wanted to know her name and where she was going, that he might provide the means for her to reach her destination and thereby gain knowledge of it himself.

The information was easily obtained. Musgrave spoke in a low voice. 'I believe the young lady is a Miss Emma Watson. I know the family well, but am not acquainted with Miss Emma. She resided until recently with her aunt and uncle in Shropshire. Her father is a clergyman in the parish of Stanton. I shall ride there without delay to inform him. It is better that I go in person, I think, rather than send word.'

'Quite.'

'The maid will take care of her,' said Musgrave.

'I might as well sit here a while longer,' his lordship replied. 'I have no pressing business elsewhere.'

Musgrave smiled at Osborne's remark. He had never seen his friend show such concern for any woman, not even for his own mother or sister.

On leaving the White Hart, Musgrave's attention was drawn to a familiar sight in the market square: Elizabeth Watson, Emma's elder sister, driving her father's old cart. Splashing through puddles and veering away from potholes, she brought the vehicle to a halt outside Mason's. Elizabeth's arrival at that moment, however providential it might have appeared, was not by accident. She had come to surprise her sister, and bring her home to Stanton.

Musgrave strode across the square to meet her. He had once fancied that Elizabeth had been a little in love with him; and had it not been for her unfashionable appearance and strong opinions, he might have been in some danger, for he had always thought her handsome. A little encouragement might even have strengthened his suit, but none was forthcoming, as she appeared, implausibly, to prefer the attentions of an unremarkable young curate by the name of Purvis. As a consequence, he had turned his attention to the other two Watson sisters of his acquaintance, Margaret and Penelope; and though he regretted his mistake almost immediately, the harm had been done. His behaviour towards Elizabeth had not been what it should have been. Yet he found reassurance in the knowledge that he had, at least for the time being, escaped the constraints of matrimony; for a single man, he often observed, was always the envy of a married one.

'Miss Watson. You have missed all the commotion. I wonder you were not one of the instigators.'

'Mr Musgrave. You are still you, I see☐ — in character if not appearance. I did not recognise you. Your hair is — ' said she, pausing to find a word, 'singular. I suppose it must be the fashion.'

'I have been told that it becomes me.'

Elizabeth rolled her eyes.

'It is all the rage in France.'

'We are not in France, Mr Musgrave.'

'Come,' said he. 'I have something for you.'

'Something for me? What could you possibly possess that I would want?'

'A heroine worthy of Mrs Burney.'

Musgrave extended his hand to help Elizabeth up the slippery steps to the entrance of the White Hart. He was aware that his gallantry gave her little pleasure and would go unrewarded as it always did. Undaunted, he gave her the briefest account of her sister's ordeal and present situation and ushered Elizabeth through to the room where Emma had been resting.

'May I? I would rather meet my sister alone.'

'Of course. I will leave you. If you need — '

'Thank you, Mr Musgrave. I am in need of nothing more than to see my sister.'

Elizabeth found Emma sitting alone by the fire, toying nervously with the trim of her cuff.

'My dear Emma, is it really you? Oh, my dear, how beautiful you are. How like our dear mama.'

'Elizabeth?' replied Emma.

'What has happened to your cloak? You will think us a neighbourhood of savages.'

'I cannot tell you how glad I am to see you.'

'I've come to take you home,' her sister replied.

CHAPTER FOUR

Dinner at Osborne Castle was a subdued affair. Miss Osborne had spent the day waiting for Colonel Beresford to call, while the colonel had spent the day engaged in endeavours of a kind that struck at the heart of the nation's security. Consequently, he was in no humour to grace anyone with his presence. Retreating to his rooms at the White Hart at a late hour, he had partaken of a simple meal in the company of the inn keeper's dog; thereafter he sat for some time by the fire absorbed in Cowper's rendering of the Iliad.

Miss Carr eagerly awaited her next encounter with Lord Osborne which was certain to take place at dinner, for Miss Osborne had assured her that his lordship was not expected to dine out. Hence, she resolved to employ her time composing clever remarks and entertaining epigrams for Lord Osborne's amusement, and she resolved to deploy the best of the collection at the dinner table.

Her efforts, however, proved to be in vain, for his lordship would not be moved. Every endeavour to captivate him failed; and once the syllabub had been served, Miss Carr was resigned to the view that Lord Osborne was in no humour to engage in amusing repartee, nor conversation of any kind.

He had been preoccupied with other thoughts, for the events of the day had given him much to ponder. There were concerns about the removal of Colonel Beresford's regiment to Reigate and the measures required to quell any further unrest. And then there was Miss Emma Watson and her forthright opinions on the matters of the day. Curiously, he was more than a little disconcerted by the way in which his encounter with Miss Watson had ended. Had not he rescued her from an angry, violent mob? Had he not taken pains to show her extraordinary benevolence? Was it unreasonable, thus, to expect that an unstinting act of kindness such as his be rewarded with more liberal expressions of indebtedness and gratitude? Indeed, he was strangely perplexed when, having recovered her composure and found her feet, she dismissed him. She had, it was true, expressed her gratitude for the service he had rendered, but she had shown no further curiosity in ascertaining the name or consequence of the personage to whom she was 'most deeply obliged'.

Once the ladies had withdrawn, Musgrave, who often dined at the Castle, returned to the events of the day.

'Beresford has his hands full,' said Musgrave. 'I daresay, we will all be rounded up and made to wear regimentals before long if matters don't improve.'

'There are riots throughout the country.'

'In Shropshire too, no doubt.'

'Shropshire?'

'Yes. I only mention it because Miss Emma Watson is just come from that county. It seemed to me that she expressed unusually firm opinions on the state of the nation. She is quite unlike most of her sisters,' said Musgrave.

'Has she more than one sister?' enquired Osborne.

'She has sisters enough to raise a regiment. Indeed, there is no foe more formidable than Miss Penelope Watson at a ball and in want of a partner. Upon my word, if the battlefield were an assembly room and Miss Penelope the adversary, the French would beat a prompt retreat. Mercifully, Miss Margaret Watson is gone away. For how long is uncertain. A full twelvemonth would not suffice for my liking.'

'And the elder Miss Watson?' enquired his lordship.

'Ah. There is a picture of malcontent if ever there was one. She spoke of my haircut in the most disparaging of terms. But that is praise enough for me.'

'How so?' asked Osborne.

'It is Miss Watson's way of paying a compliment. I daresay Miss Emma is a lot like her,' continued Musgrave, in the hope of drawing Osborne out. It was, however, not to be. Osborne was in no mood to hear more on the subject and turned his attention to the more pressing matters of the day.

When the gentlemen finally appeared in the drawing room, Lady Osborne took her son aside.

'Take a turn in the room with me, if you will,' said she.

With some reluctance, Osborne extended his arm to his mother while Musgrave made himself comfortable by the fire opposite Miss Osborne and Miss Carr.

'Miss Osborne. Miss Carr. I am at your service. Give me some employment. It does not matter what. Needlework will do. I know how to unknot silk thread.'

'What do you know of silk thread, Mr Musgrave?' exclaimed Miss Carr. 'What does any gentleman know of the matter? Perhaps we should ask his lordship to hem a handkerchief.'

'My brother is quite accomplished at darning socks,' said Miss Osborne. 'His handiwork is exceptionally neat and tidy. Mrs Blake taught him.'

'I should dearly love to see his lordship with a darning needle,' replied Miss Carr.

'I am ready and willing to learn the art of needlework if you would teach me, Miss Osborne. And you Miss Carr,' said Musgrave.

'You might employ your time more usefully by reading to us, Mr Musgrave,' said Miss Osborne.

'And what would you have me read?'

'A chapter from Evelina.'

'Ah. A charming heroine. One of Mrs Burney's finest. I can picture her now. How very odd that you should be reading Evelina. I had cause to think of her this very morning.'

'So you read novels, Mr Musgrave?' enquired Miss Osborne.

'Now and again — though I rather prefer to consider myself the stuff of novels.'

'How absurd you are!' she replied.

'Miss Carr, do you not think me the embodiment of the perfect hero?'

'Indeed she does not. Nor do I,' replied Miss Osborne.

Miss Carr's attention slipped momentarily and her eyes were drawn in another direction. As Lord Osborne took a turn in the room with his mother, she fancied that, on more than one occasion, Lady Osborne had uttered the words 'Miss Carr' and 'alliance'. She could not have been better pleased with herself for having so firm and vocal an ally.

Lady Osborne spoke to her son in a whisper loud enough to be caught by anyone with a keen ear. 'Miss Carr is not at liberty to extend her stay indefinitely.'

'I am relieved to hear it,' replied Osborne, guiding his mother to the furthest corner of the room. 'I was beginning to think she had intentions of making Osborne Castle her home.'

'Would not that be an excellent thing?' said her ladyship. 'You cannot want for encouragement.'

'Encouragement? What has Miss Carr's visit to do with me?' said Osborne, understanding his mother's meaning perfectly.

'You understand me. I know you do. When do you intend to come to the point? Let it be sooner rather than later.'

'I have no intention of coming to the point. I never had.'

'And why not? It would be a most suitable alliance. Osborne Castle is in need of an heir. Think of poor Mrs Tomlinson's brother-in-law.'

'What, pray, has Mrs Tomlinson's brother-in-law to do with anything?'

'Do you not remember how he was thrown from his horse, his life extinguished in an instant? By all accounts the corpse looked well enough. And it was not one of Mr Tomlinson's best horses.'

'That must have brought great solace to his family.'

Lady Osborne, undeterred, endeavoured to strengthen her case.

'Mr Howard heard recently of a gentleman from Margate who was caught up in the mayhem of a riot and would have been chopped to pieces with an axe had it not been for the local militia. If only you had a son, Osborne Castle would be safe.'

'How so? Consider this, Mama. The French may come at any moment — seize the livestock, raid the grain store, and slay us in our beds. Then, you see, an heir would be of little matter.'

'Butchers! All I ask is that you try your best with Miss Carr. A little effort is all that is needed. If only you were sensible of the exertions made by your sister on your behalf, you would...'

'Then please urge her to desist at once. I have no more to say on the subject.'

CHAPTER FIVE

Emma Watson gave little thought to the incident that had marked her arrival in Surrey. As Stanton Parsonage came into view, the eager anticipation she had for so long felt at the prospect of a reunion with her family had been replaced with other feelings. She was perplexed to find that her sensations on reaching Stanton were oddly mixed. Had her memory played tricks on her? The fields and the country lanes were much as she expected them to be, but the proportions of her childhood home had taken her by surprise. It was a modest dwelling, considerably smaller than the house fixed in her memory. The church, too, was not the cathedral she had imagined it to be.

On the day of her removal from Stanton, Elizabeth recalled how Emma had run away and had hidden inside the Tomlinsons' box.

'I found you weeping, hungry and cold. I remember well your angry protestations, and how you hid under the pew. You begged to let it be your bedchamber, for you were sure that no other bedchamber would do half as well. When at last I was able to coax you out, you clung to my old brown apron and would not let go until I promised to write to you every day.'

'Did I?' said Emma. 'Every day?'

'It wasn't possible, of course. But I wrote to you every fortnight.'

'Yes. And I was always impatient to receive your letters.'

Indeed, Emma's eagerness to study had been fuelled by her desire to read her sister's letters and write to her without help of any kind. It had made Mr Turner's task the lighter, for Emma had applied herself diligently to her study and had quickly made progress. Nothing would satisfy her until she no longer needed her uncle's assistance. Every letter that Elizabeth wrote, Emma kept in a special rosewood box, and the box was her most treasured possession.

Despite her apprehension, Emma received a warm welcome at Stanton. Her father, who often took to his bed, was in good spirits and came down to partake of an early dinner. 'My dear Emma,' said he, 'you must sit here by the fire for there is nothing worse than a long journey for bringing on a chill.'

There was much to say and much to be heard; memories had to be recounted, every particular of Mr Watson's state of health had to be spoken of, and enquiries concerning the journey, Shropshire and Aunt Turner's wedding had to be answered in painstaking detail.

As soon as Mr Watson had retired to his room, Elizabeth, who had said very little all evening, came and sat by her sister. Taking her hand, she said, 'We live very simply, Emma. I am afraid you may not be happy here.'

'How could you think such a thing?' Emma replied. 'What more could I wish for than to be here at Stanton with you and our dear father.'

'What more, indeed. But you are used to finer things. Our country ways must seem strange to you.'

'Then I shall be glad to learn them. I have longed for this day. Truly, I have.'

There was an alteration in Elizabeth's tone when she next spoke, occasioned by the recollection of the event that had led to Emma's return to Stanton. 'What was Aunt Turner thinking of?'

'She is Aunt O'Brien now.'

'Oh Emma,' said Elizabeth. 'When I think of what she has done. And Mr Turner not cold in his grave! She will regret it, of that I am certain. No good will come of it. And to cast you off without a penny, when we all had such hopes of you! I should dearly like to meet Captain O'Brien and give him a piece of my mind. It is not Aunt Turner but the money he cares about, mark my words.'

'Captain O'Brien is considered a respectable man. I believe they truly love each other.'

'I have made a study of such men — and there are many — men who prey on elderly widows. There is nothing more appealing to a man than a good income and a woman to provide it.'

'In that case, there is no likelihood of either of us ever becoming prey to such young men,' remarked Emma.

'Not me perhaps. But a young woman with your beauty and accomplishments — '

'My dear Elizabeth, you have nothing to fear. I have not a penny to my name. But I shall be on my guard. You have my word.'

On rising, Emma came down to find Elizabeth in possession of a note which had just arrived from Mr and Mrs Edwards. Mr Edwards was one of Mr Watson's oldest friends and it was customary for the family to invite the Watson sisters to dress, dine and sleep at their home on the day of each assembly throughout the winter. Elizabeth was obliged to decline the invitation on account of her father's ill health. And so it was left to Emma to accept the kind offer; but having little inclination to do so, she urged Elizabeth to take her place.

'I have no acquaintance there.'

'Mrs Edwards will introduce you and *among so many officers, Emma, you will hardly want partners.*'

'*I wish you had not made a point of my going to this ball.* Will you not go instead? I should prefer it. I will gladly stay at home and sit with Papa if you will go in my place.'

'Go in your place? I would never do such a thing. *I am sure I should never have forgiven the person who kept me from a ball at nineteen.* Besides, Mr and Mrs Edwards are determined to have you as one of their party. Their daughter Mary will hear of nothing else and she is used to getting her own way.'

Emma fell silent. Though she had little inclination to attend the ball, she knew that it would please her sister, and her father, and so she yielded.

'I do so enjoy the morning after a ball. It is often just as enjoyable as the event itself, for there is much to pore over,' said Elizabeth. 'And with Penelope and Margaret away, there is no chance of the gossip being unfavourable, at least where this family is concerned.'

Elizabeth instructed Emma to observe who danced with whom, who sat at cards, how the tearoom appeared, and how many times Miss Edwards danced with Captain Hunter. 'Promise me, Emma, that you will bring news of the ball. I am relying on you.'

'I shall try, but being among so many strangers, I fear my report will be found wanting.'

'Mary Edwards is a great gossip. She will make a point of acquainting you with all the important facts.'

On arrival at the Edwards' house, Emma was ushered inside *by a man in livery with a powdered head.* Elizabeth had warned her to expect it, adding, 'It will be commonplace for you, I daresay. I expect the Turners kept several such men.'

Elizabeth stayed little more than ten minutes with the family — long enough to carry the usual courtesies extended by her father and to comment on the likelihood that the ball would be a good one. Emma found that the time passed more quickly than she had imagined. The conversation was led by Mrs Edwards, a woman who was never short of something to say. Hence, from the moment that

Emma arrived until it was time to go in to dinner, Emma found herself the captive recipient of Mrs Edwards' advice and opinions on matters as diverse as the best place to buy string, to the common deficiencies of married men.

'A man, once married, must not be persuaded of the view that he is at liberty to come and go as he pleases. It is best to explain the matter early on in plain terms, for a man will agree to anything while he still fancies himself in love,' said Mrs Edwards.

On entering the dining room, Mrs Edwards embarked on a new topic: a history of the families of note in the neighbourhood, and the Edwards' place within it. Emma thought it would likely see them through the first half hour and into the second, and found that an occasional smile in the appropriate place was all that was required to make Mrs Edwards happy. The dining room was well-lit and of sizable proportions; at one end there was an imposing fireplace where a fire blazed, and at the other, a striking painting in oils of a landscape not dissimilar to that of Shropshire. Emma thought that, were an opportunity to present itself, she might enquire about the painting; but as dinner progressed, the necessity to speak diminished further. It was a new thing for Emma to be present at table where so little was required of her; but she was content to do nothing less than please her hostess and show herself a willing listener.

As the last pudding was served, Mrs Edwards embarked upon yet another subject: the dangers of curricles. 'A curricle is a dangerous contraption,' said she. 'I was once brought to my knees by one in Brighton. I might very likely have been killed.'

Mr Edwards, who had recently made it his study to compare the merits of new conveyances, with an eye to making a new purchase himself, ventured an opinion.

'My dear,' said he, interrupting her flow, 'no conveyance is dangerous of itself. It is only dangerous in the hands of a careless driver.'

'Then all such contrivances should be driven by women. I know of no man in whose hands a curricle is safe,' said Mrs Edwards. 'Mr Musgrave is the worst offender. He drives about here and there without any thought to his neighbours and thinks the country lanes hereabouts nothing but a racecourse.'

Seeing that her parents would be locked in debate for some duration, Mary Edwards took the opportunity to whisper to Emma,

'I have heard so much about you, Miss Watson, I feel as though we are not new acquaintances at all, but old friends.'

From time to time Emma had heard Elizabeth mention Mary Edwards, and although she could now claim Mary among her acquaintance, she was not yet persuaded of the view that the bonds of friendship would grow in equal measure. Before Emma had time to reply, the conversation between Mr and Mrs Edwards took an interesting turn, for the subject of carriages soon led to the mention of Osborne Castle.

'*The Osbornes will certainly be at the ball tonight for horses for two carriages are ordered from the White Hart,*' said Mr Edwards.

'I am glad of it, though *they add little to the pleasure of the evening, for they come so late and go so early,*' his wife replied.

'It is hardly worth them ordering horses at all. They would do better to stay at home,' said Mary.

'Mary. Don't be silly. Their presence *will dispose a great many people to attend the second* ball,' said her mother.

Emma observed a curious uneasiness between mother and daughter.

'Mary, I expect you to exercise prudence in your choice of partners this evening.'

'*Your father, Miss Emma,*' interjected Mr Edwards, in an attempt to avoid the business of Mary's dancing partners, '*is one of my oldest friends. I know of no one who likes a game of cards so well as he and very few people that play a fairer rubber.* If only his health would allow, I am sure he would enjoy our little whist club at the White Hart.'

'You keep such late hours, there is no wonder an invalid such as Mr Watson is prevented from attending,' said Mrs Edwards.

'Late hours? We break up before midnight,' replied her husband.

'*You would do well to break up two hours sooner.*'

Emma suspected that the whist club was an old grievance and one that Mr Edwards was not eager to pursue for the present. Consequently, she endeavoured to initiate a different topic of conversation, and settled on a subject she was certain would not cause vexation to any member of the family. 'Surrey is a beautiful county. I am sometimes reminded of Shropshire. There is an attractive painting — ' said Emma.

'Ah! Shropshire,' said Mr Edwards. 'It puts me in mind of your aunt, Miss Emma. I knew her thirty years ago. *She was a very fine woman then. I danced with her in the old rooms at Bath.*'

'That was a very long time ago,' said Mrs Edwards. 'We are all, even you, my dear, subject to the ravages of time. I am sure Mrs Turner is not quite as you remember her. I hope, Miss Emma, that your aunt is *happy in her second choice of husband.*'

'*I believe so*, ma'am,' said Emma.

'*What is her name now?*' said Mr Edwards.

'O'Brien. She married a Captain O'Brien.'

'A redcoat?' asked Mrs Edwards.

'Yes. He is an officer in the — '

'*There is nothing like the officers for captivating the ladies, young and old. There is no resisting a cockade,*' said Mrs Edwards, casting a warning glance at her daughter.

'*I hope there is,*' said Mr Edwards.

CHAPTER SIX

Charles Blake climbed the grand staircase at Osborne Castle in search of Lord Osborne and found him in the long gallery looking at the night sky.

'Well, Master Charles, are you ready for battle?' said Osborne.

'I beg your pardon, my lord,' he replied. 'Your mama and Miss Osborne wish to inform you that the horses are here and they are waiting and worn out with patience, or something of the sort.'

'Splendid. They are never better pleased than when they are hard done by.'

'Miss Osborne has promised to dance with me. *We are to dance down every couple.*'

'A wretched prospect indeed! Feign a little clumsiness. And then, you see, she will never offer again.'

'But I want to dance. *We have been engaged this week,*' said Charles.

By the time the carriages left Osborne Castle, the assembly rooms heaved with excited young women eager to secure a partner.

'You and I,' said Mary 'will not be obliged to stand up with each other like the Tomlinson girls. They never have much luck in a ballroom, though it seems there are officers enough to go round. Do you not think they appear to greater advantage in regimentals than other young men?'

'If they have manners to match their attire, I should not disagree.'

'Surely a uniform makes even the plainest young man handsome,' said Mary.

'I don't agree. Character and good manners are worth more than any fine coat.'

'Come,' she replied, not listening. Mary Edwards took Emma's arm and ploughed through a throng of young women towards a group of officers standing by the door.

'What about your mama?' said Emma. 'Should we not stay by her?'

'Mama is so tiresome. And anyway, she will not be done gossiping with Mrs Tomlinson for at least an hour,' exclaimed Mary. 'And I shall dance with any handsome redcoat who offers. Look Emma. Over there.'

'What am I to look at?' said Emma, perplexed by Mary's remarks.

'Captain Hunter I shall not refuse.'

With Mary's encouragement, Captain Hunter made his way across the room with *an air of empressement*. Emma disliked his extravagant bow and theatrical address and thought his manner insincere. Indeed, she found nothing in his demeanour, nor in the conduct of her companion, that met with her approval.

'Captain Hunter,' said Mary, 'allow me to introduce Miss Emma Watson. Miss Emma is new to the neighbourhood and yet I feel that I have known her all my life. We are so very alike.'

Emma took a different view; indeed, she was certain that they must be dissimilar in every regard.

'Delighted to make your acquaintance, Miss Watson,' said he.

The company of Mary Edwards and Captain Hunter, and the familiarity between them, made Emma uneasy. She began to wish that she had not yielded to her sister's plea to attend the ball. If only Elizabeth had come in her place! If only she had stayed at home with her father! As Emma surveyed the room, she found that the assembly held little promise of enjoyment, and began to wish away the hours until it was time to leave.

'I am come to dance,' said Mary to Captain Hunter. 'And if you will not dance with me, I shall have Mr Styles instead.'

'Then would you do me the honour, Miss Edwards?'

'Certainly, Captain.'

To Emma's relief, the music began. As Mary Edwards and Captain Hunter took their places in the set alongside his fellow officers and their partners, Emma glimpsed a look of disapproval from Mrs Edwards, who was standing with Mrs Tomlinson in the opposite corner of the room. The press of the crowd prevented Emma from resuming her place by Mrs Edwards' side and so she sought the refuge of a quiet corner to await the call some time hence to adjourn for refreshments.

After the first two dances, the sound of bustle and commotion in the passageway heralded the arrival of the Osborne set. The music stopped and silence fell as the family made their grand entrance. Emma recognised the gentleman who had come to her rescue in Delham. Being in earshot of another guest, she was able to ascertain that he was Lord Osborne and that he was accompanied by his mother, sister and a young lady named Miss Carr, on whom it was generally expected that the honour of becoming the next Lady

Osborne was to be bestowed. Emma watched as Lord Osborne led his party to the seats reserved for their use. She thought he looked ill at ease, for he neither smiled nor spoke to anyone at all. And as a suitor Emma thought him careless, for he seemed indifferent to the attentions of the young woman who was to be his bride. His awkward benevolence she had already witnessed, yet she found him, on this occasion at least, devoid of even the appearance of goodwill or affability.

In contrast, Emma was struck by the air and distinction of the gentleman who accompanied him. It was not long before she heard the name 'Howard' mentioned and learned, with interest, that he was a clergyman of the parish of Wickstead and that the lady with whom he was conversing was not his wife, but his sister. Mr Howard moved easily in a ballroom and seemed to take pleasure in the attentions of young and old alike; his agreeable air and pleasant manners set him apart, and it was soon Emma's opinion that Mr Howard was superior by far to all the other gentlemen in the room.

Tom Musgrave was also one of the party. Having the distinction of being the only crop present, a subject which provoked the firm disapproval of the older generation and the admiration of several of the officers, the Misses Tomlinson and Mary Edwards, Musgrave was well pleased.

'My dear,' said Mary, when at last she came upon Emma, more by accident than design. 'Where have you been? Have you seen Mr Musgrave's crop? Everyone is speaking of it. I think it becoming. Did you observe Miss Carr — the one in the yellow frock? She is soon to inherit a large fortune and marry Lord Osborne whenever he takes the trouble of making her an offer. I declare, I shall set my cap at his lordship if Miss Carr does not succeed, and make my dear Captain exceedingly jealous.'

'Mary, you may want to lower your voice. Your dear Captain approaches,' Emma replied.

'I am engaged to Captain Hunter for the next two dances. It seems there is no getting away from him. But I bring sad news. Colonel Beresford is shortly to take his regiment to winter at Reigate. So you see, Emma, I am to flirt my last with Captain Hunter. It will please Mama, but it vexes me greatly. How could Colonel Beresford do such a thing! By the by, I am sure Mr Styles will dance with you if you tease him a little.'

Emma had no wish to tease Mr Styles or any of the officers of Miss Edwards' acquaintance, but she was obliged to Captain Hunter for claiming Mary for the next two dances as it afforded her the means once again of parting company with her new acquaintance. As the couples assembled, and Miss Edwards marched Captain Hunter to the floor, Emma's attention was drawn to a boy standing beside her who appeared to be looking for something. She picked up a glove and offered it to him. 'Is this what you are looking for?' said she.

'Yes! Thank you. I am glad you found it, for Mama would be cross with me if I lost it entirely.'

Emma smiled at him, a gesture that encouraged the boy to take her into his confidence.

'Miss Osborne has promised to dance with me,' said he. 'We have been engaged this week and we are to dance down every couple. Miss Osborne is so very obliging.'

'And do you like to dance?' asked Emma.

'I like it better than anything, except fishing. But Lord Osborne does not like to dance. He will do anything to get out of it. I do not recommend you dance with him as he may likely tread on your toe.'

'Thank you. I shall heed the warning,' replied Emma.

To the clear delight of the boy, his partner appeared before him with a more animated air than usual; but his joy soon turned to dismay when Miss Osborne said hurriedly, '*Charles, I beg your pardon for not keeping my engagement, but I am going to dance with Colonel Beresford. I know you will excuse me, and I will certainly dance with you after tea.*'

Without awaiting a reply, Miss Osborne took her place by Colonel Beresford's side to lead the set, leaving Charles upset and confused. For some moments *he stood the picture of disappointment while his mother, stifling her own mortification, tried to soothe his.*

'I am sure Miss Osborne will keep her word,' said Mrs Blake.

'I do not mind it, Mama,' said he, biting back the tears.

Without a moment's hesitation, Emma offered herself as a substitute. 'I shall be very happy to dance with you, sir, if you like.'

The boy in one moment restored to all his first delight — looked joyfully at his mother and stepping forwards with an honest and simple 'Thank you Maam' was instantly ready to attend his new acquaintance.

'There, Charles,' said his mother. 'Can you have wished for a better partner?'

'No, Mama,' said he, smiling broadly at Emma.

Mrs Blake was anxious to know to whom she had the pleasure of being indebted. 'I do not know how to thank you for saving the day.' Master Blake received the strictest of instructions from his mother. 'Charles, Miss Watson is not used to your rough and tumble ways. Be on your best behaviour and remember — '. Her son heard not a word of his mother's entreaties for his mind was set on dancing; and with the irrepressible joy of the moment, he led his new partner to the floor before she, like Miss Osborne, had time to change her mind.

The presence of the pretty new arrival and her young partner, the godson of Lord Osborne, proved to be the focus of interest among the assembled gathering, not least among some members of the Osborne set. As they passed in the dance, Miss Osborne commented, *'Upon my word, Charles, you are in luck. You have got a better partner than me,' to which the boy answered, 'Yes'.*

Lord Osborne's curiosity in Charles Blake's partner was apparent to all as he moved closer to the couple to get a better view. His action had not gone unnoticed by Miss Carr, who was quick to come to his side and draw his attention in another direction.

'What a dull evening it is! Public balls are uniformly tiresome,' said she.

'There are, I grant you, certain unpleasant aspects to every ball, and yet sometimes a ball can be made unexpectedly agreeable,' he replied, his gaze fixed Emma.

'Come, my lord. Have you ever seen anything so ridiculous as Mrs Edwards' new gown? I declare I have not. Let you and I go and compliment her on it.'

'You may do as you wish, Miss Carr. I am happy to remain where I am for the present.'

Miss Carr could see that Lord Osborne was in no humour to speak further and knew from similar former encounters that it was fruitless to persevere. She would, nevertheless, renew her efforts in the tea room where distractions would be limited to the choice of refreshments. Although she shared his lordship's partiality for negus and port wine jelly, she most certainly did not have same view of Miss Watson.

The adjournment for tea was not long in coming. Lord Osborne was joined by Tom Musgrave at a table reserved for their party at the far end of the room where his lordship could watch other guests come and go without the necessity of engaging in conversation.

'*Why do you not dance with* Miss Watson?' his lordship asked.

'*I was determining on it*, I assure you,' replied Musgrave.

'It is not in my power to offer, though I fear she may expect it.'

'Miss Watson is hardly *overpowered with applications*. She has had but one partner all evening and that was Charles Blake.'

'Indeed,' said Osborne, aware that Emma's service to Charles was a consequence of his own sister's broken promise to the boy.

Emma, for her part, had made a new friend. To her surprise and delight, she discovered that Charles' uncle was Mr Howard, the gentleman she so admired; it was a happy coincidence that rendered the ball infinitely more pleasurable. During the course of their conversation, she was able to discover that Mr Howard was also his tutor, and taught him Latin. It was, for Charles, a cause of great consternation, for never a day went by when he was not obliged to apply himself to the task of translation. After all, what need was there for other translations of Homer or Virgil among the infinite number that already existed? A more agreeable subject was his fondness for riding, for Lord Osborne had given him a horse and he had once been out riding with his lordship's hounds.

'*When shall you come to Osborne Castle? There is a monstrous curious stuffed fox there and a badger — anybody would think they were alive. It is a pity you should not see them.*'

Emma's protestations — that she was not at all acquainted with the family, nor ever expected to be — were instantly swept aside. 'But you may come to Wickstead to see Mama and she can take you to the Castle. Look! Over there! There is Lord Osborne. Let you and I go and sit by him.'

'No indeed. I must return you to your mother and go in search of my friends.' Before Emma had the opportunity of doing either, however, Mrs Blake joined them, accompanied by her brother.

'*Your goodness to Charles, my dear Miss Watson, brings all his family upon you. May I have leave to introduce my brother?*'

Emma found that Mr Howard was even more striking than she had imagined. In her eyes he was the epitome of decorum, the measure by which all men must be judged and found wanting. His bow was gracious but restrained; his smile was engaging and yet not too broad; and his address was all that a gentleman's should be.

'Would you do me the honour of dancing the next two dances with me, Miss Watson?'

'Thank you, sir. I should be happy to,' Emma replied.

Charles was less pleased with the arrangement. 'Do you think Miss Osborne will dance with me after tea?' said he, reluctant to give up his present partner.

His mother replied that she had no reason to think otherwise, though in truth, she had no reason to think that Miss Osborne would keep her promise either.

'Ah, Mrs Blake,' said Musgrave, joining the party, 'it is too long since I was at Wickstead. I am a sad neighbour, am I not?'

'You are indeed, Mr Musgrave. Are you acquainted with Miss Watson?'

'A little, but not nearly as well as I should like to be,' said he. And then turning to Emma, he said, 'If you are not engaged, Miss Watson, would you do me the honour — '

'Oh but she is,' said Charles.

'My little friend Charles must not expect to engross you the whole evening. It is against the rules of the assembly. And I am sure Mr Howard is *too nice a judge of decorum to give his licence to such a dangerous particularity.'*

'You are right, Mr Musgrave. I most certainly should not,' said the clergyman, as he offered one arm to his sister and the other to Emma. Mr Howard took his leave of Musgrave and led the two women to a comfortable seat in the tea room.

'Ah,' said Musgrave under his breath, 'I see how it is.'

The displeasing sensations that Emma had felt at the commencement of the assembly had now been entirely replaced by feelings of another kind. Mr Howard and his sister were the most congenial of companions. The clergyman made every effort to put the newcomer at ease and took pains to explain to her matters of special local interest and custom. He even acknowledged a slight acquaintance with her father, enquiring after his health in a manner that seemed to express genuine interest and concern. Mrs Blake spoke with generosity of their neighbours, without a hint of the kind of disapproval, malice or pretence that often accompanied gossip.

To Emma's dismay, however, the conversation was brought to an end too soon by the appearance of Mrs Edwards and her daughter.

The former chided Emma for abandoning Mary and the latter declared that her own need of Emma's company was greater than that of Mrs Blake and that she could not do without her new friend an instant longer. Mrs Blake, acknowledging the prior claims of the Edwardses, yielded at once, begging pardon for encroaching on Miss Watson's time.

The dissatisfaction that her daughter's behaviour in the ballroom had given Mrs Edwards, corresponded in equal measure to the gratification she felt on observing the attention paid to Miss Watson, for, being on intimate terms with the great family, Mr Howard and his sister were regarded by the neighbourhood as important members of the Osborne set. All eyes were naturally drawn to their actions and movements in the ballroom. It seemed to Mrs Edwards, therefore, to be no bad thing at all to be seen in the company of Lord Osborne's former tutor for as long as propriety allowed. Consequently, Mrs Edwards was in no hurry to vacate her station next to Mr Howard and his sister. Mary Edwards, however, had no desire to remain by her mother's side a moment longer than she was obliged to do.

'Come Emma, I have something I must show you,' said Mary, taking her by the arm and drawing her away from the party. 'You seem rather taken with our sober-minded parson. You should hear Captain Hunter on the subject of Mr Howard. Punctilious to the last degree, says he. All worth and no wit,' laughed Mary.

'Mary, please, I beg you, hold your tongue,' replied Emma. 'People will hear what you say. It would not reflect well on you if such remarks found their way back to Mr Howard. How should you feel then?'

The only present comfort that Emma derived from Mary's company was the knowledge that it would be of short duration. Mr Howard had secured her for the next two dances and she could see that guests were already making their way out of the tea room as Miss Tomlinson was shortly to call.

Lord Osborne, who sat at the furthest corner of the room to avoid the attentions of others, was at liberty to gaze at Emma without restraint. At length he was joined by his sister, Miss Carr and Mr Musgrave.

'I wonder at you,' said his sister. 'If you made a little more effort to make yourself agreeable — '

'You are not above reproof,' he replied.

Miss Osborne understood his meaning. 'I shall make it up to Charles. Indeed, he was all smiles when I last saw him. One of the locals offered to dance with him.'

'It would add to the pleasure of the evening if we were to see you dance, my lord. Would it not please us all?' said Miss Carr. 'Though I have a horror of public balls, I have no objection to giving pleasure where I can.'

'Then you might as well give pleasure to my friend,' replied Lord Osborne. 'Mr Musgrave is free, I'm sure he would oblige you.'

'Do you not yearn to dance, my lord? Not even this once?' she persisted.

'I have not the skill,' said he.

'Nor the inclination,' whispered Musgrave into his lordship's ear.

When the dancing recommenced, Mr Howard came forward to claim Emma's hand, and Lord Osborne took up a position near to the couple in the hope of getting a better view of his former tutor's partner. Emma, though irked by the frequency with which Lord Osborne seemed to look at her, was now at liberty to study her partner. In the intimacy of a dance, the first pleasing impressions can be heightened or diminished. Mr Howard, thought Emma, was as agreeable in character as he was in countenance. He spoke on the commonest of topics, but his expression and address made them all worth her full attention. By contrast, Lord Osborne's presence nearby was an unpleasant distraction, and she wondered why it had not been in Mr Howard's power to make his lordship's manners as exemplary as his own. Emma was surprised how quickly the time passed. The two dances seemed very short indeed; and she was disappointed to find that, as they concluded the second, the Osborne set had already begun making preparations to leave.

Lady Osborne would not be persuaded to play a further rubber despite universal entreaties from the room. If only they might persuade her to stay another half hour! Her ladyship's presence at the card table was a necessity! Were she to give up now, the entire room would retire within five minutes of her departure! The evening was certain to be the poorer for her absence!

Lady Osborne acknowledged the truth of the matter; the evening would, indeed, be the poorer without her. She would not be moved, however, and having judged that she had given sufficient pleasure to the assembly for one evening, bid them all 'good night'. And the card party played on for a convivial hour and a half more until the last dance had ended, and the landlord had begged them to break up for the night and go home.

Emma and Mrs Blake parted as old acquaintances, and Charles shook her hand and wished her 'goodbye' at least a dozen times. He promised that if Emma were to visit Wickstead, which he hoped would be very soon, they should certainly go to the Castle where he would show her *a monstrous stuffed fox and badger.*

Musgrave attended Lady Osborne to her carriage, declaring that he had had quite enough of the ball and would retreat to *the most remote corner of the house and order a barrel of oysters.*

'*I shall be famously snug there,*' said he.

'*Let us see you soon at the Castle, and bring me word how she looks by daylight,*' said his lordship.

'You have seen her by daylight,' said Musgrave.

'Even so, I should still like to know how she appears the morning after the ball.'

The carriages soon moved off and splashed through mud and puddles on their slow journey towards Wickstead and the grounds of Osborne Castle beyond. Charles, pleasantly tired, slumped by his mother's side. He smiled and yawned as he thought of the events of the evening and his pleasure in dancing with the beautiful Miss Watson.

'I like Miss Watson,' said he.

His mother agreed. 'She was very kind to you.'

'I hope she will come to visit us soon, for she is most eager to see the stuffed fox and badger at the Castle and I promised that I should take her there. Do you like Miss Watson, Uncle?'

Not wishing to be drawn on the subject, Mr Howard replied only that he wished the rain would cease.

The conversation in the Osborne carriage also concerned Miss Watson, but took a rather different turn.

'I do not think her handsome,' said Miss Carr.

'She is not without charm,' replied Miss Osborne, 'for a clergyman's daughter.' After a short pause, a thought occurred to her. 'Surely she would do for Mr Howard.'

While Lady Osborne dozed, the two young women laughed at the thought. The idea was both intriguing and amusing; and they were ideally placed to offer encouragement, at least to Mr Howard, for he was ever at the Castle.

'And what say you, my lord? Would Miss Watson make a suitable bride for Mr Howard? Will she be mistress of Wickstead? When shall we wish Mr Howard joy?' said Miss Carr.

Lord Osborne gave no reply and sat in silence for the rest of the journey as his sister and her friend set the date, planned the wedding breakfast and settled on the name of the happy couple's first child.

Seeing that her daughter was about to dance with Captain Hunter for the third time in one evening, Mrs Edwards sought out her husband and demanded that the carriage be ordered immediately. Being in no hurry to leave the card table, Mr Edwards whispered to his wife, 'At this very moment? I cannot possibly make my apologies, for who else is there to make up the table?'

'*Mary is surrounded by redcoats and all from the same regiment.* She has not danced with any of our old neighbours the entire evening. You must prevent her from dancing with Captain Hunter a third time. What will our neighbours say?'

'*But, my love, if these soldiers are quicker than other people in a ballroom, what are young ladies to do?*'

'I insist that you order the carriage immediately,' said Mrs Edwards. To the amusement of the other card players, her husband gave way and did as his wife commanded. At cards Mr Edwards had the distinction of routinely outplaying his opponents; in every other pursuit, however, Mrs Edwards appeared to hold the trump card.

CHAPTER SEVEN

The next morning brought a great many visitors to the Edwards' house, curious to see the young woman *who had been admired the night before by Lord Osborne.* The morning was spent discussing the merits of the ball, and was, for Emma, made all the more pleasurable by the mention of Mr Howard and his sister. After the last visitor had left, Mrs Edwards, who had until that point concealed from all but her husband her true thoughts about the evening's events, now decided to make them known.

'You are to be congratulated, Miss Emma. Your first ball in Delham must have brought you great satisfaction. To have been distinguished by Mr Howard and his sister is a triumph indeed, for Mr Howard rarely dances, and he is very particular in his choice of partners. I confess I should have been better pleased if Mary had been honoured in such a way.' Mrs Edwards glanced accusingly at her daughter and added with displeasure, 'There'll be no more balls for you this season unless you stand up with some of our old neighbours. Redcoats indeed! After I have spoken to your father, you will see how it will be.'

As if on cue, Mr Edwards appeared at the door and, finding that the last visitor had departed, entered the room in cheerful mood.

'Papa, please tell Mama that it is not my fault that Captain Hunter prefers to dance with me rather than the Tomlinson sisters. Indeed, I danced with *Mr Norton and Mr Styles.*'

'Have you still not done with the ball? Can we not talk of something else?' said Mr Edwards.

'And who is Mr Norton, pray?' continued Mrs Edwards, ignoring her husband's petition.

'*Mr Norton is a cousin of Captain Hunter's,*' said Mary.

'Is he? And Mr Styles?'

'*One of his particular friends.*'

'There, you see, Mr Edwards,' cried his wife.

'No! I do not see. And I do not want to hear another word about it!' he replied.

'But perhaps, Mama, it will please you to learn that the regiment is to winter at Reigate. So you see, Papa — '

Mr Edwards, whose patience had all but run out, made his excuses and abandoned the drawing room for the quiet refuge of his library to escape any further mention of redcoats, ribbons, and reels.

The sound of a light carriage driving up to the door some minutes later eased the uncomfortable atmosphere in the room. Emma, believing it to be the arrival of her sister Elizabeth, sighed with relief, for it meant that she would soon be on her way back to Stanton. Her anticipation of release from her present surroundings was, however, short lived, and soon turned to disappointment as the visitor who was shown into the drawing room minutes later was Tom Musgrave. He had with him a note from Elizabeth explaining that she had been prevented from bringing Emma home as their father had found that he had need of the carriage. Mr Musgrave had kindly offered to convey her to Stanton himself.

Emma was distressed at the proposal, having no wish to be on such intimate terms with Mr Musgrave. '*I must beg leave to decline your assistance, sir. I am rather afraid of that sort of carriage.* Indeed, *the distance is not beyond a walk.*'

Musgrave was surprised by Emma's reply, but would brook no refusal. 'My dear Miss Watson, *I must not be deprived of the happiness of escorting you. I assure you there is not a possibility of fear with my horses. You might guide them yourself. Your sisters all know how quiet they are; they have none of them the smallest scruple in trusting themselves with me, even on a racecourse. Believe me,*' said he lowering his voice, '*you are quite safe, the danger is only mine.*'

Mrs Edwards, who had been unusually silent up to that point, said, '*We shall be extremely happy Miss Emma, if you can give us the pleasure of your company until tomorrow — but if you cannot conveniently do so, our carriage is quite at your service, and Mary will be pleased with the opportunity of seeing your sister.*'

Emma accepted the offer most gratefully, adding *that as Elizabeth was entirely alone, it was her wish to return home for dinner.* No notice was taken of any further protestations from Mr Musgrave, and against the silent firmness of so many women, *the gentleman found himself obliged to submit.* Musgrave was, however, in no hurry to take his leave, for he had promised his friend that he would bring a full report of Miss Watson.

'*What a famous ball we had last night,*' said he. '*Miss Osborne is a charming girl, is she not?*'

Emma, to whom the remark was chiefly addressed, replied, 'Charming? I do not think her behaviour charming.'

'Her *manners are delightful.*'

'I'm sure they are when it suits her. She would do better not to make promises if she has no intention of keeping them,' said Emma, 'especially to children.'

'You are a stern critic, Miss Watson. But what do you think of Miss Carr. *Is she not a most interesting little creature?*'

'I understand she is to marry Lord Osborne. In which case, I think they will do very well together.'

'Ah,' said Musgrave, who had not anticipated so bold a reply. 'But do you think him handsome?'

'I should be more inclined to call him handsome *were he more desirous of pleasing and showing himself pleased in the right place.*'

'*Upon my word, you are severe upon my friend. I assure you, he is a good fellow.*'

'Is he? It is a great pity then that his manners are not the equal of Mr Howard's.'

'Do you compare his lordship's manners to those of his former tutor?'

'I do,' said Emma.

'Take note, Mary. Miss Emma knows where good manners are to be found and redcoats are not — '

Miss Edwards' eyes filled with tears. She begged their pardon and left the room in haste.

'I think, Miss Emma, you are eager to return home,' said Mrs Edwards. 'I shall order the carriage. Take Mary with you and see what you can do to make her see sense.'

Mr Musgrave *was obliged to put an end to his visit.* On Emma's side, there was no time to be lost in preparing for her journey home. Mr Musgrave took his leave, uncertain as to the nature of the report he would carry of Miss Emma Watson to his friend, for she was, as he had suspected, the picture of her elder sister nine years earlier, in looks, temper and opinions.

Mary Edwards accompanied her new friend and confidante to Stanton, but as it was nearing dinner hour there, sat only a few minutes before saying, 'I should return to Delham before it gets late. Perhaps some of the regiment are still there. Not every officer, but some perhaps.'

As soon as Mary had said her goodbyes and was safely on her way, Elizabeth was anxious to hear Emma's news of the ball. *You must talk to me the rest of the day, without stopping, or I shall not be satisfied. But first of all Nanny shall bring in the dinner. Poor thing. — You will not dine as you did last night for we have nothing but fried beef.'*

'That will suit me perfectly, I assure you,' replied Emma. 'I am so thankful to be home.'

'You do not know how pleased I am to hear you call Stanton home,' said Elizabeth. 'But now tell me, why did you *not come home with Tom Musgrave?*

'*I could not wish for the obligation or the intimacy which the use of his carriage must have created. I should not even have liked the appearance of it.'*

'*You did right, though I wonder at your forbearance and I do not think I could have done it myself. He seemed so eager to fetch you, and I did long to see you. It seemed a clever way of getting you home.* But tell me Emma, how did you like our little assembly?'

Elizabeth listened in silence as Emma gave as full an account as she could. But when her sister reached the part where Mr Howard had asked her to dance, Elizabeth exclaimed, '*Dance with Mr Howard? Good heavens. He is quite one of the great and grand ones. Did you not find him very high? I should have been frightened out of my wits to have had anything to do with the Osborne set.'*

'I was perfectly at ease with him. Indeed, his manners put me more at ease than those of Mr Musgrave or his friend.'

'His friend?'

'Lord Osborne.'

'Did either of them ask you to dance?'

'Mr Musgrave offered to dance with me though I believe it was due entirely to Lord Osborne's bidding.'

'A partner by proxy! That is an honour, Emma. I have never known Lord Osborne to do such a thing.'

'Well, I wish he had not. As fortune would have it, I was saved from having to stand up with Mr Musgrave as Mr Howard offered first.'

'Mr Howard was once Lord Osborne's tutor,' said Elizabeth.

'I know. It must be a great disappointment for Mr Howard to find that his pupil has learned so little.'

'I have heard that at times he has the most engaging manners.'

49

'He stares a great deal and never utters a word. Even Mr Musgrave's manners fare well by comparison.'

'And so you really did not dance with Tom Musgrave? Not even once? But you must have liked him. You must have been struck with him.'

'His haircut caused an outcry. I own, I prefer it to powder, but I find nothing else to admire in him. *There is a ridiculousness about him that entertains me*, but that *is all.'*

'My dearest Emma, you are like nobody else in the world. It is a good thing that Margaret is not by. She would never forgive such words.'

'I wish she could have heard him profess his ignorance of her being away from Stanton.'

'I see what you mean. *And yet this is the man she will fancy is so desperately in love with her. He is no favourite of mine, as you well know.* But, *hand on your heart*, Emma, can you really say that you did not find him agreeable?'

'Indeed I can, both hands; and spread to their widest extent.'

'I should dearly love *to know the man you do think agreeable,'* said Elizabeth.

'Need you ask? *His name is Howard.'*

As daylight faded, a conveyance was heard passing through the parsonage gates.

'That must be Papa,' said Elizabeth.

Mr Watson returned…not the worse for the exertion of the day, and consequently pleased with what he had done, and glad to talk of it, over his own fireside.

Elizabeth held out little hope of hearing anything of interest, for Mr Watson was not, and never had been, proficient in the art of conversation. He rarely listened to matters he considered commonplace and when obliged to do so, would fail to recall anything of importance.

'Papa, how did Mr Tomlinson's new carriage appear?' said Elizabeth.

'I expect it appeared like all new carriages. Spotless clean and polished to a shine.'

'Have the wool stockings arrived at Mason's?'

'I did not hear the matter spoken of.'

'Is Mrs Stokes still in mourning?'

'I believe so. But then she may well not be.'

To each enquiry, and more, Elizabeth received the same unsatisfactory reply. What reason could there be, thought she, of ever going into town if not to return with news of their neighbours' joys and misfortunes? Mr Watson's powers of recall were, as ever, selective. He could recount every particular of a sermon, bible reading or theological treatise. He was, moreover, capable of reciting Herbert, Bunyan and Milton, and did so at length when his health and a little red wine allowed, which was fortuitously rare; but he had no recollection of the important news of the day.

Remarkably, Mr Watson was in excellent spirits, having attended a visitation; and by all accounts it had turned out to be a good one.

'I have never been more pleased with a visitation than today.'

Elizabeth and *Emma had not foreseen any interest* to themselves *in the occurrences of a visitation*, but when Mr Howard's name was spoken of as the preacher, they became instantly more attentive.

'Mr Howard gave us *an excellent sermon. I do not know when I have heard a discourse more to my mind, or one better delivered,*' said he. 'Mr Howard *reads extremely well, and with great propriety, and in a very impressive manner and at the same time without any theatrical grimace or violence.*'

Elizabeth and Emma exchanged glances of surprise and pleasure. Emma was delighted to hear her father speak of Mr Howard in so warm a fashion, for his words bore out the opinion she had formed of the man she had come to think of as superior to all others.

'*I do not like much action in the pulpit,*' continued Mr Watson. '*I do not like the studied air and artificial inflexions of voice, which your very popular and admired preachers generally have. A simple delivery is much better calculated to inspire devotion, and shows a much better taste. Mr Howard read like a scholar and a gentleman.*'

'And what did you have for dinner?' his eldest daughter asked, seeking to avoid a repetition of the sermon given by Mr Howard at the visitation.

Mr Watson *related the dishes* as best he could and even recalled some of what he had eaten himself. '*Upon the whole,*' he continued, '*I had a very comfortable day. I must say that everybody paid me great attention and seemed to feel for me as an invalid. What pleased me as much as anything was Mr Howard's attention. There is a pretty steep flight of steps up to the room we dine in which do not agree with my gouty foot. Mr Howard walked by me from the bottom to the top and would make me take his arm. It struck me as very becoming in so young a man, but I am sure I had no claim to expect it.*'

Elizabeth could hold her tongue no longer, and, looking at Emma who had listened intently to every word on the subject, proceeded to enquire as to whether Mr Howard had suffered any ill effects following his attendance at the assembly the previous night.

'That I do not recall, but he did ask after you, Emma.'

'Yes, Papa?' said Emma hopefully.

'I said that you were not long arrived from Shropshire. Mr Howard would ask the purpose of your stay in that county and seemed quite satisfied with my reply. And Emma, Mr Howard added a little something that might please you.'

Emma and Elizabeth waited eagerly for mention of the little something.

'But I do not quite recall what it was,' said their father.

CHAPTER EIGHT

The following morning Mr Watson sent word that he would keep to his room, fearing that a little soreness in his throat might be a warning sign of the onset of a chill, most probably due to the effects of the previous day's exertions. Elizabeth rose early in preparation for the great wash. On hearing her sister rise, Emma soon followed. It was a new thing for Emma to be occupied about the house. In Shropshire she had received every comfort, and had never been called upon to employ her time on domestic matters of any description. Emma's desire was to be of service to her sister in whatever way she could. An old frock was chosen for the purpose, and with minimum alteration to her hair, she scrambled down the stairs to offer her assistance. The sound of cheerful chatter and the clatter of lively activity led her to the kitchen. There she found Elizabeth and Nanny hard at work performing several tasks at once. The offer of assistance was gladly accepted, and it was not long before Emma found herself hidden beneath a pile of laundry, folding and sorting items according to Nanny's instructions. There was much to be done, and it was after midday before Emma and Elizabeth, having worked without respite, sat down.

The task complete, Nanny set about preparing dinner when she *was suddenly called to the front door. Charged by Miss Watson to let nobody in, Nanny returned with a look of awkward dismay to hold the parlour door open for Lord Osborne and Tom Musgrave.*

Emma, who was nearest to the door and in earshot of the visitors, heard Musgrave whisper to his companion, 'I'll wager you'll find she does not want much talking to. If she is anything like her sister, she will only want to be listened to.'

The surprise of the young ladies may be imagined. No visitors would have been welcome at such a moment, but such visitors as these — such a one as Lord Osborne at least, a nobleman and a stranger — was really distressing.

'Miss Watson. Miss Emma,' said Tom Musgrave with easy familiarity. 'May I present Lord Osborne?' said he, as though a visit from a nobleman was a commonplace occurrence at the parsonage. Lord Osborne was then properly introduced, and although his *voluble friend* found much to say, his lordship appeared embarrassed, and mumbled incoherently.

Emma took no pleasure in the visit. *She felt all the inconsistency of such an acquaintance with the very humble style in which they were obliged to live; and having in her aunt's family been used to many of the elegancies of life, was fully sensible of all that must be open to the ridicule of richer people in her present home.*

'We happened to be in the neighbourhood,' continued Musgrave.

'We are honoured, sir,' said Elizabeth nervously.

Osborne acknowledged Miss Watson and her sister with an awkward bow.

'Please,' said Elizabeth, offering a seat to their visitors. 'Our father is unwell today. I am afraid he is unable to receive you.'

'Please convey to him our good wishes,' said Lord Osborne.

'I'm afraid I have been a very sad neighbour of late,' said Musgrave with a sigh. 'I hear complaints of my negligence wherever I go. It is a shameful length of time since I was at Stanton.'

The shock and confusion that Elizabeth felt at the presence of Lord Osborne in her parlour was soon overcome. On hearing Musgrave's remark, she was herself again, for the air of self-importance that he sometimes adopted was an aspect of his character she had long taken delight in railing against.

'If I recall, Mr Musgrave, you graced us with your presence last spring. It is not yet midwinter. Anyone would say you were almost an inmate here.'

Mr Musgrave was never at a loss for words and took peculiar pleasure in Elizabeth's company, for he was never quite sure whether her raillery at his expense was spoken in jest or had a more serious purpose. He found that he was unable to resist the temptation to enquire after the two sisters absent from Stanton.

'I am surprised to find Miss Margaret has gone away. I expect she will not be long gone,' said he.

'Did you really not know? Margaret has been gone a good while,' Elizabeth replied.

'A good while, you say? How stoically you endure her absence. She must be greatly missed at Stanton,' said he. Elizabeth understood his meaning all too well and struggled to suppress a smile.

Lord Osborne, who had taken a seat close to Emma, searched in desperation for something to say. At length, his endeavour produced a general enquiry about her health.

'I hope you did not catch a cold at the ball,' said he.

'No. Not at all,' replied Emma.

Osborne fell silent once again. His attentions to Emma had not been lost on Elizabeth but most of all she was surprised to see what little trouble Emma took to put his lordship at ease.

Musgrave continued his enquiries of the family. 'And so Miss Penelope is gone to Chichester.'

'Yes. She is gone to stay with Mrs Shaw.'

'How very fortunate for Mrs Shaw to have the pleasure of Miss Penelope's company a full month,' said he. 'The absence of your sister at our assembly on Tuesday was a deprivation indeed.'

'I shall be sure to mention it when I write to her.'

At length Lord Osborne broke the silence and addressed Emma once again.

'*Have you been walking this morning?*'

Emma had little compunction about informing his lordship that they had been occupied the entire day with the business of the great wash, but in the end she gave a reply that required the least exertion, and said simply, '*No, my lord. We thought it too dirty.*'

'*You should wear half boots.*' After another pause, Osborne continued, '*Nothing sets off a neat ankle more than a half boot; nankin galoshed with black looks very well. Do you not like half boots?*'

'*Yes, but unless they are so stout as to injure their beauty, they are not fit for country walking.*'

'*Ladies should ride in dirty weather. Do you ride?*'

'*No, my lord.*'

'*I wonder every lady does not. A woman never looks better than on horseback.*'

'*But every woman may not have the inclination, or the means.*'

'*If they knew how much it became them, they would all have the inclination, and I fancy Miss Watson, when once they had the inclination, the means would soon follow.*'

'*Your lordship thinks we always have our own way. That is a point on which ladies and gentlemen have long disagreed. But without pretending to decide it, I may say that there are some circumstances which even women cannot control. Female economy will do a great deal, my lord, but it cannot turn a small income into a large one.*'

Lord Osborne was silenced. Her manner had been neither sententious nor sarcastic, but there was something in its mild seriousness, as well as in the words themselves which made his lordship think; and when he addressed her again, it was with a degree of considerate propriety, totally unlike the half-awkward, half-fearless style of his former remarks. It was a new thing with him to wish to please a woman; it was the first time that he had ever felt what was due to a woman in Emma's situation. But as he wanted neither sense nor a good disposition, he did not feel it without effect.

'You have not been long in this country I understand,' said he in the tone of a gentleman. 'I hope you are pleased with it.'

He was rewarded by a gracious answer, and a more liberal full view of her face than she had yet bestowed. Unused to exert himself, and happy in contemplating her, he then sat in silence for some minutes longer, while Tom Musgrave was chattering to Elizabeth.

The visit was brought to an end when Nanny, *half opening the door and putting in her head*, said that Mr Watson wanted to know when he was to have his dinner.

The visitors were swift to make their apologies.

'I am sorry it happens so,' added Elizabeth, turning good-humouredly towards Musgrave, 'but you know what early hours we keep.'

Tom had nothing to say for himself; he knew it very well, and such honest simplicity, such shameless truth rather bewildered him. Lord Osborne's parting compliments took some time, his inclination for speech seeming to increase with the shortness of the term for indulgence. He recommended exercise in defiance of dirt — spoke again in praise of half-boots — begged that his sister might be allowed to send Emma the name of her shoemaker — and concluded with saying, 'My hounds will be hunting this country next week. I believe they will throw off at Stanton Wood on Wednesday at nine o'clock. I mention this in hopes of your being drawn out to see what's going on. If the morning's tolerable, pray do us the honour of giving us your good wishes in person.'

The sisters looked on each other with astonishment when their visitors had withdrawn.

'Here's an unaccountable honour,' cried Elizabeth at last. 'Who would have thought of Lord Osborne's coming to Stanton. He is very handsome but Tom Musgrave looks all to nothing the smartest and most fashionable man of the two. I am glad he did not say anything to me; I would not have had to talk to such a great man for the world. Tom was very agreeable, was not he? But did you hear him ask where Miss Penelope and Miss Margaret were, when he first came in? It put me out of patience.'

To say that Emma was not flattered by Lord Osborne's visit would be to assert a very unlikely thing, and describe a very odd young lady; but the gratification was by no means unalloyed; his coming was a sort of notice which might please her vanity, but did not suit her pride, and she would rather have known that he wished the visit without presuming to make it, than have seen him at Stanton. Among other unsatisfactory feelings it once occurred to her to wonder why Mr Howard had not taken the same privilege of coming, and accompanied his lordship; but she was willing to suppose that he had either known nothing about it, or had declined any share in a measure which carried quite as much impertinence in its form as good breeding.

On leaving the parsonage, the two visitors rode for some minutes in silence. Musgrave appeared less satisfied with the visit than his companion.

'I expect we should have taken our leave sooner,' said his lordship.

Musgrave replied, 'It is well she has neither fortune nor connections.'

'Of whom do you speak? Miss Watson or Miss Emma?'

Musgrave's confusion was not lost on Lord Osborne. The novelty of it caused his friend to raise a smile and resolve to keep his thoughts on the subject of the Misses Watson in future to himself.

CHAPTER NINE

Lady Osborne's musical society was regularly attended by a distinguished company of members drawn from those families in the neighbourhood who professed to be true lovers of harmony. Whether harmony existed between the guests assembled was less certain; nevertheless, the musical evening at Osborne Castle was a celebrated occasion, and each recipient of an invitation from her ladyship considered it an honour to attend. Lady Osborne made it her business to superintend every particular of the evening. Her approval was sought on matters great and small and everything was managed by her. Indeed, she was not content to manage the practicalities of the occasion; she also took it upon herself to instruct the musicians as to the content and order of the recital pieces and how they might best be performed.

Like most of her guests, she had little command of the Italian language but, unlike many of them, she was a great admirer of Italian love songs; and although at times some of the members of the musical society might have privately harboured notions that were at odds with her ladyship's musical taste, they never gave voice to them. Complaints that the recitals were unvarying in content were never heard. The brilliance of each occasion was declared in the warmest of terms by all, and Lady Osborne was pronounced the consummate musical society hostess. Moreover, her ladyship's superior musical knowledge was universally proclaimed, and no one would brook opposition. There was no song — whether French, German or even English — that compared to an Italian love song.

On this occasion, Lady Osborne had taken particular care over the seating arrangements, and to the delight of Miss Carr and the dismay of her son, the two had been seated together.

'You are indeed fortunate this evening,' whispered Lady Osborne to her son. 'Miss Carr is anxious to translate for you. She is as proficient in the language as Mr Howard himself.'

'Miss Carr,' replied Osborne, 'need not take the trouble. The general substance of the songs is exceedingly clear to me. Have we not heard them with undeviating regularity?'

'You may say what you wish, but there would be an outcry were I to alter a single note. Come now,' said Lady Osborne, 'take your seat by Miss Carr. Mr Howard is eager to begin.'

As Mr Howard made his way to the front, a gradual hush descended on the gathering. The musicians took up their instruments and waited for the clergyman to give the signal to begin.

Miss Carr leaned towards Osborne and whispered into his ear. 'As a ray of sun, mild and serene, rests upon placid waves, while upon the deep breast of the sea the storm lies hidden — '

'Have you received news of a shipwreck, Miss Carr?' Osborne asked.

'I have not, my lord. They are the words of the song.' She continued, '…even so, a smile, gay and tranquil will wreathe a pair of lips in satisfaction and joy while in its secret depth the stricken heart feels anguish and torment.'

As the song ended, rapturous applause filled the room and, gratified by the response, Mr Howard prepared himself for the next piece in his repertoire.

'Was not that the most beautiful love song you have ever heard, my lord?' continued Miss Carr.

'I am quite deaf to the strain of love songs,' he replied. The tone of his lordship's reply left Miss Carr with little hope of securing his attention further, and the remainder of the recital passed in silence between them.

As the first part of the evening drew to a close, the guests adjourned for refreshments, and as the bustle eased, Miss Carr joined Lady Osborne and her small band of musical connoisseurs at the table. 'How do you find the evening so far, Miss Carr?' said her ladyship.

'The similarity to my uncle's musical evenings is quite extraordinary. I am completely enthralled.'

'I hope Mr Appleby gives good direction. Musicians cannot be trusted with the selection of pieces for they do not know what is best pleasing to the ear.'

'You will not find anyone as completely devoted to music as Mr Appleby. Indeed, he plays the pianoforte exceedingly well. His piano playing is considered accomplished by all the experts and is the talk of the county; it is said that he can execute entire concertos without playing a single wrong note, though I have not had the pleasure myself of hearing him play.'

'Concertos, you say? I doubt his taste in music is equal to mine,' replied Lady Osborne. If, as Lady Osborne suspected, Mr Appleby's taste in music matched his taste in interior décor, which by all accounts was singular, he was just as likely to have little true sensitivity in his delivery of a concerto as he was in the painting of the walls at Appleby Hall.

'No, indeed,' said Miss Carr, perceiving that she had vexed her ladyship. 'No one could fault your taste or your true passion for music.' An awkward silence ensued as Lady Osborne ate her soup. At length, Miss Carr returned to a subject on which she felt Lady Osborne would be in firm agreement.

'Imagine my surprise when Lord Osborne told me he was deaf to love songs. I was utterly speechless. He says that he does not hear them.'

'His deafness is entirely selective, as it is with all men, Miss Carr,' she replied. 'But it is music to their ears if there is a fish to be caught, a pheasant to be shot or a horse to be bought.'

Osborne's earlier slight of Miss Carr had not gone unnoticed by his sister. Miss Osborne, who had been occupied ascertaining news from Colonel Beresford's aunt, of the regiment's arrival in Reigate, now took her brother to one side.

'Do not slight my friend,' said she. 'Accord her the distinction due to her. That is all I ask.'

'Then, I beg you, cease to mislead her.'

'I do not know what you mean,' said she.

'I do not intend to make Miss Carr an offer. Your encouragement in this endeavour does you no credit, nor does it contribute to the contentment of your friend.'

'All that is needed is time. One day you will thank me.'

'Return to your friend,' said he. 'This matter is at an end.'

Had Lady Osborne been blessed with the ability to sing in tune, she should have been an accomplished singer of operatic arias. 'I should have been a celebrated soprano and sung with proper feeling and a tone of exquisite beauty,' said she. Indeed, Lady Osborne's voice had a resonant quality — an asset worthy of any opera singer — for it often filled the room and was discernible above every other conversation.

Lord Osborne rarely attended to his mother's discourse on such occasions, and this occasion was no exception, for his attention was drawn to a more interesting subject.

'My lord, as you know, my brother has business that takes him to town,' said Mrs Blake. 'He will be away a few days, or even a week. You may recall — though there is no reason why you should — the kindness paid to Charles at the ball by a young lady, a Miss Watson. Charles never stops talking about her.'

'I recall something of the sort,' said he with studied indifference.

'Well, I have taken it upon myself — and Mr Howard is in agreement — to invite Miss Watson to stay at Wickstead in his absence. Charles has already set to work preparing a list of things that Miss Watson might like to do. I fear I should warn her, for the list does not look too promising. I hesitate to impose on your good family, but I gave Charles my word that I would ask you if he may — we may — call on you during Miss Watson's stay. Charles should like to show Miss Watson the stuffed fox and badger he so admires in the library. My son assures me that Miss Watson has expressed an interest, though I suspect his eagerness to show them is greater than Miss Watson's desire to see them.'

'My sister, I am sure, would be happy to receive Miss Watson,' said he, in hope rather than expectation, for the certainty of his sister's happiness at such a prospect was by no means assured. He feared that a visit from the young woman whose kindness to Charles was a reminder of his own sister's broken promise would not be entirely welcome.

As the crowd moved towards the music room, the door opened to admit Tom Musgrave. His theatrical entrance eclipsed Lady Osborne's command of the proceedings as he strode into the room and offered his profound apologies for the lateness of the hour. — The shocking weather had been the cause of his tardiness. — The flooding in town was a sight to behold. — He had never seen the like of it. — No! He would not be persuaded to take a mouthful of posset. He had no appetite, not even a morsel of pie would tempt him.'

In contrast to Osborne, Musgrave appeared at first to be in buoyant mood, for he had been able to indulge his enjoyment of late entrances, not once, but twice in one evening. On further enquiry,

Osborne was surprised to discover that his friend had spent the earlier part of the evening with the Watson family.

'On my way back from town,' said he to Osborne in a whisper, 'the weather prevented me from proceeding further. I determined, therefore, to call upon the Watsons until the storm eased. Upon my word, I shall make every effort to curb any future impulse of that nature. The brother and wife were there. Miss Margaret was brought back from Croydon — and sooner than she had anticipated, it seemed. I expect the Croydon family had had the pleasure of her company long enough. Mr Robert Watson is a shrewd attorney who knows the value of money and how to come by it. He was never done with complaining about the road and how he would indict it if he lived here. He insisted on knowing the surveyor's name. His wife put me in mind of a stuffed artichoke — a woman with a complexion several shades of puce and a frock the colour of pond fodder. Indeed her whole ensemble would serve an entire troop encampment in tents a full season. I did not get too close for I was afraid of getting trapped in its folds. There was I at table, locked between Miss Margaret, whispering nonsense to me in one ear, and the elder Miss Watson, finding fault at every turn. All that was needed to make the scene complete was for Miss Penelope to arrive — which thankfully she did not. Mr Musgrave, said Miss Margaret, you must dine with us tomorrow. Miss Margaret, said I, I beg your pardon, but I am engaged the whole day with Lord Osborne. — By the by, I am now completely at your disposal. I discover I have a fondness for fishing after all. The elder Miss Watson refused to sit down with me at cards, leaving me to ward off Miss Margaret's attentions alone. She took great pleasure in arranging it so, I can tell you. And if that were not insult enough, Mr Robert made a point of apologising for *appearing in such dishabille* before me. He had not, he said, had the time to put fresh powder in his hair. Miss Margaret assured me that her brother did not mean to give offence and that he had even thought of becoming a crop himself. I very much doubt there is any truth in it, for the brother has little left up top to care about. And then Miss Watson embarked upon a discourse worthy of Mr Howard, about vanity being a serious defect of character, especially in men, as it was so often difficult to bring it under good regulation. A truly terrifying ordeal!'

'Was anyone else present?' enquired Osborne.

'Miss Emma Watson made her apologies soon after my arrival and went up to read to her father. I expect she wanted an excuse to leave them all to their own devices. Mr Robert was never done with tales of their aunt's foolishness. He blames the aunt most vehemently for marrying a redcoat and disinheriting Miss Emma. He likely wanted the management of the estate when it fell to his youngest sister. Did you know that she is sent back to her family without a penny? It is misfortune enough; but the greater misfortune, I daresay, is to find that she is dependent upon a family set on inflicting misery upon all around them. By the by, she is invited to Wickstead. It was Miss Margaret who mentioned it first, along with a multitude of complaints about her own entitlements. She was in such a temper because the honour had not been extended to her — I'll wager the family has not heard the last of the matter. I should like to see Mrs Blake's forbearance — Miss Margaret is enough to put flight to the mildest disposition.'

As the musicians raised their violins, silence fell on the gathering. 'Shall we see Miss Emma Watson at the Castle soon?' whispered Musgrave.

CHAPTER TEN

Robert Watson was *very well satisfied with himself*. He had *married the only daughter of the attorney to whom he had been the clerk, with a fortune of six thousand pounds.* — *Mrs Robert was not less pleased with herself for having had that six thousand pounds, and for being now in possession of a very smart house in Croydon, where she gave genteel parties, and wore fine clothes.* She pitied Emma; *the loss of the aunt's fortune was uppermost in her mind, and she could not but feel how much better it was to be the daughter of a gentleman of property in Croydon, than the niece of an old woman who threw herself away on an Irish Captain.* Emma *saw that her sister-in-law despised her immediately*; likewise, her brother took little trouble to welcome her, for she was *no longer likely to have any property for him to get the direction of. Mrs Robert Watson wondered what sort of home Emma could possibly have been used to in Shropshire, and setting it down as certain that her aunt could never have had six thousand pounds*, she was content to eye Emma with *triumphant compassion.*

Margaret Watson's delight in seeing *dear, dear Emma* was soon replaced with feelings of an entirely different nature.

'Imagine,' said Elizabeth, 'no sooner is our dear sister returned to us than she is off again, and into very grand company indeed. Brother, you may recall Mr Howard. He was once Lord Osborne's tutor and is now rector of the parish of Wickstead. Mr Howard and his sister are on intimate terms with the Osbornes and never a day goes by, it seems, but they are invited there. I would not be surprised if Emma were to receive an invitation to Osborne Castle herself.'

The opportunity to return several times in one evening to this interesting piece of information gave Elizabeth some satisfaction, for she was sensible of the all too painful slight inflicted on Emma by the Croydon family when first they arrived.

'What flights of fancy, Elizabeth! Emma will be sent back forthwith once the knowledge of her circumstances is exposed to the world,' said her brother.

'I have been used most cruelly,' said Margaret. 'I am sure an error has been made. Did Mrs Blake stipulate any sister in particular? Let me see the letter. I should be the one to visit Wickstead or at the very least accompany Emma. Why should she receive all the attention?'

'Because she was exceedingly kind to Mrs Blake's son,' said Elizabeth. 'And if you were a little more inclined towards performing acts of kindness now and again, you too might have your reward.'

Margaret paid no heed to her sister's remark. 'I expect Tom Musgrave calls at Wickstead every day, for he is always at the Castle, and it is not far out of his way. He is not to be trusted, Emma. Believe me, he is a great flirt. Unless you wish to expose yourself to ridicule, be on your guard. Refuse to have anything to do with him. Any encouragement on your part is sure to end in tears. It always does.'

'My dear sister,' said Emma, 'let me put your mind at rest. I have not the slightest intention of giving encouragement of any kind to Mr Musgrave.'

'That is what Penelope said, but you should have seen how she set him against Elizabeth. *There is nothing she would not do to get* a husband. And then there was Mr Purvis, the curate. He was very fond of Elizabeth, but Penelope came between them. Ask Elizabeth. She will tell you.'

Emma was not inclined to do anything of the kind and, changing the subject, turned to her elder sister, who had set about darning stockings to calm her nerves, to beg for similar employment.

'Did you notice how he called upon us last night so soon after my return?' continued Margaret. 'It is often said that absence makes the heart grow fonder. Musgrave hides it well, but I believe his heart belongs to me.'

'Believe what you will. You are welcome to his heart, if indeed he has a heart to give. Please pass me the thread, Emma,' said Elizabeth.

Elizabeth gave Emma her word that she would say nothing further on the subject of Mr Howard and his sister, and though she was sorely tempted, she also refrained from making any mention of the recent visit of Tom Musgrave and Lord Osborne to Stanton.

Mr Watson, however, had not been held to any promise of the kind, nor had he knowledge of Emma's request for silence on the matter. Having benefitted at length from a peaceful night's sleep, he was persuaded to join the rest of the family downstairs.

'Elizabeth, will you tell Nanny to bring some hot water? And would you find out if the mail has arrived? And do ask Robert and Jane how long we are to have the pleasure of their company? I hope it is not long. What was all that commotion I heard last night?'

'It was Mr Musgrave, Papa,' said Margaret, appearing at the door, having heard every word her father had said. Eager to continue speaking on her favourite topic, she came into the room and closed the door. 'He called on us after supper. I cannot imagine why his visit was a matter of such urgency. He has not visited Stanton in months.'

'But he was here not two days ago,' said Mr Watson. 'What day was it, Elizabeth? When did Mr Musgrave call upon me?'

'It was the day of the great wash, Papa. He didn't stay long,' said Elizabeth.

'He stayed for three quarters of an hour at least. Do you not remember?' said Mr Watson. 'Dinner was late that day. It was most inconvenient and quite ill-mannered to be calling at such a time. Nanny had to give him a very strong hint to leave.'

'The weather looks promising,' said Elizabeth, desirous of guiding the conversation in another direction. 'Shall we go for a walk?'

'I did not receive him,' continued Mr Watson, 'for I was not equal to it. It was a curious affair, for he brought with him young Lord Osborne. What could Mr Musgrave have possibly meant by it? *I have lived here fourteen years without being noticed by any of the family. I expect it was some foolery on his part.* What an idle fellow he is.'

'Who, Papa?' asked Margaret.

'Mr Musgrave, of course,' said he. 'And that young Lord too, I expect. I have no wish to return the visit, so Elizabeth had a note sent up to Osborne Castle. She is so very accomplished in making excuses, you know. She does it so prettily and with great economy. And now Emma is invited to Wickstead. It will do her no harm, for Mr Howard is a respectable man and very active in the pulpit. His sister seems to be a good sort of person from what I hear. I should, if my health allowed, be inclined to call upon Mr Howard.'

The look of astonishment on Margaret's face made Elizabeth smile but she drew little further pleasure from the disclosure, for she knew that it would only serve to fuel Margaret's resentment.

'Have I said something amiss?' said Mr Watson.

Margaret's *fretful displeasure* and *querulous attacks* on hearing her father's revelation, continued for the remainder of the day. She scolded Elizabeth and Emma for keeping the account of Mr Musgrave and Lord Osborne's visit hidden from her; she reprimanded Robert and Jane for keeping her in Croydon too long, thereby preventing her from having the pleasure of being present at Stanton when they called; and she blamed Aunt Turner for sending Emma back to Stanton penniless, hence ruining her own prospects of making an advantageous alliance.

Mrs Robert Watson was similarly displeased with her young sister-in-law and was not a woman used to hiding her displeasure. She was of the opinion that Margaret had a rival in her younger sister and warned Margaret accordingly; the possibility that Emma might succeed, indeed, might have already succeeded, in engaging the affections of Mr Musgrave, called for immediate action.

'My dear Emma,' said she, 'your brother and I will be returning to Croydon on Wednesday. We should be delighted if you would accompany us. I believe you will be pleased with Croydon. Indeed, I daresay you will not wish to return to Stanton once you have seen what Croydon society has to offer.'

'Thank you for your kind offer, but I am quite content to remain here for the present. I should like to be near to my father.'

'Nonsense!' said Jane. 'Elizabeth and Margaret are here. Your father had no need of you all these years. What need has he of you now? I shall not countenance opposition. You shall return with us to Croydon. You need not make a song and dance about it. A small trunk will do for your things as there is no room for a large one.'

'Please forgive me, but I am unable to accept your invitation as I have a prior claim on my time.'

'You may make your apologies to Mr Howard and his sister and tell them that it is not convenient for you to accept their invitation at present for you have recollected a more pressing engagement. Ask Elizabeth to write a note for you, for your sister, by all accounts, appears to be quite accomplished in the art of making excuses.'

'I shall make no alteration of the kind. Mrs Blake is expecting me. I shall — I must — go to Wickstead. Please excuse me.'

'When Robert hears of it, I should not want to be in the same room. Be careful not to provoke your brother's displeasure,' said his wife.

Emma left the room determined to oppose every entreaty that was put to her. She would not, could not, go to Croydon with Robert and Jane at such a time. To avoid further confrontation, she sought solace in the company of her father, a place where she could sit in *gentleness and silence*, free from the unreasonable demands and frequent reprimands dispensed by the rest of the household. She wished only for Elizabeth's company to make her society complete, and was thankful that no further calls on her time were made by Mr and Mrs Robert Watson, nor indeed by her sister Margaret, for the rest of the day.

'Jane,' said Elizabeth, when at last they were alone, 'what advantage is to be gained by inviting Emma to return with you and Robert to Croydon at this time?'

'Every advantage is to be gained by it. Emma may come to Croydon and see what she can do there. Robert has a clerk who might be persuaded to take her for very little. My husband is the very essence of generosity. He would not be at liberty to settle a great deal on Emma. Forty pounds or thereabouts, I daresay, he would part with. Mr Hemmings would think himself lucky to take Emma for twenty. He would have taken Margaret for ten.'

'Wait until Emma returns from Wickstead. Surely you cannot be insensible of the honour to Emma, and consequently to us all, afforded by such an invitation. Think of the notice she has already received from Lord Osborne himself.'

'Once these great people are acquainted with Emma's true situation, the notice she enjoys at present will come to an end. She had much better come to Croydon and let her brother do what he can to help her there. Emma has the appearance of an heiress — for I do not deny she has been brought up like one — but not the means. That is the point.'

'And how should you account for Emma's present situation to your Croydon friends?'

It was true that an absence of fourteen years must be accounted for; and while Mrs Robert Watson might exult in her comfortable situation in life among her less fortunate relations at Stanton, within the genteel society of Croydon, a penniless sister-in-law brought up by an aunt with such a history might give rise to ridicule and censure.

'Tales of abandonment by an aunt who saw fit to enter into an alliance with a redcoat young enough to be her son might raise unwelcome speculation among your Croydon circle,' said Elizabeth.

Mrs Robert Watson generally took pleasure in such narratives — most particularly those that involved rumours of scandal — yet true satisfaction was only to be had through the misfortunes of families unconnected to her own. It was unusual for Jane to be persuaded of anything by Elizabeth, or indeed anyone of lesser consequence than herself, but on this occasion she was inclined to alter her view in favour of that of her sister-in-law. Robert would also see the advantage of it once his wife had explained to him what view he should take of the matter.

'Think Jane what you might say to the Croydon set. My sister-in-law is much engaged at present at Osborne Castle. We are expecting her here at Christmas, if the Osbornes can spare her,' said Elizabeth, with only the slightest hint of derision. 'What a fine remark that would be!'

'Well, I admit there is some merit in what you say,' said Jane.

CHAPTER ELEVEN

Lord Osborne's hounds were due to throw off the day of Emma's proposed visit to Wickstead. Charles Blake could hardly contain his excitement at the prospect of a day away from the schoolroom; and the pleasure was heightened by the knowledge that Miss Watson was coming to stay. Desirous of showing their visitor the horse given to him by Lord Osborne, Charles had been the principal instigator of a plan that received warm approval from both his mother and Lord Osborne. Emma was to meet Mrs Blake at Stanton Woods where they would watch the hounds throw off before proceeding to Wickstead in Lord Osborne's carriage.

'I should like Miss Watson to see me ride,' said he. 'She will be there at the start, Mama, won't she?'

'I am sure she will. Now put on your jacket and make yourself ready.'

Despite having little inclination to meet Lord Osborne, or his hounds, Emma was eager to see Charles ride. Elizabeth insisted on driving her sister in the old chair as far as Stanton Woods where Emma would meet Mrs Blake and transfer to Lord Osborne's carriage for the journey to Wickstead.

As the old chair was brought to the entrance of the parsonage in readiness for the short journey, Elizabeth offered words of reassurance. 'Now Emma, remember that you may come home at any time. And if you happen to see Mr Musgrave, and I am sure you will, make sure — '

Elizabeth was interrupted by angry protests in the hallway.

'I have been ill-used by all my sisters! I wish Emma had never come home! She is just like Elizabeth and Penelope!'

'Oh do cease your complaining!' said Mr Watson. 'Enough! Go and make yourself useful in the kitchen.'

'Help Nanny? Why should I be the one to do all the work? I expect Emma never lifts a finger!'

Elizabeth was grieved that Emma had overheard Margaret's protests.

'Do not mind her, Emma. It is her way. Enjoy your stay at Wickstead and put Margaret out of your mind.'

'How can I?' Emma went inside to find Margaret in the hope of persuading her to accompany them to Stanton Woods, but Margaret would not be moved. She could not countenance the condescension of a younger sister, one who had, within the course of a fortnight, been noticed by *the great and grand*. Miss Margaret Watson had lived all her life in the neighbourhood and had not once received an acknowledgement of any kind from a member of the Osborne set, no matter how tenacious her efforts. Most upsetting of all was the expectation that Emma and Musgrave would be thrown together constantly. It was Jane who had first placed a seed of doubt in her mind, that perhaps an alliance had already been the subject of speculation within the walls of Osborne Castle. Had Lord Osborne given his blessing? Had that been the true purpose of his visit to Stanton? Margaret's certainty that Musgrave's heart belonged to her now gave way to doubt and, consequently, extreme wretchedness.

Emma's concern for her sister was, nevertheless, met with placid complaisance by the elder. 'You must not mind her, Emma,' said Elizabeth. 'It seems to be the way with this family. I wonder at all of us. Why should Mr Musgrave be so much thought about? He disappointed Penelope, you know. She was very fond of him, *but he never meant anything serious, and when he had trifled with her long enough, he began to slight her for Margaret, and poor Penelope was very wretched.* Margaret will recover in time. My dear Emma, do not give your heart easily. Learn from your sisters' errors — though I suspect you will have nothing to fear. Mr Howard is not a man to trifle with any young woman's affections. Did you know you have changed my view of him? Before, I could only think of him as *playing cards with Lady Osborne and looking proud.*'

'Proud? I do not find him so. He is not like Mr Musgrave.'

'Musgrave? He never struck me as proud.'

'Mr Howard and Mr Musgrave should not be named together in the same day,' replied Emma.

As the hunting party assembled, the usual greetings were exchanged; expressions of good wishes and expectations of fine weather claimed the attention of Lord Osborne, and with no immediate prospect presenting itself of paying his respects to the onlooker whose welfare had become a matter of the utmost interest to him, he contented himself, for the present, with a distant nod. The same civility was extended by his lordship to Elizabeth, an acknowledgment that pleased Emma greatly; and, accordingly, he was rewarded with a gracious smile.

'Well, Emma,' said Elizabeth, 'what will our neighbours say? Recognised by Lord Osborne in front of the world! I'll never hear the last of it from Margaret. But she had her chance. You did all in your power to urge her to join us. No one can say otherwise. It will put her in such an ill humour that I think I shall not mention it at all.'

Unshackled by the social constraints placed upon his lordship, on seeing Emma, Charles cantered cheerfully in her direction. He had been waiting with pride to show off his horse, the gift of Lord Osborne.

'Miss Watson. Do look at my horse. Lord Osborne gave it to me. Is it not the finest horse you have ever seen?'

'You are a very lucky young man.'

'Yes, I suppose I am. And I am so very happy to see you. I helped to prepare your room, you know. I picked some flowers. I hope you like them. I also found a frog, a delightful little fellow. But I cannot determine on a name for him. I thought you might like to keep him, but Mama was certain that you would not. Do you like frogs, Miss Watson?'

'I do, but I imagine that a frog, however delightful, would prefer to live in a swamp, just as your preference would be for a comfortable bed.'

'Yes. That is true. I wonder Mama did not explain it in that way. Mama said only that she would allow no frogs in the house, especially when there were visitors present. What do you think of "Henry"? Is it not a fine name for a frog? Mr Musgrave wanted to name him Louis, but I am not sure the name suits him. I expect I shall put him back in the pond eventually.'

'I think that would be a very kind thing to do.'

'Mama is over there, look. My uncle is gone to town but not for long. I will have to do my lessons again when he returns. Do girls have to learn Latin? It is so unfair that boys should. Tomorrow we are all to go to Osborne Castle. You, me and Mama. And I have a surprise for you, Miss Watson. You will never guess what it is. It was Lord Osborne's idea and it is a very good one.'

'I cannot imagine what it could possibly be.'

'Shall I tell you? But then if I tell you I shall spoil the surprise and it wouldn't be a surprise anymore and Lord Osborne would be — '

'Charles, I think you had better go. They are about to set off.'

'Oh. Please do not mention Henry to Mama, Miss Watson — I think I shall call him Henry after all. Louis is no name for a frog.'

The throng of well-wishers began to disperse as the hunt got underway. Elizabeth secured promises from Emma that she would note every particular of the drawing room at Wickstead and, should she have the privilege of seeing it, the dining room at Osborne Castle.

'Dine at Osborne Castle?' said Emma. 'I am sure there will be no occasion for that.'

'Please do not be persuaded to stay longer than a few days. I will miss you, Emma. What news you will carry with you on your return! I can hardly wait to see you again.'

The reluctance of Elizabeth to part with Emma was equalled by her desire to hear the intimate details of life among the Osborne set, and so, after affectionate goodbyes were expressed and repeated, Elizabeth left Emma to the care of Mrs Blake.

'I wonder whether a quiet drive to Wickstead would have been preferable to all this commotion,' said Mrs Blake. 'I hope you will find our home a tranquil place. Charles is a little exuberant at times, but he is a good natured boy and helpful when he wants to be. My brother's efforts to curb Charles' spirit sometimes go unrewarded, but his perseverance has no equal. Indeed, he is patience itself.'

Emma was of the view that Wickstead, despite the presence of a boisterous child in the house, would be a refuge of concord and tranquillity compared to Stanton with Margaret at home.

The day passed in pleasant conversation. Emma was given a tour of the house and gardens, and the exploration ended inside the pretty bedchamber that would be hers for the duration of her stay.

'Charles picked the flowers and placed them on the windowsill. He thought you would like them,' said Mrs Blake. 'I hope he has heeded my word and has not left you with any unwelcome gifts.'

The view from Emma's room was of Osborne Park. 'In the far distance,' said Mrs Blake, 'you can glimpse Osborne Castle's fine tower, and on a clear night, light from the tower is visible from this very window. There is a story — I do not know how true it is — that

Lord Osborne's great uncle — the younger son of his great, great grandfather — fell in love with the daughter of the rector who was once incumbent here. They were forbidden to see one another — for the match was not considered suitable — and so they burnt candles in the windows as a sign of their constancy.'

'How sad,' said Emma.

'That was not the saddest part,' said Mrs Blake. 'One night the curtains caught fire while the rector's daughter slept in her bed. She was saved by a member of the family, but her face, it was said, was so badly burned as to be unrecognisable. When her lover's father died a year later, and he inherited and was free to marry, she would not have him for she could not bear for him to look at her. It is said thereafter she kept to her room, only going out at night to walk alone in the orchard.'

'And did the young man ever marry?' asked Emma.

'It is said he died of a broken heart.'

'A tragic story indeed,' said Emma.

'The garden is the gardener's handiwork. My brother has no time to spend in the garden. He is always in his study when he is at home. He has many demands on his time. At present he has business in town, but will return in a day or two. He regrets not being at liberty to welcome you to Wickstead.'

As the day drew to a close and evening descended, Lord Osborne returned Charles safely to the care of his mother, if not neatly. Charles, exhausted by the exploits of the day, was sent to prepare himself for an early supper and bed.

'I will have no argument,' said his mother. 'Miss Watson will be here tomorrow and you may show her your fishing nets and dressing up clothes then, if indeed she wishes to see them. Have you thanked Lord Osborne for his kindness in bringing you home? I am sure he has much better things to do.'

Charles thanked his lordship, and added that the only thing that could have added to the pleasure of the day was the presence of Miss Watson throughout the proceedings. It would then have been a day without compare. Lord Osborne shared the feelings expressed with such easy eloquence by the boy, but words did not come easily to him. In that moment he wished he had been blessed with that same natural ability to articulate the sentiments of his young friend. Instead, not wishing to give alarm or to appear foolish, he clung to the safety of a general observation. 'I trust, Miss Watson, you did not encounter rain this afternoon.'

'No sir. The day was perfectly fine,' said she.

Before leaving the room, Charles obtained a firm promise from Miss Watson that they would spend the following morning by the lake in Osborne Park if Lord Osborne would not object. His lordship gave his consent without hesitation; and content with the prospect of another meeting with Miss Watson very soon, when pressed by Mrs Blake to sit a while longer, he politely declined and took his leave.

When at last Mrs Blake and Emma were alone again, the former turned to a more serious topic. 'Lord Osborne was very good to my dear husband, God rest his soul, when he was near to the end.'

Emma listened to Mrs Blake's account of the final hours spent with her husband, and offered comfort where it was needed; it was evident in every word and look that the grief of her companion over the loss of 'dear Captain Blake' was still deeply felt.

'My husband was wounded at sea. He was Captain of the Nereus. Thankfully, he was kept alive by the services of a young surgeon who attended him as far as Portsmouth or I would never have seen him again. As soon as I received word of my husband's condition, Lord Osborne placed his carriage at my disposal and accompanied me all the way to Portsmouth. Charles came too for he insisted on seeing his father. Lord Osborne arranged for comfortable lodgings, and employed the services of a respected physician to ease my dear husband's discomfort. Captain Blake clung to life as best he could; sadly, he lasted but a few days. Those days, Miss Watson, were the happiest and the saddest days of my life. I shall never love again as I loved Charles' father. And I shall never forget the service rendered by his lordship. He arranged every detail of the burial himself. You see, Captain Blake was buried at Portsmouth. He loved the sea and if he could not be at sea he wanted always to be near it.'

Mrs Blake handed Emma a miniature of her husband. 'Captain Blake was a handsome man,' said Emma. 'Charles has a look of him, I think. It is a fine portrait.'

'You are right,' smiled Mrs Blake. 'Charles is the image of his father, in both countenance and character. The likeness you hold in your hand was executed by own dear husband, for he was also a fine artist.'

'A self portrait,' said Emma.

'And one that is neither flattering nor severe. It is as truthful a representation as any portrait I have seen. But that was his nature. He was an honest man, full of kindness and good sense. I do miss him so. May I show you some of his watercolours, Miss Watson?'

'I should like that very much,' Emma replied.

'They are in the library. Excuse me while I fetch them.'

The eagerness of Mrs Blake to speak of her husband was equalled by Emma's desire to hear it; for the young woman who at five had lost a mother and at seventeen mourned the passing of the uncle who had raised her, had herself known something of the pain of loss and the loneliness of a long memory.

In the happiest of marriages, the private grief of a widow endures the longest. To be thrown back into society before the wound has had time to heal might have caused a weaker character to yield to desolation and despondency. Mrs Blake took pains to keep her feelings in check; and her generous heart, which had made her a universal favourite, was employed in the service of others and, in raising the spirits of those around her, she found that she was able to raise her own.

When the door opened, Emma expected to see Mrs Blake and was surprised to find Charles standing there instead, clothed in his nightshirt.

'Miss Watson, please forgive me,' he whispered, 'but Henry has escaped and I cannot find him anywhere. I think he is gone into your room. In case you should discover him, I have placed a little box under the bed with holes in the top where you can keep him till morning. Would you look after him until then, Miss Watson?'

'Yes, Charles,' she whispered in return. 'Now go back to bed before your mama catches you.'

CHAPTER TWELVE

Charles lamented the discovery of Henry by the scullery maid, and the reprimand by his mother which followed. It was a consequence with which he was familiar. When complaints of his misdemeanours reached his mother's ears there were always amends to be made. Before leaving for London, Mr Howard had issued Charles with a severe scolding. Having acquired a fine specimen of a sheep's skull laden with maggot eggs, Charles had placed it for safekeeping in an empty closet in his uncle's study. The closet, being near to the fireplace, drew warmth from the fire in the grate.

'And it was such a fine skull,' said Charles. 'But I was made to dispose of it and I received a very long Latin lesson in return. I do not know why my uncle dislikes maggots so. They are the most fascinating little creatures when fully hatched and very useful for fishing. There was quite a plentiful supply, but my uncle was not at all happy about their being in the closet.'

Charles insisted on Miss Watson having the use of his best fishing net and sought out the best spot for its use. He then went about finding a suitable place in the long grass to set Henry free.

Before the morning was over, Lord Osborne, having completed some business with his steward, made his excuses and set off in the direction of the lake. Miss Carr, who had observed his lordship from the window of Lady Osborne's morning room, proposed a similar plan.

'I have no greater wish than to walk by the lake this morning,' said Miss Carr.

'It will be very muddy over there,' said Miss Osborne.

'Even so, a little mud will do no harm,' she replied. 'Did not your mama commend the benefits of exercise?'

'I suppose we should make the best of the fine weather.' Miss Osborne acceded to her friend's request, and the two set out in the direction of the lake.

Charles was delighted by the appearance of Lord Osborne and at once recounted to his lordship the great injustice he had suffered and the unfairness of the reprimand he had received from his mother.

Charles had been obliged to let Henry go and wondered why it was that he was never allowed to keep anything interesting.

'Henry will be much happier by the lake,' replied Lord Osborne.

'Miss Watson said the very same,' said he. On a brighter note he added, 'Miss Watson has caught three fish already.'

His lordship smiled at Emma. 'I consider myself lucky if I catch one. You must have a talent for fishing.'

'I have an excellent teacher.'

Charles smiled at the idea of being Miss Watson's teacher. 'Shall I tell Miss Watson about the surprise?' said Charles.

'Why not? It will come better from you than from me,' said Osborne.

'Do you ride, Miss Watson?' asked Charles. 'For if you do not, I am sure Lord Osborne will teach you.'

'I used to have a horse of my own.'

'What happened to him?' asked Charles with concern.

'I was not able to bring him with me.'

'I should be very sad if I could not take my horse with me wherever I go,' said Charles. 'We are to ride tomorrow and you, Miss Watson, are to come too. Mama has found out some riding clothes for you and Lord Osborne is to lend you one of his best horses. Please, Miss Watson, please say you will come.'

Emma yielded to Charles' entreaty. She had not ridden since leaving Shropshire and the prospect of riding again, even at the instigation of Lord Osborne, was a pleasant one.

His lordship was amused by Emma's disclosure. 'Fascinating, Miss Watson,' said he. 'I remember you once said that not every woman had the inclination to ride.'

'It was a general observation, not a particular one. I used to ride a great deal.'

'Then why did you not say so?'

'At the time, if I recall, you did not ask whether I liked to ride. The answer to that question would have been yes.'

'Well, now that we have established the fact of the matter, allow me to say that whenever you have the inclination to ride, the means will be provided. You may ride one of my horses at any time.'

'That is very kind, sir, but it would be impossible for me to accept your offer.'

'Look!' cried Charles. 'There's Miss Osborne and Miss Carr!' He beckoned them over. 'Miss Osborne, do come and see the fish that Miss Watson has caught! I taught Miss Watson how to use the net and she has caught three fish already. Miss Watson says that I am an excellent teacher.'

When the necessary introductions had been completed, Miss Carr turned her attention to Lord Osborne and said teasingly, 'And where is your fishing net, my lord?'

'It is in the hand of Miss Emma Watson,' he replied.

'I thought the net belonged to Charles,' said Emma.

'It does now,' he replied.

'Osborne had it when he was young,' said Miss Osborne. 'He once chased me round the park with it. I remember it contained an enormous eel.'

'Miss Watson, do excuse my sister. Her memory is sometimes enhanced by a strong imagination and a propensity to embroider more than lace handkerchiefs. It was a dead eel. A young one. Little larger than a worm.'

Charles demanded a full account of the eel — where his lordship had caught it — if there were other eels to be caught there still — and whether a darkened closet would be conducive to an eel if kept in a pail of water, for he should very much like to look after one.

'Let us go and see what we can find,' said Osborne. Charles followed. 'We won't be long,' said he.

Emma found herself in the company of Miss Osborne and Miss Carr, but soon regretted that she had not offered to accompany Charles to look for eels instead.

'I understand that Mrs Blake is to have the pleasure of your company for a day or two,' said Miss Carr.

'Yes.'

'And Mr Howard is called to town on business.'

'That is so.'

'How unfortunate! I am sure Mr Howard's absence is a great loss, though when he is at Wickstead, he seems to be always at the Castle,' replied Miss Carr.

'I expect Mr Howard has many demands on his time.'

Miss Osborne, who had not spoken until then, said, 'Miss Watson, I understand that you and Mrs Blake are to join us for tea this afternoon. Shall we send the carriage or should you prefer to walk?'

'Thank you,' said Emma. 'We shall walk. I believe we are to call on an elderly parishioner on the way.'

'Mrs Blake is forever at the disposal of others. One wonders whether she has enough employment, though I should imagine looking after Master Charles is a piece of work,' said Miss Carr.

'How so? Master Charles is a good-natured child and very easy company.'

'And what of Mr Howard? Is he also good natured and easy company?' said Miss Carr.

'I have no reason to think otherwise.'

'How very prudent of you,' said Miss Carr. 'I'm sure you never express an opinion without knowledge of the facts or pass judgement of any kind without careful study.'

Emma was at a loss to know how to respond, for Miss Carr seemed displeased and unnecessarily quarrelsome, which puzzled her. She bade goodbye to Miss Osborne and her friend, saying, 'Please excuse me. I must see to Charles. It is time for us to go.'

As a consequence of his earlier misdemeanour, Charles was made to stay at home while Emma and Mrs Blake went to tea at Osborne Castle. On being ushered into a grand drawing room, Emma at first thought that only the ladies were present. Lord Osborne, who had been sitting in a quiet corner of the room, obscured from view, surprised the visitors by coming forward to greet them in a friendly manner. The ease of his address surprised Emma, and she concluded that it must be due to the familiarity and security of his home environment. Her uncle's disposition had been similar in some respects. He had always been more at ease in his own home than in society at large. Often at a dinner party, one he had had little inclination to attend but could not decline, he would sit in silence while Mrs Turner held sway and managed the conversation for both of them. At home, however, he was quite different. There he entertained and was happy to be entertained in equal measure.

'Had you a pleasant walk through the grounds?' said his lordship.

'Very pleasant, thank you sir,' said Emma.

'How could we not?' said Mrs Blake. 'There are no finer grounds in the whole of England.'

'Thank you, Mrs Blake. I am of the same view,' he replied. 'I hope, Miss Watson, you are not fatigued after your morning's fishing.'

'Not in the least, my lord.'

'I wonder at young ladies who profess to enjoy gentlemen's pursuits,' said Miss Carr. 'It is, I suppose, a way of singling oneself out.'

'You mistake the matter, my dear Miss Carr,' said Mrs Blake. 'Miss Watson has no greater interest in fishing than you have yourself. The morning's activity was entirely Charles' doing and at his behest.'

'There is more than one type of fish to be caught,' replied Miss Carr in a low voice to Miss Osborne. Emma heard and understood her meaning.

'We have spent a rather dull afternoon — like most afternoons spent in the country, I suppose,' said Lady Osborne. 'I do miss town. There is so much to be done there. Such varied society and all kinds of pleasures to be had. My son has been going here and there all afternoon — too preoccupied with other things to think about us. But then it is always the way with men.'

Lady Osborne was cut short by the sound of urgent steps in the hallway. They were the steps of a man, and as no one was expected at that hour, the general consensus was that they belonged to Mr Musgrave, as he was so fond of making grand entrances. The Osbornes' surprise, therefore, when the door opened to admit Mr Howard was shared by their visitors.

The clergyman's sudden appearance stirred mixed emotions in Emma. Her elation at being once more in the presence of the man she admired was somewhat lessened by conjecture as to the occasion that had given rise to his hasty return.

'What is it, Mr Howard?' said Lady Osborne. 'Have we been invaded by the French? What news do you bring? Dear me! I expect the country is in uproar. And to think that not five minutes ago were we complaining of how dull it is.'

'Oh, my dear brother, what brings you home? Has something happened? What has brought you here in so great a rush?'

'Do not make yourself uneasy. There is a simple explanation. All is well, I assure you. On reaching town, by chance I heard that the carriage of one of our neighbours, Mr Edwards, had overset itself. Mr Edwards sustained a minor injury but was anxious to return before reports of the incident were carried to Delham ahead of him. Naturally, I put my carriage at his disposal and thought it best to accompany him myself. He is now safely deposited into the care of his family.'

'You are so good. I am sure Mrs Edwards is exceedingly obliged to you for bringing him home,' said Mrs Blake.

'I doubt it,' said Mr Howard.

'And now, brother, I do hope you will delay your return a day or two more.'

'I said I would call on Mr Edwards in the morning to see how he fares, but I must return to town shortly.' Turning to Emma, he said, 'Miss Watson, I trust you are enjoying your stay at Wickstead.'

'I am, sir. Your sister has extended every comfort to me. I could not be happier or better looked after.'

Emma was made uneasy by the smile that was exchanged between Miss Osborne and Miss Carr, a gesture that did not go unnoticed by Mr Howard and his sister.

'Charles has been up to his pranks again. But he means well, I think,' said Mrs Blake. 'It is "Miss Watson this" and "Miss Watson that". You are certainly a favourite in our household, my dear Emma.'

Lady Osborne was anxious to return to Mr Edwards' accident.

'It is well that Mr Tomlinson purchased a new carriage from our maker. I do not know the particulars of Mr Edwards' carriage, but he should be careful about his purchases in future,' said her ladyship. 'We will give you the name of our man and you may pass it on to Mr Edwards.'

'Mr Edwards' carriage is, I daresay, perfectly adequate. It is the roads that need attention,' Lord Osborne said.

'After so much rain, it is a wonder there are roads left at all,' said Miss Carr. 'If it continues to rain as excessively as it has done this last fortnight, I might be detained at Osborne Castle forever.'

Lord Osborne, who had been standing by the fire, moved towards the window to look out. His overriding priority became clear; he would take it upon himself to ensure that the roads in the borough were, in future, well maintained at all times.

'Mr Howard,' said Lady Osborne, 'do sit down and take your tea and tell us what news there is from town. Has Lady Forbes appointed a new painter for music room?'

'I'm afraid I have no news of Lady Forbes. I dined last night with Mr Edwards and his brother.'

'Mr Edwards has a brother? Have I met him?' said his sister.

'I think not. He is a churchman of some repute.'

'A parson all the same,' said Miss Carr. 'I understand your father is a parson, Miss Watson. You will be familiar with matters of the Church.'

'I am not. I spent most of my life in Shropshire. I was brought up by my aunt and uncle.'

'Did I hear you say Shropshire, Miss Watson?' said her ladyship. 'Good heavens! Do you know that there is not an ounce of flour to be had in the whole of Shropshire? Not one. Mrs Tomlinson had it in a letter from her sister. Is that not the most extraordinary thing you have ever heard? Indeed, who would live in Shropshire? A most deplorable county, by all accounts. Miss Carr, has not Mr Appleby a house in Shropshire?'

'He has a large house in Shropshire, as well as a vast estate in Yorkshire, though he is not often there. But I must protest. I have never heard of such a thing. There is no truth in it at all,' cried Miss Carr. 'Flour is abundant in all the great houses. My uncle has more than enough of it and declares he is sick of the sight of it. He fails to understand what all the fuss is about.'

A brief silence fell on the room.

'I am glad to hear it,' said Lady Osborne. 'Mrs Tomlinson must have been mistaken. I expect she meant Yorkshire. Forgive me, Miss Watson. Flour is plentiful in Shropshire after all.'

'For some perhaps. But the price of flour is beyond the means of many,' said Emma.

'You appear to be an expert in all manner of things, Miss Watson. What do you know of the price of flour? said Miss Carr.

'I know only that a shortage of flour increases its price.'

'How interesting,' said Miss Osborne.

'It seems Miss Watson is an authority on the economy as well as fishing,' said Miss Carr.

'I am no such thing. I merely state a fact,' Emma replied.

'A young woman who speaks her mind. Well, well,' said Lady Osborne, lighting up.

'Miss Watson is right,' said his lordship. 'But then, her knowledge of female economy is equal to none.' His tone, far from being disdainful, was respectfully playful and approving. Miss Carr was silenced on the matter.

When Lord Osborne spoke again, his words were measured and thoughtful. 'Every man, woman and child should have bread to eat. I intend that it should be so, at least in this parish.'

'The poor are uniformly indolent,' said Miss Carr. 'One does not wish to make them more so.'

'Indolence,' replied Emma 'is considered a virtue in some circles.'

'Are not the poor always with us, Mr Howard?' said Miss Osborne. 'Was it not the subject of your sermon three Sundays before the regiment removed to Reigate?'

'The poor are always with us, Miss Osborne. You are quite right,' he replied. 'It is well to remember that. My lord, do you propose to raise poor relief?'

'Yes.'

'And make the poor good for nothing?'

'Mr Howard,' said Emma gently, 'were it in your power to prevent it, would you see the poor of this parish go hungry?'

'It is not as simple as that, Miss Watson,' said he.

As the time to leave Osborne Castle approached, Lord Osborne placed his carriage at the visitors' disposal.

'There are black clouds to the west that threaten rain again,' said he.

'We will be back at Wickstead well before the rain sets in,' said Mrs Blake.

'Perhaps Miss Watson prefers the carriage,' her brother replied.

'I should prefer a walk,' said Emma. Though a little fatigued from the morning's activity, Emma had no wish to be deprived of Mr Howard's company.

To the relief of Miss Carr, and the regret of Lord Osborne and his mother, the visitors took their leave. Lady Osborne, who had found the company of Miss Watson refreshingly novel, invited her, together with Mrs Blake, to dine with them the following evening. She expressed her hopes that Mr Howard would also be one of the party, for she was in agreement with her daughter and Miss Carr: Miss Watson was just the sort of young woman who would make a suitable match for a clergyman. Were they to be thrown together under her direction, she might do what she could to bring about a union that would be pleasing to many, not least to Mr Howard's sister. More importantly, Miss Watson would not appear out of place in the dining room at Osborne Castle; and her addition would be an advantage, for even her son had uttered more words in one afternoon than she had sometimes heard from him in a month.

Mrs Blake took the arm of her brother, and without hesitation, Mr Howard surrendered the other to Emma, a gesture that met with sincere gratitude and delight. Mr Howard spoke easily, and with the authority of a scholar, the history of Osborne Castle being the chief subject of his narration.

'Osborne Castle is grand, I grant you, Miss Watson,' said he. 'But I understand that you spent your childhood in one of the finest houses in Shropshire.'

'I knew very little of the matter at the time for I was but five years old when my mother died. My aunt and uncle had no children of their own, so they took me to live with them. You can imagine, to a small child, even the smallest parlour seems like a palace. The only regret I have is that I was separated from my family at Stanton for so long. But my aunt and uncle were very good to me.'

'And were, I daresay, as solicitous of your care as any parent of their own flesh and blood.'

'Oh, indeed they were. I shall forever be in their debt.'

'The hand of providence, Miss Watson.'

CHAPTER THIRTEEN

Mr Howard postponed his journey to town on receiving a letter in the morning's post. The business that had at first taken him there would not now be completed as quickly as had been expected. His presence in town, for the time being, therefore, was not required. The news delighted his sister and her guest, but provoked a less pleasing response from his nephew.

'But Miss Watson and I are to ride with Lord Osborne this morning? Please Uncle, I do not want to miss it.'

'And I do not want you to miss your lessons,' said Mr Howard.

It was agreed that Charles would attend to his studies, and were he to apply himself diligently, his uncle gave his word that he would be released in time to ride with Lord Osborne and Miss Watson.

After breakfast Emma sat with Mrs Blake in the parlour. 'I expect Mrs Tomlinson will call,' said Mrs Blake. 'She has promised to bring me a pudding recipe and news of Mr Edwards.'

Emma, too, was anxious to receive an account of Mr Edwards' progress to give to her father, as she intended to write a note to Elizabeth after Mrs Tomlinson's visit. While they awaited Mrs Tomlinson in the parlour, another visitor was announced.

'I was in the neighbourhood,' said Musgrave, making himself comfortable in Mr Howard's chair, 'and found that I could not pass by Wickstead without calling to see how Miss Watson goes on.'

'I am well, Mr Musgrave, as you see,' said Emma.

'You are in the best company,' he replied. 'Mrs Blake is kindness itself.'

'Mr Musgrave, flattery is wasted on me, as you well know,' said Mrs Blake good-naturedly.

'Flattery is never wasted on anyone, Mrs Blake,' he replied. 'I wonder how they are all getting on at Stanton without you, Miss Watson. Should you wish it, I would be happy to convey a message to your sister.'

'Do you know how Mr Edwards fares after his accident? I am sure if you have news of him, my father would be anxious to hear it.'

'I have not seen Mr Edwards since the morning after our famous ball and then but fleetingly as you yourself may recall. I'm sure he has come to no harm though. He's a tough old thing. Which puts me in mind — I wonder what Miss Carr will have to say when she hears that you are to ride with Lord Osborne?'

'I have no clue,' Emma replied.

'What do you think of Miss Carr now you know her a little better?'

'Mr Musgrave, I know little of Miss Carr's character or opinions, but what I know, I cannot say I care for. I was given to understand that she is an accomplished horsewoman and I have every expectation of her being one of the party when we ride out today.'

'I expect she won't if his lordship has anything to do with it,' replied Musgrave.

'I hope, Mr Musgrave,' said Mrs Blake, 'that you do not mean to be unkind to Miss Carr. She may well turn out to be the next Lady Osborne. And I cannot think of a more perfectly matched couple,' said Mrs Blake.

'Can you not?' said he.

'Lord Osborne should pay more attention to Miss Carr if he wishes to secure her,' said Emma. 'He has too careless an air.'

'That's the point,' he replied. 'He has no wish to — Well, never mind.'

'Do you not ride today, Mr Musgrave?' said Mrs Blake.

'Not I. I am determined to call on Mr Edwards and cheer him up. I shall then carry the news to Stanton. There is nothing like a report from the horse's mouth. When anyone supposes himself to be ill, every ailment is heightened and every injury inflated in the telling. And I expect that if Mr Edwards does not make the most of it, Mrs Edwards will.'

'Shall you really go to Stanton, Mr Musgrave?'

'I shall. Have you a message for your sister?'

'I should like to send a note. Would you wait while I write one?'

'Certainly. What luck! You sister is sure to offer me a dish of tea in return for rendering such a service.'

Emma scribbled a hasty note to her sister while Mr Musgrave talked to Mrs Blake of the regiment.

'That dark horse Beresford is expected in Delham next week and no one quite knows why,' said Musgrave.

'It would please some young ladies were the regiment to return to Delham,' said Mrs Blake.

'I can't see what is so fascinating about the regiment. I might mention it to Mrs Edwards and ruffle a few feathers.'

Mr Musgrave sat for ten minutes longer until Emma reappeared with the note for Elizabeth. After remarking on the advantages of Mr Tomlinson's new carriage over Mr Edwards' conveyance, and the prospects for a fine day's riding, he finally took his leave.

'I wonder at Mr Musgrave, that he should be so willing to run errands for you, my dear,' said Mrs Blake.

'Yes. It is surprising. I daresay he has nothing better to do.'

Mrs Blake kept her thoughts to herself. She had begun to wonder whether Mr Musgrave's frequent visits and his willingness to act as a messenger between Wickstead and Stanton proceeded from some growing feeling of partiality on his side for her guest.

Charles completed his studies with ten minutes to spare, and came down in search of Emma, dressed smartly in his riding clothes.

'Mama, Miss Watson and I can walk to the Castle stableyard. There is an interesting path that is not often trod which we can go by. We will reach Osborne Castle in half the time if we take it,' said he. 'I assure you, Miss Watson, it is very safe. There is no chance of your slipping or spraining your ankle or falling into the stream, for it is only a short jump to the opposite bank.'

'Nevertheless, your uncle has ordered the carriage. It will do very well. You will reach your destination more safely than by any method you might prefer,' said his mother. 'And it will preserve your new jacket from snags and tears.' Turning to Emma, Mrs Blake continued, 'When Charles has scrambled through bushes and hedgerows he is not fit to be seen.'

It was settled. Emma and Charles set out for Osborne Castle in Mr Howard's carriage; Charles was dressed in his new jacket, and Emma wore his mother's fine blue riding habit, chosen by Mrs Blake to complement Emma's eyes.

Emma proved as capable a horsewoman as Miss Osborne and Miss Carr, and, in Lord Osborne's eyes, she had never looked finer. When invited to ride ahead with the two young women, she declined, preferring to stay beside Charles and, where care was called for, to watch that he came to no harm by offering an occasional word of warning to encourage the correct handling of his horse. On reaching the wood by the edge of the lake, Osborne dropped back to ride by Emma's side while Charles rode on to point out to Miss Osborne the best place to collect horse chestnuts.

'I understand that your visit is soon to come to an end. Will you not change your mind and stay a day or two longer?'

'I could not presume to impose on Mrs Blake now that Mr Howard's business in town has been postponed.'

'It is no imposition, I'm sure,' said Osborne. 'The company that Mrs Blake enjoys can be a little unvarying at times.'

'But she is often at Osborne Castle.'

'Exactly my point,' said he. 'And it would be a shame if you were to leave us so soon. My horse needs exercise and you handle him well.'

'He reminds me of — it is no matter.'

'He reminds you of the horse you had in Shropshire.'

'Yes.'

'And the life you left behind.'

Lord Osborne had uncovered an unsettling truth. Emma was vexed to be reminded of the life she had once known — a life of ease that never gave cause for shame, a life free from the poverty and inferiority that invites the condescension of the rich and the censure of the world. The comforts and freedoms that once had been hers were no longer within her reach, and in those brief moments she felt keenly the pain of her present circumstances. To remain too long in the society of those who possessed what she had lost would be more painful that it was pleasurable.

'Miss Watson,' said Miss Carr, positioning her horse alongside Emma's, 'it seems not only can you wield a fishing-net and speak on matters of national importance, you are quite the expert on horseback too. Is there no end to your accomplishments?'

'None, I assure you,' cried Charles who was just in earshot. 'Miss Watson can do everything.'

'Can she indeed?' she replied. As the rest of the party rode on, Miss Carr drew closer to Emma. 'Miss Watson, you make me quite envious. His lordship hardly stirs from his study most days. He is a magistrate, you see, and is always engaged in some scheme or other, and has never a moment to spare for his family. I declare, if I were family I should tease him endlessly about his sorry neglect.'

'Is it not a good thing that a man should be employed in the service of others rather than spend all his time in idle pleasure?'

'I daresay his lordship does a great deal too much for the undeserving of the borough,' said Miss Carr. 'When do you go back into Shropshire, Miss Watson?'

'It is not within my power to — Stanton is my home now.'

'How interesting.'

'After my uncle died, my aunt remarried.'

'A second marriage. That is bad luck.'

'My aunt has been given a second opportunity of happiness. I would say that is good luck, and I am happy for her.'

'But I imagine it is not the best news for you. I wonder at old women who enter into matrimony for a second time. I expect the groom had better things to do with your aunt's money than to meet any obligations to you. That seems very bad luck to me. And will they remain in Shropshire?'

'They are gone to Ireland. It did not suit Captain O'Brien that I should be of the party.'

'An Irishman? Well, well. Is he related to the O'Briens of Cork?

'I do not know.'

Emma's disappointment and concern at her aunt's lack of communication had begun to give cause for anxiety. Her aunt had promised faithfully to send word as soon as she and Captain O'Brien were settled in Ireland. Emma had received no missive of any kind, and having no means of writing to her aunt directly, had written to a local attorney into whose hands the sale of her aunt's estate had been placed on the instructions of Captain O'Brien. The response had been disappointing, for the attorney had been unable to confirm the whereabouts of Captain and Mrs O'Brien, having been instructed to deal solely with the Captain's man of business in London. Emma felt the impertinence of Miss Carr's remarks, but the matter of her aunt's removal to Ireland weighed heavily on her mind.

'Is it not a curious thing, Miss Watson, that you and I should have so remarkable a reversal of fortune? You have lost yours while I find myself in quite the opposite corner. May I offer a word of advice? Do not set your sights too high, for you will surely be disappointed. A tolerable figure is all very well, but it is less appealing to a man than a comfortable income. I expect your aunt's good fortune must be a daily reminder of precisely that.'

Emma wanted to end the conversation immediately; and as little was to be gained by showing herself vexed by Miss Carr's words, she replied coolly, 'I beg your pardon, Miss Carr. Please excuse me.'

On finding the rest of the party in impassioned debate about the advantages of returning to the Castle over riding as far as the bridge, Emma urged that the shortest route be taken.

'I agree with Miss Watson,' replied Miss Osborne. 'There is far too much mud by the bridge. There is no advantage to be gained by going there except to look at it. And one can look at a bridge at any time. It is not likely to disappear, and there are many bridges just like it. I am sure Miss Watson has no desire to see something so commonplace.'

The matter was settled. The party returned the way they had come. On the way back to the Castle, Emma remained by Charles' side while Lord Osborne led the way, reined in, one on each side, by his sister and Miss Carr.

CHAPTER FOURTEEN

Among the guests invited to dine at Osborne Castle was Mr Musgrave. His arrival, though unexpectedly early, brought amusement to at least one of the Castle's inhabitants.

'It is not true! I will not have it! Tell me it is not true, Mr Musgrave. The Watsons dine at three? Poor Mr Howard.'

'Why so, Miss Carr? What possible connection can there be between Mr Howard and the hour at which the Watsons dine?' said Lord Osborne.

'At present, none perhaps,' said Lady Osborne. 'But one might conceive of a time when — '

'When what, pray?' said her son.

'Am I the only one to think of it?' said Lady Osborne.

'I daresay it has crossed your mind, Miss Carr,' said Mr Musgrave.

'Perhaps. But not seriously, of course. Such a match would expose Mr Howard to the contempt of the world. The difference in situation between them would — '

'Stranger things have happened,' said Lady Osborne. 'When one's heart is not one's own, Miss Carr, love can do all manner of things. I remember Miss Buller, all teeth and no chin, and not two pennies to rub together. When Mr Hinchman set eyes on her, there was nothing to be done about it. It was all over for Miss Debary. I seem to remember that Mr Hinchman had a fine estate somewhere in the north country. I don't recall the particulars but I do remember that the family strongly disapproved of the match. Nevertheless, he would have her and nothing could be said against it. You can imagine what uproar it caused. Mr Hinchman was exceedingly popular among certain of the young ladies — though I did not care much for the style of his waistcoats — they never seemed to fit right — and he had a singular way of wearing his necktie. I wonder he did not strangle himself in the tying of it. But he disappointed the hopes of more than one young lady, I can tell you. Miss Debary was quite inconsolable and wept an entire fortnight until her eyes were a deep shade of purple, the very colour of a nice silk frock I once had.'

'And what became of Miss Debary?' asked Miss Carr.

'She met a young naval Captain — dashing, but, in my view, a scoundrel who was not to be relied on. The couple got engaged before the season was out, which, I grant you, raised her spirits greatly. Every arrangement was made for an early wedding — the wedding clothes bought, the date settled, the invitations issued. And then, imagine! Without a word of warning, the rascal returned to his ship before the banns were read. And that was the end of that. She never saw him again. Poor Miss Debary. I hope the ship was captured by pirates.'

'It seems to me that Miss Debary had a lucky escape,' said Miss Osborne.

'The tale of Miss Debary was often recounted as a warning to all young women who frequent watering places,' said Lady Osborne. 'But this is not a watering place and Mr Howard bears not the slightest resemblance to Mr Hinchman or any officer I have ever known. Miss Watson appears to be an unobjectionable young woman. I see no harm in offering a helping hand where I can.'

The arrival of Mr Howard, Mrs Blake and Miss Watson, silenced Lady Osborne on the matter, and once the usual salutations had been exchanged and the good wishes of one or two parishioners conveyed, the news of the day followed. Mr Howard brought good news of Mr Edwards who was now fully recovered from his injury. He had called on him earlier in the day and had found him to be in excellent spirits. The news of Mr Tomlinson, however, was less satisfactory, for his physician had recommended removal to Bath on account of his gout having worsened. Naturally, Mrs Tomlinson, who was not in the best of health herself, was to accompany her husband. She intended to set to rights her own malady: the deficiency her wardrobe had endured over several years of neglect. The remedy was straightforward and painless: a new wardrobe of the latest muslins and silks was required and would provide an instant cure to all that ailed her.

The announcement that dinner was served provided Lady Osborne with the opportunity of offering a little encouragement to more than one couple present. 'Osborne will enter with Miss Carr. Mr Musgrave, I will take your arm for a change. Mr Howard, would you be so good as to look after Miss Watson?'

To Emma's delight, the clergyman graciously complied with Lady Osborne's request; the offer of his arm, accompanied by a warm smile from the gentleman himself, brought a blush to her cheeks.

'My lord,' said Miss Carr, taking Osborne's arm, 'does it not seem quite routine, quite as it should be, for you and I to enter thus?'

'You make an admirable couple,' said Musgrave with an artful grin at his friend.

'Mr Musgrave! You should not tease us so! I forbid it!' replied Miss Carr coyly.

Last to enter the dining room were Mrs Blake and Miss Osborne.

'Miss Osborne,' said Mrs Blake in a low voice, 'I wanted to speak with you. My brother has received a note from Colonel Beresford. I wonder he did not mention it, though it may have slipped his mind. The Colonel intends to visit the neighbourhood briefly next week. He will call at Wickstead on Wednesday and stay for luncheon.'

'Oh,' said Miss Osborne.

'I wonder, do you have time to spare? May I beg a favour? I should like to consult you on the purchase of some new curtains for the dining room.'

'I should be more than happy to oblige, Mrs Blake. I have no particular engagements next week. It remains only for you to name the day and the hour.'

'Wednesday would be most convenient.'

'Wednesday would suit me very well. Very well indeed,' said Miss Osborne.

'Might you be persuaded to stay for luncheon?'

'I should be happy to, Mrs Blake.'

'Excellent.'

As they took their places at the table, Mrs Blake complimented Lady Osborne on the table arrangements and the array of dishes before them. Emma was struck by the simple elegance of the room which seemed to heighten rather than diminish its brilliance. It appeared at once stately but welcoming; the dining room in Shropshire that she had known and loved seemed almost garish by comparison.

Emma, who had been placed in close proximity to Miss Carr and Mr Howard, could not help but catch something of their conversation.

'I should find it impossible to eat a morsel at an earlier hour,' said Miss Carr.

'Whether I dine *at eight or nine*,' observed Musgrave, joining in, '*is a matter of very little consequence.*'

'Eight o'clock is not an unreasonable hour. But any earlier would be insupportable. Some days I scarcely rise before three. Miss Watson, I understand your family prefers to dine at an early hour.'

'Yes, Miss Carr. We dine early at Stanton, as Mr Musgrave is well aware. It is a matter of practicality rather than fashion, though I have no objection to dining at any hour.' She was tempted, but resisted the impulse, to add that if there were candles to burn and money to pay for them, dining at eight rather than three would be a matter of choice for the many and not the few.

'You must rise very early,' said Miss Carr.

'I prefer not to waste the day,' said Emma.

'I am in agreement with Miss Watson,' said Mr Howard. 'One can accomplish a great deal on rising early.'

Lady Osborne, who had been waiting for an opportunity to present itself in which she might offer a little assistance, said 'I expect you, Miss Watson, will be used to living in a parsonage, with all its demands and duties. You will know how it all works.'

'I am but beginning to understand what it is to live the life of a clergyman's daughter,' said she.

'I am very pleased to hear it, for there is no finer preparation for life as a clergyman's — ' replied Lady Osborne.

'Mrs Blake,' interrupted Miss Osborne, 'I expect rectory life has its ups and downs as well as its charms.'

'And its claims on one's time. I am content with such a life, as you well know, but there is always something to do,' Mrs Blake replied. Changing the subject, she applied to Lady Osborne for support. 'Please do what you can, your ladyship, to persuade Miss Watson to stay a day or two longer. She is to leave us shortly.'

'Miss Watson is to leave? So soon? Will you not extend your stay another week at least, my dear? Send a note to your father tomorrow and I shall see that it is delivered. Mr Howard, what say you on the matter? Will you not urge Miss Watson to stay another week?'

'I should be happy were Miss Watson to agree to it and I am certain that Charles would wish it too,' he replied.

'Excellent,' said Lady Osborne. 'Excellent.'

Mr Howard's plea was enough. Emma needed no further persuasion and promised to send word to Stanton the following morning.

'It appears that we will have the pleasure of your company a little longer, Miss Watson,' whispered Miss Carr. 'You've made quite an impression on all the Wickstead family. How clever of you!'

Emma ignored the remark and for a time sat in silence observing the words and looks of those around her. She noticed that Lord Osborne had spoken hardly at all during dinner, but that often his eyes seemed, unaccountably, to settle on her. Mr Musgrave seemed to be amused by Miss Carr's laboured attempts to coax Lord Osborne to speak, and how resistance on his lordship's part hardened at every turn. For her part, Miss Osborne sometimes appeared distant and pensive, and only attended when the conversation turned to news of the regiment.

Mrs Blake's convivial conversation and the warmth of Mr Howard's looks prevailed over the behaviour of the others present; and Emma found that she drew greater satisfaction from the evening than she had anticipated. As dinner ended, Lady Osborne urged the men to come through early.

'We have need of your company in the drawing room,' said she. 'Perhaps Mr Howard would be prevailed upon to sing for us. Do you sing, Miss Watson?'

'Not well. I prefer to play.'

'How very opportune! Mr Howard, you are fortunate indeed. Miss Watson will accompany you on the pianoforte. How pleasant that will be.'

'Please, ma'am, I beg leave not to do so this evening, for I have not practiced in weeks.'

'Nonsense. You can do no worse than the younger Miss Tomlinson, I'm sure. She has not the lightness of touch that some young ladies have. And I have often remarked that it would be a very fine thing to introduce her to the notion of a time signature, for I have yet to hear her employ one.'

'Mama, it is of little matter, for it is of Miss Watson we speak, not Miss Tomlinson.'

It was little more than half an hour before the gentlemen joined the ladies in the music room. Lady Osborne had marked out the music and had given Emma precise instructions on how the accompaniment should be played. 'This is a beautiful song, Miss Watson. It should be played with the greatest of feeling. Follow Mr Howard's lead. He understands every particular of the song.'

'Thank you, your ladyship,' said Emma. 'I shall do my best.'

'I expect the song is new to you,' replied Lady Osborne.

'I know it well for it is one of my aunt's favourites.'

'Your aunt has good taste, I see.'

'Miss Watson's aunt is quite the romantic,' said Miss Carr.

Emma proceeded to play the introduction to the song, stopping only at the entrance of the gentlemen.

'Well done, Miss Watson. I am sure we will do very well together. Do not stop on my account,' said Mr Howard as he approached the piano.

'I am sure you shall do very well together,' said Lady Osborne, pleased to see that her efforts had not been in vain.

The song proceeded in just the way Lady Osborne had instructed, and to her ladyship's delight, another two songs were demanded by the pair before Emma was given permission to leave the instrument.

'Do you not sing, my lord?' said Miss Carr.

'Sing? That would be a sight to be seen,' said Miss Osborne.

'Or a sound to be heard,' said her ladyship.

'But it would not be pleasant on the ears, and therefore, best avoided,' said Lord Osborne.

Emma proved her skill as an accompanist, a point that was seized on by Lady Osborne who insisted on her playing for Mr Howard again on the occasion of the next musical evening at the Castle.

'There are never any true musicians to be had when one needs them. One finds, I grant you, a player or two who can now and again tap out a tolerable tune. I am pleased to see that Mr Howard is safe in your hands, Miss Watson,' said Lady Osborne. Turning to her son, her ladyship asked, 'Does not Miss Watson accompany Mr Howard perfectly?'

'Perfectly,' said Osborne. His voice was flat and lacked commitment, and although Emma felt that she deserved better praise, she gave little heed to his remark for she had played the best she could and had been amply rewarded with a smile and a compliment from Mr Howard.

At Lady Osborne's insistence, Mr Howard sang a further two songs unaccompanied, before Miss Osborne took her place at the pianoforte with a spirited execution of two Scottish airs.

'You played those pieces beautifully, Miss Osborne,' said Mrs Blake.

'Are they not favourites of Colonel Beresford?' said Musgrave.

'I do not — that is to say, they are certainly favourites of mine,' Miss Osborne replied.

When Miss Watson was again called to the piano, Miss Carr, who had been denied any attention for almost an hour, spoke up and continued to do so for the duration of the piece. 'Were we not all diverted last night, your ladyship, when Lord Osborne read to us from Mrs Burney?'

'Indeed we were,' replied Lady Osborne.

'Is Evelina a favourite with you, Mr Howard?' said Miss Osborne.

'I never read novels.'

'Then you do not know what you are missing,' said Musgrave. 'Nothing compares to a spirited romance. And ladies are mightily accomplished in the telling of them. Intrigue, mayhem, fever, passion… Indeed, when Lord Orville declares his love for Evelina, I confess it stirs within me such feelings of felicity that "language has not the power of telling". Mrs Burney's very words, if I am not mistaken.'

'Lord Orville is quite the hero,' said Miss Carr. 'But I have always found Evelina to be a rather dull heroine.'

'Indeed? I have always admired her fortitude,' replied Musgrave.

When Emma had finished playing, Miss Osborne took up the volume and found the place where her brother had left off. 'There,' she said, handing it to Mr Howard.

'Oh do entertain us, Mr Howard. There is none like you who reads with such true style and elegance, for you get more practice than many, reading all those psalms and sermons,' said Lady Osborne.

'I fear I am not equal to the task. Mr Musgrave is a lover of novels. Let him read.'

'Nonsense. I am in agreement with her ladyship. No one reads better than a parson,' he replied.

Mr Howard acknowledged the veracity of Mr Musgrave's claim. His reputation in the pulpit was celebrated by all who heard him. He mounted no further opposition to the request and graciously accepted the volume that was pressed upon him. Having cast his eye over the text and cleared his throat, he proceeded to render Mrs Burney to the gathering with the solemnity of tone usually employed for a reading from the Acts of the Apostles.

On reaching the passage which spoke of the passion between Lord Orville and Evelina, Mr Musgrave, despite great effort, found himself unable to suppress the urge to laugh.

'My lord, cried I, endeavouring to disengage my hand.' Mr Howard continued with unusual awkwardness. The flatness of his delivery served to heighten rather than subdue Musgrave's mirth.

Mr Howard went on. 'Pray let me go,' he coughed. 'I will if you wish to leave me.'

Within seconds Musgrave was reduced to tears, his laughter uncontrollable. Emma's eyes were fixed firmly on the reader, willing him on; but, one by one, others soon gave way until the whole company descended into fits of laughter. Emma felt only the anguish of Mr Howard's situation, and there was no doubt in her mind that the instigator of the piece had been Mr Musgrave. Emma could not forgive him for playing so cruel a joke on a respectable man.

'Please, Mr Howard,' said Musgrave at length. 'Allow me to put you out of your misery.'

'Put us all out of our misery, you mean,' whispered Miss Carr to Miss Osborne. Emma was certain that Mr Howard had heard Miss Carr, and wished with all her heart that she might offer a word in his defence. It was too late. Mr Howard passed the volume to Musgrave without ceremony. 'With pleasure, Mr Musgrave,' said he.

Musgrave continued the dialogue with the type of exaggerated passion that, in Emma's eyes, rendered his performance ridiculous.

'Oh, my lord, rise, I beseech you, rise — such a posture to me — surely your lordship is not so cruel as to mock me.'

He paused to look up; the reaction of his audience, who appeared to be amused by his buffoonery, gave him encouragement to proceed. Lady Osborne said eagerly, 'Go on. Oh, do go on, Mr Musgrave.'

'Mock you,' he continued. 'No, I revere you. I esteem and admire you above all human beings. You are the friend to whom my soul is attached as to its better half. You are the most amiable, the most perfect of women.'

During Mr Musgrave's rendition of *Evelina*, it had not escaped Miss Carr's notice that Lord Osborne's eyes had been drawn towards Miss Watson most of the time; and although Emma appeared to be unaware of his lordship's attention, Miss Carr was certain that the reverse was the case. She knew that some young women liked to give the appearance of indifference in order to increase their appeal. When, therefore, an opportunity arose to expose Emma, Miss Carr seized on it.

On completing the passage, and drawing enthusiastic applause from some of the party, Musgrave remarked, 'What a fine heroine she is! Indeed, I can think of none finer that Evelina. So modest. So artless. What say you, my lord?'

Before his lordship had chance to reply, Miss Carr exclaimed, 'Young women may appear as artless as they like in novels. But I know of none so artless in my experience. You can be sure that certain young women, however they appear to present themselves, deploy every device within their power to seize a husband. It is my belief that the greater their ability to conceal their art, the greater the danger.'

'Thank you for your warning, Miss Carr. But you speak as though men have no say in the matter. Do you think us all so easily taken in?' said Musgrave.

'I do.'

'And do you include yourself among the women of whom you speak?'

'I speak only of those artful young women who have nothing to recommend them but a pretty face and a tolerable figure.'

'And what of young men who have no fortune of their own? Do they not act in the same way?' said Musgrave.

'You must ask Miss Watson,' said Miss Carr. 'I believe her family know all about such men.'

Mrs Blake saw that Miss Carr's ungenerous remarks caused her friend pain, and brought an end to the conversation. 'I think it is time for us to depart. I should like to look in on Charles before too long. Would you mind if we break up early?' said she.

The signal to leave was a welcome one. Emma was relieved to leave behind *the great and the grand*, and to return to the more modest and comfortable surroundings of Wickstead. She had found little pleasure in the evening, except for the attentions of Mr Howard. Indeed, she was aggrieved by Mr Howard's humiliation at the hands of Mr Musgrave; and the frequency of Miss Carr's attacks, which seemed to have been directed chiefly towards her, seemed inexplicable and unjustified.

When the guests were safely on their way back to Wickstead, and Osborne and his mother out of earshot, Miss Carr seized her opportunity to speak to Miss Osborne.

'And if Miss Watson should set her cap at Mr Howard, what is the harm in that? Mama is all for it,' said Miss Osborne. 'And Mrs Blake, it seems, cannot do without her.'

'I believe Miss Watson aims much higher,' said Miss Carr, gazing at Lord Osborne across the room.

'Osborne? Impossible! He would never think of Miss Watson. Do not make yourself uneasy about something that cannot happen. Miss Watson will do very well for Mr Howard, but she would not be welcome here. My dear Fanny, do not distress yourself. Osborne and Miss Watson? It is unthinkable.'

CHAPTER FIFTEEN

Wickstead was unusually quiet the following afternoon. Mr Howard was engaged in urgent parish business with the curate and Charles was in the schoolroom designing a Trojan horse of his own, in preference to working on the translation of the *Aeneid* that his uncle had set for him.

Emma was content to do no more than look out of the window of her bedchamber and entertain the dream of one day being mistress of Wickstead. The trees that lined the lane outside were almost bare, and the mud thick and deep; still, there could be no place on earth to compare to the beauty of its situation in Emma's eyes. There was one matter that cast a troubling shadow in the midst of her reverie: she had received no communication from her aunt. The mysterious silence had given rise to all manner of speculation. Had something grave occurred? Had she been shipwrecked? Had Captain O'Brien insisted his new wife cease all communication with her niece? Was Mrs O'Brien too busy with the routine of her new life to think of her? No explanation, however reasonable, seemed satisfactory.

Emma set about writing to her aunt, though without a proper forwarding address, she had no means of knowing whether a letter would do any good. She decided to write to 'Mrs O'Brien of Cork' in the hope that someone, perhaps a relative of Captain O'Brien, would make it their business to deliver the letter into the hands of its intended recipient. Emma remained at her desk until there was hardly a space left on the paper that was not filled.

Mrs Blake, who had been to visit a sick parishioner, returned to find Mr Musgrave at the door. The frequency of his visits to Wickstead during Emma's stay had been noted even by Mr Howard. It seemed that Mr Musgrave had little else to do but act as messenger between Wickstead and Stanton. Consequently, Mrs Blake was not surprised to find that he had come directly from Stanton and carried with him a letter for Emma from Elizabeth.

'I expect I should wait for Miss Watson's reply.'

'Mr Musgrave, how very thoughtful,' said Mrs Blake. 'Perhaps you should place the Royal Mail livery on your own coach.'

'Whatever do you mean, Mrs Blake?'

'You seem much employed in making the delivery of mail from Stanton a daily occupation.'

'I suppose you have a point. Indeed, now I come to think of it, there could be no better conveyance for the Royal Mail. A curricle such as mine would certainly speed things up.'

Mrs Blake took the letter to Emma directly.

'Mr Musgrave is just now arrived from Stanton with a letter for you. I must say, he is keen to — '

Mrs Blake broke off. She did not wish to make Emma uncomfortable in Mr Musgrave's presence. For the time being, she would exercise prudence, and keep her thoughts to herself.

'It is Elizabeth's hand. I did not expect a reply so soon.'

'I shall leave you to read it. Let me know if you need anything, my dear. Do come and join us for tea when you are ready.'

Emma opened the letter and read:

'My dear Emma, your letter took me quite by surprise this morning, though I have thought much of you these last few days and have been eager to hear your news. What stories you will have to tell on your return! I hope it will not be long, though I do not wish to hasten your return when matters are at an interesting point. I heard that you dined with Mr Musgrave last night at Osborne Castle and that you sat down at nine to a full table. My dear, how did you go on? Were you not even the slightest bit nervous? I understand that you played for Mr Howard. What a fine pair you must have made! As you can guess, Mr Musgrave called here this morning to bring news of your evening. But I should so like to hear the details from you for I expect it differs vastly from his account. You know what men are like for missing out the important details. And so Mrs Blake has urged you to stay another week! I cannot be happier for you, my dear Emma, though for my part I should sooner have you home with me. Margaret has never done with complaining, and even Mr Musgrave's visit this morning did little to raise her spirits when she heard what a fine time you had of it last night. Stay where you are for the present and enjoy the company of the one to whom no other compares. Papa wishes you to convey his good wishes to Mr Howard and says that he would call on him if his health allowed. And if you happen to find yourself once more at Osborne Castle, please thank his lordship for the flour. There is hardly an ounce to be had anywhere. (The manservant who delivered the basket would not be drawn out, but I spied the coachman in the lane from the landing window and the livery was unmistakable.) What a sly fox he is! I will write again in a day or two. Mr Musgrave is to return shortly and I promised to have a reply ready within the hour. He is not inclined to wait long — for Margaret is in such ill humour today. Yours very affectionately, Elizabeth. PS Lord Osborne may wish to keep it a secret, so I leave it to your good judgement, Emma, whether to mention his gift or not.'

Emma found little pleasure in the knowledge that Lord Osborne looked upon her family as an object of charity, however well-intentioned his action might appear. Such gifts were usually distributed among the poor and needy of the parish — the sick, widows and spinsters. Did his lordship think of Emma and her family in the same way? Were they to be the grateful recipients of his lordship's pity and consequently of that family's contempt? Elizabeth, it seemed, had neither pride nor scruples in accepting his lordship's gift. Unlike Emma, her sister's gratitude prevailed over any sense of shame or humiliation that she might otherwise have felt. Elizabeth could not have been better pleased that her family should have been the object of Lord Osborne's benevolence and was little disposed to keeping it a secret for long.

Emma was convinced that Mr Howard would not have acted so. He would not have marked out her father in such a way. He should not have given one moment's thought to so unworthy a cause, for he knew what was due to Mr Watson as a gentleman and an equal.

At length, Emma made herself ready and went downstairs where she found Mrs Blake and Mr Musgrave in lively dispute.

'Miss Watson, you must settle it. Do you prefer the town or the country? Does not London — or Bath — provide more amusement than the whole of the Surrey, Sussex and Kent together? Mrs Blake will not have it,' said Musgrave.

'I have no clue, for I have never been to London and I have spent but two days in Bath in my entire life. And as I had a cold at the time, I did not venture even as far as the pump rooms. So you see, I have nothing by which to compare the town to the country, though if pressed I should be inclined to agree with Mrs Blake.'

'But you have said you know nothing of the matter. On what do you base your view?'

'I base it on my knowledge of Mrs Blake's good judgement.'

'You see, Mr Musgrave. You will not get your own way on this point,' said Mrs Blake.

'If Mr Howard were here, he would support me. I know he prefers the town to the country,' said Musgrave.

'I find that hard to believe,' said Emma.

'He often goes to London,' admitted Mrs Blake. 'I expect he wouldn't make a point of it if he wished to be always in the country.'

'Precisely,' said Musgrave. 'There you have it. Mr Howard's opinion must prevail.'

Emma could not argue with that. 'I must thank you, Mr Musgrave, for bringing the letter from my sister. It is very good of you to take the trouble,' said Emma.

'Your sister is as prodigious a writer as she is a talker. I have often listened to her speeches in awe and wonder. I don't suppose she mentioned me,' said he, 'in the letter'.

'Not in any particular way. No. But I'm sure my sister would be flattered by your estimation of her oratory.'

'Tell me, Miss Watson, why your sister is so set against me. Of what does she disapprove? I am a perfectly amiable fellow.'

'Mr Musgrave finds it impossible to conceive of a woman who does not find him utterly charming,' said Mrs Blake. 'But Emma, do tell me. Are we to have the pleasure of your company a little longer?'

'I am at liberty to stay a few more days.'

'Wonderful news! Let me tell Charles. He has been anxiously waiting to hear it all day.'

The long awaited news brought Charles downstairs with the express intention of planning further adventures for Miss Watson's amusement, among them the construction of a wooden horse large enough in which to hide. The idea, in Charles' eyes a fine one, was instantly dismissed by his mother.

'Should you like to go to Osborne Castle tomorrow to look for eels? Do you remember Lord Osborne pointing out a stream where we might find them? Or if the weather is not too promising we might finish our play and make hats and swords. We might send Count Mancini to fight the Trojans! Miss Watson is helping me to write a play, Mr Musgrave. There is an almighty sword fight right in the middle of it.'

'That does not surprise me, Master Charles. You could employ Miss Watson's elder sister in the role, for if she is as good at wielding a sword as she is at wielding words, you will find no better player to act the enemy.'

'Miss Watson, shall we call on your sister to play Count Mancini? Is she a good actress?' asked Charles.

Before Emma had time to reply, Musgrave said, 'The best.'

'Really?' said Charles, brightening at the thought.

'Mr Musgrave attempts to be amusing. And if he does not cease his raillery at my sister's expense, I think you should insist that he play Count Mancini himself. Indeed, Mr Musgrave demonstrated the extent of his theatrical ability last night after dinner.'

'Mr Musgrave, you shall be Count Mancini!' said Charles.

'Well spoken, Miss Watson. I see you are more like your sister than I had at first thought.' Turning to Charles, he said, 'Have you completed your lessons today?'

'I have,' replied the boy. 'But why must I learn Latin when nobody speaks it but churchmen?'

'I cannot tell you,' said Musgrave. 'You must ask your uncle. He is the font of all knowledge.'

'I think it is better to learn how to make useful things like tree houses and wooden horses and sailing boats and boxes for collecting spiders and beetles. Do you not think so, Mr Musgrave?'

'Master Charles, the logic of your argument is indisputable.'

The days that followed passed cheerfully for Emma; the company of each member of the Wickstead family brought her the greatest happiness she had known since leaving Shropshire. Her only loss was the society of her sister, Elizabeth. Mrs Blake became as firm a friend and confidante as she could have wished for, and in Charles she found the nearest thing to a dearly loved younger brother.

Mr Howard, though a little aloof at times where commonplace concerns were discussed, was happy to be drawn on matters more ponderous; notions of principle and good governance, theological disputes and church dogma were regularly rehearsed in the dining room. Emma found Mr Howard to be intelligent and serious-minded, and in some respects, not dissimilar to her late uncle or, indeed, her father. As her stay at Wickstead drew to an end, Emma's growing attachment to the place and its inhabitants left her with an increasing uneasiness about her return to Stanton.

The disquiet she felt was largely due to the impending loss of the society of the Wickstead family; but she owned, too, that her discontent stemmed from the lack of ease she felt in the place she now called home. At Wickstead there was nothing of the volatility, selfishness and discord which Emma had witnessed at Stanton.

Most of all, Emma feared Margaret's reaction to her return. When Tom Musgrave called at Wickstead, an occurrence of some regularity, he routinely neglected to mention Margaret's name. Was it, she wondered, because he harboured genuine feelings for her sister and could not speak her name for fear of exposure? Or was the reverse true? Had Margaret misjudged Mr Musgrave completely? Was Musgrave's attachment to her sister no more than a figment of Margaret's imagination? Having considered the matter from all sides, Emma could not find any evidence in Mr Musgrave's behaviour to suggest that he had any serious intentions towards Margaret. However, a more intriguing thought entered her head. He often mentioned Elizabeth; and his playful mockery of her sister was neither truly vindictive nor hostile. She wondered whether Musgrave's interest in ascertaining the cause of Elizabeth's disapproval was more than idle chatter. On the part of her sister, she had observed that Musgrave's name was often mentioned in conversation; news of him was eagerly sought and warnings of his unreliable character customarily given. Were the affections and desires of both parties more closely aligned than either would care to admit? To all appearances they seemed ill-matched. Mr Musgrave was a man of fashion while Elizabeth had no pretentions of the kind. Indeed, Elizabeth was already twenty-nine, a spinster in all but name. Perhaps Mr Musgrave had no particular interest in any of her sisters and wanted only to be useful where he could. Curiously, that was no more convincing an explanation than any other. Emma concluded that Mr Musgrave, like other frivolous young men of fortune and situation, had no notion of how to employ his time wisely, and having nothing better to do found daily amusement in acting on a whim.

The day finally came when Emma was to leave Wickstead. Charles, unwilling to accept the inevitable, proposed a final walk to the lake in Osborne Park in a bid to stretch the time of Emma's departure to its farthest extent.

'Shall we collect feathers on the way? We should make a feathered hat for Count Mancini's sister. I know a very fine path that is usually full of them at this time of year.'

Though pressed to accompany them, Mrs Blake made her apologies. 'I must be at home today for Miss Osborne is to pay a visit.'

Mrs Blake issued Charles with firm instructions on the particular items that would not be welcome in the house. Pebbles and pine cones were acceptable, as were wild flowers; peacock feathers, frogs, worms, snails and sheep skulls were, however, strictly forbidden.

'Be on your best behaviour or Miss Watson will not wish to visit Wickstead again.'

Charles gave his solemn assurance that they would be back before luncheon.

'I do not see why you should leave at all, Miss Watson. You should stay here. I am sure Mama and my uncle would approve the plan. There is plenty of room and three more bedchambers beside. Perhaps one of your sisters might like to come and stay at Wickstead too. We should have such a famous time.'

'I'm sure we would. But it is not within my power to live anywhere I choose. There are rules that prevent it.'

'It is the same with me. I do not wish to study everyday but I am allowed no view on the matter whatsoever.'

'You may not see the benefit of it now, but in time I believe you shall.'

'If you were to marry my uncle, then you could stay at Wickstead forever.'

Charles' candid observation caught Emma by surprise. 'Your uncle may not wish to marry, and were he to wish it, he may prefer someone else.'

'I am sure he prefers you. Shall I ask him?'

'I think not. It is better to remain silent on such matters. I urge you not to say a word,' said she, in a tone of voice that was more serious than Charles was used to hearing from Miss Watson.

Charles nodded, 'I am very good at keeping secrets. I have kept many from Mama.'

At length they reached the spot where Charles expected to find the best feathers. To his disappointment, there were few specimens fine enough to be added to his collection. They decided to walk on to look for more. Before long, the lake came into view, and as they neared the bank, storm clouds threatened.

'I think, Charles, we had better turn back now for it looks like rain.'

No sooner had dark clouds threatened than the rain began to fall in torrents; and though an ancient chestnut tree provided some shelter, their clothes were soon thoroughly soaked. A farmhand who had been working by the lake urged them not to return the way they had come, but instead to go to the Castle. 'It is nearer, ma'am, and less perilous underfoot.'

'What a fine adventure!' said Charles. 'I wonder what Lord Osborne will say. I should like to see his face when we arrive all wet and muddy.'

Emma was quite certain that she should not like to see Lord Osborne's face or the faces of any of the inhabitants of Osborne Castle while clad in mud and soaked to the skin. Nevertheless, the farmhand's advice seemed the most sensible. Emma took Charles by the hand and they hurried towards the Castle to shelter from the storm.

'We shall take cover by the servant's entrance,' said Emma, 'and beg help there. I do not wish to disturb the family.'

'I am sure that Miss Osborne and Miss Carr would be very sad if we did not call on them.'

'They will get over it more quickly than you imagine,' said Emma. Having no desire to be the subject of Miss Carr's ridicule or disdain, the matter was settled; they would seek help without disturbing the family at all.

On those occasions when secrecy is much longed for, it is sometimes denied. Lord Osborne had observed Emma and Charles in the park from the window of the library and had sent word downstairs to bring fresh clothes and blankets and to serve their unexpected guests with hot soup. Strict instructions were given to bring the visitors to the library once they had been made comfortable, and no protestations to the contrary were to be listened to.

Emma's reluctance to give way to Lord Osborne's request was lessened by his reassurance that a message had been sent to Mrs Blake explaining that she and Charles had found shelter at the Castle. She felt sorry that a messenger should have been dispatched at such a time, having to ford rivers that were once roads, and wade through fields knee deep in mud, but she knew that Mrs Blake would worry in their absence and Emma did not wish to make her friend uneasy about the whereabouts of her son.

'The messenger will think nothing of it. It's an adventure,' said Osborne. 'Charles would have done the same had he been alone. I've done it many times myself. Indeed, I would have set out for Wickstead in the rain the instant you arrived had it not been for — ' He broke off.

'Please do not let us trespass on your time, my lord. We can look after ourselves,' she replied. 'May I make a suggestion? If I recall, Master Charles once said he would like to show me a stuffed fox and badger that you have in your possession.'

'Oh, yes. Yes, indeed, Miss Watson! What a good memory you have! You must see them. May we, my lord? May I show them to Miss Watson?'

'Of course,' said Osborne, 'if I may be allowed the privilege of accompanying you. I have some time to spare. You'll find the fox and badger have been moved to the gallery, Charles. Some curious notion my mother had, Miss Watson, of creating a menagerie up there — though were you to attend one of our famous musical evenings you could find no better example of one.'

Osborne glanced at Emma and caught the hint of a smile; it was enough to give him courage to go on. 'Indeed, every farmyard sound imaginable is represented there.' Emma could suppress a full smile no longer, and Osborne had his reward.

But their amusement was short-lived, for on entering the gallery, the footsteps that were heard at the other end of the long chamber were found to be those of Lady Osborne and Miss Carr.

'Miss Watson? Charles? What an unexpected surprise,' said Lady Osborne. 'We rather expected to see no one today. How good of you to brave the weather to call on us. My daughter is not here, as you see. She is gone to Wickstead to advise Mrs Blake on new curtains for the dining room. As I said to Miss Carr, I hardly think new curtains are needed. The present ones are perfectly serviceable. But she would go. I thought perhaps Mrs Blake might have sought my advice on such matters. You, Miss Watson, can be no expert on drapery, or I feel sure Mrs Blake would have consulted you, for you were immediately to hand. Will you not join us and take a turn in the gallery?'

Charles explained that they had not particularly set out to call at the Castle, but that they had been obliged to take shelter from the rain.

'We are grateful to have dry things to wear,' said Emma.

'I am glad to hear that you are not accustomed to wearing such drab attire, Miss Watson,' said Miss Carr. 'The colour of that frock does nothing for your complexion. It is quite ill-fitting on the shoulders and needs a full inch taking from the hem. How quaint! You remind me of my cousin's old governess.'

'I am grateful for the use of it, Miss Carr. It is infinitely preferable to a wet frock.'

'We have come to see the fox and the badger,' said Charles. 'But I can't see them anywhere.'

'Come,' said Osborne.

Emma and Charles went over to where his lordship was standing. Miss Carr could not resist the temptation to join them, not least because it gave her an opportunity to keep an eye on Emma.

'Don't forget to show Miss Watson the birds' said her ladyship. 'There is a particularly fine example of a woodpecker over by the window. I do so like woodpeckers. They remind me of a Miss Jenkins I knew many years ago. Married a horse trader. Her family disapproved, of course. Though it was often said that old Mrs Jenkins had as great a knowledge of the trade as her son-in-law, for she managed to marry all her daughters off to the highest bidders. I shall leave you young people to it. When you are quite done, come down for tea.'

Before leaving the gallery, Lady Osborne took Emma aside and whispered, 'Don't let Charles leave sticky finger marks on the glass cases. They have just been cleaned.'

'What do you think of the fox, Miss Watson?' said Charles after Lady Osborne had gone.

'It is a fearsome looking beast,' she replied.

'Look at its teeth. Are they not prodigious sharp?' continued Charles.

'It is a divine creature,' cried Miss Carr. 'Not the least bit alarming. And with more natural grace than one might expect to see in lesser beasts.'

111

'Do you like other lesser beasts, Miss Carr?' said Charles.

'Indeed I do,' she replied.

'Are spiders lesser beasts?'

'Spiders are God's creatures. Your uncle would desire us to appreciate all God's creation,' she replied.

'That's good, because there is a very large one crawling up your sleeve. I should so like to have it. If you do not wish to keep it, may I?'

Charles was puzzled by Miss Carr's reaction, for it was a particularly fine example of one of God's creatures, but one whose demise Miss Carr demanded immediately, while performing a curious jig to hasten its end. Charles removed the spider from her clothing.

'It is a fine specimen. How did you come by it? I wish I had such luck. It has longer legs and a bigger body than Frederick.'

'Frederick?' said Miss Carr in dismay.

'My other spider. Should you like to see him? Next time I shall bring him with — '

'No,' replied Miss Carr sharply, inspecting her frock to ensure that no other insect had taken up residence within its folds.

Charles whispered to Emma, 'I do not think Miss Carr is as fond of spiders as she claims.' Turning to Miss Carr, he said, 'Do you not wonder at the genius of spiders to weave webs in which to catch their prey?'

Miss Carr had never in her life wondered about such things; she was, however, of the view that weaving webs to catch prey was not the sole province of spiders.

'What other creatures weave webs, Miss Carr?' said Charles.

Miss Carr looked accusingly at Emma. While she could barely tolerate an afternoon in the company of Charles Blake, the presence of Miss Emma Watson was an unwelcome intrusion of a different order and served only to frustrate the promise of being shut up in cosy seclusion for the rest of the day with Lord Osborne and his mother.

It occurred to Emma that Lord Osborne may have been expecting an expression of gratitude for the flour he had sent to her family. She would, she thought, thank him in time, but not in Miss Carr's presence, for she had no wish to provide their guest with further ways to deride and scorn her family.

At length, the messenger dispatched to Wickstead returned with a note from Mrs Blake which arrived on the tea tray. It was addressed to Lord Osborne, a matter that surprised Emma, for she had expected to receive a note of her own.

'What does Mrs Blake say?' asked Lady Osborne.

'She writes,' said he, 'How good of you to send word of Miss Watson and Charles. In return, allow me to tell you that Miss Osborne remains at Wickstead. Mr Howard has just informed me that part of the lane is at present impassable. That being the case, I have urged Miss Osborne to remain at Wickstead for the night. Mr Howard is in full agreement, and Miss Osborne is convinced that this is much the better plan. We are quite full up. Mr Musgrave is here and we also have the pleasure of Colonel Beresford's company, for the road to Delham is almost completely washed away too. May I trespass on your kindness, my lord? May I request that Miss Watson and Charles stay with you tonight? I fear there is little to be gained from any journey, however small the distance, until the tempest is over. My warmest regards to Lady Osborne and Miss Carr. Postscript: Please ease any worries that Miss Watson might have regarding arrangements for her removal to Stanton. A note arrived earlier this afternoon to advise that, due to current conditions, she will not be expected at Stanton until the weather improves. Miss Watson is sure to guess the name of the messenger.'

'I can guess the name of the messenger,' said Charles. 'Mr Musgrave is always at Wickstead bringing messages for Miss Watson. It is clear to see why.'

'Is it?' said his lordship. 'Why?'

'He has a great wish to play Count Mancini in our play, especially the scene with the wooden horse.'

The arrangements suggested in Mrs Blake's note received warm approval from all but Miss Carr. Everything was done that could be done to effect Emma's comfort and convenience. One of Miss Osborne's little used gowns was placed at Emma's disposal, and every amusement was sought to occupy Charles. After several games of backgammon, and two of speculation, Charles was given supper and hot milk and sent to bed, happily clutching a book containing pictures of the anatomy of frogs and other creatures.

Emma went up to dress for dinner and was assisted by Miss Osborne's maid who had been sent to arrange Emma's hair and make slight alterations to the gown. When Emma entered the dining room, she felt satisfied that she did not appear out of place. Even Miss Carr could not easily find fault with either the arrangement of Miss Watson's hair, or the fit, cut or colour of her dress.

Lord Osborne was unusually talkative. He spoke with uncommon feeling about Osborne Castle: the extensions made to the building over time; the proposal to landscape the gardens to the west; the purchase of a new pianoforte for the music room; and the recent additions to the library. He placed, without limit, the library and the music room at Miss Watson's disposal during her stay.

The arrival of so unwelcome an interloper, especially one whose presence appeared to transform Lord Osborne into a great talker, caused Miss Carr to strive harder for his lordship's attention.

'My lord,' said Miss Carr, 'you speak as though we are, all of us, to be held captive for a month, not a night.'

'Then we had better make the best of it,' said Lady Osborne. 'We are in luck this evening, Miss Watson. My son is not often disposed to be agreeable, but when he opens his mouth he can be very droll indeed.'

'How is your aunt, Miss Watson, and that dashing young Irish Captain of hers?' said Miss Carr.

'Oh. What intrigue!' said Lady Osborne. 'Let us hear more, Miss Watson. It puts me in mind of a very dashing Irish Captain who was, for a brief time, an acquaintance of mine. Had his teeth been tolerable, I think I should have been in some danger.'

'Miss Watson's aunt has abandoned her completely and gone to Ireland. Her bridegroom must be quite the most dashing of all young officers, for who would do such a thing to one's own niece? Do tell us, Miss Watson, what special charms he possessed that, being so fortunate as to capture the heart of your aunt, he also persuaded her to bestow on him your inheritance?'

Lord Osborne saw that Emma did not wish to speak of the matter, and said, 'It is not for us to judge the rights and wrongs of the situation. We do not know all the circumstances. Unless Miss Watson expressly wishes to speak of it, let us leave the matter alone.'

'Never mind, my dear,' said her ladyship. 'Things usually turn out for the best in the end even though we cannot see it at the time. My husband, God rest his soul, might not have taken possession of Osborne Park had it not been for his elder brother. They said my brother-in-law was carried away by a weak constitution and a broken heart, but it was a fondness for gaming tables and strong wine that did it. The loss of a brother-in-law *must be felt or we should be brutes*, but, in truth, it was quite the best thing that happened to us all. The estate was near collapse, but was brought under good governance by my dear husband and was saved, you see. And look at Miss Carr, who might six months ago have been obliged to take up a post as governess. You see how circumstances change. Had the ship carrying Mr Appleby's son not been lost, Miss Carr would not enjoy this happy state of affairs.'

'I hardly think Mr Appleby would consider it a happy state of affairs,' said Emma. 'To have lost an only son in such tragic circumstances must have caused him the deepest anguish.'

The dining room fell silent. Emma wished herself anywhere but Osborne Castle. The company of her sister Margaret would have been more easily tolerated than that of the persons with whom she was obliged to dine. Her greatest wish was for the storm to end and the roads to be mended; and though many would deem her fortunate indeed to be hold up at Osborne Castle, in Emma's eyes it came at a great price.

Miss Osborne's evening at Wickstead passed off more pleasantly than expected, for Mr Howard was less inclined to sermonise when men were present. The presence of Tom Musgrave always added a certain promise of amusement, but it was the addition of Colonel Beresford that made the evening most agreeable. Outside the confines of Osborne Castle and away from the prying eyes of her mother, Miss Osborne was at liberty to speak freely with the Colonel.

Mrs Blake had, sometime ago, observed Miss Osborne's preference for Colonel Beresford. But it was at the first assembly of the season, when Miss Osborne failed to keep her promise to Charles, that Mrs Blake was certain that she had not been mistaken. Miss Osborne was in love; and it took little time for Mrs Blake, who rarely missed a look or a gesture in a ballroom, to ascertain that Miss Osborne's feelings were reciprocated. She knew that young people in love sometimes acted in ways that appeared curiously out of character, and she had long forgiven Miss Osborne for breaking her promise to Charles. For his part, Charles had been disappointed, but the disappointment had been momentary, and had it not been for

Miss Osborne's lapse, the pleasure of making Emma's acquaintance would have been denied. That being the case, when the opportunity of bringing together two young people in love presented itself, Mrs Blake was happy to oblige. The curtains would remain as they were for some time to come, for the plans and desires of two lovers were in greater need of restoration and refreshment.

Mrs Blake had known only too well the pain of separation. When first she was married, she had been obliged to spend a winter at Portsmouth waiting for news of Captain Blake, not knowing from one day to the next whether he was dead or alive. But she was happier to be married than not, even though the hardships associated with the kind of life she must lead were great; for a woman in love would rather be the widow of such a man, and bear his name, than remain unmarried and separated from him forever in the eyes of the world.

After dinner Colonel Beresford was quick to join the ladies in the drawing room. 'Please forgive me, Colonel,' said Mrs Blake, 'I am not a great talker when I have yarn to unravel. Miss Osborne told me a most interesting piece of news today. I am sure you would not object to hearing it. There is a very comfortable seat over by the fire where Miss Osborne sits. I will sit over here nearer the light.' Colonel Beresford did not object, and Miss Osborne's gratitude was apparent to anyone with a keen eye.

Tom Musgrave was less inclined to move into the drawing room so soon. Rarely did he speak with Mr Howard alone, and rarer still did he relish the prospect, for they had few shared interests and even fewer common virtues or vices. Although Mr Howard had an air of elegance, he was not a fashionable man. Indeed, he disdained Musgrave's crop and at times had found his views on matters of the day too liberal. Likewise, Musgrave had never shown enthusiasm for Mr Howard's insistence on the need to strive against the sin of vanity, or his view of the French situation, and although this instance was no exception, he had other reasons for remaining behind to speak with him in private.

'This is perilous talk indeed. You must see that in time the monarchy will be restored and France will prosper again. It is but a matter of time,' said Mr Howard.

'Nevertheless, the news points to the reverse.'

'God is our strength. There is no circumstance, no obstacle too great, that cannot be overcome when one has right on one's side.'

'How foolish of me! Of course God is on our side. How could he possibly defend those French Catholics?' said Musgrave. After a brief pause, he continued. 'Miss Watson appears remarkably sanguine in view of the grievous circumstance that brought her into Surrey.'

'What grievous circumstance?'

'I speak of the alteration to the young lady's expectations. Surely you know — '

'What is your point?'

'The point is that she has no expectations. Not a penny. — How did her brother put it? *Sent back a weight upon her family, without a sixpence.* Your Christian charity serves you well. There are few men in this world who would settle for fifty pounds a year, but to take a woman for next to nothing is an act of true benevolence.'

'If this is a ploy of yours to ascertain my intentions towards Miss Watson, rest assured, there is no understanding between — that is, I have never given Miss Watson reason to believe otherwise.'

'Her being under your roof is likely to confirm it. I'll wager Lady Osborne has even named the day.'

Miss Carr rose unusually early and found on entering the breakfast room that it was empty. She had expected to find Lord Osborne there, for he was generally the first to rise. When the door opened, her hopes of seeing his lordship were dashed; Charles, enlivened by having already been to the stables to look at the horses, burst into the room in high spirits. He too had expected to see Lord Osborne at the table, but on finding himself alone with Miss Carr, and seeing that she was not disposed to making conversation, he sat quietly for two minutes and gulped down his food. Charles Blake was not used to sitting still for long; even a minute's silence seemed an interminable length of time when there were nests to be discovered, curiosities to be collected and larders to be raided. He ate as quickly as he could, made his excuses, and crept down to the kitchen to see if cook had any pudding, jelly or tart left over from dinner the night before.

When Lord Osborne finally made an appearance, he was surprised to find Miss Carr in the breakfast room at such an early hour.

'What a fine morning it is, my lord. I do hope your sister will be returned to us very soon. How inconvenient to be imprisoned at Wickstead a whole night,' said Miss Carr.

'My sister may take a rather different view of the matter,' he replied.

Shortly afterwards Emma came down. His lordship was able to ascertain through a series of enquiries that Emma had slept for six hours at least, that she had felt no draft at any time from the window of the bedchamber, that the fire had lasted much longer than any fire in the grates at Stanton and that the bed had been exceedingly comfortable and warm.

'Now the rain has stopped, I expect you will be anxious to return to Mr Howard and his sister,' said Miss Carr. 'I should be happy to accompany you and Charles as far as Wickstead, Miss Watson. And if a carriage were to be placed at my disposal, my lord, I might bring Miss Osborne home at the same time and save Mr Howard the trouble of sending his conveyance.'

'I expect a report on the condition of the roads by noon. Let us wait until then before making any decision.'

'Has Charles been down?' said Emma.

'He was here earlier,' said Miss Carr. 'Someone should tell that boy to chew his food properly and show better manners at the table. I wonder why Mr Howard allows that boy's behaviour to go uncorrected.'

To the surprise of them all, Lady Osborne entered the room and caught some of Miss Carr's speech.

'It is in the nature of boys to mount rebellions. Mr Howard made little impression on another pupil of his. You were quite the rebel in the schoolroom, were you not, my dear?' said Lady Osborne playfully, turning to her son.

Osborne made no comment.

'Miss Watson, I believe you are in agreement. I remember one afternoon when we were having tea, Mr Musgrave entertained me with your view of his lordship's manners,' said Miss Carr. 'And we know how Miss Watson's opinions carry the day. "I wonder why Mr Howard was unable to make his pupil's manners as exemplary as his own." I believe those were your very words, Miss Watson. Or did Mr Musgrave make it up?'

The shame and embarrassment caused by Miss Carr's remark, was felt by all who heard it. It was one thing for a mother to tease her son, a sister, or even an equal, but that Miss Watson should pass judgement on his lordship, and in so critical a tone, was quite another. Yet while Emma felt shame and embarrassment, her accuser did not enjoy the triumph of the moment. Even as the words were spoken, Miss Carr knew that the impropriety of such a remark, instead of revealing Miss Watson's imprudence, signified her own callous disregard for the feelings of all parties present.

'Of course, Mr Musgrave may have been mistaken. We cannot always rely on his reports. We have often thought him prone to embellishment, have we not?' said Miss Carr, in an attempt to offer amends.

'I confess, I did make such a remark,' said Emma. 'But it was groundless, uninformed and unfeeling. Please forgive me, my lord. I have received nothing but kindness from you and your family. Charles and I will leave as soon as it is possible to do so. Please excuse me.'

Until then, Emma had borne Miss Carr's taunts and censure with studied composure, but to expose her in front of the family whose hospitality had been unstinting, was mortifying. Mr Musgrave's part in the matter also deserved reproof; what little regard she had for him had gone, for his behaviour had been anything but that of a gentleman. Most of all she blamed herself. She was the real author of the piece; she had been the one to judge where judgement should have been suspended. Had she been fortunate to possess Mrs Blake's generosity of spirit, the remark would never have passed her lips, nor would the thought have entered her head. And yet, had not her uncle always said that correct behaviour is not a matter of fortune, but of constant practice? In the end, as she knew so well, the fault had been hers and hers alone.

For the remainder of the morning, she sat in her room contemplating the consequences of her actions, wondering whether any other thoughtless remarks that had so easily passed her lips had reached the ears of those to whom they were directed. The part she found most painful was in comparing herself to Margaret. Emma saw that she bore a stronger likeness to her sister than she would otherwise have cared to own.

A knock on the door roused Emma from her reverie.

'Miss Watson,' whispered Charles, his lips pressed to the keyhole, 'there is something I should like to show you. I am sure you will be amazed when you see it.'

Emma got up and opened the door, expecting the boy to have in his hand a creature that he had found under the bed or in Miss Carr's hair.

'It's in the library,' said he.

Emma's reluctance to enter any part of the house that might bring her once again into the company of its inhabitants was put aside with some difficulty; but she had neglected Charles all morning, and would not disappoint him further. Charles, for his part, would not be drawn on the surprise that awaited her in the library except for assuring her that it was so very fine a thing, that if she did not see it, he was sure she would regret it forever.

Emma stepped lightly down the stairs to avoid any sound or disturbance that might bring her into contact with Lord Osborne or his mother. On entering the library, Charles exclaimed, 'There, Miss Watson. Is it not the finest ship you have ever seen?'

The object, a model frigate, was displayed in all its splendour on a table by the window. Precise in every detail to the original, it had been commissioned by Lord Osborne and built by the hand of a skilled craftsman.

'Well, Miss Watson?' said Charles.

'It is very fine indeed.'

'It's a frigate. The Nereus. You can count the guns. It is a model of Papa's old ship. When he was Captain of it and anchored off the French coast, he nearly captured a French frigate twice her size. I begged Papa to take me to see her, but it was not possible. And now she is a wreck at the bottom of the sea,' said Charles. 'Lord Osborne had this model made from Papa's own drawing.'

'And why is it here and not at Wickstead where you can see it?' said Emma.

'Lord Osborne is to have a glass case made to preserve it. And once it is complete, his lordship has promised to have it sent to Wickstead. I can't wait to show Mama.'

As Charles described every detail of the ship, Emma forgot about the incident in the breakfast room, but when Lord Osborne came into the library, ostensibly to look for a journal he had misplaced, her embarrassment and confusion returned.

'See. Twenty guns, sixth rate, one gun deck, three masts, full rigged. And here is the quarterdeck where — ' said Charles.

'Charles, cook wants to know if you would like a piece of tart that is fresh from the oven,' said Lord Osborne. 'She said you were down earlier looking for something of the sort.'

'Yes, but there was nothing left.'

'There is now. So off you go.'

'Excuse me, Miss Watson,' said Charles. 'My lord, I haven't explained the bells or the rates or the ships of the line yet. Miss Watson, I must tell you that Papa's ship was not a ship of the line, but you must know that it wasn't a sloop either. And if I should ever be a ship's Captain, I should — '

'Charles, if you should ever be a ship's Captain, you will expect your men to act on your orders immediately. The Captain in this house is cook. If you delay much longer there will be no pie left at all,' said his lordship.

'Oh yes,' said Charles. 'Excuse me, my lord. Excuse me, Miss Watson.'

Emma continued to examine the ship.

'Well,' said Lord Osborne. 'Where shall we start? Ships of the first rate have — '

'My lord, forgive me. I regret deeply what happened earlier. I — '

'Miss Watson, if it will make you easy, you have my forgiveness, but in truth there is nothing to forgive. Indeed, my mother and sister are in full agreement with your view and have been for as long as I can remember. But may I ask you in all earnestness, what part of my behaviour at our local assembly displeased you the most?'

Emma knew not how to reply to Osborne's candid enquiry.

'Nothing. Really. I cannot say.'

'An honest reply is all I seek. The question is sincere. I truly wish to find out. And I believe that you are more likely to speak the truth to me than anyone I know.'

Emma was taken aback by Lord Osborne's request. His tone was earnest and not sarcastic, and though she struggled to find the right words, she suspected that he would not be satisfied with a hollow reply.

'Very well,' she replied, 'I noticed that for some time you sat alone in the tea room, out of reach of your own party and far away from all the other guests. Your demeanour seemed to express the manner of a man who wished to be a million miles away. And though at times some young women were obliged to stand up with each other, you did not stand up at all, not even with any of your own party. Had you been at cards, such behaviour would have easily been explained, but you were not.'

Osborne smiled at the thought of Miss Watson having made such a detailed observation of his behaviour. Any observation was better than nothing. It was encouragement enough for him to go on.

'I am an inferior card player. And I dislike ballrooms. I never learned to dance, nor had any inclination to do so.'

'Then perhaps you would find yourself more at ease in a ballroom were you to learn,' said Emma.

'To learn?'

'To dance.'

CHAPTER SIXTEEN

It was with a mixture of relief and dissatisfaction that Emma returned to Stanton. Mrs Blake expressed every hope of calling on Emma as soon as it was in her power to do so, and Charles made his friend promise that on her next visit she would stay a month at least. It was, however, Mr Howard's behaviour at her departure that had perplexed Emma. He had expressed his hope that she had enjoyed her stay at Wickstead, but seemed to suggest that it would be some time before they would be likely to have the pleasure of her company again. His business in town could no longer be delayed — it would necessitate his absence for some weeks — the curate would manage things while he was away — Mrs Blake was to accompany him to London — Charles, for the sake of his studies, would go too.

The manner of his parting was curiously unsatisfactory, being neither warm nor callous. There was a kind of aloofness about Mr Howard that spoke of indifference, or at least of an urgent desire to put some distance between the Wickstead family and their guest. Indeed, Mrs Blake had made no prior mention of their impending move to town, and seemed a little unsettled by the prospect herself.

Mr Howard had been alarmed by the information regarding Miss Watson's expectations, or lack of, that Mr Musgrave had imparted on the night of the storm, and though he had quickly put an end to the subject at the time, he had thought of it several times since. As time went on, Mr Howard's view of the matter seemed to harden; and after much soul searching and quiet reflection, he came to the conclusion that he had been the subject of a calculated deception on the part of the young lady. To avoid any further intimacy, or the appearance of it, a move to town was required for a few weeks at least.

Emma was convinced that the curious alteration in Mr Howard's behaviour stemmed from some flaw in her own actions; perhaps Mr Musgrave and Miss Carr had exposed her in some way, had distorted her words or made her opinions appear foolish in his eyes. She tried her best to keep in check her sadness at Mr Howard's departure and the manner of their parting; yet his conduct, in Elizabeth's eyes, was not easily accounted for, and quickly earned her reproach.

'It is perfectly reasonable that Mr Howard should attend to his business in town,' said Emma.

'No, Emma. It is all wrong. Mr Howard singles you out — receives you at Wickstead in the most cordial fashion — his sister becomes a trusted friend in no time at all — and then, on a whim, he ups and leaves and takes them with him.'

'It is only for a few weeks,' said Emma.

Margaret, who had been listening for any mention of Tom Musgrave, now spoke. 'He gives you no promise — makes you no offer. Come, Emma, the whole neighbourhood was expecting it. I saw Mrs Edwards in Delham last week. She was certain an announcement would be made shortly. Certain of it. Everyone speaks of it in Delham. Indeed, I find it hard to believe that you could spend almost a fortnight in the home of Mr Howard — who has never in his life invited a woman of any description to stay — and not make the most of it.'

'I was the guest of Mrs Blake.'

'It is the same thing. There must have been something wanting in your behaviour. I expect you did not give him enough encouragement.'

'Margaret, do hold your tongue. Can you not see how it upsets Emma when you speak of Mr Howard so?' said Elizabeth. 'Emma, dear, it is true. I own, I have heard some of our neighbours mention it.'

'Well, I wish they would not. I beg you, do what you can to quell any rumour of the kind. There is no truth in it.'

'None whatsoever?' asked Elizabeth.

'Mr Howard's behaviour towards me was in every respect gentlemanly, but he never gave me hope. The hope was entirely mine. I am the one at fault.'

'You see, Elizabeth,' said Margaret. 'Emma admits it. Not only does she lose an inheritance, she seems unable to secure a perfectly respectable man even though the opportunity falls squarely into her lap. If you don't try harder, Emma, we will all end up spinsters — just like Elizabeth. And I, for one, do not want *to be poor and laughed at.*'

Emma could no longer suppress the misery she felt, and, finding little comfort in the company of her sisters, retired to the peace and privacy of her room. She had harboured hopes of Mr Howard, but now she chided herself for giving way to them, and for allowing herself to think of a day when she would be mistress of Wickstead.

On one point she felt great shame. In comparing Lord Osborne's behaviour to that of his former tutor, Emma had not only accused Mr Howard of failing to bring his lordship's behaviour under good regulation, but she had revealed her preference for him to the world despite having received no indication that her partiality was, or ever would be, reciprocated.

As dinner drew near, Elizabeth brought up a tray for Emma and placed it on a small table by the window.

'You must eat.'

'Elizabeth. Stay a moment. There is something I need to say. I believe Mr Howard's departure was my doing.'

Emma had not intended to tell Elizabeth what had occurred at Osborne Castle and what had led to her present sorrow and disgrace, but the burden of concealment was too great. Elizabeth listened as Emma related the incident that weighed heavily on her mind.

'You are mistaken, Emma. Why would Mr Howard uproot his whole family for the sake of such a trifle? But I must say, Mr Musgrave's behaviour is wholly reprehensible. I shall give him a piece of my mind when I see him.'

'Please, Elizabeth, do not speak of it to Mr Musgrave. I shall say nothing to him in future, for I do not trust him.'

Elizabeth did what she could to allay Emma's anxieties.

'Miss Carr should never have done such a thing. She is as bad as Tom Musgrave.'

'No Elizabeth. Don't you see? It was my doing. I should never have spoken as I did. And Miss Carr must be so very pleased with herself. I cannot like her, Elizabeth. I have tried, but I cannot.'

'Why should you like her? She is nothing to you. She is nothing to any of us. And I do not think Lord Osborne cares for her,' said Elizabeth.

'I believe you are right, but she is determined to get him if she can.'

'Emma, should you like to walk into Delham tomorrow? There is a little path through the woods that never floods. It adds but ten minutes to the walk each way, but I think a little exercise would do both of us good. Some new lace has just arrived at Mason's. I should like your opinion of it. Margaret won't come. She is convinced that Musgrave will call, and I have no wish to see him.'

'Nor I,' said Emma.

The next morning, the two sisters set off for Delham with instructions from their father to call at the post office to ascertain whether a parcel, a book of sermons, of which he had been awaiting delivery for several weeks, had finally arrived.

While Emma waited outside the post office, and Elizabeth enquired within, her attention was drawn to a smart carriage stationed outside the White Hart. The window was pulled half down and a woman's hand appeared; it seemed to beckon Emma to approach. The passenger was seated with her face hid from the light, and though at first Emma thought it was Mrs Blake, she was sure that Mrs Blake would not have been so furtive. Having been unable to ascertain to whom the hand belonged, Emma approached the carriage with increasing curiosity.

'Emma. I am so glad to see you,' cried Miss Edwards.

'Mary. Are you unwell? What is the matter? Has something happened?'

'Oh, Emma. It is Papa.'

'Has Mr Edwards taken a turn for the worse?'

'Not at all! It is much worse than that. Papa is very well indeed. He and Mama are too cruel! I am to be sent away. I have the worst luck of all.'

'How so?'

'I have suffered the greatest injustice.'

'I am so sorry to hear it. But what is it Mary? Can I be of service in any way?'

'Yes, Emma, you can.'

'It was Mama who at first discovered my secret, for she is never satisfied until she knows everything there is to be known. Congratulations, by the way, on securing Mr Howard.'

'I am not engaged to Mr Howard, Mary.'

'But you soon shall be.'

'I shall not be. Mr Howard has not made me an offer and I do not expect to receive one.'

'I am sorry to hear it. Are you very disappointed?'

'I — Do tell me your news, Mary.'

'It is the worst kind of news imaginable. Mama insisted I tell all, and had I refused, she threatened to send me to stay with Grandmamma. I could not bear such a dreary old place. I had no choice. I feel so wretched. And Captain Hunter had already ordered the horses and paid for them. He is most put out, I can tell you.'

'You meant to elope?'

Mary nodded tearfully. 'And now I have no prospect of seeing Captain Hunter ever again. Emma, please promise you will write to me.'

'Of course.'

'And send me word of Captain Hunter when you can. Mama, I am certain, will give you my address in town, for she trusts you. I cannot tell you how I suffer.'

'Mary, this is shocking indeed. I do not know what to say. But I am certain that you have had a lucky escape. You may feel pain now, but consider what suffering might have awaited you had you eloped with this man. There is no means of knowing whether he would have made you happy, or indeed made you his wife — '

'He loves me.'

'Love is a word easily misused.'

'You must go now for Papa approaches. I thought he would be at least half an hour in the White Hart. Please don't let him see you. He insists on accompanying me every inch of the journey. I am but a prisoner. My life is over. Keep my secret, Emma. Please.'

Emma was astounded by Mary's revelation and had little opportunity to absorb the shock of her disclosure before Elizabeth's return. To Emma's surprise, Elizabeth emerged from the post office with her father's longed for parcel, and in the company of Mrs Edwards.

'Mrs Edwards has just informed me that Mary is to go to London to visit her uncle. What a happy thing for Mary! I imagine there is more amusement to be found there than in the whole of Surrey,' said Elizabeth.

'The visit has been planned for some time,' said Mrs Edwards. 'It falls at a most convenient time for my brother-in-law. Mary can hardly wait to get there, you see. Her father is to accompany her on the journey in our new equipage. May I be the first to offer my congratulations, Miss Emma? Any woman who can secure the affections of a man like Mr Howard is truly worthy of praise. You do credit to your family. I hope to see Mary in a similar situation before long.'

'Mrs Edwards, your felicitations are misplaced. Indeed, you have utterly mistaken the matter. There is no understanding between Mr Howard and myself. And I should be grateful if you would do me the kindness of quelling any rumours of the kind. Mr Howard has not made me an offer and I do not expect to receive one.'

'Pardon me, Miss Emma. How strange? I seem to have been misinformed,' said Mrs Edwards. 'Give my good wishes and those of my husband to your good father.'

The walk to Delham had not the effect on Emma that Elizabeth had wished for. She was sure the exercise would have raised Emma's spirits had it not been for Mrs Edwards' untimely good wishes. Although Elizabeth was apologetic over her lack of forethought, she could not reproach herself entirely, for there had been little opportunity to acquaint Mrs Edwards with the facts while they were engaged on other matters inside the post office. It was her hope, now that Emma had spoken plainly, that the matter would be laid to rest.

On their return, Margaret, who, from the parlour window, had seen them approach, met her sisters at the door. 'Tom Musgrave called while you were out' said Margaret rushing down the stairs. 'He threatened to stay for ten minutes at most and refused to take tea but when pressed he stayed five minutes more — and in the end was prevailed upon to stay for twenty.' Convinced that his affections had heightened or returned — though she was sure they had never ceased completely — Margaret was in high spirits.

'He asked to see you, Emma,' said Margaret. 'But I think he was almost relieved to find you absent. I could see it in his face. He brought some fruits from the hothouse at Osborne Castle. I expect he didn't want them himself. And now he is off to town on some errand and he would not be drawn on what his business was.'

'I should think not. That is his affair, and I hope he stays there for good,' said Elizabeth. 'Upon my word, is everyone gone to London? First, Mr Howard and his sister, and then Mary Edwards, and now Mr Musgrave — there will be no one left hereabouts but ourselves. I suppose he didn't mention how long he would remain in town — not that I care to know.'

'A day or two. But that signifies nothing,' Margaret replied. 'He will say a day and mean a month. I thought I might return to Croydon for a week or two as I'm not needed here.'

'Well,' said Elizabeth, 'unless you have the means to pay for the journey yourself, you will have to make the best of your present situation. Anyway, it is Emma's turn to visit Croydon.'

'How could you be so unfair? I shall write to our brother directly. Robert will not refuse me!' said Margaret. 'You're very quiet, Emma. Are you still thinking of Mr Howard? If you want my opinion — '

Emma had not the least desire to hear Margaret's opinion. And when her father's supper tray was ready, she begged to carry it up to his room; and there she remained in quiet conversation for much of the evening.

CHAPTER SEVENTEEN

The pleasure of London society and the prospect of one of Lady Forbes' famous balls kept Tom Musgrave in London longer than he had intended. A few days stretched to a week, and a week extended into a fortnight. During his second week in town, he happened upon Mr Howard in Grosvenor Square. The chance meeting gave little satisfaction to either party; indeed, Mr Howard appeared somewhat agitated and less inclined than usual to be drawn on the news of the day. The necessary enquiries were hastily made and disposed of — the Osbornes were said to be in good health several days ago — Mrs Blake had been laid low with a cold — Charles had also shown symptoms.

'You left Wickstead rather suddenly.'

'I have business here that requires my attention.'

'And when do you propose to attend once again to your flock?'

'When my business is complete, Mr Musgrave. The parish is well looked after for the present. I've heard no complaints of the curate. I shall return when I have settled things here.'

'Shall you attend Lady Forbes' ball this evening?'

'I may look in on it.'

'Then perhaps we will meet again. Give my good wishes to Mrs Blake. I am sure she will be pleased to know that Miss Watson was well when I last saw her.'

Musgrave returned from London several days later having carried out a commission given to him by Lord Osborne. He had employed the services of a Mr Webb, a dancing master of some repute, whose pupils were known to move in the first circles. Mr Webb was accompanied by a Mr Foote, a violinist whose mastery of country dances was second to none. The two had been employed on the recommendation of Lady Forbes, a woman whose skill in a ballroom to call, rally and direct proceedings, was known to draw the respect of every officer of rank who had ever fought on a battlefield.

'What use is a dancing master,' said Lady Forbes, 'without a musician? One cannot dance in silence. Mr Foote and Mr Webb will serve you well. But tell me, what scheme is this? What is Osborne up to, employing a dancing master? Is he quite himself?'

'Can you not guess, my lady?'

'How stupid of me! Of course! But are you quite certain? Is Osborne in love? Come, you must tell all there is to tell. Has Mr Appleby's piquant little niece toppled him at last? There is no accounting for taste, I suppose. You should see Lady Norton's new beau. I have heard, by the by, that Miss Carr's expectations may not be quite — well — it is hardly my place to say so — but word has it that her uncle has run up debts. Let's hope he can pay them off before the grim reaper comes to call. One doesn't wish to speak ill of a man preparing to meet his maker, but I hope Osborne knows what he is doing. Being in love is all very well, but when bills are to be paid and there is nothing left in the kitty, love is quick to fade, like the new silk wallpaper in Lady Bridges' drawing room. I have never seen anything like it. If I were her, I should ask for my money back. And what of you, Tom? How many more hearts have you broken this last while? Miss Pugh was rather taken with you at the ball. A word of warning — Mrs Powlett, her chaperone — three chins and eyes like a hawk — is no admirer of crops. But I think you are quite the most handsome man in town. Your mother, rest her soul, would be proud. By the by, if you are inclined to think of Miss Pugh, I can vouch for the family. The father is all for making a profit wherever he can and with a vast estate in the West Indies there will be plenty to settle on his daughter. But if you don't secure her soon, I fancy Mr Reed will have her.'

The return of Tom Musgrave to Delham, accompanied by two unusually flamboyant looking gentlemen, one with a violin, the other with a pink and white striped waistcoat, did not pass without comment, not least because it was rare to see Musgrave and his wardrobe outdone by any man in the neighbourhood. Once installed at the White Hart, Musgrave set the hour at which the two gentlemen were to arrive at Osborne Castle.

Musgrave's own arrival at the Castle the following day gave him the greatest of pleasure, for it was met with universal complaints of his absence and neglect.

'Have you been all this time in town?' said Lady Osborne. 'Tell me, how does Lady Forbes appear? Did she employ a domestic painter for the walls in the blue drawing room?'

'I believe so,' said Musgrave. 'For they are no longer blue. Bright yellow seems all the rage.'

'And is he to paint the dining room walls? They are more in need of restoration than anywhere.'

'They looked perfectly decent to me.'

'I daresay,' said Osborne, *'when the walls no longer need touching up, he will be otherwise employed about my lady's face.'*

'My lord,' said Musgrave, 'may it please you to know that two gentlemen — tradesmen — await you in the ballroom.'

'Are you now to act as footman, Mr Musgrave?' said Miss Carr. 'How diverting!'

'Two tradesmen you say?' said Lady Osborne. 'Are we to have the walls painted in the ballroom? Osborne, let yellow be the colour. Yellow is just what is needed to brighten it up. And you may consult your sister on the purchase of curtains, for she seems to be an authority on such matters.'

Osborne and Musgrave left the ladies to deliberate on the subject of styles and silks, ballrooms, colours and wall coverings.

'There is little point in such a scheme,' said Miss Osborne, 'for the ballroom is never used. It would be more practical to paint the music room.'

'Then perhaps we should urge his lordship to give a ball,' said Miss Carr.

'Yes, indeed! A ball would be a fine thing.'

'I doubt my brother would agree,' said his sister. 'You know how he dislikes such things.'

On entering the ballroom, Musgrave whispered to his lordship, 'Mr Webb was once dancing master to the Prince of Wales'.

'Was he? And is that a recommendation or a warning?'

When the introductions had been completed and the manner of teaching established to Mr Webb's satisfaction, the pupil was ready to begin his lesson. Mr Foote raised his violin in readiness as Mr Webb prepared to call, 'We will begin with the Barley Mow. It requires little exertion and displays the body to great effect. One can never go wrong with the Barley Mow.'

Mr Musgrave's services were called upon by Mr Webb to demonstrate the correct positioning of the body from the outset.

'Excellent, Mr Musgrave. Excellent,' said Mr Webb. 'My lord, Mr Musgrave's figure is perfectly aligned as you see. May I humbly request your lordship to follow his example?'

The renown of the dancing master had spread throughout the capital, and was in no small measure due to his attention to detail.

'My lord, if I may — ' Mr Webb delicately lifted Osborne's chin with the tips of his fingers. 'The head must be upright, without being stiff. The shoulders fall back to give greater grace to the body. The arms hang by the side. The hands like so. Neither quite open, nor quite shut. The left foot is placed foremost, as you see, and the right is ready to move.'

As Mr Webb gave Mr Foote the nod to begin, his lordship cast a look of exasperation at his friend. Musgrave was convinced beyond doubt that Osborne's forbearance was the surest sign of a serious partiality for the young lady who had once decried his friend's *careless air* and lack of ease in a ballroom.

At the end of the first measure, Mr Webb offered a word of encouragement. 'Excellent, my lord. And may I say, dancing becomes your lordship very well. Very well indeed. May I also say, my lord, that dancing is not often thought so necessary as it really is. As I once observed to His Royal Highness, the Prince of Wales, it is by dancing that we dispose ourselves gracefully in the world. Our great nation is much distinguished by it.'

'He took it to heart then,' whispered Osborne to Musgrave. 'How fortunate for His Royal Highness to have the benefit of Mr Webb's counsel on matters of state. If only the French would dance to our tune, all would be well and we would rest peacefully in our beds.'

'And now, your lordship, let us continue,' said Mr Webb, wafting his handkerchief like a fan, 'with another country dance that is a great favourite with the ladies. It provides those little occasions for the dancing couple to say a word here and a word there. Your lordship may wish to prepare, prior to a particularly desirable pairing, one or two expressions to entertain the young lady.'

On finding it necessary to ascertain the current arrangement of the ballroom before embarking on any detailed plans for its improvement, the ladies were rendered speechless at the spectacle that greeted them on entering within. The discovery of Osborne's secret was met with universal astonishment; indeed, the sight of his lordship being put through his paces in a jig gave Lady Osborne as much cause for concern as for optimism.

'Is he quite well?' asked her ladyship.

'I hardly know,' replied Miss Osborne.

'Perhaps he has had a blow to the head. Should I send for Mr Morton?'

'No Mama, he doesn't need a physician. It is probably one of Musgrave's pranks, though perhaps it might serve us well. You should like to give a ball, shouldn't you?'

'I certainly should!'

Lady Osborne decided to take the most optimistic view. Her son's unusual behaviour might easily be accounted for. That a declaration would shortly follow, and that Miss Carr was soon to reap the rewards of patience and persistence, seemed the likeliest explanation. For what other reason could there be to restore the ballroom to its former glory and for its owner to master the steps of an Irish jig?

Lord Osborne's intention had merely been to learn to dance and, in so doing, surprise the neighbourhood at the next local assembly. The idea of holding a ball at Osborne Castle had not entered his head. Gradually, however, he was persuaded of the advantage of the scheme. The full restoration of the ballroom would be an extensive and protracted undertaking, but some minor adjustments here and there were easily manageable and would add both to the comfort and elegance of the arrangements. And there was none more willing than his mother, his sister and her friend, to take command of the scheme. The plans for the ball were settled with remarkable speed, and the enthusiasm that accompanied them served only to bring forward the date of the ball. As soon as the date had been named, Miss Osborne wrote to Colonel Beresford with the news, in the hope of securing his attendance; Miss Carr employed a dressmaker with the strictest instructions that only the latest fashion in ball gowns would do; and Lady Osborne sent for large quantities of paper and set about making lists. There were lists to be made of guests to be invited, tradesmen and musicians to be employed, dishes to be decided upon, servants to be instructed, dances to be chosen.

Lady Osborne had never been happier. The late Lord Osborne, like his son, had had little interest in dancing or giving balls. It was twenty years at least since the last ball had been held at Osborne Castle and, as it might well be twenty years before the next, Lady Osborne intended to make the most of her present good fortune.

CHAPTER EIGHTEEN

In the days that followed, Mr Howard was never far from Emma's thoughts and her need for employment had never been greater. Gradually, the solution presented itself through the distraction of reading, as her father began to request Emma's company in preference to that of his other daughters. When reading passages from essays and sermons, her tone of voice was confident and clear, and her compassion for his state of health sincere. Emma made it her daily routine to bring up his dinner tray and stay to read to him whenever his health allowed. In time, Mr Watson began to recover his strength, and Emma, whose arm he would most often lean on, was content to walk with him to the church for daily matins. As time went on, Emma saw a change in her father. He would ask to take an additional turn in the garden, and sometimes he walked as far as the lane, before retreating to his room for the rest of the day. The tranquillity of his chamber was his refuge; and had there been less discord downstairs, his health might have undergone a remarkable, immediate and full recovery.

Mr Watson's illness lay in his desire for a peaceful life. Among his finest sermons were those that called for the strengthening of bonds within the Christian family, of unity and concord; it was, therefore, a matter of deep regret that he had long abandoned all hope of bringing the same accord to his own family.

Mr Watson's return to health was to be of short duration. The cause that brought on a state of rapid decline was the unexpected arrival of his other daughter, Penelope. The surprise announcement, which was made by Elizabeth one afternoon in December, was met with dismay.

'Papa, whatever shall we do? Penelope is come. Emma, you had better come and meet your sister.'

Mr Watson, who found himself suddenly in the throes of a fever that required immediate rest and quietude, instructed Elizabeth to see to Penelope and prevent her from squabbling with Margaret. Only after peace was restored should she send her sister to his room for five minutes after dinner.

But Penelope had not been five minutes in the house before the quarrelling began. Elizabeth and Emma lingered in the hallway as a heated exchange between Margaret and her sister broke out.

'I trusted you. And you set him against me with a view to gaining him yourself!' said Margaret.

'I did nothing of the kind,' replied Penelope. 'It is your own bad temper that drove him away.'

'You shall not ruin my chance of happiness again. I wish you had never come back.'

Elizabeth, who was used to Penelope and Margaret's squabbles, entered the room and called for calm.

'I wish you would not argue so,' said she. 'How many times have I told you, Penelope? There is no point in listening to Margaret's taunts.'

'I have heard nothing but the name Musgrave since I arrived. Wretched man! A fine welcome this has turned out to be.'

'Come and meet your sister, Emma,' Elizabeth replied.

Penelope looked Emma up and down; Emma smiled nervously at her sister.

'Let me look at you. Let me look at the nonsensical creature that let Aunt Turner's fortune slip through her delicate little fingers. How you can bear to live in this house after enjoying all the comforts of life in Shropshire, I do not know. I am sorry that Aunt Turner has abandoned you, Emma. I always thought her a silly woman. What does she mean by marrying a man half her age? He is bound to outlive her.'

The sister who was nearest to Emma in age bore the least likeness to her in appearance. The manner of Penelope's greeting did not alarm Emma, however, for, having lived in the same house as Margaret, she expected no less; and Elizabeth had taught her not to anticipate the degree of sisterly affection that one ought to expect within a family. Strangely, Emma was disposed to like Penelope, if only because of her impatience with Margaret's constant lament over Musgrave's neglect.

Emma went to sit by the window. The silhouette of a stranger in the garden, standing by the blackberry bush, caught her attention.

'You do know that I am married, do you not? You received my letter — the one I sent from Chichester three days ago.'

The sisters looked at each other in astonishment.

'No. Nothing has arrived from Chichester this last week,' said Elizabeth.

'Then perhaps Dr Harding forgot to send it. Anyway, it is of little matter now.'

'Married?' asked Margaret. 'Good God! I can't imagine how you managed that!'

'May I be the first to wish you joy, my dear sister,' said Emma.

'Save your breath. Indeed, save your good wishes for Margaret, though I expect you will never have cause to give them. She is convinced Musgrave will have her. But he won't. You will see.'

'Who is that elderly man in the garden? He must be sixty if he is a day,' said Margaret.

Penelope sighed with exasperation. 'Mrs Shaw assured me he would breathe his last before the fortnight was out. Two weeks! It is six weeks and he is amazingly well. I am the one who suffers. I have been completely taken in by Dr Harding. He has the constitution of an ox. It would be just my luck were he to outlive me. This is all you're doing, Emma. What were you thinking of? You had it in your power to raise all our fortunes.'

'But it was not in my power to prevent my aunt from falling in love.'

'Falling in love? How could she be so foolish?'

'Aunt Turner foolish?' said Margaret. 'And when did you first acknowledge the violence of your affections for old Dr Harding?'

'Love is of little matter. When Dr Harding is gone to meet his Maker, I shall have a comfortable income and an elegant house by the sea. I shan't depend on the scraps from Robert's table, nor be daily reminded of my lot by that pretentious, conceited wife of his. Aunt Turner has done you a great wrong, Emma. I hope she suffers for it.'

'I suppose what Penelope means is that our aunt did not need to marry,' said Elizabeth. 'But you know, Emma, *we must marry. I could do very well single for my part. A little company and a pleasant ball now and then would be enough for me, if one could be young forever.*'

'Margaret had better forget Tom Musgrave and take Robert's willing clerk while she can,' said Penelope.

'*I could never marry a man I did not love,*' said Emma.

'I daresay you will have little choice. If you are lucky enough to receive an offer at all, you must take it,' said Penelope.

'Let us introduce ourselves to Dr Harding,' said Margaret. 'I hope he has a good income, for he will surely need one.'

The following morning, Margaret and Penelope, having temporarily put their differences aside, walked into Delham. Appeased by Penelope's offer to buy lace for Margaret's new bonnet, the two went on their way almost as friends. As a newly married woman, Penelope was eager to receive the due acknowledgements and felicitations of her neighbours and to spend as much of Dr Harding's allowance as her conscience would allow. Margaret had the same view of her brother-in-law's money, but with even fewer scruples about inducing him to part with it. The prospect of meeting Musgrave was Margaret's other purpose, for she knew that he often frequented the White Hart on Wednesdays. Dr Harding, to Penelope's satisfaction, declined the invitation on account that his arthritic knee did not dispose him well to walking long distances.

'Allow me, Dr Harding, to place my modest conveyance at your disposal while your horses rest,' said Mr Watson. Being of similar age, education and temperament, Mr Watson seemed satisfied with the new addition to the family; and when Dr Harding expressed a wish to visit the church rather than spend the morning surrounded by stockings, lace and silks, his father-in-law insisted on accompanying him in person. Every detail of the church's history was discussed and debated, points of doctrine were clarified, and the lack of spiritual and moral observance among youth people was agreed on and lamented. Indeed, there was agreement on every matter, and at the end of the morning Mr Watson found himself well-pleased with his new son-in-law. He would brook no opposition: Dr and Mrs Harding must stay until the Christmas festivities were over before the word 'Chichester' could be mentioned again.

'Let your curate manage things while you are away. That is what they are there for, Dr Harding,' said Mr Watson. 'There is nothing more appealing to a young parish curate than to hold sway from time to time, as long as he does not get carried away with too many new ideas, or gain the ear of the archdeacon.'

'Quite right, Mr Watson. Quite right,' he replied.

'I hope Dr Harding has deep pockets, for he will need them where Penelope is concerned,' said Elizabeth when she and Emma were alone again. 'But how shall we manage now that they are to stay a month, Emma? Penelope and Margaret will not last five minutes without a fight. Perhaps it would not be such a bad idea for Margaret to return to Croydon for Christmas after all.'

The sudden sound of Musgrave's voice and the brisk footsteps in the hall gave Elizabeth and Emma little time to straighten the parlour in preparation for his entrance.

'Miss Watson, Miss Emma. You both appear in good health, I see.'

'Mr Musgrave,' said Elizabeth, 'this is an unexpected — '

'Pleasure,' he replied.

'Surprise was the word I was looking for,' said Elizabeth.

'I daresay your surprise will turn to pleasure when you hear my news,' said he. 'There is to be a ball at Osborne Castle, and all your family are invited. It is to take place two weeks hence and will be a very grand affair.'

Elizabeth could hardly contain her excitement at the news. 'Imagine the Osbornes inviting us to a ball and at the Castle. Whatever next? Oh! So many things to think about! But who will look after Papa?' said she. 'Indeed, I have no gown decent enough to be seen, though I should very much like to go. Margaret will have to lend me one of hers, for she is the nearest in size to me. You have many beautiful gowns, Emma. You will not want for choice.'

'There, you see. Has not my visit brought Miss Watson untold pleasure, Miss Emma?'

'I believe it has, sir,' said Emma, with little expression in her voice. Elizabeth may have forgiven Mr Musgrave his indiscretion, but Emma could not forgive or forget as easily as her sister.

'Never have I seen Miss Watson in such good humour. If the Osbornes were to give a ball every day, your sister and I would get along famously, would we not, Miss Emma?'

Elizabeth went to find Nanny and tell her that Mr Musgrave would stay for tea. Emma, who had harboured some resentment towards Musgrave since the unfortunate incident at Osborne Castle, was guarded in her reply.

'My sister has the kindest heart of any of us.'

After an awkward pause, Musgrave looked intently at Emma and said, 'I believe I owe you an apology. I caused you pain and embarrassment. Can you forgive me?'

Emma softened a little when she saw that Musgrave appeared to be in earnest, for his look and the contrition in his voice seemed sincere.

'I believe I can now, Mr Musgrave. The error was also mine, for I spoke out of turn. My judgement was at fault.'

'It won't happen again.'

'Then let us say no more about it.'

The room once again fell silent. After a while Emma remarked, 'I believe you are acquainted with my sister Penelope.'

'I am indeed,' said he. 'How is Miss Penelope?'

'She is Mrs Harding now. My sister is lately married to a Dr Harding from Chichester. Dr Harding is with my father at present. They went to the church earlier. Penelope is gone into Delham with Margaret.'

'I am sorry I am not able to wish your sister joy in person.'

'I'm sure another occasion will present itself,' said Emma. 'I wonder, have you any news of the Wickstead family? I hope Mrs Blake and Charles are well. I have not heard from Mrs Blake since the family left for London, though I expect she has many engagements at present.'

'I met Mr Howard unexpectedly a fortnight ago in Grosvenor Square. He mentioned that Mrs Blake had a cold.'

A less satisfactory reply Emma could not imagine, but she curbed every inclination to enquire further. Her impulse to know whether, during the course of their encounter, Mr Howard had mentioned her name, was regulated by a greater consideration: the desire to curtail any possibility of gossip relating to her or her family reaching Osborne Castle.

Elizabeth returned with Nanny who brought in the tea tray. 'I have never in my life heard of a ball given at Osborne Castle. I wonder what the occasion is.'

'Christmas, Nanny,' said Emma.

'Perhaps Miss Osborne is to announce her engagement,' replied Elizabeth. 'Her name has been linked to that of Colonel Beresford, I believe. Only the other day, Emma mentioned that — '

Emma glanced sternly at her sister. Elizabeth understood her look, and continued cautiously, 'the soft fruit at Osborne Castle is second to none.'

As Elizabeth poured the tea, Emma noticed how Musgrave often looked at her sister as though there was something he wished to say. Emma was disinclined to sit with them for long, and excused herself from the room on the pretext of asking Nanny if she needed help with the fowls.

'I worry about Emma,' said Elizabeth. 'She bears it well, but all this business over Aunt Turner's marriage to Captain O'Brien weighs heavily on her. We have heard nothing of our aunt since she left for Ireland. Emma will not hear a word against her. Such tardiness is insupportable. And now Mr Howard is gone away for who knows how long.'

'There is something I must tell you.'

'Oh?'

'It concerns Mr Howard.'

'Mr Howard?'

'While your sister stayed at Wickstead as a guest of Mr Howard and his sister, he was in ignorance of your sister's situation,' said Musgrave.

'I don't understand.'

'He believed your sister to be an heiress.'

'I am sure she gave him no such impression.'

'He made the assumption himself,' said Musgrave.

'I see.'

'I was compelled to — I felt it only right to — '

'Put him on his guard? Did you do such a thing? Please tell me it is not true. Did you, Mr Musgrave? Are you the cause of my sister's distress?'

'It was not like that. Indeed, it was not. I do not mean to imply that Mr Howard's interest in your sister was entirely mercenary.'

'Excuse me, sir, but that is exactly what you imply.'

'I did what I thought was for the best.'

'The best for whom?'

'Judge me as you will. But I entreat you, Elizabeth — Miss Watson — submit Mr Howard's actions to similar scrutiny.'

'Mr Howard was guided by you.'

Musgrave found it impossible to suppress a smile.

'I see it affords you great amusement.'

'No indeed. It is just the thought of Mr Howard submitting to my counsel. But seriously, had I the slightest influence on the man, I should have urged him to follow his heart.'

'I am not a fool, Mr Musgrave. You would never act so yourself.' Musgrave was silenced. Elizabeth had exposed the defect in his argument. Whatever his feelings might be, he would never be tempted to make an offer to any woman in Emma's situation.

When Emma returned, she was surprised to find Elizabeth alone. 'Is Mr Musgrave gone already?'

'Yes. He is. He is gone. I hope he is gone for good.'

'Has he said anything to upset you? For I can well believe him capable of it.'

'No, Emma. Nothing beyond his usual — he has said nothing at all.'

The return of Margaret and Penelope from Delham was far from the ordeal that Emma had anticipated. The two sisters were in cheerful mood: Margaret was delighted with her purchase of white lace and fine stockings; and Penelope, a newly married woman, was well pleased with her elevation in the eyes of the world. She had received such extraordinary kindness from their neighbours. Dr and Mrs Harding had been invited to dine by no less than three families. Her pleasure was made all the greater when Mr Edwards offered to send his new carriage for the occasion. The Watson sisters had always occupied an inferior position in relation to the Edwardes, and were ever seen as recipients of that family's patronage. Penelope's power to decline their offer was a delight she would savour for days to come. The satisfaction of knowing that Dr Harding's carriage was superior to the new conveyance purchased by Mr Edwards was all that was needed to make her joy complete.

Margaret's brightness, however, was soon extinguished by the knowledge that Musgrave had called. Convinced that her sisters had contrived it, in a fit of temper, she threw her new stockings at Penelope the moment the door opened to admit Dr Harding. The sight of Dr Harding's head, adorned by a pair of stockings, was as entertaining as it was regretful. The scene before her proved too much for Penelope, and her attempt to suppress a fit of hysterics failed utterly.

'My dear,' said Dr Harding to his wife, 'I, I…'

Penelope removed the offending articles from Dr Harding. 'Let us think no more of it,' said he, mildly.

Mr Watson, however, was not so temperate and, for once in a very long time, admonished his daughter in the strongest of terms in front of them all. Her father's reprimand was fully felt, and Margaret was sent to her room in floods of tears, vowing to leave Stanton for good at the earliest possible moment.

Margaret kept to her room for the remainder of the week, appearing only when her father and Dr Harding were absent.

Little was to be gained, thought Elizabeth, by preventing Margaret's return to Croydon. And so, having made up her mind that it was for the best, Elizabeth wrote to Robert. His response was not long in coming; Robert approved the plan immediately. Margaret should and would return to Croydon as soon as arrangements could be made for her removal. Indeed, the plan suited Robert perfectly for Mr and Mrs Robert Watson were expecting a new arrival of their own, and as his wife's confinement was imminent, Margaret would prove a useful companion to Jane while she was in a delicate state.

With the benefit of reflection, Margaret saw that the material comforts enjoyed by Penelope and Jane were infinitely to be preferred to the misery of her own existence. Disappointment in love was bad enough, but the evils of spinsterhood were certain to be far worse. Miss Margaret Watson left Stanton within the week with one aim: to return a married woman. She would accept Robert's clerk as soon as he offered and make of it what she could.

When the letter from Croydon had been read, and the surprise and pleasure at Robert and Jane's announcement pronounced, Elizabeth set about making arrangements for her sister's departure. Margaret expressed a wish to leave for Croydon at the earliest opportunity, and none of the other inhabitants of the parsonage put up any objection to the scheme. Rather, it was deemed desirable by all, though Emma was less eager than some to hasten her sister's departure, for despite her sister's crossness and constant complaints, she had no wish to increase Margaret's distress and isolation. To Emma, to feel friendless and forsaken must be a terrible thing.

'Dear sister, may I write to you?' said she, as Margaret bade them all a subdued 'goodbye'. 'I hope we can part as friends.'

Margaret said nothing, but looked back at Emma with unusual mildness and gave a slight nod of the head. Emma rushed to her and put her arms around her; still Margaret said not a word, but neither did she raise her hand to resist Emma's farewell.

Among the other post that had arrived on the same day as Robert's letter was one from London, addressed to Emma. Elizabeth was as eager as Emma to learn of its contents for it seemed certain that the address was written in Mrs Blake's hand. Emma quickly perused the letter. Mr Howard was hardly mentioned, but the contents established that the family were in indifferent health due to heavy colds and the lack of Surrey's fresh country air. One piece of news, however, raised Emma's spirits.

'My dear Emma, please accept my sincere apologies for my unspeakable tardiness. I have been much occupied with all manner of engagements that one cannot easily avoid in town. I must say that I prefer the quietude of Wickstead to the constant bustle of these busy streets and thoroughfares. One cannot easily find peace in this place for there is commotion and disorder at every turn. Not long ago, the King's carriage was attacked on its way to Parliament. The King suffered no ill effects, but protests continue daily. There is such violent opposition to war as one cannot imagine, and accounts of looting are commonplace. Something must be done about the shortage of bread, but I do not know what can be done. And so when my brother informed me that we were to return to Wickstead, I cannot tell you how glad I was to hear it. If our Divine Master is pleased to spare us, we shall arrive in time for the Osborne Ball. Charles insists on my asking if Miss Watson will be there for he would very much like it if you would dance with him. I told him that he should not be disappointed if Miss Watson had given her word to another, as she is not likely to break it.'

Emma's delight at receiving Mrs Blake's news was tempered by some measure of apprehension concerning Mr Howard. The nature of their parting had caused Emma pain. Still, she was determined that their return would not do likewise. She dared not raise her expectations too high, nor did she expect a renewal of his friendship on the same intimate terms as before. A friendly acknowledgement, from one acquaintance to another, an enquiry after her father, a request to join him in a reel would suffice. She asked no more than this. As the time drew near, she found, along with Elizabeth and Penelope, that her sense of excitement and expectation increased by the day.

Penelope, who knew little of the acquaintance between Emma and the Wickstead family, insisted on a full account of the connection from Elizabeth.

'Emma in love with Mr Howard? What does she see in him? All that pompous solemnity! It wouldn't do for me, I can tell you. When I have seen him at a dance he has always appeared to be on the point of delivering a sermon.'

'Nevertheless, she has set her heart on him, and now that he is shortly to return, one can only hope that so long an absence might have brought him to the point. Why else would Mrs Blake announce their return in time for the ball? I should like to think that he would make Emma an offer, if not at the ball, then very soon afterwards.'

'I know little of the man. But he doesn't strike me as the type who would take a woman for nothing. You must have seen the way he makes a point of acknowledging everyone in a vacant sort of way but speaks to no one properly unless they are very great.'

'I believe he is a good man,' said Elizabeth. 'But there is another, you know — whether better or not, I cannot say. Lord Osborne has been uncommonly kind to Emma.'

Penelope burst into laughter. 'Great people revel in romance and intrigue, but they hardly ever marry for love.'

'I do not think Lord Osborne is like most great people.'

'And I do not think Emma is like most paupers. For why settle for a parson when a lord is at hand? I own, I have a great desire to attend the Osborne Ball, and an even greater one to encourage Dr Harding to stay at home.'

CHAPTER NINETEEN

Within the neighbourhood of Delham and beyond, all talk was now of the ball. Each day that passed brought news of one kind or another: the families in receipt of invitations were named, new orders placed at the haberdasher's were recounted, the most fashionable colours in muslins and silks were disputed, and the number and variety of dishes for so grand an occasion were anticipated with delight. Lord Osborne and Miss Carr were frequently mentioned in the same sentence, together with the expectation that theirs would not be a long engagement. There was general agreement in the neighbourhood that, after the wedding, more balls would likely follow.

Elizabeth, having no money to buy a new gown, made up one of Margaret's old ones with some fresh lace and, pleased with the result, showed the gown to her sisters.

'It is not the latest fashion, but I expect it will do,' said Penelope.

'It becomes you very well,' Emma added. 'But it needs a little something to make it complete.' Emma left the room and returned holding a pair of long white gloves.

'There,' said Emma.

'Oh Emma,' said Elizabeth. 'They are so very fine. I could not possibly wear them.'

'Please,' she replied, 'put them on and do not say another word.'

'Well,' said Penelope. 'What a transformation. You look almost young again.'

Penelope had little trouble persuading her husband of the advantages of remaining at Stanton with his father-in-law over attending the ball of the season. 'My dear, have you not often said that balls give you little pleasure?'

'Have I, my dear?'

'I cannot begin to count the number of times you have mentioned it. And think of poor Papa. He would be left all alone. I am sure he would be so very obliged to you were you to give him the pleasure of your company.'

'But Nanny is here.'

'Yes, my dear. But Nanny is not company for Papa as you are,' said Penelope. 'And you know how balls can be very noisy affairs. They constantly overflow with people and, as you are well aware, people carry with them all manner of diseases. Besides, it is by no means certain that you will find a seat by the fire. Castles are so often damp and drafty places. You may very likely catch a chill. My dear, you must take care.'

'You are right, as always,' said he. 'You never think of yourself, my dearest one, but only of my welfare. How very good you are to me. Yes, very good indeed.'

Mr Watson, though not opposed to the plan, expressed concern about the practicality of it, not least because of the dangers that befall young women who move about at night unprotected.

'Papa,' said Penelope, 'Dr Harding's carriage will take three with ease. It is very sturdy and there is not the least likelihood of any mishap on the road.'

'Then make sure, my dear, that when you arrive, you seek out Mrs Edwards and stay close by her. Under her care you will not come to harm. I insist on it.'

'Papa, you forget. I am a married woman. Elizabeth and Emma have no need of Mrs Edwards. I shall be their chaperone. I shall look after my sisters and they shall do as I say.'

The preparations for the ball had occupied the ladies of Osborne Castle without pause since the scheme's inception; and when a final inspection of the ballroom was made, and every particular thoroughly checked and declared satisfactory, they congratulated themselves on their accomplishment.

'The arrangements are certain to meet with universal approval' said Miss Carr. 'The ballroom looks very fine. I have rarely seen its equal. My uncle would commend every improvement.'

Lord Osborne had been content to leave the detail to the ladies, and though he had heard the word 'ball' more often in the course of a month than he would normally have allowed in a year, as time drew near, he too looked forward to the occasion. It was with some misgivings, however, that he allowed himself to be persuaded by Musgrave of the advantages of becoming a crop.

'There is not a single argument that can be made against it. It is easy to wear and needs no touching up. It saves time and money. Everything must be in its favour. And where you lead, my lord, every man in the borough will follow. There will be not a single ounce of powder purchased in Delham by Easter.'

Osborne was persuaded. He was reckoned by all *a very fine young man*, but the transformation wrought by a haircut was astonishing. Even Musgrave was amazed by the alteration in his friend's appearance.

'Remarkable! Quite remarkable! What a stir you would cause at one of Lady Forbes' balls! Her ladyship would not recognise you. What a joke that would be! But I confess I am quite put out, for I shall no longer be thought the most fashionable man in the neighbourhood.'

As guests gathered in the ballroom, and musicians prepared to strike up a familiar air, Emma found herself separated from Elizabeth and Penelope. The press of the crowd and the flurry for the best view of the proceedings meant that Emma was swept along by the flow and had no means of seeking out her sisters. After some time spent scouring the room for a friendly face, she heard someone call her name and turned to find Mary Edwards cutting through the stream of guests to join her.

'Mary. This is a surprise. I thought you were still in London.'

'Well, now I am here, as you see. Quite the penitent. It accorded my only means of escape. Have you noticed how clergymen are excessively fond of repentance in others but never see the need of it themselves? Where is Penelope? Is it true? Is she married?

'Yes.'

'Mama says Dr Harding is very old and keeps a carriage and will die before too long. Oh, how I have missed you, Emma. It seems so long since we last met. My dear Captain bears it well, but he is quite lost without me. Why did you not send news of him?'

'Because I had no news to send. I have heard nothing of Captain Hunter — '

'Well, let me tell you, I have seen him twice. In London, of course. Though she had not the slightest idea, Mrs Blake provided me with the perfect excuse.'

'Mrs Blake? You met with Mrs Blake in town?'

'Yes and no. She was laid up for days without a soul to speak to, so it was not difficult to persuade my uncle to let me go. Of course, I met my dear Captain instead. He couldn't easily be spared from his duties, but he did what he could.'

'And what of Mr Howard? Did — '

'Do not speak of him! I have had my fill of Mr Howard and his sister — all the way from Reigate. He spoke not five words the entire journey. His sister spoke five at a time and not once drew breath. And that wretched child would not stop coughing and sniffling.'

Emma was anxious to discover how Mary, of all people, happened to be in Reigate with Mr Howard and his sister. Mrs Blake had made no mention of Mary in her letter, and yet the degree of acquaintance between them appeared to be greater than it had seemed prior to their removal to London. There was no time to ascertain the particulars as the music commenced, filling the ballroom and sending the signal for couples to gather.

Mary made it perfectly clear that she had no desire to speak further about such dreary matters as Mr Howard. 'Come Emma! I see Elizabeth and Penelope have found Mama. Let us go and rescue them. Oh! If only people would not get in the way! Why do they not let us by? It is like market day in one of those northern towns.'

As the music began, the crowd fell silent. Mary Edwards tugged at Emma's sleeve, dragging her closer to the spectacle that was on everyone's lips: Lord Osborne, who had never danced in his life before, led Miss Carr to the floor. Such an unexpected sight as this drew whispers of approval and gasps of amazement from the throng that gathered to witness it. Card players left their tables, chaperones their charges and servants paused in their duties.

Adorned in the finest silk, and an abundance of feathers and frills, Miss Carr carried the triumph of the moment in her face. It was a moment she intended to savour and one of which she would remind his lordship continually once they were married. As she assumed her place at his side, she indulged her audience with a rare and complacent smile which spoke of the honour of opening the ball being entirely and rightfully hers. There could now be no doubt that her efforts, which had for so long seemed fruitless, had not been in vain.

'Good gracious! Look Emma! Look at Lord Osborne! How handsome he looks as a crop! I can hardly believe it. And he is going to dance. I never thought I should see the day. Miss Carr looks pleased with herself. I am glad she does not often smile, for one would be obliged to smile back and I should not be equal to it. She is such a cross little thing.'

Emma was no less surprised to see the man who had professed little inclination for dancing endeavour to do so in a way that belied his assertion. It was an intriguing spectacle. Not desiring to be seen by his lordship, but wishing to get a better view, Emma inched nearer the floor.

'What are they doing here so early?' said Mary, glancing across the room. 'There's Mr Howard and his sister. I promised to dance with him, though I wish I had not. I suppose I'd better go and get it over with.'

'Mr Howard asked you to dance?' said Emma.

'I doubt he could avoid it. His sister wouldn't stop talking about the ball the entire journey. I'll tease him about not being a crop like Lord Osborne — for he disapproves of anything modern, you know — and then he won't offer again. Oh, Emma! If only there were more officers present.'

Mrs Blake and Emma greeted one another as old friends. Emma was pleased to find that there was no awkwardness between them; it was as though the intervening weeks had been but a day. Mrs Blake gave Emma a brief account of their journey from London and expressed the pleasure of being home once again among friends. Wickstead was just as she had left it, with all the comforts of peace and tranquillity that the country afforded. She owned she had no wish to leave it for a good while hence, or indeed ever again.

'I must apologise for Charles' absence,' said Mrs Blake. 'He is quite unwell tonight. These last few weeks he has suffered one cold after another and, I'm afraid, borne it badly. He does so hate staying in bed. His temperature is high and he can hardly speak — and the house is quieter than you can imagine — but he is well looked after by Lord Osborne's physician. Charles would insist that I give you his apologies in person, but I shan't stay long. I cannot settle while he is poorly. Oh, my dear Emma, it is good to see you and it is so very good to be home.'

Mrs Blake's attention was soon claimed by a neighbour who was eager to know how Charles fared. Emma, seeing an opening in the crowd as more dancers took to the floor, seized the opportunity and made her way to Elizabeth and Penelope.

The details of Mary Edwards' return to Delham had already been related in full to her sisters by Mrs Edwards.

'And so Mary Edwards travelled to Delham under the care of Mr Howard and his sister,' said Penelope. 'What do you think of that, Emma?'

'I see Mr Howard has claimed Mary Edwards for the first dance,' said Elizabeth, looking at Emma to ascertain the effect her words had on her sister.

'It is more likely that Mary Edwards claimed Mr Howard,' said Penelope.

'No. Mr Howard was obliged to ask Mary. It seems he could not avoid it,' said Emma.

'There is plenty of time for Mr Howard to ask you to dance,' whispered Elizabeth. 'What do you think of Lord Osborne? How well he looks! Everyone is speaking of it. And who would have guessed how well he would appear in a ballroom. He is a better dancer than I ever expected to see.'

'Are Lord Osborne and Miss Carr soon to be engaged, Emma?' said Penelope. 'She always meant to get him. I admire her. Such determination is an example to us all.'

'I do not know,' said Emma, 'but I expect so. He must love her despite his appearance of indifference.'

At the conclusion of the first two dances, Musgrave who had been engaged to Miss Tomlinson, returned his partner to her charge, and joined the Watson sisters.

'What a pleasure it is to see all the Misses Watson,' said he.

'All the Misses Watson but one,' said Elizabeth. 'Margaret is not here.'

'Does Musgrave not know that I am a married woman?' Penelope whispered to Elizabeth.

'Miss Emma, what do you think of Lord Osborne now? How does he compare to Mr Howard in look and manner? You must find him much improved.'

'Mr Musgrave, I know you too well to make plain any judgement on such matters, for I have no certainty of knowing where my words and opinions might come to rest.'

'You are very wise to keep your counsel. I doubt Miss Penelope is able to keep hers. Ah! Miss Penelope, what a surprise to see you here,' said he.

'It is Mrs Harding,' she replied.

'Married? Excellent! Well done! That must be a great relief — blessing — for your family,' said Musgrave. 'Is your husband not with you this evening?'

'He preferred not to come,' said Penelope.

'Or did you prefer to come without him?' he replied. 'I know how married women like to leave their husbands at home whenever they can.'

'Penelope, Mr Musgrave knows very well that you are married. He made Dr Harding's acquaintance the other day while you were in Delham with Margaret.'

Musgrave smiled. 'I hear Miss Margaret is gone to Croydon again,' he continued.

'She is happy there,' said Elizabeth.

'We are all hap — '

Elizabeth cast a severe look at Penelope to silence her.

'You look radiant tonight, Miss Watson,' said Musgrave. Unmoved by Musgrave's compliment, Elizabeth replied flatly, 'Do I?'

'Now it is your turn to compliment me,' said he.

'I'm afraid that is not possible. I do not have your talent for flattery, Mr Musgrave,' Elizabeth replied.

'Practice, as the saying goes, makes perfect. You may practise on me.'

'Were I to practise every day for the next fifty years, I should never attain your degree of accomplishment in the art.'

'Thank you, Miss Watson. That is a better compliment than I could ever give.'

'I did not mean to pay a compliment, Mr Musgrave,' said Elizabeth.

'Then dance with me instead and I will give you leave to find fault to your heart's content with all that I say and do.'

Elizabeth took Musgrave's hand and said, 'Well, it is a ball. And I have come to dance. I may as well dance with you.'

As Musgrave led Elizabeth to the floor, Emma said, 'Poor Elizabeth. She does not wish to dance with Mr Musgrave but she could not get out of it. I expect she did not wish to give offence, though I am surprised he offered.'

'Oh, Emma! Everything hidden is exposed in a ballroom. And you see none of it.'

'I don't know what you mean.'

'I know, for example, that the gentleman over there wishes to dance with the lady in the pale blue frock standing by the door, but he has not the courage to ask. And I suspect that there is an understanding — or very soon will be — between Miss Osborne and that officer over there — the redcoat, the tall, handsome one.'

'Colonel Beresford.'

'So that is Colonel Beresford,' said Penelope. 'How interesting! And I can see that Mrs Edwards is tired of her husband neglecting her and wishes he would leave off playing cards and ask her to dance. I also know that Elizabeth is as happy in Tom Musgrave's company as he is in hers.'

'How can you be sure?'

'I look at how something appears or how someone wishes to make it appear and then consider whether the opposite might be the case. We are all perverse creatures, Emma. Even you. We hardly ever say what we mean, nor act according to our true passions. It is clear that Lord Osborne is not in love with Miss Carr. Whether he intends to make her an offer is another matter.'

Mr Edwards was pleased to have the distinction of sitting down at cards with Lady Osborne. Their table comprised the best players in the room; among them Lady Osborne was known for playing a tolerable rubber. There was, however, little agreement among the players on whether bridge, whist or vingt-un should be the game of choice.

'Let us agree on something, for the evening will be gone before the deck is shuffled,' said her ladyship.

'I confess, I have a fancy for Speculation,' said Mr Edwards.

'Speculation?' said her ladyship. 'I have heard of it, but I have never played it. You must show us how it is played. We all play it endlessly at the Castle, but not as a card game,' said she, unable to suppress a chuckle at her own amusing remark. 'I have a great desire to learn it.'

'Mrs Edwards spends many an hour at speculation, and so does my daughter. An unprofitable endeavour, if you don't mind my saying, your ladyship. Were they to apply themselves to cards, however, I believe their time would be better employed.'

Emma had entertained expectations of an evening quite different from the one that had begun to unfold. Perplexed by the behaviour of Mr Howard, she struggled, and failed, to find a reasonable explanation for what might be perceived by some to be a slight. Mr Howard danced with Mary Edwards the first two dances, and then sat down to cards. Penelope was sure that an understanding between the two must exist, for it was the only possible explanation for so evident a particularity. Elizabeth and Emma could not agree, but neither could they proffer an alternative explanation. Nor had the actions of Mr Howard gone unnoticed by Lord Osborne. The behaviour of his former tutor towards Miss Watson surprised and displeased him.

At the earliest opportunity, he took Mr Howard aside. 'I wonder that you do not ask Miss Watson to dance. Indeed, I may not be the only one to wonder at it. She has been without a partner these last two dances. I see Mrs Blake has gone home, but I fancy your sister would not wish you to slight her friend. Surely Miss Watson has a claim on you, given the degree of acquaintance.'

'Her ladyship wishes me to join her at cards, my lord. Please excuse me. The table is waiting. I have been asked to deal.'

Lord Osborne, who had until then been unable to offer himself as a partner, went in search of Emma and found her by the door, standing alone, watching the dancing couples. Penelope, unaware of Lord Osborne's approach, was engrossed in a conversation with an old school friend whom she had not seen since they had left school almost ten years ago.

'Miss Watson,' said Osborne, 'Would you do me the honour of dancing with me if I promise not to tread on your toes?'

Emma smiled. 'With such a promise, how can I refuse?'

Miss Carr's vexation at the sight of Emma being led to the floor by Lord Osborne was acute. She resolved to do all in her power to prevent his lordship from making a fool of himself; she must seize her moment, for her power to act would be determined by her readiness to do so at the crucial time.

'I have heeded your words, as you see,' said Lord Osborne to Emma. 'How do I appear? Have I mastered the steps?'

'You dance as well as any gentleman in the room and better than some,' Emma replied.

'Then I am not, in your estimation, the best dancer.'

'No, but with practice there is every chance that you might become so,' said Emma.

'You are, as always, candid, Miss Watson.'

'I see no point in being otherwise with you, my lord.'

'I'm relieved to hear it.'

'May I ask — in learning to dance, have you learned to enjoy more fully the pleasures of a ballroom? Are you more at ease than once you professed to be?'

'You may be the judge of that. But as far as enjoyment in a ballroom is concerned, I believe it very much depends on the choice of one's partner.'

'I believe you are right. But that means a man will always enjoy a ball, whereas a woman may not.'

'Why so?'

'A man may choose his partner, whereas a woman must wait to be chosen.'

'Is that so very bad?'

'It is for young women who are never chosen. Their whole lives are afflicted by their failure to secure a partner in a ballroom.'

'And can you support such a claim?'

'Indeed I can. Alliances are made in a ballroom; and the woman who never receives an invitation to dance, rarely receives an offer of marriage. Her neighbours will always speak well of her, and in time she may become the chaperone of other, younger women; but she will remain, for the rest of her life, an observer, incapable of directing her future and powerless to prevent herself from sinking into a life of poverty and obscurity. And a woman with neither looks nor fortune fares worst of all.'

'It is a bleak view of the world.'

'But a true one. I did not always think as I do now. I have lived for too long sheltered from the world.'

A door to the terrace was opened to lessen the heat of the room. As the music came to an end and the company broke up for refreshments, Lord Osborne led Emma outside where guests in need of air gathered to look at the night sky. A shallow layer of snow, like fragile lace, lay on the ground.

'Have you seen the stars tonight?' said Osborne.

'No,' Emma replied.

Osborne pointed to a constellation directly overhead.

'Orion,' said Emma.

'You know the constellations?'

'My uncle taught me.'

'Do you know the story of Orion and Artemis?'

'I know that Artemis was the sister of Apollo and that Apollo was jealous of their love.'

'Yes. Jealousy is a terrible thing, is it not? It can make one act cruelly. One day, so the story goes, Apollo pointed to an entity in the sea and challenged Artemis to hit the object with her arrow.'

'And did she?'

Lord Osborne nodded. 'But when the object floated back to the shore, she found that she had killed Orion.'

'Poor Orion.'

'Poor Artemis.'

'But what is the moral of the story?'

'Can you not draw your own conclusions?'

'That jealousy is a dangerous weapon?'

'When you understand someone's character, Miss Watson, you better understand their motives. Consequently, you are less likely to allow them to do you harm.'

'Do you understand the motives of those around you?'

'Utterly. Do you?'

'I'm not sure.'

'You asked me whether by learning to dance I was more at ease in a ballroom.'

'I did.'

'Whether in a ballroom or a drawing room, I find myself most at ease with persons of like mind.'

Emma smiled and said, 'Persons of like mind?'

'It is why I often sit alone.'

Emma's eyes were drawn to Mr Howard who was standing at the far end of the terrace in earnest conversation with Mrs Edwards. Osborne followed the line of her gaze.

'My lord, I may regret my words as soon as they are spoken — as well you know — but I am curious to discover — have I, to your knowledge, offended any of my friends at Wickstead?'

He replied, 'No, Miss Watson. The offence is not — '

Osborne began to proffer an explanation, and Emma was eager to hear it, but her curiosity was not to be satisfied. Miss Carr, who had watched and waited long enough, decided that the time had come to act.

'My lord,' said she, approaching the pair in a great rush, 'Lady Osborne requests your presence at once on a matter most urgent.'

'What matter could be so urgent as to require my immediate attention? Is she taken ill?'

'I only know that it is imperative that you go now, sir.'

Obliged to take his leave, Osborne expressed his regrets that it should happen so, and went in search of his mother.

'Miss Watson, let you and I take some refreshment. The negus is the best you will find in any of the great houses.'

'I have found one glass of negus to be much the same as any other, whether served in a great house or a cottage.'

'Allow me to issue a word of warning, Miss Watson, as a friend. Do not set your sights too high. Neither his lordship's family, nor his friends, would ever countenance so imprudent an alliance.'

'I confess I am astonished that his lordship's family and his friends have so low an opinion of him to believe him capable of imprudence. I find Lord Osborne neither wanting in sense, nor good judgement.'

'I see your opinion of his lordship is much improved from what it once was.'

'You are right, Miss Carr. It has. It has improved. I grossly misjudged Lord Osborne. Thank you for providing me with the opportunity of correcting my opinion of him,' replied Emma. 'Please excuse me.'

Lord Osborne entered the salon to find his mother seated at the card table, engrossed in a game, and in the middle of recounting one of her tales of former days.

'And Miss Taylor was made to marry him! And that was the end of the matter! What do you think of that? Ah! There you are,' said Lady Osborne to her son. 'Mr Edwards has introduced us all to a new round game. Speculation. I, for one, hardly know *how to leave off.*'

'I believe you sent for me on a matter of urgency.'

'Indeed I did not.'

'Miss Carr said that you asked for me.'

'Then she is mistaken, for I haven't had cause to mention your name all evening. We've been far too busy learning to play

Speculation. As if we were not all experts already! Speculation, you see! Am I not able to raise even a smile? What is it?'

'It is of little matter,' said her son.

'Now that you are here, you may join our table if you will. Speculation must be the best game I have ever played. Come and sit down.'

'I think not.'

'Have you no desire to learn?'

'There would be little point, for I should never play the game as well as you, Mama,' said he.

Mary Edwards derived some comfort from the knowledge that she would not be required to stand up with Mr Howard again during the course of the evening. She drew very little comfort, however, from certain reports that were circulating of Captain Hunter's forthcoming nuptials. The lady in question, the sister of a fellow officer, had been introduced to Captain Hunter shortly before the regiment's removal to Reigate. Miss Styles, who had relatives in the town, found it imperative to pay them a visit and bestow on them the pleasure of her company, without providing them with a proposed date of departure. She extended her stay six weeks and a day until Captain Hunter, a regular visitor to the house, was persuaded to come to the point. And when he did, his offer of marriage was promptly accepted, and Miss Styles was obliged to continue her stay until the banns were read, giving further delight to her relatives and to Reigate.

'Miss Styles?' said Mary. 'Impossible! Miss Styles is a thin little thing with bad breath. She may have three thousand pounds, but I am certain he would not take her for so little. Indeed, I do not believe, by the look of her, he would take Miss Styles for less than thirty. Three thousand pounds! It is a shockingly poor amount!'

'Redcoats have been the ruin of our family,' said Penelope.

Elizabeth could see where the conversation was leading, and gave Penelope a cross look.

'Well, they have,' she insisted.

'Do you think Lord Osborne admires Emma?' asked Mary.

'It would make no odds if he did,' Penelope replied.

'I wish you would hold your tongue, Penelope,' whispered Elizabeth, on seeing Lord Osborne and Tom Musgrave approach.

Penelope had not seen them; and Mary, to whom no admonishment was given, was unaware that Lord Osborne was in earshot. 'Emma doesn't give a fig for his lordship,' said Mary.

Penelope was in full agreement. 'It's Mr Howard she's in love with.'

'And she is welcome to him,' Mary replied.

As the ball drew to a close and the guests prepared to leave, Tom Musgrave accompanied Elizabeth and Penelope to their carriage, while Lord Osborne followed with Emma. Any hope that Emma had entertained of Lord Osborne returning to the subject of the Wickstead family was dashed. She would not mention it again, although she had hoped to discover Mr Howard's whereabouts for she had seen so little of him all evening. Emma had hoped to bid him goodbye and send her good wishes to his sister and Master Charles, but it was not to be.

'I bid you goodbye and wish you a safe journey, Miss Watson. Please convey my good wishes to your father,' said his lordship.

The more formal manner of his lordship's farewell seemed to belie the easiness of their earlier exchange. She bade him goodbye as he handed her into the carriage. And as it moved away, and Elizabeth and Penelope began their lengthy examination of the merits of the ball, Emma sank into her seat, breathed a sigh of relief, and closed her eyes. It had been an evening of peculiar contrasts. Mr Howard's actions had surprised more than Emma, though none had found them as perplexing as she; but it was Lord Osborne who had been the greatest surprise of all, looking and behaving in so altered a fashion as to astonish and please all his guests.

The conversation soon turned to Mr Howard, and Penelope could not help but seek Emma's opinion of his conduct.

'Elizabeth said you once thought his manners exemplary. Do you still think him — '

'I do not know what to think. He is changed since he came back from London,' said Emma. 'He is not as he used to be. Perhaps something perplexes him. We cannot know what it is.'

'Mr Howard's behaviour changed before he set out for London. You know how it gave you pain, Emma,' said Elizabeth.

'And what of Tom Musgrave? Are his manners more pleasing to you now than once they were, Elizabeth?' said Penelope.

'Not in the least,' said her sister.

'I see that we will have great difficulty drawing you out. I shall have to be content with that. At least I shall have something to report to Mrs Shaw.'

Emma noticed a tear on Elizabeth's cheek which was quickly wiped away. She took hold of her sister's hand and asked, 'What is it? Has Mr Musgrave been unkind?'

'It is after midnight. It is Christmas Eve,' said Elizabeth.

'Then we should wish each other the felicitations of the season,' said Emma.

'I think, Emma,' said Penelope, understanding her sister's meaning, 'Elizabeth is thinking of something else entirely.'

'I didn't think of her once. Not once. I was so caught up with the ball, I forgot Mama.'

'We all forgot Mama,' said Penelope.

CHAPTER TWENTY

Christmas Eve brought a succession of visitors to Stanton. The first to arrive was Miss Edwards who was in a heightened state of agitation. Nothing was right, nothing could satisfy, and no one, least of all her mama and papa, had any understanding of what she had to endure. Emma received Mary alone in the parlour, for Elizabeth and Penelope were late to rise.

'The ball was so disappointing,' said Mary. 'There was hardly a redcoat in sight, except for Colonel Beresford. I don't see why Captain Hunter was not invited. It was probably Papa's doing. I expect he told the Osbornes not to invite him.'

'I hardly think your papa had any say in the — '

'Oh, Emma. You do not know what he is capable of. Or Mama. I may stay with you no more than fifteen minutes. On Mama's orders. And I am to return home directly, without so much as an 'hello' or 'goodbye' to any other living soul.'

Seeing Mary's present state of mind, Emma thought it not such a bad thing, but made no reply. Indeed, no reply was necessary, for Mary, who was sure she had been exceedingly ill-used, wanted only to vent her feelings about her cruel parents.

'Emma, you cannot imagine what I suffer. Every letter that enters the house must pass through Papa's hands before I receive it. I look out of the window and Mama bids me come away. She was determined to come to Stanton this morning, you know; and had Mrs Tomlinson not called on her before she had put on her coat — my only piece of good fortune in days — I would have had no peace at all. I expect you know that the Tomlinsons are just arrived from Bath. Mr Tomlinson is much recovered. Mrs Tomlinson has promised to give Mama an account of all the latest intrigues. I should like to go to Bath. And I am sure my dear Captain would too. I do not believe he cares one whit for Miss Styles, you know, for I'm sure there occurred something amiss. Indeed, it is quite possible that Miss Styles persuaded my dear Captain to make her an offer he had no intention of making. Or perhaps one of his fellow officers put him up to it, and I am sure one or other of them will take her off his hands before long. I know what I shall do, Emma,' said she.

'What shall you do?'

'I shall return to London by one means or another, for the chances of meeting Captain Hunter are greater there than they are here. Do you not see?'

'Mary. How can you say such a thing? Captain Hunter is engaged.'

'Miss Styles must have tricked him into it. You do not know her as I do. Dear Emma, my life is not my own. I suffer daily. I know I am likely to do something very foolish. I hope you will find it in your heart to forgive me.'

'Forgive you? Why should you have need of my forgiveness?' replied Emma.

'I don't. But were I to need it one day, I should like to know that you would grant it,' said Mary.

'We are all capable of acts of folly. I expect I should forgive anything so long as it was not vicious. But please act cautiously, Mary,' said Emma. 'Is Captain Hunter so utterly deserving of your regard that you would risk everything for his sake?'

'He loves me. Truly he does,' said Mary.

'If he loves you, how came he to propose to Miss Styles? Where is his constancy? Where is his honour?'

'If you knew him,' said Mary, 'you would not question his constancy or his honour.'

'I know that his behaviour is not what it should be, and in your heart, I believe you know it too.'

'It is Mama and Papa who are at fault!' said she. 'Oh! Look at the time! I should go before Mama sends half the neighbourhood to search me out.'

Emma found little to satisfy or cheer in Mary's visit. How was it possible, she wondered, that a young woman of Mary's understanding could be drawn in by a man so faithless and unworthy? But perhaps it was not only young women who were swayed by such men. Emma's fears for her aunt increased by the day; and the thought that she might have fallen victim to the charms of another Captain Hunter began to give Emma anxiety.

No sooner had Mary bid Emma goodbye, than the second visitor of the day appeared and was shown into the room by Nanny. It was Tom Musgrave.

'Nanny,' whispered Emma. 'Would you rouse Elizabeth? Tell her that Mr Musgrave is here. You need not disturb Penelope.'

Musgrave had brought with him apologies from Lord Osborne. His lordship had been prevented from accompanying him to Stanton, but trusted that Mrs Harding and the Misses Watson had arrived home safely and that they had not suffered in any way from the lateness of the hour, the snow on the ground or the chill in the air.

'Did he really say so?'

'He said something of the sort. His lordship is solicitous of your care, as you well know.'

'Then please convey our thanks and good wishes to Lord Osborne and tell him that we are all quite well.'

'And how did you find the ball? Was it to your liking? Were you not surprised to see so marked a change in him?'

'I confess, I was.'

'A change for the better?'

'Yes.'

'I cannot imagine what induced his lordship to learn to dance, for he has never before shown any desire to do so. He took great pains to learn, you know. If only you could have seen the curious look on his face when put through the steps of a jig! It was not easy for him.'

'It is to his lordship's credit that he took the trouble to learn, and though it may not have given him the greatest of pleasure, everyone was delighted with his efforts.'

'But Miss Carr seemed rather out of sorts, don't you think? Did you observe how — '

The appearance of Elizabeth caused Musgrave to break off.

'Mr Musgrave,' said Elizabeth. 'How good of you to call. I had no idea that you rose so early after a ball.'

'And how did you find it, Miss Watson? Miss Emma was just expressing her appreciation of Lord Osborne's endeavours in the ballroom.'

'For one who is not used to dancing, he managed remarkably well,' said Elizabeth.

'A great number of young ladies were won over by him, I can tell you. I imagine there will soon be broken hearts in need of mending.'

'And you know all about breaking hearts, Mr Musgrave, so I'm sure your advice, when called upon to give it, will not go amiss.'

Musgrave could not make out whether Elizabeth meant to censure or to praise.

'Miss Watson,' said he to Elizabeth, 'A man's heart is just as likely to break as a woman's, but a man is better at concealment. A man may do his best, but without any sign that he has a hope of succeeding, he will eventually give up.'

An awkward silence ensued. Emma, believing that her presence in the room was no longer required, was at the point of making some excuse to leave, when Musgrave stood to his feet, bade them both 'good day' and wished them the felicitations of the season. The abruptness of his departure sent Elizabeth to the window where she remained until he disappeared from view.

'How strange that he should leave in such haste,' said Emma. 'It is not his usual way. Isn't it often the case that some hint is required to move him?'

'It is strange, indeed,' Elizabeth replied. 'I wonder what he means by it.'

'Perhaps he spoke of himself. Perhaps he is in love and the object of his affection refuses to give him encouragement.'

'He spoke only in general terms, not specific ones.'

'Dear Elizabeth, you know him better than I. I expect you are right,' Emma replied.

The information that Lord Osborne had inadvertently been party to on the night of the ball had led to much deliberation on his part over the days that followed. It now seemed certain that Miss Watson had formed a serious attachment to Mr Howard; and as much as he wished it were not so, he endeavoured to accept it and do all within his power to bring about a union between them. He resolved to seek out Mr Howard and offer him an additional living, one which would provide a comfortable income and the means to marry, without the necessity of making Miss Watson's lack of fortune an obstacle.

On entering the rectory, his lordship found Mr Howard at his desk reading a commentary he had written the previous evening.

'The miracle of the loaves and the fishes should be approached and expounded with care,' said he. 'Do you not agree that in times of shortage, the notion of feeding bread to the multitude has the power to inflame passions and incite revolution?'

'Happily, I believe I may safely say that I know of no congregation less likely to be roused to revolution than yours. Delham may need more careful handling.'

'It is fortunate then that epiphany beckons.'

'Are you sure? Wise men bearing gifts from afar? But I am not come to debate matters of faith,' said Osborne. 'You know that Delham is soon to be vacated.'

'I do,' Mr Howard replied.

'The living should not be vacant long. That is my wish.'

'I see. And you desire me to recommend a replacement. I expect Mr Granby would do. Indeed, I believe he may be expecting it.'

'I had rather hoped to persuade you. Would you consider taking Delham? With an additional two or three hundred pounds a year, you might settle comfortably. You would keep Wickstead, of course.'

'May I ask what has prompted this offer?'

'An additional income would remove any obstacle of a material kind — a young lady's lack of fortune, for instance — were you to contemplate matrimony.'

'You wish to give me Delham in order to provide me with the means to marry.'

'Yes.'

'Your lordship is too kind, but it is not in my power to accept Delham and I have no plans at present to make any particular young woman an offer of marriage. If I have given the wrong impression to any young lady, then I am sorry that my actions have given rise to unfounded expectations.'

Mr Howard could not have spoken more clearly. Lord Osborne was surprised as much by the passion with which Mr Howard spoke as with the content of his reply. A year ago, even last Michaelmas, Mr Howard would have been glad of the extra income that Delham would have afforded him.

On his return to the Castle, Miss Osborne came to greet her brother.

'Where have you been? Colonel Beresford and I have been watching for your return this last hour or more.'

'I have been for a walk. That is all.'

'Well, I have news that cannot wait.'

Miss Osborne had two pieces of news to impart: the first was the announcement of a death; the second, an offer of marriage.

Miss Osborne had, that morning, received an offer of marriage from Colonel Beresford — it was the greatest surprise — quite unexpected — the Colonel had awaited his lordship's return in order to speak with him on the matter — he was still in the library — he could not stay long for he was due to return to his regiment within the hour. Fortunately for the Colonel, Osborne's absence had afforded an additional hour in the company of the woman he loved; hence, he was not unduly troubled by having to await his lordship's return. Lady Osborne was overjoyed by the news. She had expected it — indeed she had approved the match from the start — and added her congratulations to the growing chorus.

Miss Carr, on first hearing of the engagement, was delighted in equal measure, for it provided the opportunity to hint at the prospect of a double wedding at Osborne Castle. Her hopes, however, were dashed almost immediately by the arrival of a letter, the contents of which were apparent before the seal was broken. The news was precisely what she had longed for, but the letter had arrived at a most inopportune time.

Mr Appleby had passed away more suddenly than had generally been expected — it had been a peaceful death — he had died in his sleep — the corpse looked peaceful — he had expired at half past four in the morning — and he had been attended by his physician until the end. It was now incumbent upon Miss Carr to arrange her immediate departure from Osborne Castle, though the thought of leaving at such an interesting time left her with mixed emotions. Mr Appleby's timing was vexatious indeed — if only he had lingered another week or two. To be obliged to leave her friend at such a time was a cruelty beyond words.

Condolences were expressed and preparations for Miss Carr's departure were concluded within a day. Miss Carr was to leave Osborne Castle the following morning, and it was by no means certain that she would have the pleasure of returning before the autumn. Though tempered by the knowledge that she was now a woman of means, her disappointment on failing to secure Lord Osborne on so extended a visit was profound. The carriage that was to convey her to Yorkshire moved off. Curiously, as the Castle faded into the distance, she found that she could bear the disappointment better than she had at first supposed. Her consequence, her place in society was secure, and her rights as an independent woman to come and go as she pleased began to take hold in her mind and cause her to give way to cautious optimism.

'We shall all lament Miss Carr's departure,' said Lady Osborne. 'Mrs Blake is as agreeable a woman as one might find in the sister of a clergyman, but she has not applied herself to Speculation half so well as Miss Carr.'

The invitation to the Wickstead family to dine the following evening at the Castle was politely and surprisingly declined. Mr Howard and his sister had, it seemed, a prior engagement, one that could not easily be avoided. Lady Osborne was perplexed to find that any prior engagement could so easily take precedence over dining at the Castle, not least when her only daughter had just announced her engagement, and Miss Carr had departed for Yorkshire that very morning.

'I suppose Mrs Blake must please everyone, whether high or low. I expect they are gone to dine with the Tomlinsons,' said she. 'And yet I was not of the view that Mrs Blake was one to savour accounts of scandals and seductions in Camden Place. Perhaps I should have invited the Tomlinsons to dine here instead.'

The evening came, and the Osbornes dined alone. The absence of Miss Carr would on any other occasion have rendered it a very quiet one, but the arrangements for Miss Osborne's forthcoming marriage carried the conversation as far as the sweet; and there was every expectation that it would remain the main topic of debate for many dinners to come. Indeed, with the ups and downs of all such plans, it was likely that the arrangements for the wedding would see them safely through the winter.

CHAPTER TWENTY-ONE

Since returning from London, Charles Blake's indifferent state of health had kept him from Osborne Castle. London had afforded him little pleasure, for he had missed the chance of fishing and riding with Lord Osborne, and the prospect of dancing with Miss Watson again. Indeed, theirs was the company he had missed the most. Miss Watson would send him notes from time to time containing conundrums and puzzles to keep him amused, and when Lord Osborne called he would challenge him to a game of backgammon; but it was not same. He needed his old amusements. He needed to be free and he needed to be outdoors. Despite the attentions of Lord Osborne's physician, Charles seemed unable to shake off the cold that had first laid him low in London.

Until he was once again at liberty to climb trees, collect creatures, dead or alive, ride his horse and challenge imaginary pirates to sword fights, he would have little pleasure in anything. Eager for everything to return to the way it was, he protested that he was in the best of health. His malaise and high temperature, however, told another story, and though he wished with all his heart to be well again, he was powerless to make it happen.

A matter that also perplexed him was why Miss Watson had not paid a visit to Wickstead, especially when she had promised faithfully to do so. The answer came unexpectedly one morning as Charles, unseen, happened to eavesdrop on a conversation between his mother and Mr Howard. As angry tears began to flow, Charles went up to his room and threw himself on the bed. It was not long, however, before an impulse to act caused him to formulate a plan.

As soon as his uncle moved into another part of the house, he crept downstairs and climbed through the window of the study and over the wall into the lane. He stumbled, coughed and spluttered his way through wind and sleet, and trampled across fields towards Osborne Castle.

Lord Osborne had just concluded some business with his steward when a footman entered with an urgent message concerning the boy. 'Send word to Wickstead that Master Charles is here,' said Osborne, 'and that no mishap has befallen him. Bring the boy to me and have hot some milk sent up.'

Some minutes elapsed before Charles was shown into the room, his shoulders wrapped in a heavy woollen blanket.

'Come and sit by the fire,' said Osborne.

Charles' eyes welled with tears. 'I am to go to school,' he coughed.

'School?'

'When my uncle is married.'

Osborne received the news with a mixture of pain and resignation. It now seemed certain that Mr Howard had heeded his words and had made Miss Watson an offer. The deed was accomplished and there was nothing more to be said or done. She had accepted him, and the parishes of Wickstead and Delham would soon have a newly married incumbent. For the moment, he was obliged to put aside his own feelings.

'It is right that your uncle should marry. And surely you cannot object to something that must bring so much happiness to you and your mama,' said Osborne.

'But I do not like Miss Edwards. I like Miss Watson.'

'Miss Edwards? Your uncle is to marry Miss Edwards? Are you certain? How did you — ? Did your uncle tell you this?'

'No.'

'Then your mama?'

Charles shook his head.

'Charles?'

'I happened upon them. The door was open. Just a little. A very little. And I heard my uncle say so in his own words.'

'And did your uncle and your mama know that you were listening at the door?'

Charles acknowledged with some measure of shame his culpability in the matter, and although it was of fleeting duration, his remorse could not have been more sincere.

'Perhaps you mistook the matter,' said his lordship.

'No, my lord. I swear I did not. It is all true. And I am to go to school in Ramsgate or Reigate or some place that ends with a "gate" — to a Mr Hamster.'

'Mr Hampson of Ramsgate is a distant cousin of your uncle.'

'There. You see, my lord. I did not make it up. Every word of it is true. It was like this. Mama said — '

Before Charles had time to give a full account of the conversation, footsteps were heard in the hall.

'Say nothing for the present,' said Lord Osborne. 'I shall speak to your — '

His lordship had expected Mr Howard to enter, but when the door opened, it was Mrs Blake who was shown into the room.

'I am so very grateful to you, my lord. You cannot imagine how worried I have been.' Mrs Blake turned to her son. 'Charles, what do you mean by this? Have you no thought for your poor mother? I have been sick with worry. What if anything had happened to you on the way? You are not well.'

Beyond expressing the anxiety that any mother would feel at such a moment, Mrs Blake had no desire to chastise her son for running away. She understood perfectly the reason for his action but was powerless to do anything to relieve his present distress. Her brother had made his decision. Mrs Blake and her son were obliged to comply with his wishes. Captain Blake had left his family with little to live on and, hence, no power to direct their own affairs.

On his death, Captain Blake had had but a modest allowance to leave to his family, having been less successful than other officers in the Navy of securing a fortune in prize money. Without the shelter and protection of her brother, Mrs Blake and her son would have been reduced to a life of hardship. Forty pounds a year or thereabouts, in a country where prices and taxes seemed to multiply by the day, offered little hope of future comfort or security.

Charles gave his word that he would curb every impulse to eavesdrop on any future conversations that his mother and uncle might have. Moreover, he assured his mama that he would never again behave in any way that gave her cause for complaint. The greater his protestations, however, the more skeptical she became, for she knew her son had every intention of keeping his promise, and every likelihood of breaking it.

Lord Osborne instructed Charles to remain by the fire while he spoke to Mrs Blake in private. His object was to obtain a full and accurate account of all the circumstances, and although he meant to offer assistance where he could reasonably do so, he also had a peculiar curiosity of his own for ascertaining the details of the matter. Charles' information was found to be accurate in every particular but one.

'I cannot agree to Charles going to school,' said Mrs Blake. 'But in other respects I suppose it is a prudent match. Mr and Mrs Edwards seem well placed to settle on their daughter a sum — but of course that is not my concern.'

'Make no further plans for the present as far as Mr Hampson is concerned and try to dissuade your brother from doing so.'

'I shall do what I can.'

'And what pray is to become of you?'

'A school friend made a very kind offer some time ago in anticipation of such an event. She has a small cottage in Guildford and an empty room that would make a comfortable bedchamber.'

The resentment felt by Lord Osborne towards his former tutor on hearing the extent of the disruption that awaited Mrs Blake and her son was tempered by the news that Mr Howard was to marry Miss Edwards and not Miss Watson. That Miss Edwards had accepted him was surprising enough, and though he could not be but relieved, he was not insensible of the fact that the news of the engagement, which gave him hope, would likely dash the hopes and expectations of Miss Watson.

Osborne took the first opportunity that presented itself — the end of a meeting at the White Hart — to confront his former tutor.

'I made her no promise,' said Mr Howard.

'Your attentions to Miss Watson were marked and witnessed by all.'

'She deceived me.'

'Miss Watson is incapable of deceit. You believed her to be an heiress.'

'She gave every appearance of being so.'

'Dear God! And you are entrusted with the cure of souls!'

'I have to live like every other man. There is no shame in that.'

'No shame in knowing that you have destroyed, perhaps forever, the happiness of a woman of true worth?' said Osborne.

Mr Howard strode over to the window. 'And what of your actions?' said the clergyman. 'How long did Miss Carr reside under your roof?'

'I made it perfectly plain from the outset that I had no intention of making Miss Carr an offer. Any expectations she might have had were her own, not mine.'

'And yet everyone in the neighbourhood spoke of it.'

'At Miss Carr's prompting. But there is one other difference. Miss Carr did not leave Osborne Castle with a broken heart, for it was never mine to break. Her heart was set on a title. I expect she will succeed in securing one in time, but it will not be mine.'

Mr Howard had nothing further to say and desired the interview to come to an end.

'Perhaps your estimation of Miss Watson's character will not be so high when you see this.'

Mr Howard drew his lordship's attention to a stranger outside, a gentleman of means, locked in heated conversation with a young woman in the market square. There was no mistaking Miss Emma Watson. The manner of her address seemed to speak of her having had a prior acquaintance with the gentleman, and gave every appearance of former intimacy. Anyone who had occasion to observe the couple would have drawn the same conclusion. From all outward appearances Miss Watson and the stranger seemed to be engaged in a lover's quarrel. 'Perhaps you will now be obliged to reconsider you opinion of Miss Watson's candour,' said Mr Howard.

Lord Osborne left the White Hart with feelings as unsatisfactory as those with which he had entered the building. Once outside, he observed that the stranger was in great haste to depart. Curiously, Miss Watson appeared unwilling to leave off and followed him to a smart carriage that stood outside the post office. Although the man ceased to acknowledge her seemingly impassioned entreaties, she persisted until the door of the carriage was closed and the instruction to 'drive on' had been issued. Emma's distress, occasioned by the incident, drew the attention of several onlookers.

'Miss Watson! May I be of service in some way? You seem distressed,' said his lordship, drawing near.

'Forgive me, my lord. I — Forgive me. I must go home at once.'

'Then allow me to send for my carriage.'

'No, sir. I would rather walk. I have no wish to inconvenience you.'

'You do no such thing. Indeed, I had exactly the same thought and was about to set out for a walk myself.'

'But in quite a different direction.'

'The direction of travel is of little matter. May I accompany you? I shall be silent if you desire it. I am not a great talker, as you know. Nor am I a great listener, or so I have been told — in which case, had you the desire to speak, I should give the appearance of having listened and yet would forget everything that was said the moment the words had been uttered.'

Emma smiled. Osborne's careless, undemanding company seemed to ease her agitation.

'Thank you,' said she. 'It is not the first time you have come to the rescue.'

'And I should be sorry were it to be the last — that is to say — please do not mistake my meaning — I wish you no harm, Miss Watson.'

'I understand your meaning, sir,' said she.

They walked on in silence. Lord Osborne had no desire to speak further, and although he was curious to discover the identity of the stranger, he did not wish to press Emma for an explanation.

After some minutes his wish was granted.

'My lord, the gentleman to whom I have just spoken is known to me as the husband of my aunt. Captain O'Brien.'

'But — '

'He feigned no knowledge of ever having met me.'

'And you are certain that you were not mistaken?'

'Quite certain, my lord.'

'And what of your aunt? Where is she? Did you speak with her?'

'The woman in the carriage was unknown to me. I have had no word from my aunt since Michaelmas. I am afraid that something dreadful has happened to her. Captain O'Brien swore that I had mistaken him for someone else. He said he had no knowledge of ever having met my aunt.'

'Has he a brother, a twin?'

'Not to my knowledge, sir. But it is he. Truly it is. I have not mistaken him for another. If you do not believe me, I — '

'I should never doubt your word,' said Osborne, softly.

'Thank you,' said she.

'Do you have any idea where he is going?'

'He would not say. But I believe I heard the coachman mention Deal, though whether the Captain had come from there or was on his way there, I do not know.'

For some minutes they walked on in silence. At length, Osborne spoke, 'Miss Watson, you have a brother, an attorney, I believe.'

'Yes. His business is in Croydon.'

'He should be informed of the particulars. Write to him directly. He will know how to act. And in the meantime — in the meantime — Give me your hand.'

'My hand, sir?'

'The grass is wet. I would not wish you to slip and break your ankle on the incline.'

The shock occasioned by Emma's chance encounter with Captain O'Brien had driven all thought of Wickstead and its inhabitants from her head. Osborne, though desirous of informing Emma of Mr Howard's news, found neither the opportunity nor the courage to do so. As Stanton came into view, and as much as Osborne wished to remain in Emma's company, he would not be prevailed upon to enter the parsonage. In bidding Emma goodbye, he urged her not to lose hope. In time, he trusted, her aunt would be found and the truth of Captain O'Brien's actions exposed.

'Please give my regards to your family.'

'Thank you, my lord.'

'Write to your brother directly. There is not a moment to be lost.'

CHAPTER TWENTY-TWO

While Emma was in Delham, Elizabeth had received another visit from Mr Musgrave. The engagement of Miss Edwards to Mr Howard had begun to spread quickly due entirely to the eagerness of Mrs Edwards to impart the news to all her neighbours. Mr Musgrave, being one of the first to hear the announcement, went directly to Stanton to convey the news in person to the Watson sisters. There he found Elizabeth alone in the parlour.

'Is not Miss Emma at home today?'

'My sister has gone into Delham this morning, Mr Musgrave, and Penelope is gone with her husband to visit an old acquaintance of his who has settled a mile or two south of here. My father is in his study. You find me quite alone.'

'I expect Miss Emma intends to call on Miss Edwards.'

'That is a strange remark.'

'I was merely making conversation.'

'She did not mention it, though it is possible, I suppose. I expect she is gone to see if a letter awaits her from our aunt, though I believe she will be disappointed. It seems Aunt Turner has forgotten Emma. I do not know what will become of my sister. She is not happy. I can see it. Aunt Turner, I daresay, is full of the delights of Ireland. I doubt she will give Emma a second thought now.'

'I fear I must be the bearer of some news — bad news — that will surprise and shock you. I take it you have not heard the news from Wickstead?'

'Wickstead?' said Elizabeth. 'Heard what pray?'

'Mr Howard has made Miss Edwards an offer of marriage.'

'Mr Howard?' said Elizabeth, 'and Mary Edwards? There must be some mistake. That cannot be — for I know Mary. I know she would not — '

'Mr Howard's offer of marriage has been accepted.'

'I cannot believe it. Surely, you have been misinformed.'

'I had it from Mrs Edwards this morning.'

Elizabeth could hardly contain her shock at the news.

'But they are different in every regard. I know for certain that Mary — '. Elizabeth broke off. She realised that she was certain of very little where Mary Edwards was concerned.

'It seems that we have all been taken in. Mr Howard is to leave Wickstead owing to a happy circumstance that requires his presence in London,' continued Musgrave.

'What happy circumstance?'

'Miss Edwards' uncle, Dr Edwards, a clergyman with influence in the highest circles, has secured a stall for Mr Howard at Westminster. And together with Miss Edwards' five thousand pounds, Mr Howard appears more than satisfied with his choice of bride.'

'This cannot be. Surely this is some mischief on your part.'

'For once I wish it were.'

Musgrave's look was sincere, and there was gravity in his tone that Elizabeth had witnessed only on rare occasions.

'If only Papa's brother had been a bishop,' said she. 'Oh, my poor, dear Emma.'

'It may not turn out to be as bad as it appears.'

'Do you think Miss Edwards may change her mind?'

'No. Given time, I have every hope that your sister will change hers.'

After leaving Lord Osborne in the lane, Emma wished to be alone to collect her thoughts. She walked to the church and entered by the main door. Finding it empty, she sat down in a side pew and offered up a supplication to the Almighty for her aunt's safe return. There she remained in silent contemplation until dusk. When Emma finally entered the house, she found Penelope, who had not long returned with her husband, mixing a spoonful of tonic into a glass of warm water. The tonic, which had been recommended by Dr Harding's friend, an apothecary by trade, was said to be a 'cure all' for every symptom, including low spirits.

'Is Dr Harding unwell?' asked Emma.

'Nothing ever ails him. He only pretends to be ill from time to time to secure my attention,' her sister replied. 'I am the one who suffers.' Penelope drank down the mixture without pausing to take breath. 'A note has arrived for you.'

'From whom? From my aunt? Where is it?'

'Elizabeth has it. She's in the dining room.' Penelope followed her sister into the room, for she had a great desire to be privy to the contents of the note herself.

As they entered, Emma thought that Elizabeth appeared agitated, but Penelope was all eagerness to discover the contents. She observed that letters, more often than not, brought bad news, and for some reason the misfortunes of others made her feel very much better.

'Should you not take Dr Harding his medicine?' asked Elizabeth.

'No,' replied Penelope. 'It will do after dinner. I am not my husband's nurse maid. You have no idea what I have had to endure today. Dr Harding had to examine every ingredient of every potion and pill in the establishment. I would not mind, but he has every one of them at Chichester — and more. Indeed, I believe Dr Harding has more pills and potions than one can buy in the whole of England. He might as well set up as an apothecary, for his sermon making never seems to do anyone any good. Well, Emma, are you going to open your letter?'

Penelope sat down beside Elizabeth, as curious to hear its contents as Emma herself.

'It is Mary's hand,' said Emma. She began to read. 'News indeed. Mary is to be married.'

'So Captain Hunter has succeeded at last,' said Penelope.

'You knew about Captain Hunter?' said Elizabeth.

'It was a secret,' said Emma.

'And so it was,' Penelope replied. 'Only half the neighbourhood knew of it.'

Emma's surprise at the news turned to dismay. 'Captain Hunter is not the man.'

'Then who?' said Penelope, glancing at Elizabeth. 'Not Musgrave, surely?'

Emma handed the letter to Elizabeth, who, knowing the nature of its contents, said simply, 'Mary Edwards is to marry Mr Howard'.

'Mr Howard and Mary Edwards?' replied Penelope, who had not anticipated such startling news, 'Mary Edwards a parson's wife? How delightfully absurd! Is Mr Howard aware of his beloved's amorous adventures with the Captain?'

'There were other inducements, I believe. Other considerations have brought him to the point. But Emma, I am so very sorry. The news must be distressing for you. I cannot imagine so ill-matched a couple as Mr Howard and Mary Edwards. Who would have thought it?' said Elizabeth.

Emma sat in silence for some minutes trying to take in the news. It had been a day of surprises, unpleasant and shocking surprises.

'Please excuse me,' said she.

'You want to be left alone, I know. But if you do not appear at dinner, I shall come and find you,' said Elizabeth.

Emma's shock at the news of Mr Howard and Miss Edwards' engagement was not as great as it once might have been. There had been signs at the Osborne Ball — inconsistencies in the words and behaviour of both parties that had perplexed Emma. Mr Howard's manner towards her had been formal and distant; Mary had danced with him, despite her strong objections and her opinions of his character. Mrs Blake, though clearly constant in her friendship, had seemed almost apologetic at times. The earlier intimacy Emma had enjoyed as a valued guest of the Wickstead family had, it seemed, given way to a less satisfactory one, that of a commonplace acquaintance.

It was now clear that Mr Howard had no regard for her. Whatever her hopes might once have been of securing Mr Howard's affection, they were now to be extinguished. She would make every effort to eradicate all thought of him from her mind forever. The name Howard would not pass her lips, not even in ordinary conversation; nor would she engage in conjecture of any kind on matters pertaining to his choice of bride. And if she were at some future point in time to happen upon Mr Howard unexpectedly, she would greet him with a naturalness and civility that belied all other feelings. It would be as though she had never had the slightest regard for him. She could and would be indifferent to him, for he deserved no better.

Emma lay upon the bed as night began to draw in. When Elizabeth entered with a dinner tray, the room was in complete darkness.

'Good gracious, Emma,' said she, lighting a candle, 'it is dark and cold in here.'

Elizabeth poured her sister a glass of water. 'We will soon have no need of a dining table. I have just now taken up a tray to Papa, for he would insist on having his dinner upstairs, even though he was perfectly well earlier. Dr Harding seems to follow where Papa leads. He wanted nothing more than some fried potatoes and a boiled egg and for Penelope to take it up to him. And now you, my poor dear Emma. So you see, we will be very quiet this evening — just the two of us at table — though I suppose it will save a candle or two. This whole business must have been a terrible shock for you.'

'How is it possible?' said Emma, forgetting every vow she had made to put Mr Howard from her mind. 'I cannot believe there is any affection on Mary Edwards' side. She is never done talking about Captain Hunter.'

'Captain Hunter would never have gained Mr Edwards' approval. Mary Edwards is a headstrong young woman, as you well know, but she is not stupid. An alliance with a man of Mr Howard's standing will serve her well. She will have an entrée into London society when they are married, and the kind of independence she can only dream of in her present situation. You think that as a clergyman Mr Howard might have espoused loftier ideals — that he might have married for love. It is all very well, my dear Emma, for those who are fortunate enough to be born to a life of ease and privilege. He is not Lord Osborne, you know. His lordship may marry whom he pleases without thought to fortune or connections. No, Emma. Mr Howard's behaviour does not shock me. Most men in his situation would do the same. And there is no better example than Captain O'Brien.'

'Elizabeth, what you say is as disheartening as it is true. I confess, I had not thought Mr Howard capable of so great a misalliance, though I do believe Mary capable of it,' said Emma. 'From this moment, I shall not speak of him again. My dear sister, you must help me in this.'

'Of course,' she replied. 'These feelings that seem so real to you now, will be overcome in time. Of that I am certain.'

'What a day it has been!' Emma took her sister's hand. 'Do not be alarmed, Elizabeth, when I tell you that I have news, even more disturbing news, of a very different nature.'

'What is it? What can possibly — '

'I have seen Captain O'Brien. I came upon him unexpectedly in Delham today.'

'How so? How can that be? Aunt Turner has sent no word. Are you sure? Might you have been mistaken?'

'I could not be more certain. Elizabeth, prepare yourself,' said she. 'Captain O'Brien feigned ignorance of ever having known me, and denied all knowledge of our aunt. I believe that Aunt Turner could be in some danger.'

Startled by the news, Elizabeth would not leave Emma's side until every detail of the incident had been recounted.

'I must write to my brother directly.'

'Yes. Yes, indeed,' said Elizabeth. 'It is exactly the thing to do. I do not know why I did not think of it. Robert is sure to know how to act. Nothing would give him greater pleasure than to expose Captain O'Brien and his dealings. But tell me, Emma, is there any doubt in your mind, any doubt whatsoever, that the gentleman to whom you spoke was Captain O'Brien?'

'You must believe me, Elizabeth.' With some hesitation, Emma proffered an additional piece of information. 'He bears a scar on his right hand. He once spoke of it in my presence. I saw it today, as plain as anything. There is no mistaking the man.'

CHAPTER TWENTY-THREE

There was one aspect of Emma's past connection with Captain O'Brien which she recollected with mortification. Her aunt had first met the Captain when Colonel Moore's regiment had wintered in the neighbourhood. It was not long before he became a regular visitor to the house. Aunt Turner, whose regard for him had not gone unobserved, had encouraged his visits. His amusing tales of Ireland, his smile and handsome looks, made him a favourite in Shropshire, and ladies, young and old alike, had nothing but praise for him.

Had Emma been better acquainted with the ways of the world, rare but revealing glimpses of a less agreeable side of his character might have aroused suspicion. There was one such occasion on which she now reflected with some dissatisfaction. During a card party one evening shortly before the wedding, Emma overheard one of Captain O'Brien's fellow officers say to the other, 'He preferred the niece at first, but the aunt had more to give.' She had dismissed the remark as a thoughtless, cruel falsehood, unworthy of consideration, for her aunt and the Captain had given every appearance of mutual devotion. Had she exercised greater discernment, had she entertained doubt, she might have protected her aunt and saved her from ruin.

Emma found that she could not erase the incident from her mind. The man she had met in Delham earlier that day was indeed the man who purported to be Captain O'Brien in Shropshire, but the character of the man bore no resemblance to the one she had known in that county. The description Emma had given to Elizabeth of her encounter with Captain O'Brien had one omission. For reasons known only to herself, Emma chose not mention Lord Osborne's knowledge of the incident.

On reflection, she wished he had not been there to witness her confrontation with the Captain. She could only wonder what his lordship must think of her and her family. What further evidence did he need to declare the Watsons a family beset by scandal and intrigue? To laugh at and scorn the very name 'Watson' would no doubt afford the Osbornes endless amusement! What entertainment would be provided at the Castle over the telling of such a narrative! The derision and contempt of that family, and consequently the world, must now be complete.

Elizabeth bade Emma goodnight and left her in peace to write to Robert. 'Perhaps you would remind our brother of his promise to send five pounds. There are household bills to be paid. Papa is too proud to mention it.'

The following morning brought grave news from Chichester. The younger brother of Dr Harding had died suddenly of a stroke. The news brought a flurry of activity to the parsonage as Dr and Mrs Harding prepared for immediate departure.

'Well, Emma,' said Penelope, 'I am needed in Chichester, though I would have preferred to stay here a month or two longer.'

'I am so very sorry to hear of Dr Harding's loss.'

'No more than I, I'm sure. It is just my luck to have married the wrong brother. And there is no need to look so shocked. I am not so very bad. I should dearly have loved to stay longer — to spend my confinement here at Stanton.'

'Penelope?'

'I'm as surprised as you, and not best pleased. Elizabeth knows of it, though I have said nothing to Papa, or to Margaret. I expect Elizabeth will give them the news when the time is right. Goodbye then, at least for the present. Let us see you in Chichester when circumstances allow,' said Penelope, embracing her sister. 'And Emma, if Mr Musgrave should renew his addresses to Elizabeth, urge her to accept him. Margaret will take it badly at first, but she will come round in time.'

'Has Mr Musgrave made Elizabeth an offer?'

'Yes, but he said it in such a way that she did not believe a word of it.'

'Yet you think he was in earnest?'

'There is nothing a man loves more than a woman's indifference towards him. I should know.'

As the carriage moved off, Elizabeth and Emma waved Dr and Mrs Harding goodbye. 'Emma, Papa asked if you would read to him,' said Elizabeth. 'He's in his room. I expect he will stay there the rest of the day now that he has no Dr Harding with whom to rehearse his sermons.'

'I will go to him then,' said Emma. 'Penelope said that Mr Musgrave had made you an offer.'

Elizabeth scoffed at the idea. 'It was said in jest. You know what he is like. Penelope only heard the latter part of it and she shouldn't have been listening in the first place. *He never means anything serious. Tom Musgrave will never marry unless he can marry somebody very great.* By the by, we have been invited to a party, though I am resolved to decline the invitation. It's from Mr and Mrs Edwards. You can guess the occasion.'

'Oh,' said Emma.

'I have no wish to go, and I am sure you have not.'

Emma found Mr Watson in reflective mood. 'When I am gone, my dear, I do believe you would get on better were you to live with your sister Penelope. You'd be better off there than in Croydon, I think. I do not know what Elizabeth will decide upon. I expect she will flit between the two of you.'

'Papa, please do not give way to such melancholy thoughts.'

'I will not live forever, and so it is only right that we speak of it now. There may come a time when I am no longer able to carry out my duties here. I may be obliged to give up the parish altogether.'

'Where would we go then, Papa?'

'I am given to understand that Mrs Shaw knows of a very respectable and inexpensive house not far from Dr Harding's residence. I must confess, my preference is for Chichester. I do not know how I would get along in Croydon with the squeal and squawk of an infant all day long.'

Emma judged that it was not, perhaps, the most opportune moment to impart the news of Penelope's impending confinement.

As the day drew on, and Emma's attentions to her father had been discharged, she found Elizabeth in the parlour writing a letter.

'I am writing to Mary Edwards, Emma.'

'Elizabeth, I believe we should accept the invitation. To refuse would seem churlish and wrong. Mr Edwards is Papa's oldest friend.'

'I meant only to protect you.'

'I do not need protection. And if we stay away, it will be noticed. I believe we should go and wish Mary and Mr Howard joy. Whatever I may feel, I should at least like to show myself indifferent.'

'Very well, if you are sure,' said Elizabeth, taking a fresh sheet of paper from the desk.

'I am.'

The day of the engagement party soon arrived, and it was with some apprehension that Emma entered the Edwards' house. Elizabeth's only anxiety was the concern she felt for her sister; all other disagreeable thoughts and sensations she endeavoured to suppress for Emma's sake. Serene and cordial, Emma played her part well, while Elizabeth fought a constant inward battle to keep her emotions in check.

'I wish I had not come,' said Elizabeth.

'Nor I,' said Musgrave, who had been standing behind the door, hidden from view. Elizabeth and Emma were surprised to find him there.

'I did not think you would come, Mr Musgrave,' said Elizabeth.

'Are you surprised to find that I am invited?' said he.

'Yes. I suppose I am. I never thought of you as a favourite of the Edwardses or of Mr Howard.'

'Nor are they favourites of mine. Mr Edwards I can tolerate, I suppose. I expect I was invited in order to add an air of fashion and consequence to the occasion,' said Musgrave dryly. 'It certainly needs something. Don't you agree, Miss Emma?'

Emma had been watching the happy couple as they received, one after another, the good wishes of their neighbours. 'They look happy enough,' said Emma, in an effort to speak well of the match.

'There exists between them no true affection — nothing worthy of the name "love",' he replied.

'And what do you know of love, Mr Musgrave?' Emma asked.

'A great deal, in fact.'

Elizabeth raised her eyebrows.

'Your sister does not believe me,' he continued.

Emma sought to guide the conversation back to Miss Edwards and Mr Howard. 'They will learn to love each other. They will be happy.'

'They will make the best of it, I suppose,' said Elizabeth.

Musgrave laughed. 'They will learn to despise the very sight of one another. I give them a week at most.'

'Where is Mrs Blake?' asked Emma, falteringly.

'I expect she is stricken with a severe dose of disapproval,' said Musgrave.

'What will become of her, I wonder? Do you know, Emma?' said Elizabeth.

'I have heard nothing from Mrs Blake. I've heard nothing at all of the matter.'

'How strange,' Elizabeth replied.

'Mrs Blake is not to follow her brother to town,' said Musgrave. 'And Master Charles is not to go to school. They are to move to that charming little cottage on the edge of Osborne Park.' Glancing at Elizabeth, he added, 'The one by the brook, near the little stone bridge that you once admired.'

The look that passed between Elizabeth and Musgrave at that moment was fleeting, but to Emma it spoke with more eloquence than words; the degree of intimacy between them must once have been greater than she had imagined.

'Would you excuse me? I must speak with Mary. I must wish her joy,' said Emma.

Mary, who had been engulfed by guests eager to impart their felicitations, began to look weary and impatient. Mr Howard stood by her side with an air of stately complacency as guests congratulated him on his forthcoming nuptials and his elevation within the ranks of the Church. Emma waited for the crowd to thin before claiming Mary's attention.

'Emma. You look pretty tonight,' said she.

'Miss Watson, how good of you to join our gathering,' said Mr Howard, as though addressing a member of his flock after Sunday service. 'My sister is not here this evening. Alas, she is indisposed, but wishes you to know that when she is quite recovered she has every intention of — '

'My dear, do go and see to old Mr Tomlinson. If he is not careful he will spill wine all over Mama's new table covering and she will not be best pleased,' said Mary.

Mr Howard saw to it immediately. Emma had never been so struck by the change in him. That Mary should have it within her power to direct Mr Howard to act on her orders, seemed astonishing; that he, a distinguished clergyman, should comply was more so.

'What do you think, Emma?' said Mary, once Mr Howard was out of hearing. 'Miss Carr is not to marry Lord Osborne. She is gone away. Mr Appleby is no more. Perhaps I should have set my cap at his lordship instead. Do not be cross with me. I hope, in time, you will forgive what I have done. I should never have accepted Mr Howard had I thought he might make you an offer. He never would, you know. I am sorry to say it, but there it is.'

'Then why mention it at all?'

'Because it is the truth,' continued Mary. 'He cares only for the money and the connection. He gets on famously with my uncle and is to join him at Westminster. More fool him. I expect I shall hardly see him at all. But I am perfectly content. I shall live in town and own a carriage. It suits me very well, you see. Did you know that Captain Hunter is to resign his commission? He has a brother in town, and intends to visit him very often. I daresay our paths will cross from time to time. By all accounts, Miss Styles has no wish to reside in London. She is determined to live in Redhill. Redhill! Of all places!'

'Mary. Allow me to advise you, as a friend, to cease all communication with Captain Hunter. Have you no thought to the consequences should you be discovered? For the sake of your family, for the sake of your bridegroom, if not for your own sake, do what you know in your heart to be right. It is not too late to change your mind.'

'Change my mind? No, indeed! But I know what my heart tells me, Emma. And my heart is never wrong.'

'Then we are so very dissimilar, and I am sorry for it.'

Mary's disclosure left Emma shocked and dismayed, for there could be but one interpretation. Emma felt compelled to dissuade Mary from so reckless a course of action; and Mary, for her part, had taken the advice very badly indeed.

Impatient to leave, when the hour of departure finally arrived, Emma quickly made herself ready. Elizabeth, though less anxious to give up her seat by Mr Musgrave, saw that Emma was eager to be gone, and followed her lead. Mr and Mrs Edwards thanked them for attending their modest evening party, and begged Miss Watson and Miss Emma to convey their regards to Mr Watson and to express their hope that his health would soon improve.

Elizabeth had found the evening more pleasant than she had anticipated; the food had been cooked to perfection, Mrs Edwards had complimented her on her new frock, and Musgrave's company had been more tolerable than usual. On the journey home, therefore, she was less inclined to speak ill of him when she spoke of him at all.

'Mr Musgrave mentioned something that might interest you, Emma. Did you know that Miss Osborne is to marry Colonel Beresford very soon? At first they were to marry in the summer, but Miss Osborne could not wait. They are shortly to marry in London. It seems that Lord Osborne and his mother have already left for town. It is to be a quiet wedding. The happy couple will stay the wedding night with Lady Forbes, and travel back to Reigate soon after, and there they will remain until July at least. I should not wish to be the wife of an officer. What a life they lead,' said Elizabeth.

'And will Lord Osborne remain in town?'

'I believe so. Mr Musgrave says that Lady Osborne's musical evenings are always well attended there. Emma, I must say, you acquitted yourself admirably. No one who saw you this evening would have guessed you had ever thought of Mr Howard. Mary seems quite content with her situation.'

'Yes. I hope — '. Emma broke off. 'If only it were within our nature as human beings to act with the purest of intentions. What a different world it would be!'

'Indeed it would. But we can all be perverse creatures at times. Listen to me — I sound like Penelope. But I wish Mr Musgrave would be serious for once. There is none more perverse than he.'

'Except Mary Edwards. I never thought I should feel so little for Mr Howard. How fickle the heart is! I do not wish him harm, but I am quite certain that my feelings for him are now nothing beyond those of a commonplace acquaintance. And I am once more at peace. I believe I can think of Mr Howard and Mary Edwards without any pain at all. Mr Howard is not the man I thought he was. How could I have been so utterly convinced of his superiority, his goodness? Where was my judgement? I thought him better than any man that walked the earth. And I've always supposed myself to be a rational being, but it seems this brief while in Surrey I have lost my powers of reasoning completely. How could I have loved Mr Howard at all when I know that I do not love him now? Surely true love never loses its constancy.'

'Even true love can dissipate and die,' said Elizabeth. 'I am not sure that I know what true love is, or what it is not.'

The news of Lord Osborne's departure from the neighbourhood had taken Emma by surprise. She found it odd that he had not spoken of it when lately they had met; and though there was no particular reason for him to make his plans known to her, the acquaintance between them was such that it would not have been out of place to bid her farewell. She knew not when he would return to the Castle, nor when she would see him again; but she felt that the neighbourhood would be the poorer for his absence, and that, in future, walking into Delham would not be quite the same.

CHAPTER TWENTY-FOUR

The news from Croydon was not encouraging. Robert had made a number of enquiries at coaching inns on the road from Deal to London in the hope of ascertaining the whereabouts of Captain and Mrs O'Brien. His efforts, however, had been to no avail. There was but one line of enquiry remaining. Mr Hemmings, Robert's clerk, whose eye for detail was second to none, had been commissioned by his superior to make extensive enquiries at boards and offices in Somerset House, and to conduct a thorough examination of any items of documentation that he might find there pertaining to Captain O'Brien. Robert undertook to send news if and when there was any change to report. In a postscript to the letter, he added, 'Jane has been safely delivered of a baby girl. Our daughter is to be named Harriet. You will be pleased to know that Margaret has accepted an offer of marriage from Mr Hemmings. Not all is bad news, you see.'

Elizabeth and Emma were delighted to hear of the birth of their niece, and, though surprised by the announcement of Margaret's engagement, were just as pleased about their sister's good fortune.

'I must tell Papa, and then I shall go into Delham to tell our neighbours the good news. It is a fine thing for Margaret. I have never met Mr Hemmings but I believe he is a gentle, modest sort of person. I hope he knows what he is doing. You know what Margaret is like. Shall you join me, Emma? I do not expect to stay in Delham above an hour,' said Elizabeth.

'I believe I must reply to our brother directly. I shall stay here.'

'Of course. Then write on my behalf, and give him my good wishes too.'

An hour passed in peace and quietude. Eventually, Nanny came in to say that there was only cold beef and potatoes for dinner.

'I am sure that is sufficient, Nanny,' said Emma. 'Papa has very little appetite, and Elizabeth and I will not require a full plate.'

The sound of an approaching carriage drew Emma's attention to the window.

'Nanny, will you see who it is?'

Her first thought was of Robert, but when the door opened, and Mrs Blake was announced, Emma could not have been more delighted.

'I am not alone,' said Mrs Blake. 'Charles is in the carriage. Should you like to see him?'

'Indeed, I should.'

'Let me call him.'

Charles Blake had grown at least two inches since Emma had last seen him. And though he had lost none of his good-natured boyish charm, his boisterous manner had given way to a more subdued air.

'I should not have recognised you,' said Emma. 'How you have grown! You are quite the young gentleman.'

Charles bowed graciously.

'Mama and I have such news. May I tell Miss Watson, Mama?'

'You may.'

'We are to move to Osborne Cottage next week. Do you know it? There is a stream that passes by the garden, and when you come to stay, we shall go and fish there. Lord Osborne says there are plenty of fish to be caught.'

'His lordship has been so very kind. He has thought of everything,' said Mrs Blake.

'It is your goodness and kindness that causes your friends to act in such a way. Your neighbours cannot do without you,' Emma replied.

'Such benevolence, such kind-heartedness from all my friends! How can I ever repay them?'

'There will be no escaping Lady Osborne's card table now.'

'No indeed.'

'Do you know how long the family mean to stay in London?'

'Whenever they go, they usually stay for a month or two. As for my brother, well — I understand that he and Miss Edwards are set on a town wedding.'

'A double wedding then.'

'That would never do. The acquaintance between Miss Osborne and Miss Edwards is not so very marked. My brother insists on a modest wedding with little fuss or pomp. Miss Edwards' uncle is to conduct the ceremony. It is my brother's wish that Charles and I attend, though we shall not stay long. I should not wish to stay more than a day or two. I do not know Mr and Mrs Edwards' plans.'

Mrs Blake and her son sat for over an hour at Stanton as the former ease and friendliness that the three had once enjoyed returned. Charles would not leave without securing a promise from

Emma that she would visit Osborne Cottage very soon. 'It is a good half mile closer than Wickstead, is it not Mama?'

'I believe it is.'

'And when Lord Osborne returns we shall go riding again. Should you like to ride again, Miss Watson?'

'I should like it very much indeed,' said Emma.

'And so should I. My horse is stabled at the Castle for the present, but when everything is prepared, his lordship says I may keep him at Osborne Cottage. Do you know, Miss Watson, I don't think I shall miss Wickstead at all.'

Whatever Emma's feelings now were towards Mr Howard, the friendship that she had once enjoyed with his sister and nephew had undergone no change. During their visit to Stanton, Mr Howard's name was hardly mentioned. Instead, Mrs Blake spoke of the plans she had for their new cottage, and Charles gave assurances that he would plan many adventures for Emma in the weeks to come.

'There are so many things to do and places to explore. I have not seen better trees anywhere for climbing.'

'When we are quite settled, we should be pleased if you would be our first visitor,' said Mrs Blake.

'The pleasure would be entirely mine,' Emma replied.

Shortly after the departure of Mrs Blake and her son, Nanny brought in the afternoon post. Among the letters delivered was one from Penelope. Emma was surprised to find that it was addressed to her and not to Elizabeth. She quickly opened it and read, 'My dear Emma, I have some news that I must relate to you without delay. It concerns Captain O'Brien. My good friend Mrs Shaw recently buried her husband and in doing so had the misfortune of acquiring a multitude of distant relations. When there is a will to be read, you can be sure that the whole world is eager to hear it. (As I said to Dr Harding, had he chosen the law as his profession, he would have had no difficulty making himself heard. Everyone would flock to hear him. As it is no one pays the slightest attention to his sermonising.) The late Mr Shaw's cousin, a man whom neither Mrs Shaw nor her husband had seen for many years, happened to mention his connection with a Cork family by the name of O'Brien. "O'Brien?" said Mrs Shaw, "perhaps you are acquainted with a Captain O'Brien." And so Mrs Shaw related every detail of the matter to the gentleman

— and what do you think? Although he was on intimate terms with the O'Brien family, he had no knowledge whatsoever of a Captain O'Brien, certainly not one who had recently married a widow by the name of Turner. Here is the interesting part. My late husband's cousin recalled, three summers ago, meeting a gentleman at Fishguard by the name of O'Brien who professed a connection with the Cork family. "Indeed," said he, "then we must be related by marriage, for my wife's brother is married to a Miss O'Brien of Cork" — the very same family, you see. The information had quite the opposite effect on the gentlemen than the one anticipated. He was exceedingly guarded in his response and soon took his leave on account of a pressing matter that apparently necessitated his immediate attention. There was something in his manner that made Mr Shaw's cousin think he was not to be trusted. I have written to Robert to inform him of the facts; I understand that our brother has taken it upon himself to find Aunt Turner. And so he should. Indeed, it will give him no trouble at all, for he is the first to appear when there is money to be got. That is the way with all attorneys — and redcoats. It would not surprise me if Captain O'Brien, whoever he is, has run off with more than a young woman in a barouche.'

On hearing Penelope's news, Emma now knew that Aunt Turner must be in some danger. She was determined to find her aunt by whatever means was available to her. As soon as Elizabeth returned from Delham, Emma related the contents of Penelope's letter to her.

'Surely there is something I can do,' said Emma.

'There is nothing you can do. You must allow Robert to act. He is best placed to discover the truth, and I am sure he will, given time. Hard as it may seem at present, you must be patient, Emma,' said Elizabeth. 'Our aunt will be found and Captain O'Brien will be brought to account. Robert will make sure he is. This could all work out very well in time.'

'But not, I fear, for my aunt. What will become of her?'

'Let us remain hopeful, at least for the present. Worry will contribute nothing to the situation.'

'Yes. Yes, you are right. But I do not know how I can stop myself from worrying. What if our aunt has come to harm?'

'Then prepare yourself for the worst, but hope for the best. Until all hope is extinguished, we must carry on. We must not despair.'

Musgrave decided to follow the Osbornes to London and put all thought of the elder Miss Watson out of his mind. London, he believed, would provide the kind of distractions that Delham could not. There he would be able to escape any thought of Elizabeth, and, with Lady Forbes' assistance, would be thrown into the company of more eligible young women — young women of fashion and consequence.

A card party at Lady Forbes' residence, the day after his arrival, did little to raise his spirits and served only to remind him of Elizabeth.

'Do tell us Tom which young lady has affected so great a change in his lordship,' said Lady Forbes.

'You are mistaken if you think Miss Carr did anything of the kind,' said Lady Osborne. 'She did her very best. She afforded him many opportunities to make her an offer but he simply would not. And now see where his tardiness has got him. I am sure there are many young ladies of your acquaintance who might do — '

Osborne drew Musgrave aside. 'You seem out of spirits this evening, yet I am the one whose peace is disturbed at every turn.'

Musgrave gave the briefest account of the incident that had brought him to London.

'And she refused you? Again? Yet you anticipated a favourable outcome?'

'I did. She is not likely to receive a better offer. I expect her sister, Mrs Harding, has set her against me. Elizabeth — Miss Watson — does not — will not — believe I am in earnest. She was more concerned to hear whether the rain had got into the closet upstairs than to hear me out. That was how it was a fortnight ago. And then, I broached the subject again at the Edwards' party. Said she, what do I possess that could possibly tempt you? Then you'd better say yes before I change my mind, said I. But she was determined to think that it was a piece of foolery on my part, even though I swore to her it was not. I begin to think that it is Miss Watson who means to mock me, for I am not the wit in this case.'

'You might consult the Colonel. Beresford had none of the trouble with my sister that you speak of.'

'I expect your sister was swayed by the regimentals. Perhaps I should have joined the Regulars. I shall ask my tailor to make up a new jacket instead, in a military style. Miss Watson may turn out to be like any other woman. I fear they all have a penchant for redcoats.'

'From what I have seen of the elder Miss Watson, I should not count her among them.'

'Nor the younger, perhaps?'

Emma waited every day for three weeks for news from Croydon.

'I must go to my brother, Elizabeth,' said Emma. 'I cannot rest, I cannot remain here a moment longer. I must —.'

'Robert will do all he can. What more could you do by going to Croydon yourself? Surely, you would not enjoy the society of Jane and Margaret — and if there were no news, or even if there were bad news, I cannot imagine what comfort their company would afford.'

'If only I might be of assistance in some small way, if only there were something to be done. I have searched my mind for some clue to their whereabouts, and I can think of nothing. Captain O'Brien only ever mentioned Ireland in the vaguest of terms, that is, when he spoke of it at all. I wonder how we could have been so blind, so unguarded.'

'You are not to blame. I doubt you would have acted as our aunt has done,' said Elizabeth.

'I do not know what I should have done. Had Mr Howard — but then, what point is there in speaking of him.'

The next morning, a commotion outside drew Elizabeth's attention. She looked out of the landing window and, seeing a familiar carriage, breathed a sigh of relief. 'There may be news after all. Thank goodness Robert is here.'

'Emma,' said Elizabeth, knocking at the door of her bedchamber, 'Are you awake? Make haste! Robert is come!'

'Robert?' said Emma. 'Let us hope he carries good news!'

Robert Watson would not wait to be announced. He threw down his hat, coat and gloves and marched into the room in a state of heightened irritation.

'*By God, Emma. A pretty piece of work your aunt has made of it.*'

'What news is there, Robert? Please tell me.'

'*A woman should never be trusted with money. I always said she ought to have settled something on you as soon as your uncle died.*'

'*But that would have meant trusting me with money and I am a woman too.*'

'*It might have been secured to your future use without your having any power over it now. I hope the old woman will smart for it.*'

'*Do not speak disrespectfully of her. She was very good to me and if she has made an imprudent choice, she will suffer more from it herself than I can possibly do.*'

'What a fool she has been! And *I thought Turner had been reckoned* a rational man. Tell me, Emma, *how the devil came he to make such a will?*'

'Why speak of a will at such a moment? What news is there of my aunt?'

'Had Turner acted wisely, none of this would have happened.'

'*The most liberal and enlightened minds are always the most confiding.*'

'Nonsense!'

'Robert, mind your tongue. Please do not speak to Emma so,' said Elizabeth.

'*My aunt may have erred — she has erred — but my uncle's conduct was faultless. I was her own niece, and he left to herself the power and the pleasure of providing for me.*'

'*But unluckily she had left the pleasure of providing for you to your father, and without the power. — That's the long and the short of the business.*'

'Robert, have you or have you not found Aunt Turner?' said Elizabeth, struggling to keep her temper.

'Not I. You are not in my debt. Though I have no doubt whatsoever that I shall likely be the one to pay dearly for it. You had better read this,' said he, handing a letter to his younger sister.

'It is not my aunt's hand,' said she.

'Open it,' Robert replied.

'The letter is from Miss Osborne — Mrs Beresford. How very odd,' said Emma.

'What does she say?' Elizabeth asked.

Emma read the letter aloud. 'My dear Miss Watson, though I hope that you will not be alarmed at receiving this letter, I fear that you may. Let me say, first of all, that your aunt has been found. She is safe, and though not as well as she might be, I have every hope that she will rally.'

'Oh Emma! What news!' said Elizabeth. 'What part had Miss Osborne in the affair?'

Emma scanned the letter and related the contents to her sister. 'It seems Colonel Beresford and his new bride had taken it upon themselves to impart the news to our brother in person on their journey from town to Reigate. It was Colonel Beresford's tailor who at first had supplied the names and addresses of other tailors in the capital whose main clients were thought to be officers. With the information at hand, Mr Musgrave paid visits to several of the addresses before making the discovery of a tailor among whose clients Captain O'Brien's name was notorious. The tailor, having supplied three coats to the same, had been requested to forward the bill to an address in an unwholesome part of town. The bill had remained unpaid for several weeks and all attempts to recover the debt had met with failure. In return for the address, Musgrave paid the amount outstanding to settle Captain O'Brien's account, and on receipt of the information, drove directly to the address supplied. There he found Aunt Turner living alone in a small, airless room, in a boarding house with little food and no money to buy candles. Captain O'Brien was not present. It appears that Aunt Turner had not seen him for some time.'

'That Aunt Turner should have been forced to live in such conditions, alone and friendless, is cruel and contemptible,' said Elizabeth.

'The depravity of the man! Vile, loathsome, wicked creature!'

'This is Turner's fault. He must have known what a foolish woman he had married,' said Robert.

'Foolish? Captain O'Brien deceived us all. No one who knew him in Shropshire would ever have suspected him capable of such evil. I must go to my aunt at once,' said she. 'Brother, will you take me to her?'

'Put on your coat.'

'But I must pack some clothes — '

'That will not be necessary. We shall not go far.'

'Where is she?'

'Put on your coat,' he insisted. 'Elizabeth, you had better stay here and inform our father. When he rises from his prayers, you may tell him that they have been answered. I only hope that he has given thought to the consequences of his intercessions. There is little chance of recovering even a quarter of Mr Turner's fortune. Perhaps the Almighty will work a miracle there.'

Emma's astonishment was made all the greater when Robert's carriage drew up outside Osborne Cottage.

'I will leave you now. I must return to Croydon at once.'

Mrs Blake, who had been expecting Emma to arrive at any moment, met her at the door. 'Calm yourself, my dear,' said she. 'Your aunt is safe, though a little tired from her journey.'

'I do not understand — and there is so much I need to know.'

'Not now, my dear. In time all will become clear. Go now to your aunt. I shall send in some tea.'

'You are very kind,' said Emma.

'I am glad to be of service,' Mrs Blake replied. 'What do any of us know of the fate that awaits us? I am sure I should not have borne the death of my dear husband had I not friends to assist me at such an hour. And look at me now. A month ago I could not have hoped to be situated so happily.'

Emma found her aunt sitting by the window, pale and thin. When Mrs O'Brien, tired and ashen, looked up and saw her niece, she said simply, 'Oh Emma, can you ever forgive me?'

Emma came forward and embraced her. 'Truly, there is nothing to forgive. All these months of worry — you cannot imagine. But of course you can, my dear aunt. I can see it in your eyes. I can see that you are weary,' said Emma, taking her hand. 'I will not press you now, but in time I must know all that you have endured.'

'There is much I would rather not tell, for I fear you will think so very ill of me. Indeed, you have every right to do so. But I could not bear it if you did.'

'I could never think ill of you after all you have done for me. But I am so happy that you have been found. You have endured all manner of unspeakable wickedness, but you are alive and here among friends and family who will protect you.'

'I was utterly deceived in Captain O'Brien.'

'Evil man! I came upon him in Delham, you know, and he denied ever knowing you. He said that I had mistaken him for another. I knew then that you were in some danger. But where is he now? Has he been discovered?'

'I have no clue. He was traced to Bristol and no further. It is possible he is gone to the West Indies. I believe he had a friend with business interests there.'

'He had better stay there.'

'My dear Emma, I am Mrs O'Brien no more. In truth, I do not know who I am or what to make of it. Mr Musgrave was very kind. He brought me here, you know.'

'Mr Musgrave? No, I did not know.'

'Yes, dear. What an amiable young man he is! I daresay, he is very fond of you, though he seemed a little out of sorts. Do not fret yourself, for I am sure he will not be satisfied until everything is settled between you. It was "Miss Watson this" and "Miss Watson that" all the way from London.'

'You mistake the matter. I am not Miss Watson here. I am Miss Emma. Elizabeth takes precedence. But it is of little matter. What does Mr Musgrave say of Captain O'Brien?'

'He tells me that Captain O'Brien — my husband who professed to have connections with all the great families in Ireland — has never in his life ventured nearer to its shore than Fishguard.'

'Fishguard? But how came you to — '

'Captain O'Brien is an imposter. He is a Mr Pegg of Liverpool — or rather, that is one name he is known by. I am told that he may have others. How many is uncertain.'

'I cannot believe it. He must be found. He must face justice for what he has done. You may not be his only victim.'

'I am certainly not his only victim. But what can be done to bring him to account? Very little, I fear.'

'I am sure Robert will do what he can to recover all that has been taken from you unlawfully. His treachery and deceit must be made known. Robert is a lawyer. He will know precisely what is to be done.'

'Your brother thinks so very ill of me — and why should he not? He cannot bear the sight of me.'

'He will come round. It is as much in his interest to assist you in this matter as it is in yours to recover your loss.'

Fifteen minutes passed without interruption before the maid brought in some tea.

'I beg your pardon, ma'am — Miss — ' said she. 'My mistress says that luncheon will be served in the dining room in an hour, but that if you prefer, a tray can be made up for you instead.'

Emma and her aunt exchanged glances. In former days, they knew the meaning each other's looks. Without hesitation, Emma replied, 'We should be delighted to join Mrs Blake in the dining room.'

'Very well, Miss.'

When she was alone once again with her aunt, Emma began to notice, as she had not done at first, how weak her aunt looked. The sallowness of her skin, her gaunt appearance and swollen eyes were evidence, if any were needed, of the severity of her ordeal.

'My dear Emma,' said she, 'I am so ashamed of myself. I was completely taken in by him, but I think you were not. I cannot forgive myself, for you were under my protection and I utterly failed in my duty towards you. I remember your words to me — "He has every appearance of a gentleman, but what do we know of his family and situation in life?" At the time, I believed you thought only of the harm to your own prospects. What a dreadful injustice I have caused you! Your words were spoken in truth, but I was deaf to all reason. I am ashamed to say it, but I believe a kind of inexplicable madness came over me.'

'Until I have known a widow's grief and understood the life of a woman unprotected and alone, I cannot judge you. I have not suffered as you have, for I have found comfort in the company of my dear sister Elizabeth, and my father, and all the friends who have become so very dear to me here. When you know them as I do, I am sure you will love them just the same.'

'I cannot stay in Surrey, Emma. I could not bear it. I must never bring disgrace on you or your family again, nor suffer to see you brought down publicly through my foolishness. I deserve to suffer. You do not.'

'You are not well. You must return with me to Stanton where I can look after you.'

'No, my dear. That is not possible. I am indebted to Mrs Blake for her kindness, but I shall leave tomorrow. Suddenly I feel quite overcome. If you would excuse me, I shall go and lie down. Please make my excuses to Mrs Blake.'

When Charles Blake returned from a morning's fishing, he was delighted to find Emma in the dining room.

'Charles, go and see cook,' said his mother. 'She has made something for you. It is in the pantry, but you must ask permission before you go in there yourself. And after you have completed your writing you may come down and show Miss Watson the fruits of your labours. And be very quiet when you go upstairs because our visitor is resting.'

'Is Mrs Turner really your aunt, Miss Watson?'

'She is.'

'She will get better. I am now much recovered, as you see. Mama made me drink milk and honey. Shall I ask cook to make some for Mrs Turner, Mama?'

'Not now. Later, perhaps.'

Charles was about to tell Emma about the fish he had caught but the gravity of his mother's look caused him to think the better of it. He smiled and closed the door gently behind him and then tiptoed down to the kitchen in search of cook.

'Your aunt may stay here until she has regained her strength. I am grateful for the company and I should like very much to be of service in some small way. I understand how grief can cause such feelings inside one's breast. One can hardly make sense of them at times.'

'I could not wish for better shelter for my aunt at present. But how came she to be here? Why was my aunt not brought directly to Stanton? And what was Mr Musgrave's part in it?'

'When your aunt was first discovered, she was so very anxious to see you, but would not entertain any plan that might oblige you to receive her. As you know, she is fully sensible of the harm she has done to more than just her own situation,' said Mrs Blake. 'I received a letter appealing for my help in the matter, to which I immediately responded.'

'What an imposition! How could my brother do such a thing when he has not the honour of your acquaintance? He should have provided for his own aunt at such a moment.'

'It was not your brother. It was Lord Osborne who wrote to me.'

'Lord Osborne?'

'It was Lord Osborne's idea to seek out the name of Colonel Beresford's tailor. The rest you know, though perhaps you don't know that his lordship saw to it that your aunt was removed immediately from the establishment. She spent a day or two in the care of Lady Forbes — therein lies another story — until arrangements were settled to bring your aunt into Surrey. Mr Musgrave insisted on accompanying her.'

'How is such kindness to be repaid or such wickedness to be punished? That Lord Osborne should have played so great a part in my aunt's discovery! I must thank him. My brother must write to him directly.'

'Wait a little while. I am sure an opportunity will present itself when the time is right.'

'Of course,' said Emma. 'Dear Mrs Blake, I cannot thank you enough. I should dearly love to see Captain O'Brien's — that is to say, Mr Pegg's — character exposed to the world. His callous dealings and his ruin of my dear aunt's reputation and fortune should be a warning to others. If only it were possible, in so doing, to protect Aunt Turner from public humiliation.'

'It would appear that he has covered his tracks well. It is unlikely that he will travel under the same name in future, and there is every possibility he has already left the country.'

'That such iniquity should go unpunished! He is a master of disguise and perpetuates deceit of all kinds on the innocent and unsuspecting. I fear that it will not be the last time that he acts in such a way,' said Emma. 'But how came Lady Forbes to be involved? I have heard her name mentioned from time to time by Mr Musgrave but I know nothing more of her than that.'

'Several years ago, Lady Forbes' sister, ten years her junior, suffered a similar fate at the hands of such a man. Sadly, she was not discovered until it was too late. So you see, my dear, when Lady Forbes heard of your aunt's plight, she could do no other than to offer sanctuary. She is convinced that some lack of vigilance on her part was responsible for her sister's demise. Ever since, she has sought to find the man in question,' said Mrs Blake. 'Indeed, I have wondered whether Lady Forbes' famous balls have another purpose, for one comes across gossip and intrigue of every kind there and Lady Forbes knows it all. Very little escapes her ladyship's attention. If anyone could discover Captain O'Brien's whereabouts, I believe it would be Lady Forbes herself. But the connection does not end there.'

'The connection?' said Emma.

'Yes. The connection between Lady Forbes and your aunt.'

'Is there one?'

'I should say Lady Forbes, your aunt and Lady Osborne.'

'Lady Osborne?'

'In former days, yes. Am I right in saying that your mother was Mr Turner's sister?'

'She was.'

'And is it also the case that your uncle, Mr Turner, met and married your aunt, a Miss Morris, in Basingstoke from whence her family originated?'

'There was little family to speak of, as I recall. My aunt was an only child, brought up by her father's family. Her own parents died in a house fire when she was very young.'

'Did you ever hear your aunt mention a Miss Debary?'

'No, not at all,' replied Emma.

'Your aunt, Miss Morris as she was then, was a great friend of Miss Debary and the two were very fond of the old rooms at Bath. Among their acquaintance all those years ago were Miss Tilson and Miss Green — Lady Osborne and Lady Forbes.'

CHAPTER TWENTY-FIVE

A fortnight passed before Mrs Turner was given leave by Mrs Blake's physician to move to Stanton. The daily presence of her niece at Osborne Cottage, and the unstinting ministrations of Mrs Blake steadily restored Mrs Turner's strength and spirits. Emma could see that although each day brought some improvement, her aunt was changed, subdued, pensive.

'I loved him so very dearly,' said she, one day as they walked in the garden at Stanton. It was the first mention of the man who had brought about her ruin. 'I have done you so great a wrong and I am powerless to make amends. I must leave Stanton as soon as it is possible to do so. I have an old friend who lives near Shrewsbury. She has kindly offered to take me in. Her health is poor and she requires a companion. If it is in my power to do some good, I must do it now.'

'You must not punish yourself so. A man of such cunning and propensity for deceit must by his very nature act in entirely plausible ways. It is his art to make everyone believe him.'

Their walk had hardly begun when Elizabeth came in haste from the house to find them. In her hand was a letter.

'It came this instant,' said she. 'It is for you, Emma. It bears Lord Osborne's seal.'

'Shall we leave you in peace to read it?' said Mrs Turner.

'No, indeed, for I have hopes it may bring news,' Emma replied.

'Let it be good news,' said Elizabeth.

Emma opened the letter. 'Lord Osborne expresses his hope that you now much recovered.'

'How very kind of him,' said Mrs Turner.

'He writes on behalf of Lady Osborne who has expressed a wish of renewing an old acquaintance. We are invited to the Castle tomorrow to take tea with her ladyship.'

'Well, what do you make of that?' said Elizabeth. 'Shall you accept the invitation?'

'I think we must,' said Emma. 'Dear Aunt, please say if the journey is too much. Lady Osborne would surely understand. And I should be just as happy to suggest a postponement.'

'No. That will not be necessary. I should very much like to see Miss Tilson — Lady Osborne — again. Indeed, I was hoping for an opportunity to thank her son in person for his extraordinary kindness to me.'

The passing of thirty years may sometimes seem but thirty days. When old friends renew acquaintances the years between appear to vanish. Emma watched in speechless amazement as a transformation in her aunt took place in Lady Osborne's drawing room.

'No, indeed! You quite mistake the matter. I had no fear of minuets. None whatsoever! You are thinking of Miss Debary.'

'She was a great friend of yours,' said Lady Osborne. 'I recall her father. He had a pretty estate in Somerset.'

'So he did. He chased all the young ladies — ' said Mrs Turner.

' — whether they were out or not. What fun, what laughter was to be had then!'

'There is nothing to compare to the old rooms at Bath.'

'Assemblies are not what they used to be,' said Lady Osborne.

'Indeed they are not!'

'It is not uncommon these days for a young woman to reach the age of three and twenty without a single conquest to her name. You must tell me how you secured Mr Turner in the end. Was he not a favourite with all the young ladies?'

'He followed me all the way to Basingstoke, you know.'

'I can believe it. Did not Miss Debary set her cap at him one season?'

'I expect she did.'

'She set her cap at most eligible men as I recall. Whatever happened to her?'

'Did you not know?'

'I am sure Lady Forbes would have mentioned something of it if — '

'Miss Debary ran off to France with a French nobleman. I do not know what became of her after that.'

'Dear me. Nothing very bright, if one is to believe the news from Paris,' said Lady Osborne. 'If only that dreadful man who robbed you of all but the very clothes you stand up in — if only he were to pass himself off as a French count. Then justice would be served. That would settle things as far as I am concerned.'

'Perhaps he will one day, and then he will be sorry.'

'The guillotine is too good for such a man. Oh! How you have cheered us all up! Indeed you have. You must join us for dinner tomorrow evening. I will brook no opposition. Tell me, did you by chance hear what happened to Miss Fowley after she cried off? You remember Miss Fowley, I'm sure. Mr Marshall would not hear a word against her. He was quite the tragic hero. I fancy he might have turned his hand to poetry.'

'He had a way with words.'

'And I could never understand a word he said.'

'Perhaps that was why Miss Fowley cried off.'

'She saw how it would be.'

'She would never get a word in edgeways.'

'So thought the better of it — '

' — and probably married a — '

Lady Osborne and Mrs Turner continued without pause for almost an hour while Emma and Mrs Blake looked on in silent bemusement, occasionally exchanging looks of wonder and disbelief.

'Well, Emma. I confess, I am surprised,' whispered Mrs Blake.

'It is as much a surprise to me as anyone. I had no knowledge of there being any degree of acquaintance between my aunt and Lady Osborne in former days.'

After a moment's pause, Emma continued, 'I had expected to see Lord Osborne. Is he away from home? I hoped to have the opportunity of thanking him.'

'I expect he has business to attend to in the borough.'

'Of course.'

'And if you do not see him today, you will have another opportunity tomorrow evening.'

Emma was as relieved as she was disappointed. As the time had drawn near to visit the Castle, she found that Lord Osborne had been uppermost in her thoughts. It was he who had witnessed the depths to which her aunt had plunged. Would he now judge her aunt harshly for her folly and indiscretion? And by association, would he conclude that the propensity for poor judgement exhibited by the aunt must also be present in the niece? Had Lord Osborne purposefully avoided her?

All that she had planned to say by way of appreciation for his kindness had been in vain, for he did not appear. Every sound, every movement, every footstep in the hall, served only to heighten the strange nervous anticipation that had taken hold of her.

At length the carriage was called. Fond goodbyes were exchanged between the two former friends, as were hopes that the following day would afford further opportunities to reminisce.

'It's strange to say it, but it is only now that I know how happy I was then,' said Mrs Turner.

'We knew little of what life would demand of us,' her ladyship replied. 'The old days were the best of days.'

The following morning, Elizabeth and Emma set out to walk into Delham while Mr Watson entertained Mrs Turner to an exposition of the biblical story of Samson and Delilah. 'We think little of the evils posed by young women who encourage young men to cut their hair. What is the world coming to, Mrs Turner? These young men rattle about without a dab of powder up top. And hereabouts they all follow where that young coxcomb Musgrave leads.'

'He is a fine young man, though not so very young, I fancy. He must be thirty if he is a day,' replied Mrs Turner. 'I find him quite charming. He was very attentive to me, you know. And were it not for his fine style in jackets and greatcoats and knowledge of tailors and the like, I daresay I should not have been discovered at all.'

'The young lady he finally settles on will have a life of it, I should imagine.'

'And a very good one too. If I were ten years younger — but then — never mind that.'

On completion of their purchases at Mason's, Emma and Elizabeth came upon Lord Osborne and Tom Musgrave unexpectedly in the market square. As pleasantries were exchanged, Emma struggled to suppress the confusion she felt on seeing Lord Osborne.

'Do you mean to walk back to Stanton?' said Musgrave.

'We do,' replied Elizabeth.

'Then perhaps you would allow us to join you,' said Lord Osborne.

Osborne offered his arm to Emma as Elizabeth and Musgrave walked on ahead. After some minutes, the distance between the two couples was such that only private conversations were possible.

'How pleasant it is to walk along country lanes,' said Musgrave.

'I'm surprised at you, Mr Musgrave. You are not dressed for country walking, and I know that you are usually very particular about that sort of thing,' replied Elizabeth.

'Not at all, I assure you.'

'How contrary you are! You would walk knee-deep in seaweed to prove me wrong.'

'Without a moment's hesitation, Miss Watson, were you to accompany me,' said Musgrave. 'I hear Miss Margaret is soon to be married.'

'Quite soon, I believe.'

'Will she stay in Croydon?'

'I think she must. Mr Hemmings is my brother's clerk.'

'And I expect your youngest sister will soon follow.'

'Go to Croydon? I think not. It is by no means certain, however, that Emma will stay at Stanton once Mrs Turner's affairs are settled. If any part of our aunt's estate is recovered, I should not be surprised if Mrs Turner were to take Emma with her.'

'Does your sister still think of Mr Howard? I happened to see him recently.'

'She does not mention him. How are Mr and Mrs Howard?'

'In marrying Miss Edwards, I suspect Mr Howard has paid a very high price for his elevation within the ranks of the Church.'

'How did he appear?'

'Resigned. Tired. He had the look of an old married man who had made the greatest mistake of his life.'

'And now he must live with the consequences. Poor Mr Howard. He should not have married her. But I believe Mary's discontent will be greater than his.'

'You would not marry for the sake of expediency.'

'Mr Musgrave, it is unlikely that I shall marry at all.'

'And that is your preference?'

'I am merely stating a fact.'

They walked on in silence. It was several minutes before he spoke again.

'I might as well come straight to the point. This time, Miss Watson, I beg you, believe me to be in earnest. I know that you love me, Elizabeth. You need not deny it.'

'How can you say such a — '

'As I love you,' he continued, raising his hand gently to her lips to prevent her from further interjection. 'I have always known it. And I know that I could be happy with no one but you.'

Elizabeth was struck by the serious look in his eyes, and although her natural impulse was to doubt his every utterance, this time she could detect no hint of mockery in his address.

'I do not jest,' said he. 'I am in earnest. Marry me.'

'But we are so very dissimilar.'

'In essentials we are much the same.'

'I am not one of those fashionable young women of your acquaintance who — '

'I know you who you are. You have always been truthful in your dealings with me. Indeed, I know few women whose forthright opinions can be relied on as completely as yours.'

'I can believe that.'

'And I suspect you know me better than any woman of my acquaintance. I can brook your disapproval better than any man. And you need not change on my account. Besides,' said he, 'your father has already given his consent and I have no wish to seek it again.'

'My father has given his consent?'

'With some reluctance, I might add. Now, will you put me out of my misery once and for all? I won't ask again.'

Delight, confusion, wonder and disbelief rendered Elizabeth speechless; but when she raised her eyes to meet his, Musgrave was rewarded with a smile that said what words could not express at that moment.

'Well,' said he. 'It was a long road, but we finally got there.'

Emma found Lord Osborne less disposed to speak than she had hoped or expected. It had been some time since their last meeting, and much had taken place since then that seemed to require explanation, at least on her part.

'Thank you, my lord, for all that you have done for my aunt. I do not know what might have befallen her had it not been for you.'

'My part in your aunt's discovery was slight. Others had a greater hand in it.'

'I do not believe that. I have heard how it was.'

'Then believe what you will but let us not speak of it again,' said he. 'I understand we have the pleasure of your company this evening.'

'I expect you are aware of the degree of acquaintance between your mother and my aunt in former days.'

'My sister and I have for years been regaled with colourful chronicles of the old rooms at Bath.'

'Then you will not expect too much from the evening.'

'I never expect a great deal.'

'Can all their stories be true?'

'I expect a little light and shade has been added for effect over the years. My father's recollections of the past were dissimilar in every way to those of my mother.'

'But they were happy memories?'

'There are different paths to happiness. I have discovered, like my father before me, that it is sometimes necessary to put one's feelings aside and act in accordance with the wishes of others. Surprisingly, duty is a form of happiness,' said he.

'I believe you are right.'

'Miss Watson,' said he, 'there will be more than one addition to the party this evening. Colonel Beresford and my sister are expected, and Miss Carr is to accompany them.'

Emma understood Lord Osborne's meaning; there could be no other view. Whatever affection his lordship might once have had for her — and of that she had never been quite certain — must now be put aside. Miss Carr's period of mourning would soon expire and the marriage that was long wished for would take place. No one could say that it was not was prudential for both parties. Besides, his lordship would not now connect himself with a family that had sunk so low in the eyes of the world.

'There is one piece of information — '

'Please, my lord. There is no necessity to — ' In that moment Emma realised that Lord Osborne meant more to her than she had imagined. She loved him. It was too late, but she loved him.

'Have courage,' said Osborne.

CHAPTER TWENTY-SIX

Mr Watson was the first to receive the news of Elizabeth's engagement to Mr Musgrave.

'Let me go to him. It is best that I speak to my father alone,' said Elizabeth.

'Let us hope your father does not take a turn for the worse on hearing that you have accepted me at last.'

'I am sure he will be just as delighted as everyone else,' said Elizabeth.

'I doubt it. I expect he has been at his prayers imploring the Almighty to save him from such a son-in-law.'

'Surely Tom, any son-in-law is better than none. Papa will be overjoyed at the prospect, for he will no longer have to provide for me.'

'And I thought you loved me for my charm and fine features.'

On hearing Elizabeth's news, Mr Watson was more sanguine than his daughter had anticipated.

'Congratulations, my dear. You have surprised us all. Nine and twenty, and not a penny to your name! Some may think Musgrave a fool — indeed it has always been my view. But I must say I find he is not quite the idle fellow I took him for. I should not have given my consent quite so readily, Elizabeth, had it not been for your sister. Now that I have Emma to look after me, you have no need to worry on that score. Now that Emma has got used to my ways here at Stanton, we shall do very well without you. I believe I shall hardly notice any change at all. And when Robert finally settles your aunt's affairs and she is gone back into Shropshire, all will be just as it should be. Emma and I will manage very well, you see, and there will be peace in this house at last.'

'Papa, it is not likely that Emma will stay at Stanton long,' said Elizabeth. 'Should she receive an offer of marriage, and I have every expectation that in time she will, you must release her.'

'Emma is quite content as she is. All that is needed is for you to acquaint her with the necessary particulars — the housekeeping and the best suppliers. And you may find, from time to time, that you are able to send a basket of provisions from Mr Musgrave's estate to stock the larder. Your sister will not be unhappy for she will have charge of the house. She will be mistress here. I expect you will see her most days, one way or another. And when I am gone you may take her in. If you do not want her, I am sure your sister Penelope will have her at Chichester.'

'No Papa. That cannot be. Emma must be allowed to marry if and when she chooses.'

Mr Watson did not agree, and he was not to be reasoned with. To have three daughters married was fortune enough. Had Penelope or Margaret been left on his hands, his prospects of securing a comfortable existence in his later years would have been less certain. But Emma would suit him perfectly. She had shown herself to be solicitous of his health, unlike Penelope; the tone of her voice was not shrill like Margaret's; and when she read to him, whether poetry, a philosophical treatise or a religious tract, she did so with just the right degree of inflection. Indeed, he had, on occasion, admired her delivery to the point that he had almost supposed her capable of understanding the substance of the text itself.

Her father's obstinacy in light of the changes that were soon to take place at Stanton gave rise to certain misgivings in Elizabeth's mind. His implacable selfishness caused Elizabeth to doubt the wisdom of her own actions. How could she be happy knowing that she was the cause of Emma's unhappiness? Had Emma not suffered enough? Elizabeth knew her father of old and she had learned Emma's character well; Elizabeth had every reason to suppose that Emma would comply with their father's wishes. Her sister would not see their father left to manage alone; Emma would not abandon him. For the present, Elizabeth decided to remain silent on the subject of her engagement to Tom Musgrave. After wishing Emma and Mrs Turner a pleasant evening, she went up to her bed chamber early. There she was at liberty to contemplate in peace and quietude the unforeseen consequences of her good fortune.

The day that had brought the greatest measure of happiness Elizabeth had ever known now ended in despondency. For the sake of her sister's happiness, Elizabeth was persuaded that one course of action, and only one, would suffice. Marriage was impossible. She would — she must — break her promise to Musgrave, and swiftly, while no one but her father knew of her engagement. Mr Musgrave must not be subjected to public humiliation; she would bear all the shame and disgrace should her actions be made known. She resolved to conceal every aspect of the affair from her sister, and should

Emma ever discover any part of it, she would never reveal why she had been compelled to act in such a way.

The thought of Miss Carr's presence at Osborne Castle that evening left Emma wishing that the invitation had been neither issued nor accepted. She had little desire to go, and would have gladly stayed at home had it not been for Mrs Turner who had spoken of little else since the renewal of her acquaintance with Lady Osborne.

While Mrs Turner kept watch by the window for the arrival of the Osborne carriage, Emma observed Elizabeth leaving their father's room looking pale and disturbed. Her sister had seemed in a state of agitation after their walk from Delham. Emma wondered whether Mr Musgrave had made some thoughtless remark that had given her pain. It was unlike Elizabeth to keep to her room on such an occasion as the expected arrival of so grand a carriage at the front door of the parsonage. Emma ran upstairs to her sister's room and found her quietly sitting by the window in the half light.

'Are you unwell?' said Emma. 'Shall I stay? I should be happy to have any excuse not to go. Truly, I have no wish to dine at Osborne Castle this evening.'

'You must go, Emma — if only to bring me a full account of every dish served at dinner, and her ladyship's improbable stories of past conquests. You will have a pleasant evening. I am certain of it. And be assured, I am well. Everything will be — everything is as it should be. How does Aunt Turner look? Did you find her something suitable to wear?'

'She looks very well in the gown Penelope left behind. The fit could not be better.'

'Then go and fill your head with conquests, cotillions and unrequited love.'

'I should rather stay at home with you and Papa.'

'No, Emma. You must take every opportunity to be seen. Think of all the invitations you have received from Osborne Castle. You are the envy of every young woman in the neighbourhood. What could possibly be disagreeable about that?'

'Whenever I expect something to be agreeable, it almost never is.'

'Expect something very disagreeable then, and you will be pleasantly surprised.'

'On this occasion, I doubt it.'

Mrs Turner was in excellent spirits. Her health had made so great an improvement that Emma thought her almost herself again.

'Emma, my dear,' said Mrs Turner, climbing down from the carriage. 'Do give me your hand. The sleeves of this gown are so tight that I do believe they will tear if I stretch my arm any further.'

The prospect of spending an evening at Osborne Castle in the company of her old friend raised Mrs Turner's spirits, and by the time they had stepped out of the carriage she almost skipped up the steps towards the waiting footmen. Emma lagged behind, her eyes drawn to the well-lit window of the large drawing room. There was Lord Osborne and Miss Carr standing together by the window, deep in conversation.

'Take care on the steps,' said Emma. 'They are a little deeper than they appear.'

'I hardly notice them at all,' said Mrs Turner. 'What an evening we shall have! I haven't had hope of such convivial company since the day of your uncle's funeral.'

The guests were announced and shown into the drawing room where the family members were assembled. Emma saw that Lord Osborne and Miss Carr were still locked in conversation while Lady Osborne and her daughter appeared to be in the midst of a lively debate with Colonel Beresford.

Mrs Turner was immediately at ease in her surroundings. She was just as her niece had known her of old, in Shropshire, in the days before her uncle's death, full of sparkle and wit, and ready to please and be pleased. In that moment Emma was less certain of herself than she had ever been, for the sight of Lord Osborne and Miss Carr together, seemly at ease with one another, talking and smiling, was no longer a matter of indifference to her. She hesitated and held back, choked by feelings that were strangely disconcerting.

After the usual salutations had been given and received, Miss Carr, who was no longer in mourning, took Emma to one side. As mistress of her late uncle's estate, she was now a woman of consequence and exuded an air of stately self-importance. To Emma, her condescension was unrelenting.

'Miss Watson,' said she in a whisper, 'I hear all manner of tales about your family, the half of which would keep St James' Court entertained an entire season.'

'I am sure those who frequent St James' Court have tales enough of their own to keep them amused. And I have no interest in hearing them.'

'Feign disinterest if you will. It is always the way with persons who envy those who move in the first circles. For my part, I cannot wait to hear more of your aunt's escapades.'

Lady Osborne and Mrs Turner resumed the lively tête-à-tête they had begun the previous afternoon. 'And so you see, Mrs Turner, Colonel Beresford was good enough to take my daughter off my hands three months earlier than planned,' said her ladyship. 'They are not long married, as you see, for the fires of romance still burn bright. My dear late husband, you know, had not a whit of romance in him. When eventually I persuaded him to make me an offer, I had no knowledge of it having taken place. Well, said he, I expect we had better get on with it. Get on with what? said I. But once we were married, I never let him forget it. Husbands, as I said to my daughter, should never be left in doubt as to their own shortcomings or they are likely to get puffed up notions of their own usefulness. I have often come across men who believe all that is needed to please their wives is to keep out of the way. And when they think they have made their wives happy, you can be sure that they begin to think themselves appealing to other women as well.'

'You are right. Indeed you are,' said Mrs Turner. 'What you say puts me in mind of Miss Giddings. You must remember Miss Giddings. You always had *a very good eye for spotting an adultress* and invariably fixed upon the right one from the first. I never had your skill.'

'So I did. And what a sight it was to behold. How can anyone forget Mrs Moody in pursuit of the pair? I have never seen anything quite so amusing as that woman running around the room after her intoxicated husband and his brightly painted mistress. And everyone thought her the perfect match for Moody. As attributes go, in name at least she chose well.'

When dinner was announced, Emma was pleased to find that she was not seated next to Miss Carr; Mrs Beresford was in easiest reach of conversation and seemed disposed to talk to her. Desirous of avoiding any mention of Mrs Turner's present predicament, Emma wished at least to convey her gratitude to Mrs Beresford for her recent assistance in the discovery of her aunt in London.

'Colonel Beresford and I were glad to be of service. Had that imposter been a member of the colonel's regiment, he would not have — well, perhaps it is best left unsaid.'

The two spoke easily for fifteen minutes of Reigate, the regiment and the weather, before Mrs Beresford's attention was claimed by Miss Carr.

'Do not you recall the day we dined with the Earl and Countess of —'

Emma's eyes were drawn to Lord Osborne who was listening to Colonel Beresford's account of the perils of night travel in Kent. It seemed remarkable that she had spoken of him so unfavourably when she had first entered the neighbourhood. He had rescued her, advised her, ridden with her, danced with her, defended her, admired her; and she had preferred Mr Howard.

When Emma compared herself to Miss Carr, she found her judgement wanting. Miss Carr had always preferred Lord Osborne; she had seen qualities in his lordship that Emma had been slow to discover. Miss Carr had been the better judge of character. Reluctantly, Emma had to concede that in many ways it was Miss Carr who was the more deserving of his lordship's affection.

Lord Osborne appeared to hear every detail of Colonel Beresford's account of the perils of night travel in Kent; his attention, however, was divided. He was aware that Emma had glanced briefly in his direction, not once, but twice during dinner. He had wanted to speak to her but the distance between them at table prevented it. And when she looked once more in his direction, he returned her gaze; though his face bore no hint of a smile, the intensity of his look caused Emma to turn away. Her confusion at once surprised and captivated him. The silent exchange between them had not gone unnoticed; Mrs Beresford had seen it, and so had her friend.

'I understand,' said Mrs Beresford, breaking the spell that Emma seemed to be under, 'that your sister is soon to be married.'

'Yes, my sister will marry from my brother's house in Croydon.'

'Croydon? Have the arrangements been made already? It was only this afternoon that Mr Musgrave mentioned it. I confess, I had assumed that —'

'Mr Musgrave? What does Mr Musgrave know of my sister's wedding?'

'He told me of it. I came upon him in Delham just after he had left your sister. He was quite delighted with himself, though perhaps he said more than he had intended.'

'He spoke of his own engagement?'

'To your sister.'

'To Elizabeth?'

'Your elder sister,' said Mrs Beresford in a whisper. 'If I have spoken out of turn I apologise. Please forgive my indiscretion. I thought you knew. And I gave Mr Musgrave every assurance that I would not mention a word of it to anyone. Even my brother is not aware of it.'

Emma felt Lord Osborne's eyes upon her as she absorbed the astounding news. The nature of the conversation between the two women perplexed him, and he was curious to know what his sister had said to bring about so marked a change in Emma's countenance.

Emma was astonished by the news, but the part that seemed inexplicable was the knowledge that Elizabeth had not confided in her. Elizabeth's demeanour earlier that evening now seemed to Emma peculiar in the light of Mrs Beresford's disclosure. It must be true, she thought. There could be no reason for Mrs Beresford to spread false information concerning Mr Musgrave and her sister. But it was strange that when Emma left Stanton, Elizabeth had seemed dispirited and anxious.

Emma wondered whether there might be another explanation. Had their father refused his consent? Despite her father's avowed disapproval of Mr Musgrave's haircut, a sign in his eyes of the frivolity and foolhardiness of all idle young men, the match was advantageous in every respect. She could not imagine that her father would be so unyielding. Such an engagement would be regarded as an extraordinary achievement. That Elizabeth had been able to secure Mr Musgrave where many women had failed must be a triumph in anyone's eyes.

Emma could no longer find fault with Mr Musgrave. His choice of Elizabeth was evidence of his fine character and good judgement. She could now wish for no better brother-in-law, and conceded without reservation that her own earlier judgement of his character had been hopelessly flawed.

Emma was eager for the evening to end for she wished more than anything to see her sister and to congratulate her on her good fortune. In Emma's eyes there was no one in the world more deserving of happiness that Elizabeth.

Any hope of an early return to Stanton was dashed when, after the gentlemen had finished their port, Lady Osborne suggested a game of cards. Miss Carr spoke enthusiastically in support of the idea and the two were soon joined by Colonel and Mrs Beresford, and Mrs Turner.

'Do you not play, Miss Watson?' said Miss Carr.

'Thank you, no. I have no interest in cards.'

'Come, my lord, and sit by me,' said Miss Carr.

'You know perfectly well that my brother won't play. If he plays at all, he will play whist, though he will sit for half an hour at best and fidget throughout,' said Mrs Beresford.

'Then let us play whist. If Mrs Turner would give up her place, I should be happy to partner his lordship,' said Miss Carr.

'But we are five. Speculation is better suited to our numbers,' said Lady Osborne.

'It would be better still were his lordship to join us,' continued Miss Carr, unwilling to leave off.

'We will get on much better without him, I assure you,' said Lady Osborne.

'I have no intention of playing cards this evening,' said he. 'Enjoy your game, but leave me out of it.'

Lady Osborne was eager to begin, and setting the deck on the table, said, 'Colonel Beresford, would you be kind enough to deal?'

Miss Carr had contrived the arrangements badly. For the present, she could do no other than endure the displeasure of seeing Lord Osborne and Miss Watson engaged in private conversation, without the opportunity of being party to it.

'It is unlikely they will rise before midnight,' said his lordship to Emma. 'Allow me to provide shelter for the night. I shall, of course, send word to Stanton.'

'Thank you, my lord. But I believe we must return. I should be grateful if you would discourage my aunt from sitting at cards too long.'

'I fear it would not be safe to return, even at this hour. I shall save you Colonel Beresford's stories of travel by night in Kent. I doubt we fare much better in Surrey.'

'I must see my sister.'

'Have you some particular concern? Is your sister unwell? I shall instruct a messenger to bring word of her.'

'No, that will not be necessary. But — '

'Then it is settled?'

'I really think we — that is to say my — Thank you, my lord. If my aunt agrees — '

'Do you think she will object?'

'I think not. My aunt is herself again. This evening I am reminded of our former life,' said Emma. 'Do Colonel and Mrs Beresford stay long?'

'The Colonel returns to Reigate tomorrow. My sister and Miss Carr will follow in a day or two.'

'Oh.'

'Your aunt appears to have made a remarkable recovery these last two days.'

'I believe so. She has rallied better than anyone might have expected. I believe Lady Osborne has done more to raise my aunt's spirits than I ever could.'

'My mother has a naturally happy disposition which has no doubt been shaped by the easy circumstances of her own situation. In that regard, I count myself very like her. She — we — find it hard to comprehend the measure of adversity visited on others.'

'If I may say so, sir, I believe you judge yourself and your mother more harshly than you should.'

'Many would think not harshly enough,' said he. 'My mother may appear to disregard the consequences of your aunt's situation, but I fear her understanding is flawed. To my mother, the unfortunate affair concerning your aunt is little more than an adventure — the stuff of novels — a subject on which she claims to be an authority. It is a serious business though, and if my mother appears to make light of it, I hope that it will not cause pain to you or your aunt.'

'Making light of it seems to have raised my aunt's spirits. I do not think any harm will come of it, but I would like to see a resolution of the matter soon, for my aunt's sake.'

'Of course.'

There was now no awkwardness between Emma and Lord Osborne, and although the lively conversation from the card table at times filled the room, she caught none of it; his was the only voice she heard.

'I expect Mrs Blake has mentioned to you that Mr and Mrs Howard are to visit Delham next week.'

'Mr Howard?' said Emma.

'Yes. Mrs Howard is to accompany him.'

'I should like to see Mary again.'

'Should you?'

'Yes.'

'Forgive me, but I thought there was a time when, that is to say — they will stay with Mr and Mrs Edwards.'

'Yes, of course,' said Emma. 'There was a time when I might have viewed their marriage less contentedly than I do now, but for some time I have been perfectly reconciled to it. I have no misgivings about meeting Mr and Mrs Howard again.'

The party rose from cards just before one o'clock, and though Lady Osborne had urged them to continue for another half hour, none would hear of it.

'Mama, you forget — we are weary travellers. I, for one, am ready to retire,' said Mrs Beresford.

'You young people have not the energy we had in our youth,' replied Lady Osborne. 'I recall travelling from Andover to Bath in one day and spending the whole evening at Lady Blackstone's ball. I danced every dance and when finally we returned to Camden Place, it was six o'clock in the morning. I felt as fresh as a daisy.'

'And you probably did not rise until five in the afternoon,' said her daughter. 'We are expected in Reigate tomorrow by four.'

'Colonel Beresford perhaps, but surely you will stay a day or two longer. I believe that was your plan,' said her mother.

'I should prefer to travel with my husband.'

As the party bid goodnight to one another, Mrs Beresford took Emma aside. 'Miss Watson, do forgive my earlier indiscretion. I spoke out of turn. May I sincerely wish your sister joy. I own, I have never seen a happier man than Mr Musgrave, except Colonel Beresford, of course.' Lowering her voice still further until her words were barely audible even to Emma, Mrs Beresford added, 'Miss Watson, while we were at cards I was able to observe my brother and, as I know him better than anyone, there is no doubt in my mind that — .' Miss Osborne paused. 'Miss Carr is a dear friend, but I know that she would not make him happy. True happiness is as rare as it is precious. I have been more fortunate than I dare have imagined. My wish is that my brother may have the same good fortune. It was my intention, and Miss Carr's, to stay here a day or two longer, but I believe you will get on better without us.'

Emma was saved the necessity of a reply as Colonel Beresford, who was waiting for his wife, appealed to her to bid everyone goodnight.

'Make haste, my dear. If you are indeed set on returning to Reigate tomorrow, we must leave at an early hour. Noon will not do. Half the day is over by noon.'

Mrs Beresford smiled at her husband and in his hearing said playfully, 'Excuse me, Miss Watson. My dear husband sometimes forgets that I am not a member of his regiment. He may issue as many orders as he likes on a battlefield, but they have little effect on me.'

'Thank you, my dear,' said the Colonel smiling broadly. 'I am wholly conversant with the chain of command on the home front. Nevertheless, the carriage will be ready and waiting at six and if you are not in it, it will not be my fault.'

'Six o'clock? Impossible! It is the middle of the night.'

'There is nothing impossible about it. We leave at six and that is the end of the matter.'

The affection between the Colonel and his wife was plain to see, and while each teased one another, neither did so with serious intent, nor did either party feel the need to triumph over the other. Mrs Beresford made no effort to acquiesce with her husband's plans, and her husband showed little inclination to insist on her doing so.

CHAPTER TWENTY-SEVEN

Emma spent a sleepless night thinking about all that had occurred. Her feelings for Lord Osborne had taken her by surprise, and Mrs Beresford's revelations had stirred in her all manner of conflicting emotions until her mind was giddy. The discovery, in one evening, of Elizabeth's engagement to Tom Musgrave and of her own feelings towards Lord Osborne was too much to comprehend. What possible explanation could there be for Elizabeth's low spirits in the light of such wonderful news? Would the happy couple be married from Stanton? How would Margaret react to the news of Elizabeth's engagement? Why had it taken Elizabeth so long to give her heart? Had she truly given her heart or had she accepted Musgrave's proposal for other, more pragmatic reasons? Every unusual sound, every ray of moonlight, every object made distinguishable in the half-light, and every question and idea in Emma's mind was studied ten times over. By morning she was left with even greater doubt and confusion, and a deep fatigue that would not leave her.

When the chambermaid entered to light the fire, Emma was awake, sitting by the window.

'Goodness me, Miss,' said the chambermaid, 'you will surely catch a cold if you sit there, for there is such a draft in that corner from the north wind. You will be chilled to the bone. Let me make up the fire.'

Lost in her own thoughts, Emma heard hardly a word. 'Can you tell me, have Colonel and Mrs Beresford left yet — and Miss Carr?'

'Yes, Miss. Mrs Beresford's friend, Miss Carr, accompanied them. They left a little after seven o'clock.'

Emma smiled at the thought that the Colonel hadn't entirely got his own way. 'Have the rest of the family gone down?'

'The master is downstairs. Her ladyship will not rise early.'

'And Mrs Turner?'

'Mrs Turner is still in her room.'

'Thank you.'

Emma went downstairs in hopes of finding Lord Osborne alone. She was perplexed to find Mr Musgrave in the breakfast room and in a state of agitation. On seeing Emma, he got up to leave, and said simply,

'Excuse me.'

His lordship looked on in silence as his friend strode angrily out of the room.

'I expect you are better acquainted than I as to the cause of the scene you have just witnessed,' said Osborne.

'No, my lord, I am not. I cannot comprehend — '

'Forgive me if I speak out of turn, but I am astounded by what I have just heard' said he. 'Mr Musgrave sought your father's blessing before making a proposal of marriage to your sister. Your father gave his consent and yesterday your sister accepted my friend's offer. I have known Mr Musgrave since childhood, and I have never found him to be more sincere in any matter. Last night he received a communication from your sister informing him that the promise she had made to him earlier that day must now be retracted. Miss Watson gave no explanation.'

'I cannot believe it. Elizabeth is not one to break a promise. It is so unlike her. There must be some misunderstanding, for I know that my sister would never give her heart — or her word — lightly.'

'There is no misunderstanding. The letter was perfectly clear,' said Lord Osborne. 'And now it seems that Mr Musgrave is determined to leave for London as soon as he can settle his affairs in Delham.'

'I must go to her at once. There will be an explanation, I am certain of it. Please do not disturb my aunt. I shall go on foot. If you would be good enough to convey Mrs Turner to Stanton in due course, I should be so very grateful.'

'You shall not go on foot. I'll send for the carriage.'

'But — '

'I insist.'

'My lord, in that case, I should make better progress on horseback.'

Charles Blake, who had been chasing hens into the coop, heard the sound of a horse approaching and stopped to wave. 'Miss Osborne! I mean Mrs Beresford! Hello there!' he shouted. As the rider drew near, he realised that he had been mistaken, for the rider was not his lordship's sister, but Miss Emma Watson.

'Miss Watson! I thought you were Mrs Beresford, for she has riding clothes just like yours.'

'They belong to Mrs Beresford. I have been given leave to borrow them.'

'I am so glad you have come. I'll go and tell Mama.'

'Charles — I cannot stay. There is something urgent I must attend to.'

'That's curious. Mr Musgrave passed by not half an hour ago and said that he also had something urgent to do. I wish I had something urgent to do.'

'Do you know where Mr Musgrave is now?'

'He is gone home. He was in a great hurry.'

At that moment Mrs Blake came in haste into the garden. 'Emma, I am so glad you have come. I have some news which I must tell you. I was on the point of sending word to you at Stanton. Charles, I believe you have a job to do.'

'But I have fed the chickens.'

'Then go and feed the ducks.'

'I should like to hear some news too, Mama. I never hear any news. And I should like to have something urgent to do.'

'Then go and see to the ducks. That is urgent business enough for the present. I wish to speak with Miss Watson in private.'

Turning to Emma, Mrs Blake continued, 'I do not wish to delay you, for I believe I can guess your purpose. Mr Musgrave is not long gone. He said very little and would not stay, but I was able to glean something of the matter which I believe is of some delicacy and concerns your sister. He intends to leave the neighbourhood for good. I cannot believe it.'

'There must be some misunderstanding for I am certain my sister would not give her word without intending to keep it. If you should see Mr Musgrave, please urge him to delay his departure, at least for a week or so — at least until all the facts are known.'

Lord Osborne was called on by his mother and Mrs Turner to explain Miss Watson's whereabouts. His lordship was not forthcoming, even though both women had seen Emma leaving Osborne Castle on horseback in a great rush. The incident required an explanation of some kind, and so invention was deemed a perfectly acceptable alternative to the truth.

'I confess, I like to see a young woman with spirit — charging around the countryside in pursuit of a young man,' said Lady Osborne. 'Your niece will do very well for Mr Musgrave, I'm sure. He is not without means, and I must say, he is a great asset in the drawing room for he always has something amusing to say. They will make a handsome couple. I wonder I did not spot it earlier.'

'It is as much a surprise to me as to anybody,' said Mrs Turner. 'I had thought my niece — but one never knows what is in the heads of young people these days.'

'You are right. I had no notion of my own daughter's preference for Colonel Beresford. I was the last to know. Young women nowadays think the occasional flutter of an eyelid and the exchange of some tepid pleasantry the quickest way to a conquest. It is a wonder that any of them succeed in securing an introduction, never mind an alliance.'

'Too true,' agreed Mrs Turner. 'Do you recall the younger Miss Dawlish?'

'I do. Plagued with the pox, poor woman.'

'Indeed. There was never a more ridiculous sight than Miss Dawlish in pursuit of Mr Pratting.'

'I remember it well. There was she, perched like a petrified parrot at the reins of her father's curricle — '

'That hat.'

'Oh, the hat! I never saw the like, nor have I since.'

'And when she took up the reins — '

' — the horses would not be moved!'

'I have never laughed so hard in my life.'

'What a fine joke! Everyone thought that old Mr Dawlish had substituted his pair of greys for a pair of mules on purpose to prevent his daughter's pursuit of Mr Pratting.'

'I never saw a swifter exit from Bath than the one made by that young man — except, of course, my own when Mr Edwards would not leave off.'

'Mr Edwards?'

'He was not to my taste in those days, but I must say he appears to have improved with age.'

'Our neighbour Mr Edwards?'

'It was but brief. There was no harm done.'

When Emma arrived home, dishevelled and breathless, Nanny hastened to the door to meet her.

'Miss Emma, thank goodness you have come. Miss Watson is unwell and will not eat.'

Despite Nanny's repeated pleas, and the pleas of Mr Watson, Elizabeth would not be prevailed upon to leave her room.

'Do not worry, Nanny,' said Emma. 'I will go to my sister.'

Emma went directly to her sister's room. 'Elizabeth, I must speak with you. I shall not stir until you unlock this door and let me in. And if you do not yield, I will make up my bed here on the floor until you do.'

Emma pressed her ear against the door and waited for a word of acknowledgement. A brief silence was followed by movement from within. At length, Elizabeth turned the key in the lock and opened the door.

'I have done a terrible thing.' Emma closed the door behind her and embraced her sister.

'I am sure you had no intention of doing anything terrible, for you do not have a bad heart. I believe I know what you have done, and I confess, I do not understand your reason for doing it, but I know that whatever it was, you would not have given your word lightly or withdrawn it on a whim.'

'I should not have acted so had — had circumstances been different.'

'How can circumstances change so completely from one hour to the next? Elizabeth, what causes you pain? Please do not bear this alone. I am here.'

'Nothing, truly — except knowing the pain I have given to — .'

'Do you know that Mr Musgrave is shortly to leave the neighbourhood without any thought of returning?'

Elizabeth looked away. After a brief pause, she said, 'I have no claim on him now. He is free to come and go as he pleases. I believe it is for the best.'

'For the best? How can you say such a thing?'

'In London he will be able to put it behind him more quickly than he might were he to stay here. That way we will, neither of us, be reminded of it. I should not wish, nor I imagine would he, to be constantly thrown into each other's company.'

'You would deprive him of his friends and neighbours, and deprive them of him? I own, at first I did not like Mr Musgrave — indeed, I thought quite ill of him. I am ashamed to recall it now, for I do believe he is a good man. He truly loves you, therefore he must be good.'

'I didn't mean — '

'I urge you, if you have given your heart, if he is the man you love above all others, do not falter. Go to him before it is too late.'

'It is too late. I have written to Mr Musgrave — I wrote to him last night — in the clearest of terms, to avoid any damage that might ensue had the engagement been made known.'

'I saw Mr Musgrave this morning. I have never seen a man more wounded. If only you could have seen his look, Elizabeth. Tell me that your heart is not broken too.'

Elizabeth, who had stifled her tears until then, could do so no longer. At such a time words of comfort rarely bring the intended relief the comforter wishes to bestow. Emma could think of nothing to say that would bring ease or hope to her sister. She sat in silence by Elizabeth's side, and taking her hand, stroked it gently as Elizabeth's eyes welled. When every tear was spent, Emma waited until her sister had slipped into a soothing sleep before tiptoeing out of the room. At the foot of the stairs she was met by her father.

'In heaven's name, what has come over your sister? What does she fret about? The house has been in chaos all morning. Anyone would think your sister Margaret had come to stay.'

'Papa, Elizabeth is resting now.'

'Resting? But when will I get my dinner? Nanny will not know which birds to roast.'

'Nanny will manage perfectly well without Elizabeth's supervision. I will see to it. You will have your dinner on time.'

'Good. Good. By the by, before Elizabeth enters into matrimony with that idle fellow Musgrave, I shall see to it, my dear, that she leaves a list duties — neatly, on a clean piece of paper, set out in a row and written in her own hand. She has as clear and bold a hand as I have seen. There will be no mistaking a word or phrase in Elizabeth's hand. I would not wish you to be left in ignorance of any particular. We cannot be scuttling about like headless chickens when Elizabeth is gone,' said he. 'Indeed, I find I am quite reconciled to your sister's departure for I am certain that you will see to things as well as she. Where is your Aunt Turner? Does she know of your sister's engagement? You might as well tell her. It will come better from you. Nanny does not like to hear your aunt's tittle tattle when she is busy in the kitchen for she cannot get on with things when Mrs Turner is near. And Emma, you'd better tell your aunt that a letter has arrived from London. I pray it carries good news. If Robert could but recover a fraction of your aunt's fortune, I should be happy enough, for then she could rent a cottage of her own and plague us no longer. Failing that, she should find employment as a novelist, for I daresay such fantastic tales as your aunt is wont to pass off as fact must likely stem from an overactive imagination.'

Since his removal to Osborne Cottage, Charles Blake had found little reason to devise a plan of escape, for the need to do so had not arisen. It had been an oversight on his part, and had he been better prepared, his passage from the schoolroom to the lane would have been accomplished with ease, and without any fear of detection. Osborne Cottage was, in many respects, ideally situated, but the absence of an obliging tree close to the schoolroom window was a decided disadvantage in comparison to his bedchamber at Wickstead. There was neither a conveniently placed window in a downstairs study that opened onto the lane outside, nor a mother who had an obligation to call on the old and infirm of the parish on a Wednesday morning. Fortunately, Charles had a talent for invention and used it to full advantage.

'Where are you going?' said Mrs Blake to her son.

'Mama, I opened the window upstairs.'

'And why does that necessitate stepping outside?'

'I opened the window so that I could breathe in the fresh air while writing my sentences. The air is very fresh today. Fresh air is very good for me.'

'And have you finished your work?'

'Almost, Mama.'

'When you have finished, you may go outside to enjoy more fresh air.'

'But Mama, I cannot finish my work until I have been outside.'

'Why so?'

'A bird flew into the room.'

'A bird? Where is it now?'

'It flew out again. It was a big bird with a red pointed head and black wings with specks of white in them, and it had enormous yellow claws. I wafted it with my papers to make it fly away but I dropped them and they flew out of the window too.'

'Your papers flew out of the window?'

'Yes, Mama. But if I go outside to recover them, they will not be lost. I have worked so hard today.'

'You'd better make haste. If the pigs get there first there will be nothing left to show for your efforts.'

'If I were a pig, I should prefer a turnip to a — '

'Charles, go and pick them up.'

'Thank you, Mama,' said he, hastening to the door. 'It may take some time for there are many papers to be gathered.'

'Then I will come and help you.'

'No, Mama. It was my doing and I must bear the responsibility myself. You always say I should mend what I have broken.'

'I am pleased to hear that you occasionally heed my words. Off you go! And don't dawdle. I know how easily you succumb to distraction.'

Charles quickly gathered the papers from the garden and stuffed them into the sleeve of his jacket before climbing over the wall and into the lane. He ran as fast as he could, and was half a mile away before his mother discovered he was missing. Believing him to have headed in the direction of Osborne Castle, Mrs Blake immediately set out on foot to find him in order to lay before him the prospect of going to school in Ramsgate where discipline would be harsh, fish, spiders and frogs would be scarce, and lessons would be long and arduous.

Emma was no nearer an understanding of Elizabeth's change of heart. Nothing about Elizabeth's situation appeared to make sense. It was only when she recalled the words of her father that a possible explanation presented itself. Mr Watson expected that his present infirmity would worsen with time and had no wish to spend his declining years alone. He had thought that the excellent care he had so far received from his eldest daughter would continue, for she was in that happy state of almost being old enough to be called a spinster. Another year or so and the likelihood of Elizabeth ever marrying would have been so remote as to have caused Mr Watson no further anxiety.

The return of his youngest daughter to Stanton, however, had presented him with a satisfactory alternative. Emma had many of Elizabeth's excellent qualities, as well as being an exceptional reader. This being the case, Mr Watson found that he could sanction

Elizabeth's removal from Stanton without a second thought, for there could be no better substitute than Emma to look after him when he was too weak to look after himself.

Ever since the death of their mother Elizabeth had cared for the family. It had not been easy, for she had much to learn about keeping order in the house and food on the table; and despite the grief she felt over her mother's demise, she had thrown herself wholly into her tasks. Responsibility came easily to Miss Watson and she coped as well as any elder sister might have done with the ups and downs of bringing up younger brothers and sisters. The most difficult years had been those in which Margaret and Penelope had ceased climbing trees and had embarked on climbing pursuits of a social kind. Elizabeth had assumed the duty of mediator in the face of their petty rivalries and squabbles, and no matter how trivial, more often than not it was she who was accused of provocation and it was she who had borne the brunt of any dispute.

Elizabeth's darkest day had been the day Emma was placed into the care of Mr and Mrs Turner. Her youngest sister, whose nature was mild and acquiescent, and who seemed imperturbable when chaos broke out within the walls of the parsonage, seemed lost to her forever. She was given no part in the decision to send Emma away, and the suddenness with which it had been accomplished had caused Elizabeth to grieve as much for her sister as for her mother.

When, at Robert's instigation, her father decided to let Nanny go, Elizabeth fought hard to keep her; but Robert, who was by then apprenticed as a young clerk in Croydon, thought only of the cost of feeding an extra mouth. With Emma out of the way, he argued, Nanny's presence in the house was no longer a necessity. But Elizabeth had protested strongly and had refused to eat for two days until the decision had been overturned. Since that day, Nanny had provided the practical support that a young woman of fifteen, with a home to run and a family to care for, had found indispensable.

Nanny set about preparing a dish of beef broth for Elizabeth while Emma toasted a crust of bread over the fire. A tray was arranged prettily with a sprig of lavender from the garden, a newly pressed linen cloth on the tray and a soup spoon of the best silver.

'If that doesn't tempt your sister, I do not know what will,' said Nanny. 'I do not think a morsel has passed her lips since yesterday morning.'

'I shall go to her now.'

Emma entered Elizabeth's room and set the tray down on the table by the window. Elizabeth was seated at the looking glass, making adjustments to her hair.

'Nanny has sent up some of your favourite broth,' said Emma.

'Emma, forgive me. I beg you — I do not know what came over me.'

'My dear sister,' said Emma, 'I have spoken to our father. Papa and I will do very well without you at Stanton. I am perfectly content to take your place here. And if you wouldn't mind it, I should much prefer your room to mine, for it has a most pleasing aspect.'

'How can you say such a thing? How can you sacrifice your life in such a way? You are young. You must have your chance of happiness.'

'And you must not? What of your happiness, Elizabeth? Why must you, for my sake, forsake the man whom you love and who loves you with all his heart? You have been burdened with every trouble and care since our dear mother departed this life. You have laboured long and borne it all with the greatest courage and fortitude. When, in all these years, did you ever think of yourself? When did you give yourself leave to be happy?'

'I do not wish my fate to be your fate.'

'Nor will it, for I choose it freely and gladly. You were afforded no choice.'

Before Elizabeth had an opportunity to respond, there was a knock at the door. 'Miss Emma, you are needed downstairs,' said Nanny. 'Master Charles is in the parlour covered in mud from head to foot. Goodness knows what his mother will say.'

Emma found Charles sipping a dish of beef broth in the parlour. 'This is the best beef broth I have ever tasted.'

'Charles, whatever has happened to you?'

'What a morning I have had of it, Miss Watson. But I have had such an adventure, the like of which you will never guess.' Charles recounted the ingenuity of his escape from Osborne Cottage and his chance meeting with Mrs Turner on the road to Delham.

'And where is my aunt now?'

'With Mr Musgrave, of course,' said Charles with gleeful satisfaction.

'Mr Musgrave?'

'Yes. I wanted to help your sister, Miss Watson. I didn't mean to overhear anything, really I didn't, but Mama's voice is so very clear that one cannot avoid hearing it even if one wished to. So I thought of a plan to bring Mr Musgrave to Stanton, but that didn't work. And then I happened upon Mrs Turner, though at first I thought it was Lady Osborne, for she is usually the one to travel in that particular coach. Have you seen the seats? They are very comfortable.'

'No, I haven't.'

'We were nearing Mr Musgrave's house — and we could not have been more perfectly situated — when Mrs Turner had a seizure.'

'My aunt has had a seizure? I must go to her at once.'

'She has not had a very big seizure. Indeed, it was not very much of a seizure at all really, but she was very upset when she heard about Mr Musgrave and your sister. We arrived just in time, for Mr Musgrave was about to leave for London. Mr Musgrave sent for his physician. It was fortunate that Mr Tomlinson was there too for he was able to bring me as far as Stanton Woods.'

'Does your mama know where you are?'

'I expect she does now, for Mr Musgrave insisted on sending word,' said Charles. 'Did you know that Mrs Turner is a very good actress? I have offered to show her my box of costumes. Perhaps we three could perform our play together. Are you not pleased that I have prevented Mr Musgrave from going to town?'

'I suppose I am. I know your intentions are good, but now I must ask you to do something for me. I want you to stay here with Nanny. And when my sister appears, keep her busy until I return or until your mama sends for you.'

'But how shall I keep her busy?'

'I am sure you will have no problem whatsoever. And Charles,' said Emma, smiling, 'thank you. You never know — you may well have saved the day, though I'm not sure your mama will see it in quite the same light.'

Nanny, entering the room, said, 'Miss Emma, your father is gone to Delham in the old chair to see Mr Edwards.'

'Please look after Charles. I must go to my aunt. I shall take Lord Osborne's horse.'

When Emma arrived at Mr Musgrave's residence, she found him alone, pacing the hall.

'Mr Musgrave, once again I must thank you for your kindness to my aunt.'

'My physician is with Mrs Turner now. I do not know whether it is advisable to move her. We must wait for his report.'

'I hope this incident has not inconvenienced you in any way,' said Emma.

Musgrave paused to compose his reply. 'Your aunt? No indeed. But I have no doubt that you are aware of recent events concerning your sister.'

'Yes.'

'I shall leave for London at the earliest possible opportunity. I am not an unreasonable man, but I do not have within me the power to forgive your sister at present. I hope in time to forget what she has done.'

'No man could easily forgive or forget such a thing.'

'Then you agree that your sister is the guilty party — that she is culpable?'

'My sister — my sister has nothing but the deepest regard and affection for you. Truly, she loves you with all her heart. Of that I am certain. I have every reason to believe that Elizabeth fully intended to honour her promise to you. Mr Musgrave, would you allow me a few moments of your time to acquaint you with the facts?'

Although Musgrave gave no reply, he offered no opposition to Emma's request. Deriving encouragement from his silence, she went on, 'Elizabeth is the kindest, most selfless sister of anyone I know. Last night my sister learned that, after your marriage, Papa intended that I should take her place at Stanton. It is my belief that she could not bear to see me lead the life that she has led these past fifteen years, and so she resolved to stay with our father in order to release me from her fate. Elizabeth broke her promise to you, it is true, but with a heart that will always be yours.'

'Why did she not come to me? Why did she offer no explanation?'

'How could she reveal the nature of a sacrifice she had chosen to make?'

'But she told you.'

'She did not. I guessed the truth of the matter when I spoke to Papa earlier. My sister is so little acquainted with the notion of happiness, and does not believe herself worthy of it. Elizabeth believes herself duty bound to — '

'What little trust your sister has in me! A solution might have been found — would have been found. I would have found it!'

'Indeed, there is a solution. I shall look after my father. I cannot allow Elizabeth to sacrifice her happiness forever, nor should I wish to be deprived of a dear brother-in-law. I beg you, Mr Musgrave, reason with her. I could not bear to live in this world knowing that my sister had given up all hope of true happiness for my sake.'

The door opened to admit Musgrave's physician. 'I cannot determine wholly the nature of the ailment,' said he. 'A nervous disorder is indicated. I have prescribed laudanum, and the patient is now stable.'

Emma and Mrs Turner returned to Stanton as night fell. Having placed his carriage at the patient's disposal, Musgrave delayed his departure. 'One of my men will return Lord Osborne's horse,' said he. 'I wish you a safe journey.'

On reaching Stanton, Emma found Elizabeth alone in the parlour. The embers of a fire were just warm enough to take the chill off the room, and the candles were almost spent. Emma stoked up the fire before taking Mrs Turner to her room. When she came down, she found Elizabeth with the toasting fork, toasting crusts of bread.

'Mrs Blake arrived just as we were about to dine so I invited her to sit down with us. At first she declined, but when I pressed her and explained the service that her son had rendered, she yielded. I'm afraid there's nothing left but these crusts. It was a pleasant lunch though, and to own the truth, I was glad of the company. What ails Aunt Turner?'

'Nothing that a good sleep won't put right.'

'Is she gone up for the night?'

'I believe so,' said Emma. 'She's heady from the laudanum. I think the physician was a little too liberal with the dose.'

'It was good of Mr Musgrave to — . When does he leave?'

'Soon, I think.'

'How did you find him?'

'I found him much as I find you. Troubled and upset.'

'Is he resentful?'

'Yes, I'm afraid he is.'

'He has every right to be. I have used him ill. Emma, do you forgive me?'

'I will when you make things right with him. He is at a loss to know why you did not consult him first if you had misgivings.'

'It has not been my nature to seek for solutions outside myself. I have always supposed that where it was in my power to do so, it was my responsibility to provide the answer to any crisis that might arise. On reflection, had I consulted Mr Musgrave, I wonder if an answer might have been found. I am wholly at fault. What have I done, Emma?'

'Is it foolish to hope that he might renew his addresses to you?'

'He is a proud man who has been injured by my lack of faith in him, not once, but three times. How could I expect him to renew his addresses to me now?'

'Write to him. Let him find a way back to you,' said Emma.

CHAPTER TWENTY-EIGHT

Emma indulged hopes of seeing Mr Musgrave at Stanton the next morning and of everything being properly settled with Elizabeth before the day was out. As the morning progressed, Emma and Nanny took turns at the window to keep a lookout for his carriage, but nothing was seen or heard of it; and as the hours passed, hope gave way to doubt, and doubt to discouragement.

The day, however, brought news of another kind, for the letter concerning Mrs Turner that Mr Watson had in his possession was from Robert and contained news that she had been anxiously awaiting for some time. Despite the gloom that prevailed within the house, Mrs Turner was in excellent spirits. Her elation, occasioned by the previous day's caper, combined with the effects of a generous dose of laudanum, accorded Mrs Turner a singularly bold view of the world, one that was uncommonly and irrepressibly cheerful. On reading the letter, nonetheless, her exuberance turned to frenzied indignation.

The letter contained confirmation that Mr Robert Watson had concluded his inquiries in regard to the recovery of Mrs Turner's estate, and though the outcome was less satisfactory than had been wished for, it was better than nothing. It was now quite certain that the person claiming to be a Captain O'Brien had fled abroad and was thought to be living in some style, possibly in the West Indies, furnished with funds from Mrs Turner's estate. It was probable that he had assumed a new identity, enabling him to conceal his whereabouts indefinitely.

After extensive inquiries, Robert had been able to recover a sum of money that had remained untouched. The letter went on, 'I expect the scoundrel had no knowledge of its existence, for there is not a penny left elsewhere. The amount recoverable is a fraction of the fortune Emma might have expected. Had the fund's beneficiary been designated clearly and explicitly, it would have been the end of the matter. As it was not, I shall make the following recommendation. Emma should receive three thousand pounds. It is hers by right. It is not much, considering what it should have been, but it is a reasonable sum and is likely to yield results. I daresay one of the Tomlinson's might think of her. The residue, if invested properly, would allow for the purchase of a modest house, pay off outstanding debts, and provide Aunt Turner with an income of two hundred pounds a year or thereabouts. If the arrangements outlined above meet with her approval, I should be happy to complete all the necessary transactions without further delay. Yours, etc…'

'Two hundred pounds a year? How does one live on so little?' said Mrs Turner. 'I doubt Emma will need three thousand pounds to induce one of her suitors to make an offer.'

'It is a fair and reasonable arrangement, and most providential. I must commend Robert for his good judgement in this matter. Three thousand pounds is a beneficial amount, but it is not excessive,' said Mr Watson. 'It is by no means certain that Emma will marry. She will need something to live on when I am gone, as I have nothing to settle on her myself. Mrs Turner, when you and Mr Turner took her off my hands, you vowed to bring her up as your own with every advantage of breeding and situation.'

'And so I did — we did. There was no deficiency of any kind in that regard. Emma lacked nothing that this world could offer. No comfort was ever denied, no expense spared. Indeed, Mr Turner devoted himself to Emma's education and comfort unstintingly. Had I borne him a son, he could have done no more.'

'And I am certain that Mr Turner intended Emma to inherit. I very much doubt that he anticipated any situation in which his wife would throw off her niece in order to satisfy her own needs and to follow her own ignoble passions.'

'And I am certain that Mr Turner intended Emma to marry. You speak of my requirements and yet you had no scruples in declaring your intention of keeping your youngest daughter at Stanton when you thought that Mr Musgrave would take Elizabeth off your hands. I can think of no greater illustration of placing the satisfaction of one's own material comforts above all other considerations. Indeed, should I choose to go back into Shropshire, Emma may likely follow, for all her friends are there. In the end, she may choose me over you.'

'Return to Shropshire? And suffer the disgrace, ridicule and humiliation that must follow from your utter foolishness and weak judgment?'

'My poor dear sister-in-law! What a life she must have led! I expect she was driven to an early grave. I cannot recount the times I said so to dear Mr Turner. He thought his sister well situated, and "Mr Watson" a reasonable, amiable sort of man.'

'Madam, you forget yourself. Cease these hysterics at once!'

'I expect you have no knowledge whatsoever of the events that have transpired under your own roof these last two days,' replied Mrs Turner. 'Did you know that your eldest daughter, having accepted Mr Musgrave's proposal, has since cried off? Do you know why Elizabeth has acted so? Ah! I see you know none of it.'

The objections of both parties were rehearsed for more than half an hour before the interview was brought to an end by the arrival of Mr Robert Watson, accompanied by Margaret, the new Mrs Hemmings.

'My dear sisters,' said Margaret, with all the consequence of a newly married woman, 'it has been too long since I was at Stanton. I could not wait a moment longer to see how you are all going on. When Robert said that he was to visit I told him that if he did not take me with him he would never hear the end of it. And as he has torment enough from Jane, he relented immediately. I am married, you see. Mr Hemmings could not be spared — Robert insisted that he look after things at Croydon. And if Robert does not make him a partner before the year is out, he will not hear the last of that either. And so Papa and Mrs Turner are huddled together in the study, are they? I expect they are squabbling over your inheritance, Emma. And don't look at me like that. All is not doom and gloom, for I expect you will get a portion of it, which is more than I ever had. That is why Robert is here — to insist on it — for he knows that Papa, left to his own devices, is apt to give in. Well, what news is there to tell? Not much I see.'

Margaret threw off her gloves and bonnet and sank into a chair by the fire. 'We happened upon Mr Musgrave in Delham. I must say, he looked quite downcast and was not particularly gallant towards me. I expect I have disappointed him greatly, for he did not wish me joy when I mentioned I was married. He deserves to be crossed in love after leading me a merry dance. He is gone to London, you know. I mentioned that he must call in at Croydon, but he made it very clear that he had no expectation of ever passing within fifty miles of the place. I thought that a gross exaggeration for it is impossible to — '

'Margaret, allow me to wish you joy,' said Emma. 'We are anxious to hear all the news from Croydon.'

'Excuse me,' said Elizabeth. 'I must go and help Nanny stretch dinner. I wonder Robert didn't send word ahead.'

When Elizabeth was out of earshot, Margaret exclaimed, 'Well! I expect she is in a temper because I am married. Did you notice, Emma? She didn't wish me joy. Elizabeth looks and behaves very ill indeed.'

'I am sorry that we have not the pleasure of meeting Mr Hemmings on this visit. How was the wedding?'

'It surpassed anything that could have been done at Stanton. Croydon society is far superior. Robert gave me away and, I must say, he appeared quite the gentleman. The younger son of a baronet came to the church. He is a client of Robert's. I fancy no one of distinction attended Penelope's wedding. Mr Hemmings' family are from Yorkshire and did not attend. It was no great loss. He has threatened to take me into the north country next spring, but I daresay I shall make him take me to Eastbourne instead. Where is Robert?'

'He is still with our father.'

'Well, I hope he has some luck in getting your aunt to part with her money. She had few qualms about giving it away to that imposter. You are much in Robert's debt, you know. He has paid out a great deal to recover what little remains of your aunt's estate and he will expect to be paid handsomely for his trouble.'

'I'm sure he shall be,' said Emma.

'Good Lord. What time is it? I hope dinner will not be long. I've hardly had a morsel to eat all day. I shall go up and change. Do tell Nanny to get a move on.'

Emma went in search of Elizabeth and found her alone in her room, looking out of the window, watching the lane.

'A carriage passed by some minutes ago. It was not his. I should have known if it were,' said Elizabeth. 'He is gone to London then. It is for the best.'

'Perhaps.

'It is said that time is a great healer. I wonder if the same is true of distance.'

'Where there is true love, it must surely transcend both. Allow yourself to imagine, if you will, that Mr Musgrave in time will forget you. It may happen, but it is often the case that affection is deepened by absence. When Mr Howard left Wickstead, I confess, I thought of him more than I should, even when he was lost to me forever. He never gave me encouragement, you know. Now I understand better the part I played in bringing about my own heartache. I see that his regard for me was entirely the creation of my imagination. Because I fancied myself in love with him, I believed him capable of the same. But where there is mutual affection, such feelings should not, do not die. Mr Musgrave may soon be in London but I am certain that his mind and his heart will remain in Surrey.'

The visit of Robert and Margaret did not extend beyond two days and was concluded after the terms of the financial settlements had been agreed. Mrs Turner assented to the sum of two thousand pounds being settled on her niece. Emma, however, insisted that half the amount should go to Elizabeth. 'And where is my share?' said Margaret. 'Have I no rights? And what of Penelope? — Though I daresay Penelope is not in need of it half as much as — '

'You are married women,' said Robert. 'Your husbands must have the pleasure of providing for you now. There is no certainty that your sisters will ever have your good fortune. Emma, you are a foolish creature to be parting with an inheritance that is rightfully yours, though I confess, it is an uncommonly generous deed. There are few as deserving of it as Elizabeth. It is a great shame that your aunt did not find it within her power to exhibit the same impulse. She will receive my bill in due course. Unlike you, I have no mind to be out of pocket.'

'Thank you, Robert. When I think of what might have been, this is not a bad outcome after all. I am sure Aunt Turner is as much obliged to you as I am.'

The necessary expression of hopes for a safe journey and promises of carrying the good wishes of all to Croydon completed the family's leave-taking. Mr Watson retired to his room and gave instructions that he was not to be disturbed; and Elizabeth busied herself with the household accounts.

'I need some diversion, Emma. Reckoning is as good as any employment, for it concentrates the mind as no other occupation does. I am resolved not to think of him. Shall you walk into Delham?'

'The weather does not look too promising. I should speak to my aunt. Robert and Papa were a little overbearing earlier.'

Mrs Turner readily assented to a walk in the fresh air. 'A short walk will suffice — a turn in the garden and a walk to the church is all I have strength for.'

'And if it should rain, we can take shelter there,' said Emma.

'Emma, you must think me heartless, ungenerous. Your father believes me to be so. But be assured that you — and Elizabeth — will always have a home with me should either of you ever be in need of one.'

'Thank you. I cannot think of a more generous offer.'

'In time I will learn — I must learn — to live without the comforts to which I was born. But how will I move about without a carriage?'

'You have many friends who will always be ready to assist you.'

'Here, perhaps. But I fear that I have few friends left in Shropshire,' replied Mrs Turner. 'My dear Emma, I have given some thought to where I might settle. It would not be prudent for me to go back into Shropshire after all that has transpired. Your brother's enquiries have led to much conjecture among our former neighbours. If I should decide to settle in Delham, would you — '

'My dear aunt, I can think of nothing I should like better. Not a day would pass without my seeing you. I should walk into Delham every day.'

'I thought I might ask Mr Edwards to make enquiries on my behalf.'

'An excellent idea. Mr Edwards is precisely the person to ask. I cannot wait to tell Elizabeth.'

'You may have to wait a little longer, my dear. There is a gentleman approaching — over there by the churchyard gate — and I believe it is Lord Osborne. I shall make my excuses and return to the house.'

'Surely there is no need for that. Perhaps he brings news of Mr Musgrave.'

'In which case, I am sure he would rather share it with you in private.'

The surprise appearance of Lord Osborne afforded Emma little time to prepare her thoughts, or to bring into check the curious sensation she felt on seeing him.

After greetings had been exchanged, Mrs Turner made her excuses. 'Forgive me, my lord,' said she. 'I have need to consult my niece Elizabeth on a matter that cannot wait.'

'Then let us accompany you to the gate,' said Lord Osborne.

'No indeed,' replied Mrs Turner. 'There is no need for that. Enjoy the fresh air while you can. I'm sure I'm not needed here.'

'There is one thing I wish to say,' said he. 'I understand that you may be in need of a home. There is a house, fairly situated, not far from Delham — a mile or two at the most. It is in need of repair, but these things might be easily accomplished were the house to meet with your approval. I wish only to offer my services should you need assistance in securing a property in the neighbourhood. Forgive me if the offer is presumptuous.'

'It is a very kind offer. I am deeply indebted to you, my lord. I should be delighted to see it.'

'Very well. The necessary arrangements will be made. My steward will furnish you with the particulars. And now, if you would be so kind, I should like to speak with Miss Watson alone.'

'Of course. Emma, my dear, take my shawl. A little drizzle won't harm you, though it is often the prelude to something more violent. As the saying goes,' said Mrs Turner, playfully, 'it never rains but it pours. I shall leave you in peace.'

After parting company with Mrs Turner, Lord Osborne and Emma walked in the direction of Stanton Woods. Several moments passed without a word being spoken on either side; on more than one occasion, Emma thought that his lordship seemed to be on the point of speaking, and although he had indicated that there was something particular he wished to say, when at last he spoke, it was of the weather. Unlike the rain, words did not flow effortlessly, and as they walked on in an uneasy silence, the drizzle turned to rain.

'We can take cover in the church,' said Emma. Osborne acceded to the plan. They returned along the path they had taken and reached the church porch as the deluge intensified.

'Miss Watson, you must wonder why I wished to speak with you. I hardly know how to begin,' said he. 'Please — please allow me to express the hope I have harboured for many months now, though I have hardly allowed myself to entertain it. I hope that one day you will consent to be my wife. I know that you do not love me as I love you. But it is my dearest hope that perhaps in time your feelings may change. Forgive me. I have no wish to make you uneasy. Please feel under no obligation to reply.'

Perplexed by his lordship's belief in her indifference, Emma replied, 'My lord, am I given to understand that you wish to make me an offer of marriage despite your conviction of my indifference?'

'I do,' said he. 'Is that so very strange? Marriages of the kind are common, are they not? I dislike the kind of pretence that involves false professions of affection, the kind that often occur when alliances are made with more material considerations in mind.'

'Were I to accept your offer, how could you be certain that my motive was sincere?'

'I have studied you long enough to know that you are incapable of the kind of artifice of which I speak. Had I felt less, I should have spoken sooner and done so without trepidation. But the prospect of living in this world without hope is more painful than anything else. If I do not attempt it — if I do not speak at all, any opportunity of happiness that might have been within my reach would surely be lost forever. I beg you, take time to consider. I confess, I should not wish you to — '

' — act as my sister has done?'

CHAPTER TWENTY-NINE

Osborne Castle Tuesday October 13th 1812

Aspiring heroines are often great readers. They apprehend the necessity of spending a substantial portion of their education reading novels. Mothers of aspiring heroines, though they themselves might once have entertained similar ambitions, generally have different aspirations for their daughters. When the young heroine of Osborne Castle tripped lightly down the stairs, her mother, the one whose mantle she was poised to assume and whose half-boots she was destined to fill, called to her daughter from the morning room.

'Where have you been? Your Aunt Elizabeth was here earlier and was most desirous of seeing you.'

'I did not think she would come today,' said Miss Emma Osborne. 'I went up to the lake and sat among the ancient ruins. It is so beautiful there today.'

'The ruins are not ancient. They are made to look old.'

'Oh, but it is such a romantic place. Did you and Papa ever meet there?'

'Heavens, no. Your grandmamma had them built when you were but five years old. I cannot think why, for they serve no useful purpose.'

'I called to see Grandmamma today. We had a merry time. Great Aunt Turner was there and Mrs Blake. You will never guess the name of the third visitor.'

'You are right. I have no idea.'

'Lieutenant Blake was there, Mama. It is a great shame that he cannot be spared for more than two days. But he promised to call on us, and I shall keep a look out every hour. He looks so handsome in his naval uniform.'

'Most young men look handsome in uniform. That is why young women, and I may say, older ones, find them so appealing. But that sometimes puts young women in danger of mistaking charm for character. Fortunately, Charles Blake has both, but he will not think of you.'

'Why not, Mama?' said Emma.

'You are not yet out and you have still much to learn about young men.'

'Grandmamma said that when she and Aunt Turner were young ——'

'I can imagine just what your grandmamma said,' replied Lady Osborne. 'I should prefer it if you were to take your grandmamma's stories as a caution and not a recommendation.'

'Do you think Charles Blake will marry Anne Musgrave?'

'Marry your cousin? Whatever gave you that notion?'

'He enquired after her. That is all,' said Emma. 'Did Aunt Elizabeth mention whether Charles Blake had called on them?'

'My dear child, you must not fill your head with such things. Your cousin is almost six months your junior. Charles Blake will not think of either of you.'

'What if one day he should propose?'

'I wish you would not dream your life away.'

'How did Papa propose to you?'

'In the rain, under the church porch.'

'That is not romantic. Did he go down on one knee?'

'No. We were standing in a puddle of water.'

'How was his address? Did he declare the violence of his feelings?'

'Your papa believed me to be indifferent to him.'

'And were you?'

'Indifferent? I accepted his proposal the moment he made it.'

'That is not very romantic.'

'I'm sorry to disappoint you.'

'But did you love him?'

'Utterly.'

'When did you know?'

'I have no idea. It seems so long ago. I cannot remember a time when I did not love him.'

'But you were in love with Mr Howard at first.'

'And how do you know about that?'

'It was something that Grandmamma said.'

'Was it indeed? She had no business saying anything of the kind.'

'Mrs Blake said that Mrs Howard is gone to visit her friend in Somerset. It is the second time she has done so in as many months. Do you not think it strange?'

'Strange?'

'That she should go away so often and leave poor Mr Howard on his own. Grandmamma said that if Mr and Mrs Howard had had children, Mrs Howard would have had to stay at home instead of charging about the country on her own and raising all kinds of spectacles.'

'Speculation.'

'I could see that it made Mrs Blake uneasy. And then Charles Blake arrived.' Lady Osborne's daughter sighed as she mentioned his name. 'I wish I could go to the ball on Tuesday and I wish Charles Blake would be there, and I wish that he would ask me to dance.'

'And I wish,' said her mother, 'that you would apply yourself to other things. Your grandpapa has not seen you this fortnight. I should like you to accompany me. And we shall take Nanny a basket of fruit from the hothouse.'

'May we call on Aunt Elizabeth for five minutes on the way?' said Emma. 'I have something very particular I wish to ask her.'

'Had you not run off this morning, you would have seen her then.'

'It is of no matter, Mama,' said Emma, looking out of the window, 'for Uncle Musgrave is here. And Papa is with him.'

'Your papa is come? And your uncle?'

Lord Osborne greeted his wife and daughter with the affection that a husband and father must feel when parted from them for longer than a day. Business in London had kept him from Osborne Castle for three weeks. He had anticipated a less promising date for its completion, and was pleased to find that the matter was settled sooner than expected.

Due to the fine weather, Mr Musgrave had set out to walk to Osborne Castle in search of his wife, and had happened upon Lord Osborne's carriage along the way.

'You have just missed Elizabeth,' said Lady Osborne. 'She was here earlier, but I believe she is gone to call on Mr and Mrs Edwards. They are to leave for Harrogate tomorrow. I understand Mrs Edwards' sister has recently taken a house there.'

'Then I do not think she will be in luck, for they left early this morning. I saw them as I was leaving the White Hart,' said Musgrave.

'Elizabeth will be disappointed,' replied Lady Osborne.

'I shall not be,' said Musgrave. 'Mrs Edwards is a piece of work.'

'What does that mean, Uncle?' said Emma.

'Never mind.'

'I am sure Papa said the same about Aunt Margaret.'

'Did he?' said her mother. Turning to her husband, Lady Osborne enquired, 'Did you happen to call in at Croydon on your way home?'

'I did,' said Osborne. 'But I stayed no more than half an hour. Never have I witnessed such feats of the imagination as those that trip off your sister Margaret's tongue. And Mrs Harding's countless tales of woe and tumult are enough to ruin the strongest constitution.'

'Penelope was at Croydon?'

'She was,' said Osborne. 'She seemed in excellent health and insisted on sending a tonic to Mrs Turner — though I hardly think she needs one. That boy of hers is determined to go to sea, but she will not have it. Mr and Mrs Robert Watson and all the family were away. I understand they have gone to Bath. Your brother, it seems, is gouty.'

'Uncle, did Aunt Elizabeth refuse you when you proposed? Grandmamma said that she did.'

'Did she?' said Musgrave. 'Your grandmamma doesn't know the half of it.'

'Grandmamma said that you went to London with a broken heart and stayed there for two years at least.'

'Two years? More like two weeks,' said Lady Osborne.

'Indeed I did.'

'And then what happened?' said Emma.

'Well, it was like this. Your Aunt Elizabeth was pursued by an evil villain who captured her and imprisoned her in a tower — the ruins of which you see by the lake.'

'Those ancient ruins?'

'Indeed. There your Aunt Elizabeth languished for at least a week before I chanced to pass by on a white horse, looking every bit the hero. She called to me and asked me to rescue her, and I found after several hours' deliberation that I could not leave her there to languish alone. So I rescued her. And on witnessing my gallantry (my heroism is legendary — I tore down the tower, stone by stone – that is why it is in ruins today) your aunt relented and immediately agreed to be my wife.'

Emma could not contain her laughter at such a nonsensical tale. Said she, 'Did your hands blister as you tore down the tower, stone by stone?'

'They did. But I was consumed with passion so I felt no pain at all.'

'But how is it that the ruins did not exist then?'

'Ah,' said Musgrave. 'That is the only flaw in an otherwise irrefutable tale.'

'That is not the only flaw, I am sure,' said Emma. 'But I shall ask Aunt Elizabeth, for she will tell me the exact truth.'

'I expect your aunt would tell you that I left Delham for London and returned within the month. She would say that we met by chance outside Mason's, where she had gone to buy thread, that I proposed once again, and that I was accepted without the slightest hesitation.'

'And I should believe Aunt Elizabeth's account over yours. But it is not as romantic as it should be. Please don't tell me that romance does not exist.'

'It is there, but perhaps not in the way or in the places you expect to find it,' said her mother. 'Too much conjecture feeds the imagination. And that is not always a good thing.'

'Your mother and your father are perfectly rational beings now. But it was not always so,' said Mr Musgrave.

'I was and am the most rational being that ever walked the earth,' said Lord Osborne. 'But the point is this. Just as the ruins in Osborne Park have the appearance of being ancient, but are not, so there are people in this world who have the appearance of virtue but without the attribute. Your great Aunt Turner is the world's greatest authority on such matters. If it is a happy ending you desire, remember that in novels the fulfilment of happiness is apt to end where in life it is usually thought to begin.'

'Papa, philosophy does not suit you. After we have had tea, there is something I must ask you.'

'Ask me now. There is no time like the present,' said her father.

'Very well. Charles Blake told me how you met Mama. But I do not think I believe him.'

'It will never do to doubt the word of the man you intend to marry.'

'I think he meant to tease me, Papa. But I shall forgive him, for he gave me the prettiest seashell. Look. He found it in Cadiz.'

'Or Lyme Regis.'

'Papa! It was Cadiz!' said she. 'I should like to go to Cadiz.'

'Well,' said her father, 'when I next go to Cadiz I will take you with me.'

'You never go anywhere interesting.'

'There is nowhere more interesting than to be at home with you and your mama.'

Emma sighed with frustration.

'Papa, is it true what Charles Blake said? Did you really rescue Mama from an angry mob?'

Lord Osborne smiled and said to his daughter, 'No, it is not true. It was your mama who rescued me.'

POSTSCRIPT

Over the last two centuries, fascination with Jane Austen and her fictional world has led to the proliferation of spin-off novels, continuations, sequels and pastiches commonly known as 'fan fiction'. The growth of fan fiction might be seen by some as an adulteration of the Jane Austen literary canon and unworthy of consideration. To others, it provides a means of revisiting that fictional world, exploring and imagining time and again what might have been. Jane Austen died too young and left too little, and yet the characters she created are among the most memorable and most loved in English literature. Perhaps this, in part, explains the growth and popularity of fan fiction, for fascination with her work shows no sign of abating. Arguably, Jane Austen, more than any other novelist, has turned readers into writers.

The first 'completion' of *The Watsons*, the fragment of a novel on which Emma and Elizabeth is based, was published in 1850 by Jane Austen's niece, Catherine Hubback, and was entitled *The Younger Sister: A Novel*. There is evidence that, after Jane Austen's death in 1817, *The Watsons* continued to be read in Austen family circles. Hubback, who did not work from the original manuscript, wrote *The Younger Sister* from memory. Since its publication, other novel continuations have been published, a number of which have two things in common: the 17000 word fragment is used in its entirety, and the story develops according to Cassandra Austen's account of Jane Austen's 'intentions'. (Mr Watson was to die, and Emma was to decline an offer of marriage from Lord Osborne in favour of Mr Howard.)

The original fragment remained untitled until 1871 when J. E. Austen-Leigh published *The Watsons* in his *Memoir*. Most continuations bear the same title. I have, however, chosen to call the novel Emma and Elizabeth, for at its centre, it seems, is a story of two sisters whose lives are shaped in different ways by circumstances beyond their control. In writing *Emma and Elizabeth*, I have chosen not to continue the story from the point at which *The Watsons* ends, but rather to take inspiration from the fragment, occasionally blending short passages of the original text into the narrative in an attempt to throw light on the development of themes, characterisation and plot. While I cannot claim that the integration of the original text within the narrative provides a seamless transition, the method helped me to address problems of evenness and consistency of tone.

The Watsons opens on Tuesday October 13th, the date of the first winter assembly in the town of 'D' in Surrey. A fictional town, Delham, is the setting for the story, though Dorking is the place generally regarded as 'D' in the original fragment. This provided greater freedom to imagine the geography of the town and to situate events within its environs that might otherwise appear improbable.

The reference to the day and date of the first assembly, Tuesday October 13th, in the opening sentence of *The Watsons* has led to debate among commentators about the year in which the novel was set: October 13th fell on a Tuesday in the years 1795, 1801 and 1807. In setting *Emma and Elizabeth* in 1795, I have taken account of three things. The first relates to hair powder. The year 1795 saw the introduction of hair powder tax of a guinea per annum. An interesting, though minor, detail about *The Watsons* is the unusual number of references to hair powder. Within Jane Austen's fictional works, hair powder is mentioned six times: three of those references are found in *The Watsons*. The introduction of hair powder tax in 1795 led to a decline in its cosmetic use and had a major effect on male hairstyles of the period. A miniature of Jane Austen's brother (as a 'crop') from c1796 appears to show that Francis Austen had abandoned hair powder soon after the introduction of the tax; and in a letter to Cassandra in 1799, Jane relates how her brother, Charles, had been much admired, 'neither oppressed by a pain in his face or powder in his hair' (Le Faye, 1995, p.37). In *Emma and Elizabeth*, hair powder is taken to be a symbol of the 'old order', espoused by Mr Howard and rejected by Mr Musgrave. Lord Osborne, during the course of the narrative, abandons its use; his openness to change, evidenced not only by his haircut, is seen in his relationships, in the arena of the ballroom, and within the neighbourhood of Delham. In the same way that espousing a 'crop' signals a change in Lord Osborne, so learning to dance provides him with the opportunity to relinquish the role of detached observer and become more a part of the neighbourhood. This transformation reaches its height when Osborne Castle throws open its gates and gives a Christmas ball.

In 1795 food riots took place around the country in protest at the high cost and scarcity of bread. In *The Watsons*, Emma dines with Mr and Mrs Edwards and their daughter, Mary, on the night of the assembly. On her return to Stanton, Elizabeth tells Emma, 'You will not dine as you did yesterday, for we have nothing except some fried beef'. The 'microcosm' of the Watson household, where 'the dreadful mortifications of unequal society and family discord' are played out, may, arguably, be seen to mirror the unrest within society at large.

Perhaps one of the questions that has most intrigued readers of *The Watsons* is why the novel, which for some critics appears to show promise, was abandoned (unlike *Sanditon*, which Jane Austen began writing prior to her death in 1817, and remained incomplete for that reason). Various abandonment theories have been proposed, from the 'bleak realism' of *The Watsons* in contrast to her other works, to the 'flaw' of making her heroine, Emma Watson, too low. Others have suggested that the death of her father caused her to put the novel aside.

The use of comic irony in the major novels, through which the evils of genteel society are routinely addressed, is virtually absent in *The Watsons*. In the fragment, we encounter Jane Austen 'unmasked' and glimpse the harsh realities of her world. Universal themes, such as love and duty, to which she is drawn time and again, in *The Watsons* become studies in rivalry, deception, treachery and repression. Moreover, there is perhaps an autobiographical element of a different kind. By setting Emma and Elizabeth in the year 1795, Emma would have been born in the same year as her creator. In October 1795, Jane Austen was nineteen years old, the same age as Emma Watson at the beginning of the novel.

Revisions to the original manuscript made by Jane Austen appear to cast Lord Osborne's character in a somewhat better light. These textual changes, according to Babb (1967, p.42), make the outcome less certain: 'So pointed a transformation of Lord Osborne may lead us to wonder...whether we can be positive that the fragment would have continued as the Austen family predicted.'

I have sought to raise the possibility that in writing *The Watsons*, Jane Austen had another novel in mind. (An example of this in her major works is *Northanger Abbey* which references Anne Radcliffe's *The Mysteries of Udolpho*.) *Evelina*, by Frances Burney, first published in 1778, centres on the love story between Evelina and Lord Orville. Emma, though not subject to Evelina's misadventures, bears some similarity to Frances Burney's heroine. Disinherited and brought low by the actions of others, Emma is not Lord Osborne's equal. Like Evelina and Lord Orville, Emma and Lord Osborne first meet in a ballroom; but there the similarity ends. Unlike Osborne, Orville appears to have no flaws; he proves to be a fine dancer, his manners are 'open and engaging', his appearance 'all elegance', and his conversation 'sensible and spirited'. Perhaps the obvious parallel with Lord Osborne is Mr Darcy, whose behaviour at a local assembly leaves Elizabeth Bennet with a poor first impression of the man she is destined to marry.

Two sources on which I have drawn deserve special mention: the song referred to during the musical evening at Osborne Castle is Bononcini's *Come raggio di sol*; the instructions given by the dancing master derive from *The dancing-master: or, The art of dancing explained*.

There are more stories of the Watson sisters to be imagined and told, for Jane Austen's novel fragment, and fan fiction in general, raises a myriad of possibilities. In the end, *Emma and Elizabeth* is simply an attempt to imagine one of them.

BIBLIOGRAPHY

Babb, H. 1967 *Jane Austen's novels: the fabric of dialogue*, Ohio State University, Archon Books.

Bononcini, G. B. *Come raggio di sol* (trans. Lucy E. Cross from a CD by Ramón Vargas *Arie Antiche: 17th and 18th Century Songs*, RCA, 2002).

Burney, F. 1778/1982 *Evelina*, Oxford, OUP.

Eastwood, M. 2005 *The Watsons: a continuation and screen adaptation of Jane Austen's novel fragment*, University of East Anglia.

Le Faye, D. (ed) 1995 *Jane Austen's Letters*, Oxford, OUP.

Rameau, P. 1725 (trans. John Essex 1728) *The dancing master, or The art of dancing explained, Ch.1: The manner of disposing the body.*

Also by Ann Mychal

Brinshore
(A Sequel to 'Emma and Elizabeth')

Printed in Great Britain
by Amazon